EBEN MCNINCH

BY

RANDALL PROBERT

Eben McNinch

by Randall Probert

www.randallprobertbooks.net

email: randentr@megalink.net

Cover Painting by
Eleanor Goodman
North Country Lodge
P.O. Box 323
Patten, Maine 04765

ISBN: 978-0-9852872-5-2

Printed in the United States of America

Published by
Randall Enterprises
P.O. Box 862
Bethel, Maine 04217

EBEN MCNINCH

CHAPTER 1

There were rumors circulating throughout Canada that Britain's Royal Navy had pushed the Americans too far and every Canadian was expecting the newly formed United States of America to strike out with a vengeance and declare war on England. England had been embarrassed when she had to cede defeat to the backward colonists. Backward as the Americans had been, they sure as hell were a fighting lot. The British military had not expected that an untrained and undisciplined bunch of misfits would ever fight so long and so hard.

England also knew that the new United States was almost bankrupt and the Royal Navy kept up their aggressions hoping President James Monroe would declare war against England, giving England another chance to reclaim its lost colony.

Ebenezer McNinch didn't want to be sucked into a British regiment and fight against the Americans. He wished his own countrymen had had the foresight of the American colonists to declare their independence against the British Empire. So one evening after work in late May of 1812, he told his wife, Ada, how he felt, and he was not going to fight against their neighbors.

"But what will you do, Eben?"

"There is only one thing I can think of, Ada." He paused before continuing. "In one week, we leave. Nine years ago, in 1803, the Northwest Fur Company in Montreal built Fort Williams as a mid-continent store and warehouse at a place called Thunder Bay. We leave Ottawa and board a ship to Lake Superior."

"How long have you been planning this, Eben?"

"Just this spring. I'll leave you at Fort Williams while I go north to trap. I'll be back to Fort Williams in the spring before the ice has all melted."

Ada was silent. She wasn't liking the idea of staying alone for so long, but Ada was one of those exceptional women— she loved Eben and didn't want him to be scripted into a British army to fight their neighbors. She nodded her head and said, "I do understand. And with my medical skills, I should be able to find work at the fort."

Eben breathed a sigh of relief. *That went a lot easier than I thought it might.*

Eben and Ada had been married for two years and no children yet. They both had agreed not to until they had a place of their own and had settled down. Eben had been working since he was twelve, first with his father in the stone quarries, then as a mason and then a carpenter.

Eben and Ada were both twenty-four, born in Ottawa in 1788, and they both were from Scottish ancestry. He stood five-feet, ten inches…not a big man, but he was barrel-chested and not an ounce of fat in his two-hundred and twenty pounds. He was as strong as five men. His muscle tissues were so dense, he could not swim or float. When he was eight years old, his father had decided, "You need to learn to swim, Son." And he picked Eben up and tossed him in the pond. At first Eben tried to swim, but he sank to the gravel bottom. His father stood on shore and watched as his son walked ashore under water. Eben was furious and walked up to his father and said, "You son-of-a-bitch, someday I'm going to throw *you* in the water!" Then he walked off to change out of his wet clothes. His father stood there roaring with laughter to think his son would have the audacity to speak to him like that.

Eben's hair was reddish-orange, like a fire. When he let his whiskers grow, his beard was as fiery red.

Ada had brown eyes and hair, and although she could not be considered attractive, she was very pleasing, of good nature and moderately pretty.

They sold all of their possessions except for Eben's rifle and pistols and knives, and their clothing and Ada's medicines. Their small house was easy to sell and they withdrew their savings and had a surprising amount of money...more than enough for passage to Thunder Bay and to start a new life at Fort Williams.

They didn't say anything to their friends about what they were doing. The fewer people who knew, the better. They boarded the Canadian Queen ship and a week later they had arrived at Thunder Bay.

"Where will you trap, Eben? Neither of us know anything about mid-country."

"The best way to learn the land is to befriend a band of Indians."

They were able to live at the fort and Ada went right to work in the infirmary. Her work in the infirmary paid for their living quarters, their food and accessories, and Ada still had some left each month to save.

Eben purchased two mules, one to ride and one pack mule. "Do you know yet, Eben, where you'll go?" Ada asked.

"Yes, I have been talking with Major Albert and he told me of an overland trail to a trading post to the west, called Fort Gibraltar, built in 1809 by the North West Company, and the Hudson Bay Company is building another trading post near there called Fort Douglas. Douglas is being built as we speak. This overland trail is in good shape and can be traveled with wagons. Major Albert said if I was to travel north from there, I would find prime beaver trapping. He said his trappers stay away because of the Indian settlements there, but he said if someone was to befriend the Chief, "Big Eagle", then he would have the best trapping in all of Canada."

"When will you leave, Eben?" Ada asked.

"Soon, I think. I'll need time to befriend the Indians and set up shelter."

"Are you sure about...I mean the Indians...what if they are not friendly?"

"Canadians haven't abused the Indians like the Americans have. I think they trust us more."

Eben had his mules and all of the supplies he would need to winter out in the cold Manitoba wilderness. He had decided to travel north at Fort Douglas between Lake Manitoba and Lake Winnipeg.

Ada knew Eben could take care of himself, whether he was with an Indian tribe or out in the winter cold. But still, she would miss him and she understood why he had to go.

In the short time they had been at Fort Williams, Ada, even though she was a woman, had taken control of the infirmary and she was the boss. She knew more about medicine than the quacks there who were proclaiming to be doctors. Major Albert was aware of her abilities and he had put her in charge of the infirmary.

After all of Eben's supplies were purchased, they still had a considerable amount of money left, and he entrusted this to Ada. "You save this, Ada, and someday we will have a place of our own."

As Eben was securing his supplies on his pack mule, Ada asked, "You'll be back next spring? When?"

"Before the ice is gone in the rivers."

"You'd better not take up with any pretty Indian gal or I'll cut off your you-know-what!" She was serious, but she said it jokingly. And Eben understood what she was saying. "In years to come, Eben, if there are any red-haired Indians, I'll know you didn't keep your word."

"Nah, I'd never do that, Ada...and lose your pleasing personality? No, Ada, you're the only woman for me. Besides, I'm going after beaver."

"Just make sure it's the four-legged kind." They both laughed,

"I will worry about you, Ada. Are you sure you'll be all right here alone at the fort?"

"I'll be just fine; it's you that I'll worry about."

"If I meet another trapper along the way, maybe I can get a message out to you if he is coming this way."

They kissed and hugged and there were tears in both their eyes. "I'll see you come spring, Ada." Eben mounted his mule and with the pack mule in tow, Ada watched until they had disappeared in the woods.

* * * *

The overland trail was good for the first three days out, and Eben and his mules were traveling at a fast pace. He ate a hearty breakfast each morning and made sure his mules ate well and had enough water, then he traveled all day with only occasional rest stops. The mules and he stopped about an hour before sunset each day, and he figured he had traveled more than sixty miles those first three days. From there afterward, the overland trail was not as easy to follow, but he still was making good time.

On the evening of the fifth day out, he met two brothers heading back towards Fort Williams. Eben had shot three partridge that day, and was roasting them on a stick over his fire when the two men came walking in to his camp. "Hello there, Mister. We could smell your smoke a long ways back and now those birds roasting over your fire sure do smell appetizing. Me and my brother, we ain't had nothing to eat for days now, except for a few berries."

"What's your names?" Eben asked.

"I'm Paul and this here is Ralph. Ralph is the quiet type," Paul said.

"What's your last name?"

"Smith."

"Yeah, maybe and then again maybe not," Eben said. "Where's all your gear and horses or mules?"

"We had us a bit of trouble a while back and lost everything we had."

"What kind of trouble?"

"Does it matter?" Paul replied.

"To me it does. You running from the law...although there ain't no law out here. So what did you do?"

9

"We had us a run-in with some Indians."

"It must have been some run-in for you two to be running for your lives." Eben turned the roasting partridges over the fire.

"You want some food and share my fire tonight, out with it. What did you and your brother do?"

"Ralph found a little Indian girl that wandered away from her village and he brought her back to our camp."

"And you two had your way with her.... If she was too young to bed, I'm surprised they didn't kill the both of you."

"I think that's what they had in mind. That's why when we escaped we left all of our supplies, furs and gear."

"Well, I don't condone what you did, but neither can I refuse to share my food with two starving, stupid dimwits. I'm hungry enough to eat two of the birds and the third for breakfast next. I'll give you and Ralph one bird to share, and I'll have the other and save one for breakfast."

"We thank you, Mister," Paul said. Ralph only nodded his head.

There was no conversation while they all ate. Eben kept a watchful eye on the idiots. He shook his head in disgust. It was exactly men like these that kept the Indians riled up. He chuckled then and Paul asked, "What's so funny, Mister?"

"I was just thinking to myself. If it wouldn't be so far out of my way and time I don't have, I really ought to take you two back to the girl's village and let the tribe take care of you. That probably would put me in good standing with the tribe. How fortunate it is for you two that I don't have the time."

Neither of the brothers said anything. They only grunted. When the two finished eating, they laid close to the fire for warmth. Eben sat back with his back leaning against a log, sipping his coffee and keeping a watchful eye on the two.

Sometime around midnight, Eben fell asleep, and shortly after that Paul woke his brother and whispered, "He's asleep now. We take his rifle and mules and ride out of here. You get the mules and I'll take care of our friend. Be quiet though, damn it,

Ralph, or I'll nail you to the tree and leave you."

They stood up and Ralph started tip-toeing towards the mules and Paul stepped around the fire and stood at Eben's feet. His rifle was tucked next to his side and his arm was lying on top of it.

Paul stood there wondering how he was going to get the rifle without waking him. He started to slide the rifle out from under his arm and Eben stirred and groaned and settled back. Paul's hands were shaking. He tried again to slide the rifle out and then the mules started braying and Eben opened his eyes and saw Paul bending over by his feet and he instinctively knew Paul was after his rifle.

In one fluid movement, Eben grabbed his rifle and brought it up and hit Paul in the face, knocking him over backwards and unconscious. Eben stood up and ran toward the mules. Ralph was still trying to untie their tethers.

Ralph had no idea he was being watched. "Stand still, Ralph, or I'll put a rifle ball through your head!" Eben didn't holler. He said it with a deep tone in his voice and Ralph knew better than to try and challenge him.

He stood still and put his hands above his head. "Okay, Mister, don't do nothing rash." Of the two, Eben mistrusted this one the most.

"Leave the mules alone and come over here."

Ralph did. He was too afraid not to. "We only wanted the mules, Mister. You have no idea how far we have walked."

"How about that young Indian girl? Have you once thought about what you did to her?" When Ralph didn't answer, Eben added, "Probably not. You and your brother are the most rotten, despicable people I have ever met. You sicken me."

Eben leaned his rifle down against a tree and stepped over to stand in front of Ralph. "What do you think I should do with you, Ralph?"

"Let us go and we'll leave your camp now?"

"You'll leave, alright, but not just yet."

11

With a huge right fist, Eben hit Ralph in the stomach forcing him to bend over. Then he took his right arm and broke it over his knee like a piece of wood. Ralph screamed in pain and fell to the ground. Eben reached down, grabbed him by the back of his shirt collar and hauled him to his feet, then dragged him over to the fire. Paul was just regaining consciousness.

Eben waited until he was fully awake and then he broke Paul's right arm and he screamed in pain.

"You two dimwits came into my camp and I shared my food with you, and then you tried to steal my mules and my rifle and you probably would have killed me. You'll both be a long time now before either one of you can harm anyone again, or steal. Now get on the road and leave my camp before I change my mind and kill you both. Now beat it!"

Paul and Ralph jumped to their feet and holding their broken arms ran down the road out of sight. Eben didn't know if the two would ever make it back to Fort Williams or not. But they were no longer any concern of his. He lay back in his blanket and slept until dawn.

* * * *

At Fort Douglas, being built by the Hudson Bay Company, Eben wasn't able to pick up any additional supplies, so he crossed the river to the North West Company's trading post, or Fort Gibraltar, constructed three years ago in 1809.

There he was able to purchase coffee, sugar, flour and another .44 caliber rifle. As he was putting these on his pack mule, a tall, distinguished looking man came walking over to talk with Eben.

"Good afternoon. My name is Major Wilson."

"Eben McNinch, Sir."

"Those are two fine looking animals. You'd be surprised to see how many new trappers try to bring horses into this country," Wilson said. "Are you coming up from Fort Williams?"

"Yes."

"Where are you heading? I like to keep track of the men if they intend to sell their fur to me."

"North of here, between the lakes."

"That'll be prime beaver country, but two brothers were recently run out of there. Maybe you saw them on the trail up here."

"I did, and they tried to take my mules and my rifle."

"Are they still alive?"

"Yes, but they won't be hurting anyone for a long while. I broke an arm for both of them and sent them on their way."

"I don't know what they did to Big Eagle's people, but Big Eagle and six warriors came here looking for the brothers. So you be careful up there. The Cree are naturally friendly people; don't try to cheat them and leave their women alone."

"Major Wilson, if you have any of your people heading for Fort Williams, would you ask them to get word to my wife, Ada McNinch, that I'm fine and heading north. She's doctoring in the infirmary at Fort Williams."

"She shouldn't be hard to find, then."

"Thank you."

"McNinch, the natives around here have never seen a man with red hair and beard. Just be cautious."

"I'll do that, Major. See you before the ice is gone in the spring."

Eben, for some reason, was glad to be leaving Fort Gibraltar behind. Maybe it was the anticipation of spending the winter trapping with the prospects of filling his pockets with gold coins in the spring, when he sold his fur. And part was the adventure itself and befriending Big Eagle and his people.

The trail north was nothing more than old game trails that trappers had been using for years. He was still making good time...that is, for the first two days. Then the semi-prairie land was slowly being left behind, and he had to sometimes cut his way through thick brush and stands of poplar and alders. This was beaver country. But he wanted to be further north. He didn't understand why he thought he had to go so far north. It was almost as if an unknown entity was pulling him.

Occasionally while traversing over high hills and ridges, he could still see prairie grassland way to the west. Once he found a place to set up his winter camp he might have to venture out to the prairie in search of buffalo for food and its warm robe. In a deep recess of his mind, he would like to find Big Eagle's village. Perhaps only to tell him that the Smith brothers had been punished and would never be back.

He awoke the fifth morning after leaving Fort Gibraltar to a cold drizzle, and decided this would be a good day to make a temporary camp and rest his mules and let them graze. He made a lean-to from the canvas he had brought with him and stored all of his supplies out of the rain. Then he went in search of food.

A nearby stream was loaded with frypan size brook-trout. He went back to his camp and used a sack and made a scoop on an alder branch. A fish net. "This will work."

His first scoop had a dozen nice trout. He cleaned those and took them back to his camp, then went foraging for vegetables. He found ferns growing beside the stream and dug up the roots. He found wild onions and mushrooms. This would be enough for a nice kettle of hot stew.

While the kettle full of trout and vegetables was simmering, he roasted two trout stuck on a stick over the fire. Fresh trout roasted on a stick was delicious. It was the best tasting trout that he had ever eaten. The stew didn't take long to finish cooking, and he had a bowl of that and decided this wilderness living was pretty good.

With his belly full, he decided to do some exploring. He took his rifle in case he saw a deer. He checked his compass and headed east. About a half-mile from camp he came to a clearing where he could look out over a vast forested wilderness. Earlier he had not been aware that he was at such a high prominence. He saw a large body of water at the very edge of the horizon, and decided this must be the southern end of Lake Winnipeg.

From atop the prominence, Eben turned north and hiked a mile before turning west for a mile, then south and about halfway back to his lean-to he spotted a nice crotch-horn deer and shot it. As he was cleaning it, he knew he would have to stay at his lean-to for a few more days while he smoke-cured the meat so it wouldn't spoil.

He carried the deer over his shoulders. The extra weight didn't bother him or slow him down. He had had to carry heavier stones while working in the quarry as a boy.

Back at camp, he built up his fire and then put on some green hardwood that would burn down to hot coals. As he waited for the hot coals, he skun the deer and fleshed the hide at the same time. When the fire was ready, he put the liver and heart on sticks to roast. The hide he nailed around the trunk of a large hemlock tree to dry. Twice a day he would rub hemlock bark over the fleshy side to help preserve and soften it. He had done the same to cowhides on his grandfather's farm.

While he waited for the heart and liver to cook, he cut the meat into strips for drying and smoking. In the morning he would make a drying rack over the fire. When he had finished that, he warmed up a cup of stew and the liver and heart were also done. He sat back enjoying his meal.

That night he sat up feeding the fire way past midnight. He was mesmerized by the flames and listening to the night sounds. It seemed that as soon as the sun had set, the forest came alive. As he sat watching the fire, he discovered two things about himself. One: he had never been this serenely happy in all his life. And two: he was missing his wife Ada, and how much he really loved her.

* * * *

The next morning after eating some of the liver and a cup of hot black coffee, he made a crude rack and laid the strips of meat on it to begin drying and smoking. Then he checked on his mules and led them to new grass and tethered them.

Instead of going right back to his camp, he circled to the west and then back to the trail. Just before reaching the trail he heard something to his right. He stopped to listen, realizing he had just made a big mistake if he hoped to survive. He had left his rifle at camp. He waited and after several minutes, he heard it again. But he still wasn't able to determine what was making the noise.

As he got closer he decided someone was hurt and was moaning. He stopped to listen again and the sound was clearer now and it seemed to be coming from the base of the cliff ledge. He looked over the edge and saw an Indian sprawled out on the ground. The drop was only about six or seven feet, but the Indian had obviously broken his right leg and there was a gash on his forehead where he had hit his head. He was unconscious and most probably this was a good thing. Eben slipped the pack off that he had been wearing, and he smelled of whiskey. He probably had been at the fort trading some fur for his pack of blankets and whiskey. There was broken glass next to the ledge and there was no more in the pack. Eben surmised that while in a drunken stupor, the Indian had probably stepped over the ledge.

He picked him up and put him over his shoulder and carried the pack in his other hand. His hardest part was climbing the sandy knoll, but once on top, it was an easy carry back to his camp. Eben laid him on his bedroll and checked his broken leg. It would have to be set with a splint to keep it immobile. With his axe he shaved one side of two cedar sticks so the sticks would rest flat against the leg.

As he tied up the splint, he was glad the Indian was still unconscious, as it might have been extremely difficult to do it if the Indian was awake and saw a white man working on his leg. When he had finished, he cleaned the head wound and put a cool compress on his forehead to reduce any swelling.

The Indian remained unconscious for two days. Eben kept busy tending to the meat and cool compresses for his head. In another day Eben figured the meat would be sufficiently cured.

As Eben was turning the meat strips over, the Indian began to stir. Eben decided to sit by the fire and let the Indian adjust to his circumstances before he tried to talk with him...which was going to be difficult since they both spoke different languages.

He sat still watching him as he regained consciousness, little by little. He lay there looking around him, not fully aware yet of his broken leg or surroundings. When he saw Eben sitting there watching him, he was startled and started to move, realizing then that his leg had been immobilized. Then he could feel the pain in his leg and he touched his forehead where the gash was healing nicely.

Eben got up and kneeled by his side and touched his broken leg and made the sign he was breaking a stick. The Indian understood. "I don't suppose you speak English?"

Much to Eben's surprise the Indian shook his head that he didn't, but it was also obvious that he could understand some at least. Eben talked slowly, pronouncing his words carefully and told him he had been drinking whiskey and had fallen off a cliff. The Indian nodded his head—*yes*.

"My name is Eben. How are you called?"

He tapped his chest with his fingers and said, "Neokiowa."

Eben gave Neokiowa a cup of fish chowder and said, "Eat slowly." When he had finished Eben gave him some water to drink.

"You lay back down and go to sleep. We talk more later."

Neokiowa seemed to understand and he laid back and he was soon asleep. While he slept, Eben went after more firewood. Tomorrow morning the meat would be thoroughly cured and the day after that, Eben wanted to leave. He knew he would have to take Neokiowa back to his own village first, though.

Neokiowa slept until early evening and when he awakened, Eben gave him another cup of stew and then a small piece of the smoked meat. Neokiowa seemed to like the meat more. They talked until after dark and Eben needed sleep. He learned to talk with Neokiowa by asking him questions which he could answer by shaking or nodding his head. Eben learned that Neokiowa lived at Big Eagle's village and it was two days travel, maybe three with a wounded man.

Neokiowa was impressed with the smoked meat. He had heard so many stories about the white man that he had the idea that they didn't know anything about nature or surviving in the wilderness. But what he couldn't understand was that this man's hair and beard were so red. *Red like the fire.* He had only seen a few white men, but this was bewildering to him. *Was he someone special? Someone to be feared?* He didn't think fear was what this white man was about. He had showed him so much kindness and had saved his life.

Eben picked up his axe and said, "I come back soon." Neokiowa nodded that he understood. Eben didn't have far to go to find what he wanted—a small sapling that had grown in the shape of the number 7 that Neokiowa could use as a crutch. He cut the sapling off and rough cut it to length and went back to his camp.

Neokiowa was his own height so he cut the crutch to fit him and showed Neokiowa how to use it. Neokiowa immediately understood and wanted to stand up and try it. Eben had to help him to stand and then gave Neokiowa the crutch and he knew immediately how to use it. There still was no way he could walk back to his village, but it would help him to get around camp and once he was at home. He smiled at Eben and said something Eben didn't understand, but he knew Neokiowa was thanking him. Eben smiled back and nodded his head.

Neokiowa's appetite had come back and Eben wasn't sure now if they had enough food to last the few days it would take to reach his village. The stew was gone and they ate their fill of smoked venison.

The next morning they had a cup of coffee with venison and then they started to pack up. Neokiowa was determined he was going to help. When it was time to leave, Neokiowa wanted to walk with Eben, but Eben was persistent and begrudgingly

Neokiowa rode on the mule. If Eben had understood Neokiowa, they had to travel north two, maybe three, days. Once they were close, Neokiowa would know which way they would have to turn.

Eben was glad to be on the move again and the first day he figured they traveled twenty miles or a little more. They were both tired and slept well that night.

The next day traveling was a little slower and then better the third day, but they didn't reach Neokiowa's village until midday of the fourth day out. Kids playing at the edge of the grassy clearing were the first to see. *And who was this red haired man leading the mule that Neokiowa was riding?* They ran off to tell the villages, hollering and laughing. Everyone then came out to greet them.

Neokiowa was happy to see that this red haired white man, his friend, did not carry his rifle as they entered his village. Chief Big Eagle was also aware of this, and this pleased him.

Eben helped Neokiowa to dismount and gave him his crutch. Big Eagle had always been a good judge of character and he immediately saw the goodness in this white man...whoever he was.

There was a long conversation between Neokiowa and Big Eagle. Eben surmised Neokiowa was explaining his ordeal and how this white man had saved his life.

Finally Big Eagle dismissed Neokiowa and the women rushed to his side to help him. Big Eagle looked square at Eben. . .no smile, no expression at all except understanding. He took two steps closer to Eben and said in English, much to Eben's surprise, "Ncokiowa says you saved his life. If not for you he would walk on the other side of this life. This good thing you do for Neokiowa. He says you good white man." Then Big Eagle reached up and removed Eben's hat and ran his fingers through his red hair.

"Never see white man with red hair, like fire, or red beard. All white man I see, beards are black. Not you. You different white man that all my people never see. You walk my village with no trouble, yet you carry no rifle. This is good. I think you good man, Red Beard. Come, you and me smoke pipe and talk. Neokiowa says he ride your mule, but you walked all way here. You must be tired."

Without saying a word, he made one gesture with his hands and the men were going to take Eben's mules and gear. "Wait one minute, Big Eagle. I have a gift for you." And Eben unwrapped the smoked venison and gave it to Big Eagle's woman. The fleshed and dried hide he folded and said, "For Neokiowa." Another stepped up and took the hide.

"Come, follow me," Big Eagle said.

Once inside his lodge and there was no smoke in the pipe, Eden asked, "Chief Big Eagle, how do you know the English words?"

"Before I tell you this, what is your name?"

"Excuse me, Big Eagle. Yes, of course. I am called Ebenezer McNinch."

"Ebenezer sounds like an Indian name."

"Most people call me Eben."

Big Eagle repeated this. "Eben.

"Many years ago—I was small boy—a French holy man came to live with our people. He taught me and others his tongue. He said knowing the English words would help us when the white settlers would come into our land."

"You said a French holy man, but you speak English."

"Yes, holy man's words were English."

"Okay."

"What you want in land of Cree, Big Red Beard?"

"I come to trap, but only with your permission. If you say no, then I will leave your land."

"You are the only trapper to ask before he takes the beaver. Two brothers trapped near here and stole my granddaughter and took to their camp for many days, and each had her. Now she is shamed. I sent two of my warriors to capture these two and bring them here, but they escaped."

"Tell me, Big Eagle, how these two trappers looked."

When Big Eagle had told his story, Eben said, "I know these brothers, Big Eagle. They came into my camp and I gave them food and water and they tried to steal my mules and my rifle."

"You say tried. Did you punish them?"

"Yes, I broke their arms," and Eben broke a stick in his hands. "And I told them if I ever saw them again I would kill them."

"Good, my granddaughter has been avenged.

"We have talked enough for now. You are free to walk in my village. I will council with the elders and decide if you trap on Cree land or not."

There was a gathering of children of all ages that followed behind Eben everywhere he went. When he sat to rest, some of the smaller children wanted to touch his red beard. To see a man with a beard where their own people couldn't grow beards, was one thing. . .but a man with a fiery red beard was bewildering.

After they all had eaten and everything was picked up, Eben was sitting close to the fire and Big Eagle sat down beside him. "Our medicine man says you did good with Neokiowa. The council wants to know where you want to trap the beaver."

"I do not wish to crowd you people, Big Eagle. I saw good beaver possibilities a day's travel from here, to the south. If this is okay with the council, I will agree not to trap any closer than a day's travel. Or more, if they prefer."

"Will you be alone or someone to help you?"

"I will be by myself. No one knows where I am."

"You good man, good medicine, Red Beard." They both laughed. "I share my lodge with you this night."

Eben slept well and he was surprised with how little noise there was in the entire village, even after the evening meal. Now as he laid on his back, there was complete silence and he was sound asleep.

Everybody was awake and up at sunrise the next morning. He was surprised at the length of daylight and how short the night actually was. He was now further north than he had ever been. At mid-morning, Big Eagle asked Eben to join the council on the shore at the stream.

Big Eagle, since he was the only one of them who knew the English words, was the council spokesman. "The council wants to know if you will bring more trappers to Cree land?"

Eben cleared his throat and replied, "No, I will not bring more trappers here."

"Will you tell others where to trap beaver?"

"Only my woman, who is a medicine woman at Fort Williams, many days travel to the east."

There was some discussion amongst the council, and Big Eagle said, "Your woman, you say she medicine woman?"

"Yes."

"How can this be? Is Cree custom that only man be medicine man."

"My woman, Ada, is very gifted and she likes to help people."

They talked for a long time and then smoked the pipe until there were only ashes left. There was a lot of interest in Eben's red hair and beard.

Big Eagle stood and said, "Leave us now, Red Beard. We talk and give you answer soon."

Eben stood up and walked back to the village. He went to see Neokiowa. He was resting outside of the lodge and the same two women were waiting on him. Eben figured both women were probably Neokiowa's wives.

"Hello, Neokiowa. It is good to see you are growing stronger."

Neokiowa nodded his head and indicated for Eben to sit, and then he said something to one of his women, and she brought Eben something to drink. He wasn't sure what it was, but it was a fermentation of something, and it wasn't bad. "It is good, Neokiowa, that you grow stronger." And he said goodbye and walked back to Big Eagle's lodge. Big Eagle and the council were walking up from the stream.

Eben waited for Big Eagle. "Council has decided. Council say you good man, treat our people good. Saved Neokiowa's life. You can live on Cree land and trap, and I call you brother."

"Thank you, Big Eagle. I will leave in the morning. I need to find a place to build my lodge and get ready for winter."

"You no go now. In two days, we have special feast in your honor, Red Beard."

The next day, Eben spent with Neokiowa and his family, trying to teach them to speak English. They worked at it all day, and by the evening meal, Neokiowa was able to talk a bit easier with Eben and using sign language, also.

He left Neokiowa and his women and went back to Big Eagle's lodge. He was sitting outside. "You teach Neokiowa to speak your words." Not a question; it was a statement of fact. Big Eagle was aware of everything that was happening in his village, as it should be for the chief.

"Red Beard, you need young girl to sleep with you and keep you warm. You need girl to take care of you when you trap and come back to your lodge. My granddaughter, I give you."

"Thank you, Big Eagle. I have a woman that I'll go home to in the spring. Before I left, she told me that if I took up with an Indian girl, my woman, Ada, would cut this off," and he touched his crotch with his hand.

Big Eagle thought it was funny and he laughed. He nodded his head that he understood Eben.

At the feast the following day, Neokowa's two women had made Eben a deerskin shirt. Another couple gave him a pair of moccasins, another gift was a bear hide he could either use as a rug or a blanket. There was so much food, no one went hungry, and it all tasted so good. Much of it he didn't want to know what it was. At the end of the feast, Big Eagle asked, "Red Beard," and everyone laughed, "you tell us about your world, the white man's world. You tell me; I will tell my people in our words."

He started out telling them where he had lived while he was growing up and trying to describe the huge lakes where you couldn't see land on the other side. Some of the elders had actually been to Lake Superior and they understood the greatness of the lake. He told them about the war between the American Colonists and England, and there again, some of the elders knew about this. He tried to describe towns and cities and how many people live in the white man's villages. He drew pictures in the sand of horses pulling wagons and carriages with people riding in them.

He told them that the winters are much warmer way to the south and Big Eagle said, "In the land of our brothers the Apache and Cherokee."

"That's right, Big Eagle. There they never see snow or cold winters." Eben was surprised that Big Eagle knew about the two tribes, so far away from the Cree Nation.

When the story telling was over, Eben, Big Eagle and his council smoked the pipe and talked more about the white man.

"Before cold weather, go east, hunt the caribou. Big Eagle asks Brother Red Beard to join us."

"I would be honored to join the hunt."

"When time is ready, I send brave to get you."

"How will you know where I'll be?" Eben asked.

"Big Eagle keep watch of you. Know where you go."

Eben guessed he could live with that. After all, he was a guest on Cree land.

Eben laid awake for a long time that night before going to sleep. He was really surprised at how readily he had been accepted by Big Eagle and the whole village. These were truly remarkable people. They were nothing like the stories told about them. They had a very established form of government and he guessed that when one violated one of the tribe's rules, they probably were dealt with severely.

There were so many thoughts and ideas running through his head, he knew he wouldn't be able to sleep. He got up and went outside to the communal cooking fire and stirred the coals and put some wood on and sat down to watch the flames. His first thoughts were of his wife, Ada. And he hoped she was okay, and as much as he was missing her, he knew this would not be any kind of life for her.

He started thinking then about how he would build his lodge. He had not thought much about this, but he had about three months to get it built and a shelter for the mules and put up some winter food. His biggest concern was finding enough feed for the mules. He knew he would be okay.

After a day of celebrating and feasting, he was surprised he wasn't tired. He put more wood on the fire. A wolf howled from north of the village. A bat flew across and back across the firelight chasing bugs. He looked up at the stars. God, the heavens were out bright tonight and he wondered what that star-filled belt was that crossed the sky. He looked for a shooting star. There would be many in late summer. There always was in August. He had no idea what month it was or the day of the week and he wasn't sure how long it had been since leaving Fort Williams.

He put more wood on the fire and sat back wondering if anyone had any right to be this happy.

CHAPTER 2

Ada's life at Fort Williams since Eben left had been extremely busy. First there had been a construction accident at the wharfs, then several workers had come down with the flu and the brothers had wandered into the fort with a broken arm each and they were emaciated smelling like a stray dog heap. Both breaks had started to heal and she had to re-break them, so the bones could be set properly.

Ond day at the noon meal, Major Albert asked, "Ada, would you sit with me in the dining hall today? There's something I would like to talk with you about."

Ada kept wondering what was it that Major Albert wanted to talk with her about. The anticipation was killing her. Then finally at a little after noon, she was able to break away from the infirmary for lunch.

Ada sat down across the picnic table from Major Albert. He was only drinking a cup of strong tea. "The United States has declared war on England and the fighting has already begun. British troops have entered northern Maine from the New Brunswick Province and met only a pitiful amount of resistance and are now moving on Portsmouth Harbour in New Hampshire. The British are looking for young men to volunteer. So far there have only been two who have left here to join the Brits. They're also looking for medical people, doctors. If you were interested, Ada, you would be paid twice what you are getting here."

"Absolutely not, Major. Not with my husband trapping in the wilderness and expecting to find me here come spring. It's out of the question," Ada replied.

"I thought that would be your response, but I had directives to ask all of my medical people. Frankly, I'm glad you're not leaving."

"What about you, Major? I would think with your rank you would be called to join."

"Ada, none of us here are in the military. My title as Major is merely a position of authority within the North West Company. Fort Williams is a base of operation for the North West Company, the fur trade as well as shipping. The fort was built for protection."

"From what I have heard, I'm not a bit surprised to learn that the United States has declared war against England," Ada said.

"That is my feeling exactly. I think we should be supporting our neighbor with hopes of declaring our own independence."

"Have you heard if Canadians are conscripted into the British militia?" Ada asked.

"I have heard such rumors, particularly in Eastern Canada."

Ada didn't say it, but she was now glad Eben was where he was. There would be no way of conscripting him now. She smiled to herself. And Major Albert noticed the smile, but didn't say anything about it.

CHAPTER 3

Eben was still awake watching the fire as the sun started to break over the horizon. The women were the first to emerge from the lodges, then the children and the men. Apparently he was in the women's way. Big Eagle's woman, Little Buffalo, shooed him out of the way and pointed to her lodge. When Eben didn't move she picked up a piece of firewood as if to hit him. He got up and ran. The women all thought that was funny and had a good laugh.

For breakfast Eben had leftovers from the feast and a few wild strawberries. Big Eagle and Neokiowa knew Eben would be leaving after he had eaten. They were being very subdued. Quiet.

When Eben had finished eating, he left the crowd and started securing his supplies and his mules. He had been given so many gifts he now had to use his riding mule as a second pack animal. He didn't mind walking.

Neokiowa walked over to say goodbye, "Big Red Beard, you always be my brother. Not tell Big Eagle whiskey made me fall. Thank you. One day I come visit you."

"I would like that, Neokiowa, my brother."

Goodbyes were said and Eben started south with the two mules in tow. It was a hot, windless day and he had to stop often to rest and give his mules a rest, also, and a drink of water. By walking, he figured he had not traveled a normal day's travel from the village like he had promised. Not sleeping the night before, he was tired when he stopped for the day and he slept well that night.

He was up at dawn the next day and there was a thin cloud cover which would keep the air from getting so hot. At mid-day, he stopped for a rest on a high prominence and to the west he could see a marsh, streams and heaths. This was the country he was looking for. After the mules were rested and had some water, he turned west from the prominence.

About a mile west of the prominence, he found exactly what he wanted. A cool stream marshland, dotted with small ponds and flowages. He would camp here the night and explore this area to be sure there were enough beaver here. He unpacked the mules and staked them out where they could eat heath grass. Then he made a lean-to with the canvas he had, built a stone fireplace and made supper.

After he had eaten, he walked around the area and noticed how rocky it was—not just in the stream...the ground was covered with rocks. *There are so many rocks, I could build my lodge with rocks.* He dug a small hole or cave and the walls and top stayed in place. It was clay mixed in with sand and he supposed it was the clay that held the sand in place around the hole.

He now had the plans for his lodge—now, if he could find enough beaver tomorrow.... He brought his mules back from the heath and fixed something to eat.

After eating, he squared off a block in front of the knoll. He just knew he would find beaver. He worked until midnight cutting sod into squares and removing it to where he wanted his lodge. He piled the sod squares off to one side, out of the way. He suddenly was tired and decided to stop for the night.

The sky was clear that night and filled with sparkling stars. About daylight, he woke up to one of the mules braying. He picked up his rifle to investigate. There was a gentle breeze blowing, but everything else was silent. He kept scanning the area behind the mules and up the knoll. Then he saw movement, but movement only. He waited and just when he thought whatever had been there must have moved on, he saw some bushes moving and then a black bear's head poke out through the ground hemlock bushes. His first instinct was to kill it. He could use the meat and hide, but on second thought he didn't have a whole lot of time to be curing bear meat. He had a lodge to build.

The bear kept inching closer to the mules. Eben wanted to drive the bear off and not have it come back. Simply scaring it wouldn't work. The bear would be back. So not to be cruel, he decided to shoot it in a front paw. That way it would run off, live, and may never come back. He waited until he had a good shot at the front paw and then he pulled the trigger.

The bear roared with pain and anger, but it ran off. "I hope that'll be the last we see of you!"

He reloaded his rifle and stood by the mules talking to them and patted them to calm them. Once the bear's scent was blown away, the mules calmed down. He could see it was going to be a lot of work keeping his mules through the cold winter, bears and wolves. *Maybe once I get settled here and more of my scent spread around, the varmints won't be so curious and stay away.*

He ate and staked the mules in the heath again and he took his rifle and pistol and his large sheath knife. He kept it as sharp as a straight razor. He could shave with it if he wanted to.

He followed the stream downstream and he didn't have far to go when he saw fresh beaver tracks on the stream bank. In that first mile he found six new flowages. The houses were big enough to support six or eight beaver each. He followed the stream five miles downstream and had counted a total of sixteen active flowages.

He crossed over one exceptionally tall beaver dam to the other side and made a circle back to his camp. There were indeed enough beaver flowages downstream alone to keep him busy all winter. *This would be home, then, until spring.*

* * * *

Eben was so busy building his lodge for the next three weeks, he had no idea much time had elapsed. He had carried rocks from the surrounding area and made double rock walls up against the knoll where he had dug the hole. When the rocks were too far to carry any longer, he made a sled from small cedar trees and he hitched one of the mules to it. He could haul many rocks at a time this way. He made the walls about five feet tall and filled the center with sand he dug from the hole in the bank. He dug down two feet inside the now four walls, below ground level. This gave him seven feet inside the lodge now.

He made a rock fireplace in the front wall and cemented the rocks together with clay. When the walls were finished, he dug out the hole in the bank large enough so he could stand up in it and use it for cold storage. For the roof, he cut cedar trees and laid them from the front wall back to the bank with a rounded pitch. Then he laid the sod squares on that and covered everything with canvas and covered that with sand.

He next made a rough-hewn table, chair and a bed from dried evergreen needles. When his lodge was finished he dug another hole in the bank for his mules. They would need shelter from the cold. Eben was having fun building a new existence, but he also knew survival here would become very difficult. Getting enough firewood to keep warm, feed and water for the mules and to trap beaver, and food for himself. . .he was beginning to hope he hadn't bitten off more than he could chew, as the saying went.

He made a rough-hewn door for the mules' shelter. Now he figured he was done. He would have to start looking for food. . .nuts, betties, mushrooms, onions, fern roots. He found an abundance of hazelnuts.

He figured it was probably late August and there should be plenty of edibles in the forest. He foraged for several days; he had an abundance of food and he found more in flowages upstream, and high bush cranberries…these he would pick later.

With his feed stores in good shape, he was wanting some fat trout to eat. That would be a welcomed relief from all the dried meat he had been eating. He made a two-prong spear and went upstream where he had seen large and deep pools. There was nothing in the first few pools, but then he found one with many large brook trout. He laid on his stomach on the stream bank watching the trout and waiting for an opportune time to thrust the spear. One large trout swam near the bank below Eben. This was his chance and he crept out and thrust the spear and hit the trout mid-body. He brought the trout out and broke its neck and laid back to wait for another chance. All of the trout had moved to the opposite side.

He waited and eventually the school came back and another swam close to the bank. When Eben had speared six nice brook trout, he decided that was enough for now. He cleaned those there and then headed for camp.

He ate one that evening and the others would be smoked. As he sat outside tending the smoking fire, he began to think about the coming winter. His biggest concerns were the two mules. Could they get enough food from the heath and the thick moss that grew in the evergreen thickets?

When the trout were finished curing, he decided to go back to the same deep hole for more trout. He knew he'd have plenty of beaver to eat during the winter, but a diet of only beaver might get a little tiresome. He took his backpack with him this time and before he had finished he had almost completely filled it.

While those trout were curing over a smoldering fire, he foraged in the area for more vegetables, nuts and berries. When he was satisfied he had enough, he worked on harvesting feed for the mules and stockpiling it. He cut grass in the heath, he picked moss, small poplar bushes for the bark. He had quite a pile when he was done, but he knew there wasn't enough for the mules to last the winter. He'd have to turn them loose in the marsh and heath to feed for themselves.

One day after Eben had all his food supplies stored and the feed for his mules, Neokiowa walked into his camp yard one day. "How did you find me, Neokiowa?"

"Our people been watching you for many days. Time to hunt caribou. Tomorrow you and I meet hunting party at water that goes to big lake. There we have canoes to cross lake. That is where caribou are."

"Okay, Neokiowa. We stay here tonight in my lodge. Tomorrow we go."

"Yes."

"Your words, Neokiowa, are much better now."

"Yes, Big Eagle been helping to use your words."

Eben had not shared his coffee with anyone while he had been at the village, but now he offered Neokiowa a cup, and they sat outside in chairs Eben had roughed together. Neokiowa pointed to his cup questioningly and looked at Eben.

"Coffee. Try it, you may not like it."

Neokiowa sipped his coffee without saying whether he liked the strong, acid taste or not. But he drank it all. All while he'd sipped his coffee, he was marveling over Eben's lodge. "Good lodge, my brother. Sturdy, no wind blow through." He was especially surprised to see how the floor actually set two feet below the ground and the cavern in back Eben had dug out.

Eben had picked some dandelion greens the day before and now they ate these with some trout. After eating, they sat by the fire long after the sun had disappeared. Eben told Neokiowa about the bear.

"Not good, my brother. Bear don't forget. He be back in spring; after his long sleep he'll be hungry and he'll remember the smell of the mules. He might try to eat you, my brother."

Eben had only the one bed inside, so Neokiowa chose to sleep outside on the ground. Eben gave him the bear rug to sleep on that had been given to him. As Eben laid in bed waiting for sleep to take him, he was thinking about the caribou hunt.

* * * *

Eben took his rifle, pistol, his big hunting knife and a smaller skinning knife. The brush was too thick to ride the mules, so they led them and when they reached the stream that flowed into Winnipeg Lake, Big Eagle's people were already there and temporary living quarters all set up.

"Good to see my brother, Big Red Beard. At early sun tomorrow, hunters take canoes across lake to Manigotagan River. Mules can't go. Stay here."

Everyone was excited about the hunt and getting enough caribou meat to see them through the winter. There was a huge fire that they danced around, and suddenly there was complete silence except for the crackling and snapping of the fire. The holy man was offering a prayer for a successful hunt tomorrow. Then there was more dancing and excited chatter. At midnight, there was suddenly complete silence as everyone went off to their own lodge and sleep.

The young boys, probably too young to go on the hunt, stayed up all night keeping the fire burning. Eben wasn't sure if this was a spiritual thing or not, or why the fire was kept burning. Come morning, he too was excited about the hunt and he forgot to ask about the fire.

There was no talking around camp come morning, nor while they pushed the canoes into the water or paddled across the lake. The lake was calm, like a piece of glass. All communication was done with hand signals, and each hunter knew what was expected of him. Eben followed Big Eagle and Neokiowa. Not far from the lake they came to a long, narrow meadow. Without a word from anyone, they all separated along the western side of the meadow. Eben supposed to ambush the caribou when they came through. He also surmised that there probably was a migration trail somewhere out in front of him that went the whole length of the meadow.

Just then, Eben watched as one hunter crawled out into the middle of the meadow and then crawled back to Big Eagle. Big Eagle whispered to Eben, "Only some caribou went through yesterday, not herd. They come soon, we wait."

They didn't have long to wait. Up at the head of the meadow, a few caribou could be seen ambling their way down, foraging on the way through. When those first few were about half way down the meadow, the rest of the entire herd could be seen now at the head of the meadow.

Those first few had disappeared, but Eben realized they were waiting for the main herd now, so they could box them in and improve their chances of killing many animals.

Eben was as excited as everyone else as they watched the herd pass in front of them Then as if on cue, everyone began shooting their arrows into the caribou, taking care for a good killing shot. Eben pulled his rifle to his shoulder and took aim on one that was too far away for a bow and arrow, and when he pulled the trigger his caribou dropped dead. He quickly reloaded and sighted in on another caribou at a greater distance than what a bow and arrow would be capable of. That one also dropped.

He shot twice more and then again as if on cue, everyone stopped and the remaining caribou ran off. Not all of the caribou were dead. Some were wounded and ran off stumbling and hunters went after these. There were a few still struggling to get up. Eben dispatched two with his rifle and pistol. Eben was walking beside Big Eagle's grandson, Little Claw, when a caribou they were walking by suddenly seemed to come to life and it knocked Little Claw to the ground as it was stumbling to get up.

Eben had not had time to reload either weapon. The caribou was about to gouge Little Claw with its antlers. Eben never even stopped to think about what he was doing, he just did it. He dropped his weapons and he charged the caribou and grabbed it around the neck and behind its antlers, and with all of his strength and weight, he twisted the caribou's neck and rolled the caribou to the ground, its legs kicking and flying. Before the caribou had hit the ground, Eben had his big knife out and he stuck it in the caribou's throat and with one strong pull, he cut the caribou's windpipe and the big arteries. The caribou was dead; it just didn't know it yet as it kept struggling. Eben lay across the animal's neck with all his weight. He knew if the caribou couldn't lift its head, it wouldn't be able to get to its feet. Little by little, the animal stopped struggling and lay dead.

By now many others had seen Eben wrestle the caribou to the ground and cut its throat with his big knife, and they slowly gathered around him as he laid on the caribou's neck. When he stood up, he was covered with blood, and when he turned to look at Big Eagle all he could do was grin. Then everybody, Eben included, broke out with laughter. Little Claw stood there in awe. He had never seen anything like it before. If Eben had not been a friend to the entire tribe, he would have been afraid of him after witnessing what had just happened.

Little Claw finally built up his courage and stepped over to face Eben and in his own words, Eben knew he was thanking him for saving his life. "My grandson says it is good thing you came on caribou hunt today or he would have walked to the afterlife. Little Claw says you more strong than the buffalo we sometimes hunt."

Eben knew this was Little Claw's way of saying thank you.

Big Eagle watched as Eben helped Little Claw with skinning the caribou. It took two men, one to hold the legs while the other did the skinning. The next caribou, Little Claw held the legs while Eben did the skinning and he showed Little Claw how to flesh it at the same time. His big knife was an excellent tool for skinning and fleshing. The next caribou Eben let him use his big knife and Little Claw did a fine job at fleshing.

After the caribou were skun, they were quartered and everything was hauled back to the lake. Only half of the meat had been taken across to their temporary camp before dark. Big Eagle returned with the first two canoes loaded with meat and would stay with his people on the west side of the lake. Neokiowa, Eben and Little Claw and five others stayed with the meat so bear, wolves and wolverines would not steal it. They all ate heart and liver that night, roasted over a fire.

Wolves howled all night from the meadow, but all that was left there were the innards and blood. Once in a while a wolf would venture closer to their fire and let out a series of howls and barks, but none would come into the light so they could get a clean shot at it.

By noon of the next day, all of the meat was on the other side. The hearts, livers and stomachs were washed and cleaned and what wasn't eaten on the trail back would be smoked and cured, as would most of the meat. There was some waste but not a lot. The antlers, which couldn't be eaten, were the last to be packed. Most were left. Neokiowa and Little Claw helped Eben make a travois for each mule. They could haul four times the weight. "Big Eagle, I'll only take what meat I'll need with one mule. You can use the other mule to help take this meat back to your village," Eben said.

"That would be good. Carrying all this meat now would take maybe three days on trail. What we do with your mule?"

"Can you use it to help haul wood to the village this winter, and maybe other jobs as well? If you can use it, then I'll come get it in spring before I leave."

"Yes, you come in spring for mule."

That also solved one of Eben's worries. He would not need as much feed for just one mule.

* * * *

Eben had said his goodbyes and he was a day and a half returning to his camp. He noticed the temperature was changing and the tree leaves had turned color. It wouldn't be long now before there was snow. Once he had all of the meat taken care of, he would start beaver trapping before there was any ice.

He didn't have to smoke cure all of the meat as the days and nights were now cool enough so the fresh meat would not spoil. He really enjoyed the flavor of fresh caribou meat. Before he would set any traps, though, he scoured the area for wild onions. Cooked with the caribou, they gave the meat a special taste.

It took all day to find an onion patch, but he had plenty for the winter, he figured. The next day he left early, after staking the mule in the heath, with axe, pistol and his traps. Since the walking was good, he went downstream as far as he had explored earlier. He found the tall dam he had walked across before and dug out two troughs through the top of the dam and set a trap in each, knowing that beaver often checked the dams and would repair any leakage.

Then he went back upstream to the next dam and did the same thing. He went back to the first flowage and waited until he heard the traps spring. The trap in the first trough was not there, meaning there would be a beaver in the trap at the end of its tether. He waited, though, before pulling that in. He didn't want to scare off the beaver from his second set. He didn't have long to wait. When he heard the second trap spring, he pulled his first trap in and there was a huge beaver in it. When he pulled the other trap in there was an equally large beaver.

He reset both traps and made sure the tether chain was still secure, then he put both beaver in his pack and went back to the second flowage. While he waited, he skun and fleshed both beavers and rolled the hides up and put them in his pack. If these beaver weren't caught soon, he would have to wait and skin them back at camp.

No sooner had he thought this than both traps sprung. The first trap had a large beaver and about the same size in the second trap. There was just enough time left to skin and flesh these and get back to camp while it was still light. But he had to move right along. There wasn't time to reset his traps here.

He stayed at camp the next day and stretched the hides on a large spruce tree, then he harnessed the mule to drag out dried wood from the heath for his fire. He wished he had thought to bring a bucksaw. That would have made it a lot easier to chunk the wood up. By the time he quit that afternoon, he had hauled out more wood than he thought he would have.

The next day he tended his traps and got two more extra-large beaver. He would keep resetting until he started getting the small beaver. He wanted to leave those for seed. He tended three more times before he caught one small beaver. He now had a total of fourteen beaver. He set traps on the next dam upstream and returned to camp. He had hides nailed to trees all out in front of his lodge. The days he didn't tend traps, he would work on his firewood. He also hauled in green trees that beaver had cut down and had only taken the tops and limbs. His axe was sharp and it didn't take him long to chunk up a tree.

The beaver fur looked prime, even though at home this would be a bit early for trapping. He was taking the castor and scent glands out of each beaver. The castors were worth almost as much as the hides. The oil glands he would use as lure for trapping other animals.

* * * *

Eben knew that once there was deep snow on the ground, beaver trapping would be much harder. So every other day he would go downstream to either tend traps or set up a new flowage. By the time ice started forming at night along the edges of the stream, Eben had twenty-five beaver and three otters.

One day in mid-afternoon while Eben was stretching beaver hides and roasting a beaver over the outside fire, Neokiowa wandered into his camp yard.

"Hello, Neokiowa. It is good to see you."

"Yes, it is good. I smelled beaver cooking far back. Smell good; me hungry."

"It won't be much longer." Eben poured two cups of coffee and handed one to Neokiowa. They sat close to the fire as the temperature was dropping. They talked long about the caribou hunt and Neokiowa was most interested to learn more about his friend's world.

The beaver was finally done and they each chewed on a hind leg, then the back-straps and front legs, and then wherever they could cut off a piece of meat. The meat was all gone. They each had had their fill.

With darkness, the temperature dropped and they moved inside. The firelight from the fireplace was adequate to light the whole interior. "I like your stories of your world, my friend. It frightens me. I see how our two worlds so different. Makes me afraid of losing Cree way of living. You from other world, but you come to Cree land, village, you like all Cree people. You live like Cree people. I do not think all white men are like you, though."

Eben knew what his friend was worried about and he felt sorry for him and his people. To change the subject he said, "You're English is getting better, Neokiowa, every time I see you."

"Yes, Big Eagle and I speak often together with this English, and we are teaching others to know these words."

It was getting colder outside and Eben spread his bear rug on the floor for Neokiowa to sleep on. Before they were asleep, the wind began to blow, but inside the stone lodge they were warm and comfortable. Even when the fire burned out.

* * * *

The next morning before Neokiowa left he said, "I must go now. This wind is bring in the snow. Big Eagle was worried about you alone here. When I tell him all about this—" and he spread his arms to mean everything "—he worry no more." They said their goodbyes and Eben watched as he disappeared into the forest.

Eben took care of the mule first and then headed downstream to tend his traps. Even though the temperature was cold and the steady wind made it feel colder, and there was more ice in the stream now, Eben decided that this was still better than traveling in the snow. He had brought snowshoes with him, but he didn't want to wear them out before the winter was half over.

Hiking right along and not wasting any time, he had begun to work up a sweat and he knew this wasn't good, alone and out here in the wilderness. He opened the front of his coat and slowed down. If it was -20°, he knew he'd sweat. He always had.

He had two beaver and one was small, so he pulled his traps and moved to the next flowage and while he was setting the second trap, the first one sprung. He turned around just in time to see the beaver disappear into deep water. He finished setting that trap, then pulled the first one out and reset it.

He decided to build a fire and roast some beaver meat and wait for his traps to do their work. He kindled a fire and then started skinning and fleshing. He put some meat on a stick over the fire and both traps sprung closed at the same time. He pulled in two extra-large beaver. By the time he had reset both traps, the beaver meat was cooked. In between mouthfuls, he began skinning the other two.

It was getting late, so he decided to head for camp. When he came back to tend, he would first set two traps in the flowage upstream. He cut off the castors and this time he left the oil glands. He left the three carcasses there on the bank, and headed for camp.

It was dark before he got back, but he had walked along the same path so many times he really didn't need much light. He brought the mule in, inside its cave shelter and closed the door. Even without a fire, the inside of his lodge was not uncomfortable.

Two days later when he went back to tend traps, he set up the flowage before the one where his traps now were. Then he moved downstream and this time he had the male otter. He didn't know if otter was worth as much as beaver or not. He reset those traps and went on up the bank to skin the otter. The beaver carcasses had been eaten by something and not far away he found a wolf scat. He guessed he'd better start carrying his pistol. He threw the otter carcasses into the open water in the pond. No sense giving the wolves something to come back for and running into a pack of them.

When he got back to the other flowage, he had two more beaver and instead of skinning them there, he put them in his pack and would skin them at camp. It was still daylight when he got back.

As he was skinning the beaver, he thought about the wolves and decided it might be a good idea to set some wolf traps around the camp, just in case they came looking for a meal. After he had nailed the hides up to dry, he set three traps. One upstream, one downstream and one behind the lodge on top of the knoll. He used beaver meat for bait and some castor for lure.

He wasn't sure which month it was, but the hardwood leaves had fallen. There was ice that didn't melt during the day in shady places, but the ground was not yet frozen.

When he got up the next morning, there were two inches of dry, fluffy snow on the ground. After eating, he checked his wolf traps before doing anything else. The ones upstream and on top of the knoll had been sprung, and in the third trap he had a large female wolf.

He decided if they were coming this close to camp, he'd have to be more cautious about his mule.

It was more difficult skinning the wolf than a beaver. The hide didn't separate from the flesh as easily. But it was a handsome looking fur. This one was female and the others running with it were probably this year's pups.

He reset those three traps around his camp and the next day when he tended his beaver traps, he set two more wolf traps. He had four large beaver this trip and he pulled the traps on the lower flowage.

He cooked some beaver meat at the new flowage and warmed up beside the fire. The wind was beginning to blow again. He baited his wolf traps with beaver and castor and then put one carcass in his pack to take home and eat, and the rest he put under the ice in the pond.

That night the temperature dropped so cold the water in the streams froze solid. He figured it was probably the middle of December. So far, this early into the trap season, he had done very well. He now had thirty-eight beaver and six otters and one wolf.

Even as cold as it was it didn't take much of a fire to stay warm inside the lodge. And the mule was also well protected inside its cave-like enclosure.

What hides were dry he took off the trees and stored them in cold storage in the lodge. He took the mule out to the heath and while she grazed, Eben cut more feed for the mule and took it back to her shelter. When she had had enough, the mule came back on her own and went into the shelter out of the cold.

That evening the full moon peeked up over the trees and Eben could feel the air getting colder. The wind had stopped blowing, which was good. About the time he was getting ready to sleep for the night, he heard his mule braying like something was after her. Wolves came to mind and Eben picked up his rifle and quietly opened the door and eased out. The ground was blanketed with snow and the moon was full and bright, and fifty feet away were two wolves trying to break through the hewn door to the mule.

Eben shot one and the other one, the larger of two, turned to look at Eben. "Damn it, my pistol is inside!" He had his big knife and he gripped his rifle for a club. The wolf was inching closer with its head down and snarling. Eben held the club ready and he ran at the wolf, hoping to scare it off. But he didn't scare so easily. Instead, he lunged at Eben, and Eben brought his rifle down on the wolf's head. The wolf ki-yied and fell to the ground and rolled once. Eben was on him with his knife before the wolf could get his bearings. The wolf bit Eben's left arm. Eben thrust the knife into the wolf's chest and twisted the blade to maximize the damage. The bite did little more than break the skin.

Blood was spurting from the wound and the wolf didn't have enough life in him to fight back. Eben laid down beside the wolf exhausted. *How many more damn wolves are around here?*

While the wolves was still warm, Eben skun them there in the moonlight and took the hide into his lodge and went out to see the mule and calm her down. At first the mule didn't want anything to do with him, but little by little as Eben kept talking to her, she finally let him pat her and scratch her behind the ears. "I won't let anything happen to you, girl."

That was the end of the wolves being so close to camp for a while. When he went to tend traps the next morning, he had another wolf and two more beaver. He set traps upstream in a new flowage and set another wolf trap. But after three tends, nothing came back to the wolf set. He now had four wolves. He had heard that wolves run in packs, sometimes as many as six or eight together. *Maybe the rest of them left the area, if there were any more in this pack.*

Ada had insisted that Eben take along a few medicinal things such as alcohol and clean bandages. He washed the blood and dirt off and then sparingly poured alcohol over the wound. When the skin was dry, he bandaged it. It would be stiff and sore in the morning, but he knew he'd be okay now. He went to bed and before going off to sleep he wondered just how many more wolves were around. One thing for sure, now he would not be without his rifle or pistol.

In the morning, he began working on a holster and belt for the pistol. *They won't catch me off-guard again!*

There was six inches of new fluffy snow the next morning. He had to tend traps and he thought of using snowshoes, but the snow was so dry and fluffy he could easily walk through it and snowshoes would be just added weight.

He had two more otter at the flowage further downstream and he reset those and put the otter in his pack and went back up to the next flowage, and he had one large beaver and a rock sitting in the pan of a sprung trap. "Well, two otter and one beaver isn't bad." He reset those traps and took them back to camp to skin in the warmth of his lodge. There was just enough daylight left to take the mule out to the heath to feed. She had a network of trails through the heath, like deer would have. When she had had her fill she came back to the shelter. Eben was real glad now that Big Eagle had taken the other mule for the winter. With two mules to care for, he wouldn't have half as many beaver as he had now.

He was hungry come dark. Every fifth night he would use a little of his precious flour and make bread dough to roast over the fire twisted on a stick. And he would have some onions and fern roots with the smoked caribou. He was developing a liking for caribou meat. He liked it as much smoke cured as he did fresh. With as much meat as he had now in storage, he wasn't worried about running out.

That night it was so cold Eben could feel the coolness even in his lodge. The morning was the coldest yet. That day he shoveled snow up against the lodge exterior walls. No wind blew through the rocks, but it was damn cold outside. When he tended traps the next day, both traps at both flowages had frozen. In answer to that, he dug the trough deeper so more water would flow over the traps.

This solved his problem. Two days later, he had four more beaver. He had to skin at least two because his pack wouldn't hold four beaver. He built a fire in a spruce thicket out of the wind and skun two, and while he waited for the beaver meat to roast, he decided he might as well skin the other two, and not wanting to waste food, he would take the carcasses back with him. He hadn't seen any wolf tracks in the snow since he had killed the two at camp. So he left what was left of the other two carcasses.

* * * *

More snow finally came in and it, too, was all dry and fluffy, but it was deep enough now so Eben had to use his snowshoes. But at least all of the farthest flowages that he had scouted were already trapped, so what remained were close at hand.

Working around the beaver dams and digging deep troughs for the traps, he was always getting wet. But as cold as it was, the water would freeze to his clothing before it had a chance to soak through to his skin.

His mule had to wander further in the heath also, to find enough to eat. There was still plenty of dry grasses sticking above the snow, but the mule had to wander further for it. But at least the mule's trails were being kept open.

The daylight hours were getting longer now, and there was more heat in the sunshine and the snow had settled. Eben noticed fox, squirrels, pine martin, fisher and bobcat tracks in the snow. They weren't sinking much at all. He had all of the beaver hides pulled off the trees with only one remaining flowage he wanted to trap. From the size of the beaver house, there were probably at least four extra-large beaver. Maybe more.

One bright sunny and somewhat warm day, on his way back from tending traps, he saw fresh wolf tracks on his snowshoe track. The damn bastards are back.

After he had skun two beaver and had them drying and stretched on trees, he went back along his snowshoe trail where he'd seen the tracks, and then made another trail off that into an evergreen thicket. He set one trap and baited it and then used a little castor for a lure.

Then he made another set in front of an old rotting stump in the flowage. Instead of letting the mule out to feed, he fed her some of the dry grass and brush tops and he made doubly sure the door was secured.

He was thinking about setting out bait in the camp yard to shoot the wolves, but the moon wasn't bright enough for that. Now he wished he had a window. If these wolves were some of the same pack that was there earlier, he doubted if they would come to the camp yard. He waited two days before checking the traps. Let his scent dissipate first.

There was still some daylight left, so he cleaned his lodge. Anything he didn't want to keep he burned in the fireplace.

He went to sleep that night certain he had taken all the precautions warranted, and he slept surprisingly well. For something to do the next day, Eben stayed close to the mule as she grazed in the heath. When she had finished eating, he twitched out some dried trees that he had to cut down. He hauled out one tree at a time so not to tire the mule, even though the trees were small. Then he chunked the wood into usable lengths for his fireplace.

The next day he had a sprung trap in the thicket and one wolf on the flowage. He looked around checking the wolf tracks and determined it had only been the one wolf. A male. He had two beaver and decided that was enough for this year unless he found an opportune flowage somewhere. He skun the beaver and would take the wolf back to camp and skin it there.

He now had fifty-two beaver, eight otter and four wolves.

CHAPTER 4

Eben found no more wolf tracks close to his camp and he finally pulled all of the wolf traps. The weather was changing fast. The sun was warm and in some places the snow had melted enough to expose patches of ground. But he knew that cold temperatures and snow were not over yet.

The snow was sticky and he traveled great distances west, exploring new country. He had his axe in his pack and he carried both his rifle and pistol. He found more beaver country about two miles from camp. Another stream that had many flowages on it. He would keep this area in mind if he came back to the same area in late summer. He really liked Big Eagle and his people, so in all probability he would come back. At least he wouldn't have to build a new lodge or a shelter for his mules.

He circled north and then east, making a wide arc. Everywhere he went he found numerous beaver colonies. This made up his mind to return again for the next season, and he would trap this country first before trapping close to his camp. He was toying with the idea also of building a small temporary camp over there somewhere. A one-night trapper's camp, where he could rest out of the cold. He would keep these ideas in the back of his mind and not dwell on them now.

All of this country that he had seen so far that lay between the two lakes was pretty much low, flat land. No mountains, only an occasional easy-rising knoll or hill. It was certainly beautiful country. And he had not seen any wolf tracks yet. Maybe this late in the season, they had moved to another area where the hunting was better and they would not be pursued by Eben McNinch.

He suddenly was wishing the snow to melt so he could start his trek for home. He was missing Ada.

It was almost dark when he reached the stream that flowed by his camp. He found a safe place to cross and now out of the small undergrowth his pace was faster. The snow helped him to see and he was back two hours after sunset.

He tended his mule first and then he kindled a fire in his lodge and laid on his bed waiting for the warm glow of the fire. He was bone tired and the warmth from the fire was making him sleepy. Sometime later, the fire blazing hot, he awoke to wolves howling outside. He was still wearing his pistol and holster and he picked up the rifle and opened the door.

The wolves were trying to get into the mule's shelter again. Only this time there were four of them. This was a different pack. He sighted in on one and pulled the trigger. That one dropped dead and as the others were running off, he fired his pistol. He doubted if he hit anything, and he'd wait until daylight to go see. He reloaded both weapons before going to look at the dead one.

Steam was rising into the air from the wound, and the wolf lay still. He skun it while it was still warm and dragged the carcass away from the mule shelter. Then he went inside to calm his mule. Her eyes bugged out like saucers and hair stood up on her back.

He was really beginning to hate these damned wolves. The next day he dragged the wolf carcass way off and made snowshoe tracks into the evergreen thicket and set one wolf trap, baited with beaver and castor. Then he checked the heath and set another trap, and then downstream where he caught and skun the last beaver. Then he went directly behind his lodge where he had set before.

For the rest of that and the next two days, he stayed close to camp and he wore his holstered pistol always, even when he lay on his bed.

It was a week before the wolves returned again, and in the moonlight he could see four. So if this was the same pack, there should only be three left or there had been a fifth wolf out of sight. He shot one and the others ran off. *They must be hungry.*

He checked his traps at daylight and nothing. He found their track where they had run off last night after he shot the one. He followed their tracks for a while and set two more traps. That evening as he was fixing supper, the wolves started howling, barking and growling in front of the lodge. He inched the door open. There were three about ten feet away, looking at him and growling. *Where was the fourth wolf? On top of the roof waiting for him to step out?*

There was very little he could do now except put something in front of the door to keep them from pushing it in. He finished cooking and ate in the chorus of their howling. Eben was certain now—the wolves were after him and not the mule.

Then he said, "I'll get you bastards, but there's nothing I can do tonight."

After eating, he relaxed and began laughing. He had an idea how to take care of them. He was safe here and he knew they couldn't get at the mule, only she would be scared as long as they kept howling. But eventually they got bored and left.

* * * *

After eating and drinking a pot of coffee, Eben drew a two-and-a-half inch groove, a foot long, vertical, three inches below the tip of the door, and then the same horizontally, so he had like a plus sign. Using his axe and knife he cut through the wood so he could stick his rifle out, and be able to cover the front yard with using both vertical and horizontal grades. "There, that solves that problem."

Then he went to work carefully removing rocks in the wall facing towards the mule's shelter. The clay and sand had actually solidified much like baked clay, but he was still able to dig out about an eight-inch hole. Looking through the hole he could see the shelter door and the area in front. He did have to remove much of the snow piled up against the wall where the hole was. He plugged the hole from the inside with cloth and he did the same to the door. Then he took some remains of a beaver carcass and froze them in the snow about fifteen feet in front of the lodge door.

He went outside and closed the door to look at his handiwork. He was satisfied. Then he took the mule out into the heath to feed and he stayed with her as she fed.

Not wanting his scent near the traps he had set out, he wouldn't tend until the wolves came back to torment him and the mule. If one was to get caught he might be able to hear howling. For the rest of that day, he busied himself around camp. He checked on his own food supplies and happened to think that once he left for the trip back, he would have to cure some meat to take along. He would have a few stores to take from here, but not enough. But there would be time enough for that. What would be ideal would be if he could shoot a moose. Although he had not seen one since he moved in, he had seen a few tracks. Maybe he should trap a few more beaver and smoke the meat. That he would, but not before he had eliminated the wolves or they had moved. And he doubted very much if they would move on. They knew there was food here. Himself and the mule. But he was determined to have the last laugh.

He chunked up some more wood and piled what he could inside with him to dry it out and keep it dry. He put some in with the mule also. He shoveled the mule's manure out and put it in a hollow place away from the shelters.

He cut fresh fir and cedar boughs for his bed and cleaned the sandy floor as best he could. He melted snow and made sure his water containers were full. He wished he had some grain for his mule. Maybe when they got to Fort Gibraltar, he could buy some grain from the trading post. He hoped they would pay a decent price for his fur, so he would not have to take them all the way to Fort Williams. That would mean several more days on the trail.

Using up most of his remaining wild vegetables, he made a

stew with caribou meat. It was good and he had made enough to last him a week.

He ate before sunset that day so he would be ready for the wolves. He propped his rifle up next to the door. He was already wearing his pistol. He waited and waited and they never did make an appearance that night, and there was no howling in the distance.

He wanted to stay close to camp and he was finding it difficult to stay busy. He was getting bored. He took the mule out to feed twice. Next year he was determined to bring something to read for just such occasions.

A week passed and he had not seen or heard anything of the wolves. Then one morning as he was finishing his coffee, he heard a scratching at the door, but that was all. It might have been only a mouse or squirrel, but he didn't think so. He removed the cloth from the shooting grooves, and a large wolf jumped up and tried to put his nose through the grooves. His nose was right in the center and sticking about two inches through the door. This infuriated Eben and he punched the wolf's nose sidewise, bringing blood, and the wolf backed off but was not leaving. It stood there facing the door and growling.

Eben removed the cloth from the other hole so he could see the mule's shelter. There were two wolves there. Somewhere he figured there was one more. For them to attack in the daylight meant they were hungry. He put his rifle into the hole and left it balancing there. He drew his pistol and took aim at the wolf in front of his door. The bullet took the wolf in the middle of the chest and he was dead. Eben then looked through the hole towards the shelter and those two were leaving, but not running. He fired and hit one broadside but the wolf stayed on his feet and kept going. He was sure he had hit the wolf good. He didn't believe the wolf would go very far before he lay down and then he probably would bleed to death.

What bothered him, though, was that fourth wolf. *Where was it?* Twice now they had made a deliberate attempt to get at him. *Could these bastards actually think?* If so, was the fourth wolf on the roof waiting for him to come out? Or was he being paranoid?

He reloaded both weapons and sat down at the table with a cup of coffee. He could look through the hole at the shelter and a corner through the front door. He sat in silence.

The coffee gone now and shaking with anger, Eben stood up and checked in both directions. There was nothing there. With the rifle in his hand, he eased the door open. There was nothing there. He jumped through the door and turned around to look at the roof. There was nothing there. He wiped the sweat from his face, even though the temperature was below freezing. There was nothing there. He climbed up the knoll to look for tracks. There was nothing fresh. From on top of the roof, he scanned back and forth the camp yard and beyond, looking for movement. There was nothing.

The dead wolf was another large male. The mule was braying and excited. Eben had to calm her before she hurt herself. Then he picked up the blood trail of the wounded wolf and began to follow it. He went back for his snowshoes.

The wolf was losing a lot of foamy looking blood. This meant the wound was in the lungs. He knew the wolf couldn't go far being shot in the lungs, but he was surprised that it had run off at all. Not even being knocked off its feet! He snow-shoed at a slow pace scanning both sides as he progressed, even though the blood trail was still in front of him. But if these beasts could think, then what would prevent them from circling back to attack him?

According to the tracks and blood trail, the wolf was staggering now. It was weakening. A quarter of a mile from camp, the wolf lay dead in a hollow. Eben would never understand how the wolf managed to get as far as it did. He was forming a new respect for the animal. But he still hated them.

While he was out there, he checked that trap. Nothing, but he left it. The wolves were apparently hungry and if hungry enough, they would come back. He skun that wolf there and tossed the carcass aside.

He went back to camp and skun the wolf and took care of the hides. He went downstream and one more wolf. This had probably been the fourth wolf in the pack. He got three that day and there was one more left. Would he be back? Eben had no way of knowing, but he reset that trap and went back to camp. He now had ten wolves. He had no idea what their hides would be worth.

* * * *

That was the end of the wolves for the season. Eben had made a big dent in their numbers in the area. The fur was really beautiful. The days were continuing to get warmer and the daylight hours longer. His smoked brook trout were long gone, so he decided to go fishing. The deepest pond would be behind the tallest dam where he had started trapping. He had some line and a few hooks. He scraped together some fresh meat from the wolf carcasses and with axe, shovel and rifle, he hiked downstream. He'd pick up the last wolf trap on his way back. There was nothing in it and he sprung it.

Ice had melted quite a ways away from the dam, and he rigged up one line on an alder stick and stuck the stick in snow so the tip would be off the ice. Then he went to look for another open hole. There was a spring-hole close to the opposite shore and he rigged up another line and as before, he stuck the alder stick in the snow with the tip over the open hole.

The first stick and line nearest the dam was dancing all over the place. Eben rushed to grab it before it was pulled into the water. He pulled in a beautiful brook trout, about four pounds. He rigged the line and went back over to the other line. It was okay, so he kindled a fire and before he was done, both alder tips were dancing in the air. He pulled a trout in at the dam and ran to the other spring-hole. There he pulled in another four-pounder.

He had three beautiful trout.

With both lines now reset, he rebuilt the fire and put a stick through the smallest of the three and hung it over the fire to roast. The coals were hot and it didn't take long for the trout to cook. Eben sat down with his back against a spruce tree, enjoying the hot meal. He was hungrier than he thought as he chewed the last morsel.

By mid-afternoon, he caught his seventh trout and figured this was good enough for today. He would smoke-cure these before deciding if he'd need more. The fireplace wasn't exactly what he needed to cure meat, so he had to dig out the outside fire pit and build another rack for the meat.

With the fresh scent of curing fish in the air, he sat up all night with his rifle across his lap, leaning back against his lodge. During the day he would cat-nap sitting in the same position. Every once in a while he'd have to drive off the blue jays and gorbies who were looking for an easy meal. The next day two ravens sat in the tree tops also hoping to snatch a bite and fly off.

* * * *

The camp yard was almost free of snow now. There was still enough in the forest to make traveling slow and tedious. But it wouldn't be long. There seemed to be more cold and wind this winter than snow depth. Eben would have thought there would have been more snow. The snow had all been dry and fluffy, and when it settled, he didn't believe there was more than two feet on the ground at any one time. But there was probably more than two feet of ice in the beaver ponds and lakes. It would be another two months at least before the ice was gone.

Eben was anxious to be on his way home and he already had all of the fur pieces bundled up. He wasn't sure what the price on fur was now, but he was guessing his cache was probably worth more than $1,000.00. That would be almost three years wages back home. Yes, he had made up his mind to return for another season. He hoped Ada wouldn't object too much. At least he wasn't fighting in some damn war that he didn't understand.

Some nights he was so warm in his lodge that he had to let the fire die out. The snow and cold temperatures were gone now, but as Eben lay on his bed the wind started howling, stronger than any wind during the cold months. The wind was coming from the west and it was warm.

Each day Eben would take excursions away from camp so he would know how fast the snow was melting in the forest. He went south for five miles and back. Then he went north towards Big Eagle's village. He thought he would probably be able to make the trip to the village, but bringing his mule back would be difficult. He'd wait a few more days.

The strong wind blew in warmer air that stayed around for days, softening the snow. Eben knew it wouldn't be long now. He started putting together his feed stores that he would have to take with him once he left. All of the smoked and cured meat was wrapped.

He spent the rest of the day bringing in dried grass from the heath for the mule while he let her eat her fill. When she was full, she went back to her shelter. Eben filled two water buckets for her while he would be at the village. With the wolves gone now, he wasn't worried about having to leave his mule at camp.

When he went to bed that night, he knew he would leave in the morning for the village.

CHAPTER 5

Filled with anticipation, Eben was up early and ate his fill. Then he checked on the mule and gave her enough grass to tide her over, and when he closed the door, he secured it safely. He put some smoked beaver in his pack for the trip and picked up his rifle and closed and secured his door and started north towards the village.

It would be a pleasure to see his friends again. He wished he had more time to visit. For some reason the further north he traveled, the less snow there was. The ground was still frozen and he didn't have to detour around marshes or wade the streams. He was actually making good time. Part of the reason might have been the fact that after hiking and trapping all winter, he was now in excellent shape.

Only once in a while did he have to check his compass, even though nothing now looked familiar. Just as the skyline was turning gray Eben could hear the chatter at the village and kids playing. The kids were taking turns riding his mule. The kids were the first to notice him and one ran to tell Big Eagle.

Eben walked directly to Big Eagle's lodge, saying hello to everyone along the way. Big Eagle and Neokiowa were sitting in front of Big Eagle's lodge. They stood up to greet their friend. "It is good you have come, my friend Big Red Beard."

"Big Eagle, Neokiowa, I am happy to be here. How are my friends?"

"We good," Neokiowa said. "You had good winter? Good trapping?"

"Yes. It was fun."

Big Eagle and Neokiowa looked questioningly at each other. They didn't understand living alone in the cold of winter and having fun. They simply accepted it.

"Come, you been walking all day. You must be hungry. Come, you eat," Big Eagle said.

Everyone was glad to see Eben return, but no one could understand why he was alone. There was a lot of chatter as Eben ate. "You had good trapping?" Big Eagle asked.

"Yes. Did your people get any beaver?"

"Yes. Not as many as you."

"Would you like me to take the furs with me and sell them? But I won't be back until late summer," Eben said in between mouthfuls. "Money probably wouldn't do you any good. What would you like me to trade them for?"

"I not know that. You decide. You know what we could use."

"Do you have only beaver or do you have any wolves or otter?"

"Just beaver. You have wolves and otter?"

"Yes. The wolf hunted for me all winter. I killed ten," and Eben held up both hands so Big Eagle could count his fingers.

"No wolf here. Must be all near you."

Eben took off his coat and rolled up his shirt sleeve and showed him where the wolf had bitten his arm.

"Wolf did this?"

"Yes."

"Tell me how this happened. You let wolf get so close to you," Big Eagle said. Then he noticed Eben was laughing.

"You attack wolf," Big Eagle said straight-faced, and then began to laugh also. And he had to tell everyone that Big Red Beard had attacked a wolf. Then he wanted to hear the story.

After Eben had finished telling his story, Little Claw said, "Neokiowa, he fights with caribou and throws it to the ground to kill it with that big knife to save my life. He now attacks a wolf and fights it to the ground and again with big knife he kills it. He good man, but who is he? He lives alone and walks the land alone, unafraid. Me glad he like our people. He not afraid of anything!"

Neokiowa stood up and instantly everyone was quiet. "Big Eagle, Little Claw and me talk. Big Red Beard not afraid to fight caribou to ground to save Little Claw's life. He fight wolf, take him to ground also. Not afraid of wolf. Our friend not afraid of anything. Little Claw and me call our friend by new name: *Big Red Beard Not Afraid.*"

Everyone was nodding their heads that they agreed. "Okay, it will be. You are known as Big Red Beard Not Afraid."

Everybody was going back to their own lives and lodges. "You come my lodge. We smoke." This time it was just the two of them and Eben suspected Big Eagle wanted to talk more seriously about something.

Big Eagle chose to sit close to the fire and then Eben sat down. After the pipe was smoked, Big Eagle spoke. "I not know what brought you to Cree land. You say trap beaver. You trapped beaver. You not like what others say white men are like. You good to my people and I glad you came. I think you yourself not know why you come here. You big medicine, I think, where you travel. Others stop and watch you pass. You walk this land not afraid of anything. You have great spirit who walks beside you and protects you. Always. No one, white man or red man can walk alone like you and not be afraid some. That why you have great spirit that walks with you."

As Big Eagle was talking Eben was thinking that the idea of a spirit guiding him never before now had occurred to him.

"When snow leaves, I send young runners to other tribes to tell about Big Red Beard Not Afraid. You can travel any land now without trouble."

"Thank you, Big Eagle, for your kind words. You know more about the spirit world than I do. I would never have thought about a spirit guide walking with me. Big Eagle smart chief, good for his people."

"Mule helped us haul wood from long way. Made work

easier. Maybe next year you leave mule here again," Big Eagle said.

"I will return, Big Eagle, late summer before the leaves turn color and before you hunt the caribou. I would like to leave my mule here for winter and help your people."

"You see any white trappers?"

"No. I saw no one. Big Eagle, when I leave here, I will go to trading post where Neokiowa go last year. I will not tell anyone where I trapped beaver. I will not tell anyone about my friends. I have friends here. I don't want other white trappers coming here and causing you trouble."

"This is good."

"I don't want to bring your people trouble by my being here, so I give you my word I will not tell anyone except my woman."

They talked for a long time into the night. Big Eagle wanted to learn about the ways of the white man. And Eben had to retell the story about him charging the wolf with a club and then throwing it to the ground.

* * * *

The next day there was another feast in Eben's honor. And again he had to retell the stories of the wolves. The people were enjoying them as much as they had the first time Eben told them.

Eben decided that he had better contribute to the feast also. Although he had only a little smoked meat, it was appreciated. Someone had found a honeybee hive before the winter storms and now as desert, everyone was enjoying fresh honey and wax.

When the feast was over, Neokiowa and Eben tied the beaver hides together. There were twenty. "You leave tonight?"

"No, at first light tomorrow. I need to get back and take care of my other mule."

"You come back for caribou hunt, Big Red Beard Not Afraid," Neokiowa said.

"I'll be back in time for the caribou hunt," Eben replied.

Everyone was up at daylight to say goodbye to their friend. Before disappearing into the forest, Eben turned and waved goodbye. He would miss these people. They were not at all like the stories told of the natives.

Eben really wanted to get back and take care of his mule. Having to lead this mule slowed his pace. The moon wasn't full, but it was bright and he continued on in darkness. Once he found the stream that ran by his camp he knew he was almost home.

The mule he was leading started braying before he could see the camp. He could smell the other mule and he knew he was home also. Eben put both mules in the shelter and fed them and watered them. He carried the beaver hides inside and stored them with his.

He was tired, but he was more hungry. He kindled a fire and warmed up some caribou meat. There wasn't much left. It was good he would be leaving soon.

He laid down after eating. Too tired to put more wood on the fire, he went to sleep. His bed was not soft by any means, but he was comfortable.

After eating the next morning, he staked one of his mules in the heath to feed, while he hitched the other one up to the rock sled. Before leaving he wanted to rock up the entrances to the shelter and his lodge to keep the bear and wolves out. Some of the rocks were still frozen to the ground and he had to range quite far to find enough to do the job. Then he staked that mule in the heath also.

He sat on the stream bank with his rifle leaning up against a tree, watching the mules. They were doing more playing than feeding, so he got up and put them back in the shelter.

"I smell. Maybe it's time I had a bath and washed my clothes." He wasn't about to sit in the cold stream water. It was still mostly covered with ice. He filled the buckets and put them by the fire inside to warm up. It would take a while to warm up, so he fixed a cup of coffee and then put more wood on the fire. He found a piece of cloth he could use for a washcloth. He had no soap or towel. That would be corrected when he returned. His clothes he put on the bed and would wash those when he was done. He pulled out his extra pair of pants and shirt and long underwear.

He felt of the water and it was warm enough. When he dipped his washcloth in he saw he had scooped up a bit of gravel. No problem. But as he was turning away something had caught his eye and he looked again. He found a gold nugget about the size of a pea. There was just the one. He checked the other bucket. It too had a handful of gravel in the bottom...but no nugget.

Wow. I'll be go-to-hell! There has to be more of those in that stream. I wonder why I never saw it last year before it froze over?

He scrubbed up real good, got dressed in clean clothes and washed out his old ones. He put the wet clothes outside to dry and then he went down to the stream where he had dipped his buckets. He got down on his hands and knees. There was nothing laying on top of the gravel He scooped up a handful and washed the silt out and he had another nugget about half the size. *God, that water is cold!*

He went and got his black fry pan. He washed three pansful before he found another nugget about the same size as the first one. He worked all along the stream-bank until almost dark. He had found eight nuggets in all...most about the same size as the first.

If'n the weather is good come morning, I'm leaving. But I'll sure remember this when I come back.

After eating, he made a small cloth pouch for the nuggets and then he buried that in the sand in the wall where he had made a hole to shoot through. Then he laid the rocks, when put back in place, look natural. He checked the outside wall also. He was satisfied. He figured he probably had ten or fifteen ounces of gold.

* * * *

Early the next morning he packed both mules. He was leaving behind what he could. He had food, hides, and rifle, pistol, bed roll, clothes. Everything else he had left in the lodge and then locked up both doors. "Okay, mules, let's get out of here." Neither mule was loaded heavy but there still wasn't room for him to ride.

The further south he went the less snow there was. But the streams and lakes were still solid with ice. Every once in a while he'd check his compass to make sure he was staying on course. There was no way he could possibly miss Fort Gibraltar. If he went too far to the east, he would come to the Red River. If he went too far west, he would come to the Assiniboine River. Gibraltar was at the confluence of the two rivers.

The third night out, it snowed a few inches of wet snow, and for some strange reason partridges were still roosting in fir trees at mid-morning. Eben took advantage of this and shot four of them. He wasn't sure how much further he had to go, but he was figuring on a week to reach Gibraltar.

On the eve of the fifth night, he made camp beside the Assiniboine River across from the fort. He just thought it would be safer to be on that side of the river instead of mingling with other trappers at the trading post. He made camp far enough back from the river so his campfire would not be seen.

After eating and seeing to the mules, he wrapped a blanket around his shoulders and sat down leaning against a huge spruce tree. The air was warmer here and he took a deep breath and smelled all the wood scents. It was like perfume to him. He sat there all night catnapping and occasionally putting another stick of wood on the fire.

He crossed the river before daylight so no one would know from which direction he had come. Once inside the fort, he went directly to the trading post to settle his business first.

"Good morning, sir. If you're a trapper, you've beat the rush. Most trappers don't get back until much later. They try to pick up some spring beaver," Oliver Stone said.

"Well, I thought about that, but I'm tired of cutting ice and getting wet. I'll have to be satisfied with what I have."

"How do you go by?" Oliver asked. "I'm Oliver Stone. I run this trading post for the North West Company."

"I'm Eben McNinch. Pleased to meet you. Can you tell me the date?"

"Sure thing. It's April 2, 1813."

"Thank you."

"McNinch? Never heard of you before. You must be new."

Eben let it rest there. "I have two bundles of beaver. The smaller bundle of twenty, I'll want a voucher on account. I'll use that to outfit in late summer when I'll head out again. The other bundle, there is fifty-two beaver, ten wolves and eight otter."

"Holy shit, McNinch! You have quite a catch. Let me do some figuring. The government is paying a $5.00 bounty on each wolf hide, plus $10.00 each; otter is almost double from last year. The ladies in Europe are wearing them around their necks, $6.00 each. The beaver I'll have to sort by size." A few minutes later Stone said, "You have forty super blankets; that's $25.00 each. The rest—twelve—are large. No small beaver at all. Most first timers will have more small beaver than large. The large beaver are $20.00 each. Do you have the castors?"

"Yes, I almost forgot. I'll have to get them off the mule. I have forty. The others I used to bait the wolves."

"$2.50 each castor times forty is another $100.00. The otter is $128.00. Your grand total is $1618.00.

That's a big sum of money, McNinch. I have that much here if you want cash. Where are you heading from here?" Stone asked.

"You're getting a little personal, aren't you?"

"If you're heading for The Company's base at Fort Williams, I could give you a voucher and you can get paid there. It would be safer than carrying that much money around with you," Stone replied.

"Would I get more money if I waited and sold at Fort Williams?"

"Yes, but only another ten percent. In your case a little more than $160.00."

"I guess I'll take your voucher, Mr. Stone. And another voucher for that first bundle."

"Well, let's see what you have in that one." It didn't take Stone long to size them. "You have ten super blankets and ten large, that's a total of $750.00.

"Not to be nosy, but where did you trap, McNinch?"

"You said let's not be nosy, and leave it at that, okay?"

"Okay, young fella. Not to change the subject, but last summer I heard quite a story that came back by two neophyte trappers like yourself. It seems as how only a few days out of Fort Williams they came upon two men, brothers. They were walking and had no supplies, furs, weapons or food. They were about starved. Oh, yeah, they each had broken right arms which were never splinted and their bones began to set on the trail. They said a man robbed them. He had red hair and beard like yours...and with two mules."

"That was me." There was a long pause before either of them said anything. "I didn't rob them. They came into my fire one night, hungry and thirsty. I fed them and they told me about running from some Indians because they had taken an Indian girl to their camp and they both bedded her. Then during the night they tried to rob me. I thought it fair pittance to break their arms. I could have killed them both and no one would have blamed me."

"No, sir, McNinch. I guess not. Here are your vouchers."

Eben looked at them. "You forgot to sign them, Mr. Stone."

"Oh, yes, certainly." His hands were shaking.

"Now, I need me some supplies: ten pounds of bacon, one pound of coffee. Do you have any fresh bread?"

"My wife is baking now."

"I'll take four loaves wrapped, ten pounds of grain for my mules. And it looks like rain coming. Do you have any slickers?"

"Yes."

"One slicker. You have these ready to go and I'll go have breakfast. How much do I owe you?"

"For everything, $11.50."

"That's expensive."

"Everything is expensive here, McNinch. We have to freight everything in overland."

"I guess that makes sense. I'll be back soon."

Before going to breakfast in the mess hall, he stopped at the livery. "I'm stopping only long enough to eat breakfast. Could I leave my mules here until then and can you give them each some grain?"

"Sure thing, mister. That'll be fifty cents each."

Eben gave him the money and walked away. "Thank you. I won't be long."

When Eben entered the mess hall, every one stopped what they were doing and silence hung over everyone's head. Eben paid no attention and found a table in the corner. A stout woman dressed in men's clothes asked, "You wanting breakfast, mister?"

"Yes, ma'am—"

She interrupted Eben with an annoying laugh, "Do you hear that, fellas? We have us here a real gentleman! He called me *ma'am.*

"What would you like, honey?"

"Eggs, ham, home fries and a pot of coffee. Four eggs and over easy."

"My name is Chelia and I'll get you that pot of coffee. Usually guys only ask for a cup. What's your name?"

"McNinch."

While he waited for his breakfast, he drank coffee. All the while others kept looking at him. When he would look directly back at any one of them, they would turn back to their own business.

Chelia came back with his breakfast and said, "Here you go, mister. Seconds if you're still hungry. The first helping cost enough. Where you heading, honey?"

"Fort Williams."

"Talkative sort, aren't you."

He didn't reply.

The eggs, ham and home fries were delicious, but he decided against seconds. Some of the men there had trouble written all over them. He finished eating and stayed long enough to finish the pot of coffee.

"That'll be $2.00, mister."

Eben paid it and said, "It was worth it."

Eben stopped at the trading post to pick up the supplies he would need on the trail to Fort Williams. "Mr. Stone, I have never done business like this before—vouchers saying someone owes a great deal of money. Because you represent the North West Company, I'll take your word on it. But if this turns into a lie and you have stolen my fur, I can assure you I'll make a special trip back here to square the account."

"Yes, sir, Mr. McNinch, everything is as I have said."

"Good day, Mr. Stone," Eben said as he left the trading post.

With grass in their bellies, the mules were frisky. He put on his new slicker, just in case.

* * * *

He didn't stop until the sun was overhead and he gave each mule a handful of grain and he had what was left of his smoked meat. He changed mules and rode until about two hours before dark. He chose an out-of-the-way place to make camp that night. The mules were helping themselves and Eben fried up some bacon and warmed up some fresh bread. Expecting trouble, he sat against a tree with a blanket around his shoulders. He slept some, knowing the mules would start braying if man or animal came near.

He slept through most of the night and was awakened at daybreak by a noisy raven cawing at him over his head, perched on a tree limb. He gave each mule two hands full of grain and then fried up bacon and had some more fresh bread and coffee.

It had drizzled during the night but under the spruce he had remained dry and didn't know it had drizzled. He wiped his mule off before saddling up. The mules were feeling frisky again and he made good time once he was back on the trail.

Three days later he met two men camped by the road at noon. Camping this early made him suspicious. He pulled the pistol out of the holster and laid it on his lap. The rifle he rested across his legs.

The two men walked over to the edge of the road, and Eben reined up. "Nice looking mules, mister. No luck trapping or are you a company man?"

Eben looked straight at the one who had spoken and he said, "My business is my own. I'm not looking for any trouble but if you two idiots are looking for trouble, I can surely give it to you."

"How are you going to do that, mister? There's two of us and only one of you."

"Well, stupid, if you look real close you'll see I have a pistol pointed at you right now."

"Yeah, maybe you do and maybe you don't. The way I sees it, we don't have much of any choice. We've been down on our luck for some time now and we want everything you got, except your life. And if you're smart you won't sit there and run your mouth anymore."

"Well you have a point there. But if you think for one second that I'm going to just hand over my mules to you two pukes, then you're crazier than hell. You want my mules, mister? Come get 'em." He sat in his saddle, not moving or pointing his rifle towards them.

The two didn't know what to think. He could be bluffing. But he sat there pretty damned confident.

Eben didn't think the one who was doing all the talking was in any hurry to do something stupid. But the other one who hadn't said anything was slowly cocking the hammer back.

Eben cocked his pistol and then his rifle. They weren't leaving him any choice. Eben heard his rifle fully cock. When the quiet guy raised his rifle to Eben, Eben shot him in the chest with his pistol. Now his friend was cocking his rifle and bringing it up. Eben shot him in the chest with his rifle. They were both dead, steam rising in the cool air.

His first instinct was to simply leave the bodies here. There wasn't much law in this part of Canada yet. But then he knew he'd have to do the right thing and take the bodies into Fort Williams with him.

He put a body on each of their horses and secured them. All they had was a little food and their rifles. "Stealing ain't much of a living, boys, and you two ain't very good at it."

As he rode on with the two horses in tow, he started thinking how much he had changed. He had never killed a man before and now he was having no regrets. He had given them a way out and they didn't take it. He was sure he would have some explaining to do once he was back at Fort Williams.

The wilderness out here demands that a man be on his guard at all times against both man and animal. If not, you're not going to survive. He supposed that's what the natives had discovered a long time ago. And the white man coming into this country still has that to learn. He wanted to feel bad about having to shoot both men, but the truth was he didn't. He wished it had not had to happen, but it did. He was learning to survive.

Ten days later he met two separate parties heading for Fort Douglas, a Hudson Bay Company facility across the river from Fort Gibraltar. When asked about the two bodies, all Eben would say was, "They didn't make it out here."

CHAPTER 6

It was a rainy day on April 20th when Eben rode into Fort Williams. He was wearing his slicker and tired. It had been a long, hard trip. People everywhere were staring at Eben and the bodies in tow. He stopped at the livery stable. "You Bill Wilcox?" Eben asked.

"Yes, sir. What can I do for you, mister?"

"You can take care of my two mules and give both a heaping portion of grain. They have earned it. And I'd like to leave these horses with the bodies here until I see Major Albert."

"Yes, sir."

Eben dismounted, stretched, took his pack, rifle and pistol and walked into Major Albert's office. The door was open and he walked in. He was still wearing the slicker. He looked like a rough-tagged trouble-maker.

"Who are you and state your business," Major Albert said.

Eben removed his slicker before saying anything. "My name is Eben McNinch and I prefer to have people look at me when I talk with them."

Major Albert stood and apologized for his bluntness. "You're back earlier than I expected. How was your trapping?"

"For my first year out, pretty good. Here's a voucher from Oliver Stone at Fort Gibraltar."

Major Albert took the voucher and looked it over and said, "Yeah, for first time out I'd say you did okay, considering you were alone. How do you want this? On account with the North West Company, paper money, silver or gold?"

"I don't trust paper money. I'll take $1000.00 in gold and the rest in silver, please."

Major Albert didn't quibble. He went in the adjoining room and withdrew the money from the safe. He gave Eben the money and said, "There's a matter of the brothers who came in here last summer, not long after you left. They both had their right arm broken and said someone with a red beard and hair robbed them."

"I broke their arms because they tried to steal everything I had at gunpoint." Then he told Major Albert the whole story.

"I never liked those two and I found it difficult to believe that you would rob them."

"Are they still here, Major?"

"No, they spent some time in the infirmary and then I told them to leave. Your wife did a pretty good job of fixing them up." The Major started laughing and then continued. "Their arms had started to mend and Ada had to re-break both arms and reset them properly. I guess they had it coming. Is the Indian girl okay, Eben?"

"She's fine. Oh, there is something else. I left two dead bodies at the livery. I told Wilcox to leave them on their horses."

"What happened with these two?"

"They jumped me between here and Gibraltar. I tried to talk them out of it. It was their choice."

"Well, Eben, I'm not the law. In fact there is no law in this wilderness. I'll write up a report to the main office with my monthly reports."

"Major, what I have seen at Fort Gibraltar, in my opinion it is filled with misfits and trouble makers. They could be causing a lot of trouble with the natives. Everybody I saw except for Oliver Stone was no good. If they trap for North West Company, they are a poor representation. If they work for you, they should be told to hit the road. That's only my opinion.

"Now I think I'll go find my wife. Good day, Major."

"Good day, Eben."

Eben closed the office door and Major Albert sat back at his desk smiling. "One year out, Eben McNinch, and already you have a solid reputation. There's no old timer that'll ever come close to you. This was your first year; I wonder what you'll be like five years from now." Major Albert was pleased with Eben and he was wishing he had a dozen trappers just like him, instead of the no-good pukes that Eben had described at Fort Gibraltar.

* * * *

Eben quietly opened the infirmary door and walked in. Ada was tending to someone; when she turned around, she screamed, dropped what she had in her hands and ran to Eben. He caught her in his arms and they hugged and kissed and hugged some more. "You're home early."

"Well, I was all through trapping and traveling was good, so I couldn't see any reason to stay out any longer."

"How did it go?"

"Better than I expected. I'll tell you all about it, but not here."

"I'll be off at noon. You go back to my room and take a bath and change your clothes. You smell."

He laughed and hugged her again and said, "You sure I need a bath? I had one before I left my camp in the woods."

"How long ago was that?" She asked good naturedly.

"Well...maybe six or seven weeks ago."

"No wonder. You go on now and clean up."

He was laughing as he closed the infirmary door. "She always did have the last word. Nothing has changed here," and he laughed all the way to her room.

He picked up some clean clothes and went to the bathhouse to bathe and have his hair and beard trimmed.

Cleaned up with clean clothes on, Eben surely didn't look like a trapper. Then he went to check on his mules. "Hello, Mr. Wilcox."

"My, you look different all cleaned up."

"I won't be needing my mules for a while. Do you pasture animals?"

72

"I do, just west of town I have some pasture land."

"How much?"

"There's not much tending. How does $5.00 a month sound?"

"Pretty good, Mr. Wilcox. How much to keep them here until you can pasture them?"

"$1.50 a week, but that doesn't include grain."

"Well, they won't be needing any more grain. But after their hooves heal up a bit, in a couple of days, I want new shoes all around for both," Eben said.

"That's $1.00 per shoe."

"Okay, you let me know when you pasture them and then I'll settle up with you. Will you need some money now?"

"Is Ada McNinch your wife?"

"She is."

"Then you can wait until I turn them out to pasture. Your wife took out my appendix. I almost died and she saved my life."

When Ada went back to her room and met Eben again it was as if for the first time. They hugged and kissed and held onto each other. "My, you sure do look different—better, and you don't smell!"

Ada locked the door and pulled the shade and then, without saying a word, took her clothes off and lay on the bed. For the first part of the afternoon, they each were only fulfilling their animalistic desire for sex. Then their sexual ecstasy became lovemaking with tender caresses.

Exhausted, they both laid on their backs, Ada snuggling close. Eben put his arm around her to hold her close. They talked for hours, not even getting up to eat supper. He told her all about his life as a trapper and Big Eagle and his people. Even about the wolves that had stalked him and his mule. The only thing he didn't mention was the gold nuggets he had found.

* * * *

Ada's happiness at having her husband home again was obvious at work and in how she greeted others. She had never been so happy. But she also knew that he would be leaving again towards late summer.

To keep busy and pay his keep, Major Albert asked Eben to help out at the trading post with hides coming in. Occasionally a loud and boisterous crew would come in and for a while Eben would let them have some fun and hoot and holler, but when it started to become a problem, he wasn't long putting a stop to the shenanigans. Occasionally one of them would want to test his temper with Eben, and ultimately ended up on the short end. It wasn't long before Eben had gained a reputation around the fort: not to mess with the red-haired guy.

One morning while Eben and Ada were eating breakfast, Major Albert joined them. "Good morning, folks. Eben, word is that there won't be any more problems with the trappers bringing their hides in. Everyone has heard about you all the way out to Fort Gibraltar and Fort Douglas. You're setting an example with some of the trappers, anyhow, how to act more responsible. And there is one thing that trappers hate more than anything is a thief. And a lot of the thievery between here and Gibraltar has stopped. I'm not getting as many complaints as previous years."

"Major, what is the news about the war?" Major Albert didn't have to ask what war.

"Not so good for the Americans. The British pushed south through Maine from New Brunswick down to New York. The northeast is no longer any threat. The Louisiana battles are going better for the Americans, but England has more manpower and money. It'll be a costly war no matter who is victorious."

"Well, that settles that. I'll definitely be going back to Manitoba to trap."

* * * *

Once in a while during the summer, someone would ask where he had spent the winter trapping, and he would always say, "West of Fort Gibraltar along the Assiniboine River." The only person who knew where he trapped was his wife Ada. He had given his word to Big Eagle and he intended to keep it.

"Do you really like it up there, Eben? I mean so alone and so far away from everything. I worry about you."

"I worry about you also, Ada, but this trapping life isn't any kind of a life for a woman. Big Eagle and his people have helped me a lot. They're good people, Ada. Nothing like the stories you hear around here about the natives. I have never known a group of people who are so honest and responsible. I don't think they could lie if one of them wanted to. Everyone always lends a helping hand to others. Maybe someday, Ada, when this war is over, we can move out that way somewhere and build us a life."

"I would like that, Eben. But until then, I'll go on missing you."

* * * *

By mid-July all of the fur from the company trappers had come in. There were still wagon-loads coming once a week from Fort Gibraltar. A few trappers had brought in a couple of wolf hides each, but no one had as many as Eben had. The price on all fur had gone up about ten percent since he sold in April and the market was looking even better for the following year.

One day when Eben started putting together some gear for the trip up, Ada asked, "You're leaving soon, aren't you, Eben?"

"Yes, in a week. Today is the last day at the trading post. Ed doesn't need any extra help now."

He had been working on a list of supplies he would need:

Two bucksaws
A calendar
Three books for reading
Nails and wire
Enough glass panes to make the windows
More flour this year

More coffee
Canvas
One lantern
Towel and washcloth
Canned vegetables, depending on room
A draw-shave

Ada had made him two new pullover shirts, one laced with rawhide just below the neck. The material was a special heavyweight cotton, one green and one brown. He bought new boots, a new winter coat and a light coat. Everything fit in his pack and the pack-mule would have a light load, so he would be able to travel faster.

Eben gave Ada all of his money except for $100.00. "I'll need to pick up a few more supplies at Gibraltar."

"We have a tidy sum now, Eben. I'll ask Major Albert if he will lock our money up in his safe."

"If you do, Ada, get a voucher from him. Just in case."

"Do you have everything, Eben?"

"I think so. What I'll get for Big Eagle I can get at Gibraltar."

Their last night together they lay in each other's arms all night. "Be careful, Eben."

"I will and I'll send word back with someone when I reach Fort Gibraltar."

CHAPTER 7

Eben left the next morning before most of the folks at the fort were even up. As much as he hated leaving Ada behind again, he was excited about getting back. It was July 20th and with good traveling, he hoped to be there in six weeks. Less if the traveling was really good.

He was on the road for fifteen hours that first day, stopping briefly at noon to rest and give the mules a rest, feed and water. He guessed he had traveled maybe thirty miles that day or a little more. He pushed hard the next day also and covered another thirty miles.

It was dry that summer of 1813 and he didn't encounter any rain all the way to Fort Gibraltar. He made it in three weeks and he and the mules were tired. He tied up at the livery and asked Francis, "Will you give them a good feed of grain and bag a hundred pounds for me to pack?"

"Sure thing, Mr. McNinch."

"How do you know who I am?"

"Everybody knows about you, Sir. You're the only red-haired trapper up in this country."

Eben walked over to the trading post and Mr. Wilson recognized him immediately. "Welcome back to the fur country, Mr. McNinch."

"Mr. Wilson, here is a list of what I need."

"How much bacon?"

"Fifteen pounds."

"Blankets?"

"Ten."

"Knives?"

"Six."

"You must be going to do some trading with the Indians."

"Something like that."

"Tobacco?"

"Two large cans."

"Anything else?"

"That'll have to be all. At least that's all the room I have."

Wilson was busy putting everything together and wrapping the bacon. Then he spent several minutes adding everything up.

"That all comes to $253.00. That will leave from your voucher, $147.00. How do you want that?"

"On account, please."

"Yes, sir, and thank you for your business, Mr. McNinch."

After Eben had his supplies secured to his mules, he would have to walk now. He went to have breakfast at the dining hall. He was hungry and he knew it would be months before he could have eggs again. He ordered four eggs over easy, home fries and ham and a pot of coffee.

He paid for his breakfast and went outside to start his journey north. Just as he was untying the mules from the hitching rail, he saw two men standing and watching, who both had had too much to drink. After all, it was 6 a.m. They spoke with a nasal twang, which Eben guessed they had come up to Canada from somewhere in the southern United States. "He don't look so tough to me, Fred," his brother Joe said.

"Ain't he suppose to be that bad ass'n guy people are all talkin' about?"

"His purty red hair onliest red hair I seen here'n these woods. Must be him, Joe."

They took a couple of steps closer to Eben and Fred said, "Hey, you!" and he almost shouted which got everyone's attention. Eben tried to ignore them.

"Hey you!" Fred shouted again. "I'm talk'n to you, you son-of-a-bitch!"

Now Joe joined in, "Hey, mister, you this bad ass guy we'n been hearin' about?" When Eben didn't answer, Joe took another step closer. Eben's silence was angering Joe. "Hey, mister, ain't you'n get back enough to answer?"

"Look, you two pukes, you're both drunk. Why don't you go crawl off in some pigpen and sleep it off before you get yourselves hurt."

Joe didn't like being talked to like that, and he took another step closer and Eben could see Joe was about to swing a punch at him. He was prepared and he side-stepped just as Joe swung at Eben's head. Eben grabbed hold of him and lifting him completely off the ground, threw him out into the yard.

While he was doing this, he noticed Fred had started to look through the pack on his mule. Eben came up behind him and grasped Fred's arm and broke it like a piece of dried kindling. Fred screamed with pain.

Joe got to his feet and rushed head down at Eben. He caught Eben in the stomach and much to Joe's surprise and disgust, this head bunt didn't even make Eben back up one step or even seemed to faze him. Joe knew he was in trouble now, and there wasn't one thing he could do. But Eben didn't hit him, like the on-lookers thought he would do. Instead he literally picked Joe up off the ground and carried him to the other end of the compound and threw him into the pigpen in the deepest corner of pig shit. "I told you two to crawl off into a pigpen and sleep it off. Now you stay there until I leave town. Do you understand me?"

When Joe didn't answer, Eben said again a bit more forcefully. "Do you hear me, Joe?" he said in a deep voice.

"Yeah."

Fred was still screaming.

Eben led his mules up to the trading post and Mr. Stone was outside watching like most everybody there. "Mr. Stone, would you see that this letter gets to Fort Williams with your next freight wagon?" And he handed Oliver a letter.

With his mules in tow, Eben left Fort Gibraltar.

* * * *

Eben was glad to be leaving Fort Gibraltar. It seemed that place was a magnet for undesirables and trouble makers. The class of people he didn't want to find the Cree land and his trapping grounds. He had thought maybe some trapper or two might try to follow him and he kept a watchful eye on his back-trail and randomly changed course. He marked off each day on the calendar.

Five weeks to the day after leaving Fort Williams he arrived at his camp. Everything was as he had left it.

He cared for his mules after he unpacked them and removed the rocks from both doors. The mules were as tired as he was. After unpacking, he kindled a fire in the outside fire-pit and then he sat under one of the spruce trees to relax.

He staked the mules in the heath. He needed meat so he went hunting. Two days away from camp he had started to see a lot of moose tracks and droppings. Apparently the moose had moved into the area that summer. So he went looking for a small moose. About a yearling would do. Bull or cow.

Not far from camp he found two yearlings heading for the heath to feed. He shot the little bull and skun it while lying on the ground like he had seen Big Eagle's people do with the caribou. This was actually a much cleaner way to take care of it.

When he was finished skinning, he hitched one mule up to the rock drag and hauled the meat back to camp. For now he put it all in cold storage and made a bigger smoking rack. Later that evening as the meat was curing, he ate roasted heart, stick bread and a few raw onions he had found in the heath.

He sat up by the fire all night tending to the fire and meat. He was really enjoying himself. He liked this rough wilderness living. He ate heart and liver every day until it was gone. He had kept a small amount of fresh meat in cold storage and everything else was now cured.

His next project was to make two window frames, a small one in the door and one looking towards the mule shelter. The moose hide he lay on the ground and rubbed wood ashes into the hide to rid it of insects. Then he soaked it in the stream for a day and then staked it out on the ground to dry. He would use it for a rug next to his bed. The caribou hide from the previous year had to be thrown away.

Now it was time to forage in the heath and forest for mushrooms, onions, berries and nuts. After two days he figured he had enough and spread them out in the sunshine to dry. He had a devil of a time to keep the squirrels out of it.

After everything was dried he decided it was time to go visit Big Eagle's village. He packed one mule and would ride the other when he could. He didn't want to leave one behind. He didn't know how long he'd be away.

* * * *

It was evening before he arrived and everyone was happy to see him. "Is good you come back, Big Red Beard Not Afraid."

"I am happy to be back and I have missed my Cree family."

Eben unloaded the mule and placed everything on the ground so everyone would see what he brought. He handed Big Eagle the rifle and ammo and his eyes bugged out as large as silver dollars it seemed. Big Eagle gave the rifle to Neokiowa. Then he picked up a can of tobacco and asked, "What this?"

Eben opened the can and gave it back to Big Eagle. Big Eagle knew what it was then. "Tobacco for pipe. Good."

Little Claw was looking at the bucksaw, wondering what it was with so many sharp teeth. "Little Claw, go get a log about this long." And he spread his arms about four feet. Little Claw came running back with the log on his shoulder. Eben showed them how to saw through the wood for the fires. Little Claw could not be happier. They knew what the axe and knives were and the women were fondling the blankets. "I wanted to bring more, Big Eagle, but there wasn't room on the mules. You still have money on account at the trading post." Big Eagle just shrugged his shoulders. He had no idea of money or what Eben had said. But everyone was happy and it would be up to Big Eagle to see who got what.

That night when Big Eagle and Eben were alone in his lodge, Eben showed him the map of the North American Continent. Once Big Eagle recognized the two lakes, Manitoba and Winnipeg, he pointed on the map the location of his village. Eben pointed about where he had built his lodge.

Big Eagle swept his hand over the map and said, "Big. Big country."

Eben showed where Fort Gibraltar was and the trading post and Fort Williams near Lake Superior.

"I been this lake once when boy," and he pointed to Lake Superior. "Not see land on other side."

The next day was declared a feast day for Eben's return. "You go on caribou hunt this year?" Neokiowa asked.

"Yes, I would like to."

"Okay. I come get like last year. You and I shoot many caribou with rifle. Maybe leave one for Big Red Beard Not Afraid to wrestle before he kills caribou."

Eben felt more at home with these people than he did at Fort Williams. That doesn't mean he didn't miss Ada, because he did. She was the best woman for him that he could imagine. There was never any false pretense here with these people. They had so readily accepted him as one of them.

* * * *

Eben returned from the village. There wasn't anything needing his immediate attention and out of curiosity, he took his fry pan down the stream and in no time he had a handful of nuggets. All about the same size as those first few. The size of green peas. He had to make a bigger pouch and he buried it in cold storage.

The next day after tending to the mules and then shutting

them up in the cave shelter, he put some bacon in his pack with his axe and carrying his rifle he checked his compass and headed for the new beaver country he had found in the spring. He wanted to build a temporary shelter there. It was only about a two mile hike, but he would be time limited if he was to travel back and forth in daylight and do any trapping.

He found a good place where there were many small spruce and fir trees, only about three to four inches. He worked until just before dark before stopping for the night and then again until noon the next day. He was done except for a fireplace. It was rough, but it would do for a night at a time.

He returned in two days and finished the fireplace. There was plenty of scrap wood left from his building so there would be plenty of firewood for his occasional overnight stay.

With that temporary camp completed, he concentrated on working up firewood and found it so much easier to chunk the wood up with the bucksaw rather than having to chop each piece with the axe. And the mules needed a workout also. In a few days he figured he had plenty of wood.

Then he worked on gathering food for the mules. It was back breaking work cutting the tall marsh grass with his knife. He brought in enough to fill the storage area inside the shelter. Besides he would only have the one mule during the winter.

He went fishing downstream in the biggest and deepest flowage. There were a lot of new beaver workings and there was another big house.

He spent all day fishing there and roasted the first trout caught and nibbled on it while it cooked on the stick. He carried a dozen three or four pound trout back with him. He finished eating the fish he had roasted during the day and now he filleted each trout and put it on the rack to smoke and cure.

Then he went to cut down a green becchnut tree. Green wood would smoke more and the beechnut would give it a good flavoring. This would probably be enough smoked fish until maybe later in winter.

With his axe, bucksaw and draw shave, he made more substantial tables. One inside and one for the outside. He made two wooden chairs also.

When he didn't have anything to keep him busy, he would spend time on the stream with his fry pan. Each time, he would find almost a handful.

The water was only cool and he thought this would be a good time to take a bath. He took his clothes off and waded out to the middle of the stream. The water didn't quite come to his waist. Against his bare skin the water seemed Gawd-awful cold. But he finished his bath and then washed the clothes he had been wearing and hung these on the trees to dry.

He thought about brushing out his trail downstream to the last flowage, but thinking better on it, he didn't want any cleared trail leading back to his camp.

The autumn leaves were just beginning to show some color. He knew it was almost time for the caribou hunt. With all the moose meat he had, he really didn't need the entire caribou. Maybe he'd only take half of the animal and Big Eagle could have the rest.

The days were getting shorter and it was beginning to be too cold in the evening to sit outside and watch the fire and listen to the breeze whisper through the treetops. He hadn't heard a wolf howl since being back. Maybe they won't return this year. But somehow he doubted that; there was at least one left from the pack. He was sure of that. He would know better as soon as there was some snow on the ground and he could see their tracks.

Two days later Neokiowa arrived carrying his new rifle. "Me like this rifle. Me shoot bear and moose far distance. Big help."

The next morning, each riding a mule, Neokiowa led the way east to the rendezvous at the river. From there everything was a repeat of the previous year except Eben did not have to wrestle any caribou to the ground. Eben explained to Big Eagle that he had shot a moose earlier and didn't need the entire animal. He took only one hind quarter and one shoulder. "That is enough, Big Eagle. You take the rest."

"You want hide? It belong to you. You shoot caribou," Big Eagle said.

"No, you keep the hide, Big Eagle. I'll see you in spring same as last year," Eben said.

Eben tied the two quarters to his mule and led her off for home. He turned to wave goodbye. He was sad to have to leave them, but he must. The sky was turning gray like it might snow before he got back. So he pushed himself and the mule harder. He would reward her with some grain.

It was always good to be back at camp. The snow never came and by morning a cold wind had blown the gray clouds out. He saved some of the best steaks fresh and in cold storage. The rest was cut into strips and dried, again using green beechnut for flavor. It took a week to smoke it all. With everything else done, it was time to trap. He let the mule out to graze while he put his gear together. He only packed a little food, intending to eat beaver.

He used the same routine as last year; setting up close by the flowage and set in troughs on the dams. He worked back and forth all day and caught six large beaver. He was up late skinning the last beaver. He was glad he had built the small camp. Only big enough for a small fireplace and a bed.

He left to head back to camp at noon with nine beaver—all skun and the fur rolled up and castors and hind legs cut off and wrapped in one hide.

"Yes, this is going to work out just fine."

He spent two days at camp taking care of the beaver hides, the mule and storing the beaver meat in cold storage. He knew it wouldn't last long without smoking it, but fresh beaver was delicious.

That night as he checked his calendar in the glow of the lantern, it was the end of October. Having the lantern made all the difference inside the otherwise dark lodge.

He kept up this schedule until the last of November. He had thirty-two beaver and four otter from the flowages to the west.

He was done with his temporary camp and when he left he made sure it was closed up tight and he had taken everything with him.

There was plenty of daylight left and he knew he'd get back before dark. There was a northwest wind blowing in storm clouds. There was a cold chill in the air also, and he knew this was going to be a bad storm.

The two mile hike back he made in record time. He didn't run, but his pace was almost as fast. He just made it to the camp yard and wind driven snow blew across the yard. He took care of the mule before going in. His lodge was cold as ice, but it would warm soon. There was frost on some of the rocks.

He lit the lantern first as the storm had darkened the sky. Even after the fire had been burning for a while it was still cool. In his absence and with no fire, the rocks were as cold as ice and it took all night before the rocks were again warm. As he laid in bed listening to the wind howl outside, he was glad he had had the foresight to trap to the west first. Now he was done there and could concentrate on the flowages downstream.

There was a foot of dry snow on the ground in the morning. He checked his calendar to see what the date was. November 28th. The wind had stopped blowing during the night. He was smiling when he got up and decided to have a breakfast of bacon and toasted stick bread and of course, coffee. Even after he had eaten, he was still in a jovial mood. He was simply feeling good about his life there.

* * * *

He set traps downstream exactly like he had done last year and he tended his traps every day, and he would plan to be back in time so to stretch the hides on the trees. By the end of December he had another twenty-five beaver and four more otter. He already had a few more beaver than last year and he didn't want to over-trap the area so he would pull his traps after he caught two more super large beaver.

The first of March rolled down from the artic like a lion. The wind blew day and night and the temperatures dropped so low all Eben wanted of the outside was to tend to his mule. He was glad he had put up so much grass earlier. There was maybe five pounds of grain left and he would save that for now.

As if the cold and wind wasn't bad enough, it began to snow. At least it was dry and fluffy and the wind pretty much blew it into the trees. His trapping was obviously over, unless a thaw came behind this artic weather and opened the water near the dams so it would flow through the troughs. With nothing else to do he stayed inside and read. He was sure glad now he had thought to bring along the books and with the lantern and the windows the inside of the lodge was light enough so he could read. Otherwise he would have gone stir-crazy contained in such a small space with nothing to do.

The day before the artic blast blew in he had taken all the hides off the trees and they were now bundled together in cold storage.

The wind blew and it snowed for a week. When it stopped much warmer weather returned. There was no way of knowing how much snow had fallen, being so wind driven. He was hoping Big Eagle's people had survived the storm. Then he said out loud, "Of course they did. They have been surviving weather like this for centuries. They're probably worrying about me."

At the only flowage downstream that he had not had the time to trap, the water around the dam was open. Three more beaver to make it an even sixty. While he was working the second trough, the first trap snapped closed. Whatever it was had gone back in the water under the ice. He waited to pull it in until he had finished with the second trap.

When he did pull it in, it was an otter. He caught two otters before any beaver. He had his quota, so he pulled his traps and stored them in cold storage and stretched the hides to the trees.

The daylight hours were warm enough now so he could leave his door open so to air out the inside. And the mule returned to foraging in the heath.

He was surprised that the wolves had stayed away this year. He had naturally thought he would have had the same problem.

With March 15th came warm, almost hot sunny days and the snow was melting fast. He prepared to leave. He made the same preparations as last year only this year he took his mule with him so he could stay longer.

He was glad to see his family and they all were glad to see him. The day after his arrival there was a feast and he had brought along a lot of his smoked meat that he knew he wouldn't be using.

Big Eagle had twenty beaver to send back with Eben. The same as last year. "This year I will bring back something special for the women, Big Eagle."

He stayed for three days before saying goodbye.

"You come back?" Big Eagle asked.

"Yes, I come back before the leaves turn color."

"Good."

* * * *

The next day Eben put his food in his pack along with clothes. The pouch of gold he buried in cold storage.

The next morning he and the mules were ready to leave. He took one last look to make sure everything was done. While on the trail south the weather turned a little colder. At least it wasn't snow or rain. He was still making good time. When he'd stop to rest, he'd give each mule a handful of grain.

When he reached the juncture of the two rivers there was a little water on the ice. Not much, but Eben decided to cross now in the daylight instead of waiting for early dawn.

The price for fur didn't go up like he had expected it to. Some said the war between the United States and England kept the price down from paying what it did last year. "No wolves this year, Mr. McNinch?"

"They left me alone this year."

"$1200.00 for your beaver, $160.00 for the otter and $110.00 for the castors. That totals to $1470.00. How would you like that, Mr. McNinch?"

"Same as last year. And this bundle of twenty on account, with a voucher, of course."

"Certainly, Mr. McNinch. Here are your two vouchers. Will you be back the same time in the summer?"

"Yes."

Eben left his mules at the livery so they could eat and he went for breakfast. While he ate, two real rough looking fellows got up and left. Eben watched them cross the compound and head in the same direction he was going. He had a feeling he'd have to be cautious of those two.

Eben thanked Mr. Wilcox for feeding his mules and he was on his way again. He rode with his pistol in his lap. If they were going to jump him, it wouldn't be so close to the fort. He didn't have any money on him, only the vouchers, which no one could draw on except him. By the time he stopped for the night he hadn't seen anyone on the trail, but he still made camp out of sight of the trail and he built his fire behind a large rock so that wouldn't be seen either.

He gave the mules grain that he had gotten from Mr. Wilcox. Water would have to wait until morning. If anything was going to happen he expected it to be at night.

He pushed his mules that morning until noon, when he caught up with the two he was concerned about.

"Hello, mister," one of them said.

His mules needed a rest and water so he had to stop. He ate some smoked beaver while the mules ate grass. Eben was keeping a sharp eye on the two, never letting one of them get behind him.

When the mules were rested he saddled up and one of the men asked, "Do you mind if we ride along with you, mister?"

"Yes, I do mind. I don't want either one of you close to me. The two of you pukes are just looking for a chance to jump me. Let me warn you, if you do and if I don't kill you, I'll hurt you so bad you'll wish you were dead. I strongly suggest that wherever I make camp tonight that you don't come into my camp. In my opinion you two are two worthless pieces of crap."

Before Eben was out of sight he said, "Remember what I said."

"That son-of-a-bitch, talking to us like we're nothing but a dog turd," Chad said.

"Are we just going to let him ride off?" Lex asked.

"I know a way we can get ahead of him, but we'll have to hurry," Chad said. "Come on, let's move it."

The trail swung north up ahead to get around some marshland. Chad had found a shorter route detouring to the south. They followed behind Eben out of sight until they came to the cutoff. "From here, Lex, we'll have to lead the horses."

When Chad and Lex were back on the trail, Chad checked for tracks. When he didn't see any he said, "We're ahead of him now. We'll find a good place to ambush him." They rode on. Just as they disappeared, Eben rode up over a knoll and all he saw was the hump of a horse disappearing ahead of him.

They must have another way around that marsh. He dismounted to walk his mules to see if he could see where they had come back onto the trail. He found where two horses had come onto the trail from the south side. At least he knew where they were and that they were probably going to ambush him. He only went a little further on the trail when he stopped and tied the mules to a bush and gave them some grain to keep 'em from braying.

With his rifle in hand, he slipped into the woods on the high side of the trail. He expected the two to be on the high side also and if possible he wanted to be above them.

He had only gone about a mile when he spotted the first about thirty feet off the trail behind a waist-high rock. *There was one, now where was his friend.* He had to be down the trail in case Eben slipped by. *I'll deal with you in a few minutes.* Eben took off and with his rifle he inched down toward the first thief. There was thick moss underneath and not dry branches to step on and snap. He made sure he always kept a tree between him and the thief. Eben inched along, not even breathing heavy. He was now directly behind the guy and he whispered, "Hey, you."

The guy turned around and Eben punched him hard in the nose, driving him over the rock and he lay unconscious on the ground. He took his rifle and jammed it in the ground, plugging the barrel. "Now, where is your friend?"

Eben went back up on higher ground and continued on parallel with the trail. He found him about two hundred feet down the road. And like his friend, he was about thirty feet off the road behind a large spruce tree.

He left his rifle propped up against a tree and withdrew his pistol and he began inching his way down to this guy. When Eben was about twenty feet from him, for some unknown reason the guy turned around. Eben knew he had made no noise, but instinctively the guy brought his rifle up to fire at Eben and instinctively Eben leveled his pistol at the man's chest and fired. He went down in a crumble and moaned several times and then was quiet.

Eben walked up the trail to the first man and he was just coming around. He was finally able to stand. Eben punched him again and he fell unconscious again. Then he sat down and waited for the man to regain consciousness. It took several minutes before he stood up. He said, "Don't hit me again, mister, please."

"Give me one good reason why I shouldn't just shoot you now. That's what you were going to do to me."

"I know, mister, but it wasn't my idea. It was all Chad's. Where is Chad?"

"Chad is dead. I shot him."

"What you gonna do with me then, mister?"

"You're a royal pain in the ass and you're useless. I should just leave you out here with nothing. Not even your horse. But I have a better idea. I'm going to haul your ass back to Fort Williams and have you shipped off to a provincial jail and let you sweat it out for a few years making small rocks out of large rocks. Now get up. Where's your horse?"

"Chad tied 'em both up down below him somewhere."

"Then we'll have to walk back for my mules. Let's go.

"What's your name?"

"Lex, Lex Buford."

"What was your buddy's last name?"

"Humphrey."

"Okay, Buford. Mount up on that mule." He did without arguing.

When they found the horses they had to go back and get Chad's body. Eben threw him over one of the horses and tied him securely. "You ride the other horse. I'm not going to tie you up because that will only slow me down. Let me warn you about doing anything stupid. You will regret it. Let's move it; we have half a day to make up because of you."

Eben kept moving into the night as long as he could see the trail. When he did stop, he had no choice but to share his food with Mr. Buford and the grain with the two horses so they would not fall behind.

Every day was the same routine and the mules seemed to sense Eben's urgency, where the horses had to be prodded to keep going.

Eben still arrived at Fort Williams within his own timetable. He took Buford to Major Albert's office.

"Sit down, Buford."

They walked into Major Albert's office and Eben closed the door. "Hello, Eben, you're right on time. Who is your friend?"

"Yes. Not a friend, sir. He and his partner tried to ambush me between here and Fort Gibraltar. I want him arrested for attempted murder and piracy."

"I have no authority to arrest him, Eben. The only thing I can do is send him out with the next ship to Ottawa with my report and an affidavit from you. Where is his partner?"

"He's dead, tied to his horse outside."

Major Albert wanted an explanation.

"He tried to shoot me and I shot him."

"Who is he?"

"Chad Humphrey"

"What's your name?"

"Lex Buford."

"So what were you two going to do, Buford?"

"Take his mules and gear and money. It was Chad's idea to kill him."

"We have our own security people here, but they have no authority outside this fort. But we have accommodations for you, Buford. If you'll wait here, Eben, I'll go get security to take charge of this one."

In a few minutes Major Albert returned with two security guards. "Take him to the blockade. He'll be shipped to Ottawa on the next ship.

"Sit down, Eben." He did and Major Albert brought a bottle of whiskey and poured two glasses. "Here, Eben."

Eben didn't reject the drink.

"You know, Eben, we lose a few trappers each year. Some from piracy between here and Fort Gibraltar, some to Indians, some succumb to the weather. But you are the only trapper who brings bodies back here. You are apparently the only trapper who survives piracy attacks."

"Major, how is the war going?"

"Not good for the Americans. British troops now occupy New York, and Boston and most of the northeast. England brags that they'll end the war by the end of the year."

"Do you believe that, Major?"

:No. These Americans are like—how do I say, England might as well had kicked a hornets' nest. I believe these Americans will win in the end. In the south there is a very good military leader, American General Andrew Jackson and there is a French pirate who has come to his aid. A Jean LaFitte. He is a notorious fighter.

"Do you have your voucher, Eben?"

Eben gave it to Major Albert.

"Um, no wolves this year...."

"No, sir, they left me alone. I'd like $1200.00 in gold coin, sir, and the rest in silver."

Eben went to the bathhouse first and then had his hair and beard trimmed, before going to see Ada.

"I heard you had made it back. Where have you been?"

"Well, I didn't want you to tell me I smelled, so I cleaned up first."

"And quite nicely, I must say. Mary is going to take over for me for the rest of the day."

* * * *

They lay exhausted in each other's arms, talking. "How did you do this year?"

"I caught three more beaver and two more otter and no wolves. They left me alone this year. The final total isn't quite as much as last year. Close, though."

"Will you be going back, Eben?"

"Yes," and he told her about his responsibility towards the tribe to see that he traded their beaver for things they needed.

"I'm not sure about a fourth year. From what I have heard, the Americans are not fairing so good in this war against England and it might be over soon. By then, Ada, we'll have saved enough money to get our own place."

He told her all about the piracy occurring on the trail to Fort Gibraltar and why he had to shoot that one fellow. "You know, Ada, it isn't as dangerous living in the wilderness or with the natives, as it is when I come back into the white man's world.

"From what I have seen, the tribes would not allow

94

dishonesty, stealing or what the white man thinks is okay as long as he isn't caught. They have a different sense of value about them than we do."

"Will you be leaving about the same time as last year?"

"Yes."

"Well, I guess I can't complain any. I have you every day for three and a half months and we never quarrel. There are a lot of women who aren't so fortunate. But I like the idea of our own place."

She told him all about her work at the infirmary and how much she liked working there. "I'm the boss there now, and I like that."

"You make a good boss, Ada. You can use me for a reference." She laughed and poked him in the side.

The next morning Ada took the money and had Major Albert lock it up in the safe. "I would like a voucher also, please."

"Certainly."

Eben drank coffee in the mess hall while he wrote out a report justifying shooting Chad Humphrey and bringing Lex Buford in. It was a lengthy report as he included every detail. When he had finished he gave the report to Major Albert.

"Thank you, Eben. The ship leaves tomorrow and I can assure you Mr. Buford will be on it. He'll never see this wilderness again."

CHAPTER 8

Ada helped Eben pack his gear and supplies. During the winter she had made him two more green pullover shirts with rawhide laced v-necks. "You know, Eben, try to understand what I am about to say. I might stumble over the right words some. I love you dearly, but I'm not sad to see you go. You were made for the wilderness life, not what we had back home. Here you are always happy and this makes me happy. When you return each spring we both are so happy, and happy to be with each other every day, I think. It makes up for the time you are away. Can you understand what I'm saying?"

"Yes, Ada, and I love you more than anything and I have always known you are the best woman I could ever hope to find."

Then laughingly she said, "And no Indian girls."

"No Indian girls," Eben repeated.

"Because you know what I said...."

There, she had the last word again.

Eben left after breakfast the next morning and kissed Ada goodbye.

"You be careful out there, Eben."

"I will."

"You better." She had the last word again.

* * * *

The trip to Gibraltar was uneventful. "I'll need:
4 fry pans
10 blankets

1 rifle, .45 calibur
3 axes
Cooking pots and pans
2 cans of tobacco

"You figure up how much all this is and I'm going to load my mules and see if there's room for more."

"Okay, Mr. McNinch."

There wasn't much for weight and the blankets took up most of the space. "Okay, I can take a little more:
2 more axes
6 more knives
2 more fry pans
Another set of pots and pans …and that'll be enough."

"That'll be $373.00, that'll leave you with just over $200.00 on account."

"Okay, I'll need 15 pounds of bacon."

"It's always a pleasure to do business with you, Mr. McNinch."

"There is one more thing, Oliver. Last spring two lazy-ass pukes tried to rob me. I killed one and sent the other one to prison in Ottawa for a good long time. You spread the word, Oliver."

"Yes, sir, Mr. McNinch, I surely will."

After breakfast and the mules had also eaten, Eben left the fort and headed north. He was feeling good, being back in the wilderness. He was anxious about seeing his friends in the village.

Two days north of Fort Gibraltar, he came upon horse tracks left in mud that had dried. He figured they were about a week old. Trespassers in his private trapping country infuriated him. As it would any trapper. He decided to follow their trail and if he caught up with them, drive 'em out and off Cree land.

There were times when their trail seemed to disappear. Then he'd check his compass and continue on in the direction they were traveling and eventually he came across their tracks again. The trail, if they kept their course, would take them to the last beaver colony that he trapped.

It looked like two men on horseback and one pack animal. To bring horses up into this country he surmised the two were neophytes and knew little about what they were doing. And he surely didn't want them to find gold in the stream, then this country would be overrun with gold seekers, and that would cause a lot of hardship for the Cree as they would try to drive them off their lands. And eventually, they would fail.

Eben knew he was getting close to his trapping country, maybe a whole day's hike away. He stopped to check the tracks and smelled wood smoke. He tied the mules and left his rifle. The pistol he always wore now. He started following the smoke scent. He didn't have far to go. They were down over a little rise next to a stream, probably the same stream that he was camped on.

Only a fool would go charging in. He lay on his stomach to watch. There were just the two of them and it looked like they were going to make this their camp. They were about his age, taller by four inches and they spoke English with a French accent.

Their rifles were leaning up against a tree. This was good. They each were wearing a big sheath knife but no pistols. From the look of the gear maybe they only had intentions of trapping only until there was snow and cold weather.

He crawled back out of sight and worked his way to the right to come in behind the rifles. He wanted to get between the rifles and the two men. He laid behind a rotting log and waited for an opportune time to go in.

They were about forty feet away from the rifles now with their backs turned. This was the best advantage Eben was going to get. Very quietly he got up and walked right in to their camp. Placing himself between them and their rifles. He was about twenty feet from them when they turned and saw him, one of them jumped backwards and screamed, "Sacré Anglais!"

The other one was a little more composed and said, "Why you just come in to our camp, monsieur, like a ghost? What you want, monsieur?"

The other one who had hollered was trying to get behind Eben to the rifles.

Eben pointed at him and said, "Hold it right there, mister. You stay away from the rifles."

"What you want? You want to steal what we have?"

"No, I don't want anything. This is my trapping country, not yours."

"You own this country? Thought not. We stay, me."

"No, you don't stay. I have permission from Chief Big Eagle of the Cree Nation to be here. You do not."

"What if we don't want to go?"

"Then I'll make you go." While Eben was talking the one to his right was inching closer. The man was close now and Eben knew what these two had in mind.

The guy took one more step closer and said, "We ain't going no where, monsieur."

About then, Eben turned and back-handed the guy so hard the blow drove him backwards and over backwards. The other guy was rushing to Eben with a closed fist. Eben stepped aside and drove his iron fist into the guy's stomach, doubling him over but not down. He recovered before his friend, and he came at Eben again. But Eben was quicker and hit the guy on the end of the nose, flattening that and blood sprayed all over his face. Now he was really mad.

The first one was up now and a little dazed. He rushed at Eben and Eben double-fisted him on the back of his neck, breaking the collar bone. He heard the bone snap. The guy screamed in pain. The second guy could focus now and he swung a wild punch at Eben. That only grazed the side of his head. Eben wasn't even fazed. He hit the guy on the chin and broke his jaw. But he didn't do down. Eben punched him in the stomach again and in the face. This laid the guy out flat on the ground.

Eben had had enough of this and when he saw the guy's right arm stretched out straight on the ground, he stamped on his wrist and it broke and he howled with pain. That ended the fight. Eben sat down until the two had calmed down and composed themselves.

"Now are you two going to leave on your own or do we continue fighting?"

"No, monsieur, we go. But some day we fix you good."

"What's your name?"

"Guy Tardiff."

"And your friend?"

"Reynold Terrion."

"If I ever see either one of you two again, I'll continue this beating. Now take my advice. Stay off Cree land and tell your friends to stay off. And to make sure you two don't follow me and try to back-shoot me—" He walked over to their rifles and swung them against a tree, breaking them.

"Now get on your horses and get out of here before I lose my temper."

Eben watched them leave and followed behind them for a short while to make sure they kept going.

Since he was that close to his camp, he kept going, since there was plenty of daylight that time of year. He unpacked the mules and took care of them. By now it was dark and he went to bed without eating. He was exhausted.

Two days later he repacked the mules and went to Big Eagle's village. As usual, they were happy to see him and to see what he had brought with him this year. This year the rifle was given to Little Claw. The women all cried with joy when they saw all the fry pans and pots and pans. They knew how to use them.

Big Eagle said, "Come, we smoke this tobacco. Neokiowa, Little Claw, you come to." Not a word was said until there was nothing but ash left in the pipe.

"Big Eagle, I followed two white trappers from Fort Gibraltar to the stream where I trap. I told them they had to leave, that this was Cree land."

"Did they go willingly?"

"With my help."

"They come back?" Big Eagle asked.

"I don't think so."

Big Eagle started smiling. "You wrestle them to ground like caribou and wolf?"

"Something like that."

Then Big Eagle laughed. "You take care of Cree. Good. You more Cree than white man."

Then on a more serious note, Big Eagle said, "This war between America and England not go good for Americans. England burned American big city where white chief is."

Neokiowa said, "Big Eagle means the big house where the white chief is in a place called D.C. I don't know what D.C. is."

"D.C. is actually Washington D.C. Big city, many people and the white chief or President works in the capitol. But how do you know this?"

"You know about runners that go from tribe to tribe. Runner was here before you arrived. Told us many things. I sent runner to Ojibwa village west of here. When he returns, he brings news from there."

"Okay, guess I can understand that."

"We know from runner that you have big name in white man world. Many have tried to take what is not theirs. You kill one and take other man to jail. Runner said you say good about Cree friends. Cree runner takes word Big Red Beard Not Afraid can travel anywhere on land belonging to tribes and no-one bother you. You become legend because you help Cree people and not afraid."

* * * *

Eben made sure, first of all, that his temporary camp to the west was okay and made any repairs necessary. He worked up enough wood for the season and then he scouted out the flowages he had trapped last year. They all were showing signs of activity and new lodges.

He worked up grass for the mule, firewood, gathered edible food and dried them. He caught a pack full of fish and dried them. Then he caught more and dried those. He didn't have moose meat this year. When everything was done, he panned for more gold and found it downstream this year. He had quite a pouch full of nuggets now and decided he had enough.

* * * *

The caribou hunt came and now there were three men with rifles which made the kills cleaner and not so many lying wounded. Those with the new knives were surprised how well they could skin the animals and strip the meat for curing.

With his caribou meat curing on the smoke rack and some fresh meat in cold storage, Eben was ready to start trapping at the out-camp. Every day until the meat was cured Eben stayed close to keep green beechnut wood on the fire.

The day came when he put the now cured meat in cold storage and he put together what he would need the next day to trap at his out-camp. He worked it as he had the previous year and each day he was catching four super blanket beaver.

He continued this routine until there was six inches of snow on the ground. Then he pulled all his traps and gear and returned to camp. He already had thirty beaver and five otter.

Trapping downstream from his camp was as lucrative. By the end of November he had twenty more beaver and four more otter. There still wasn't much snow by mid-December but it was cold and the ice was getting thick. When he had to break ice in front of the dam so beaver could swim to the troughs, Eben figured it was time to pull his traps. By the end of December he now had sixty beaver, like last year, and two more otter.

The temperatures really got cold during January, the coldest he had ever seen. Water in buckets in the mule's shelter froze each night. Eben would have to put more wood on his fire three or four times each night. The sap in the evergreen trees was freezing and the bark and wood would explode like a rifle report. Ravens stopped flying, squirrels stayed in their burrows.

Then in February the temperature warmed up and it snowed eighteen days out of twenty-eight. He was glad he had stopped trapping.

Spring was late in 1815 and when Eben counciled with Big Eagle, Neokiowa and Little Claw, "I don't think I'll be back this time. I can't explain it, but I feel there is something that I must do." Eben, as he was saying it, didn't know what that was. It was only a feeling.

"When I take your beaver to the trading post at Fort Gibraltar, I will tell them to put the account in the names of Neokiowa and Little Claw. I'll make sure that you won't have any trouble at the trading post.

"Someday I will return, Big Eagle. My woman, Ada, would also like to come out here."

"When you come, you and your woman can live on Cree land where you wish. You are always welcome on Cree land. You one of us now."

The beaver hides were secured on one mule and Eben said, "Goodbye, my friends, for now. I will return someday."

* * * *

As Eben made his way to Fort Gibraltar he was not aware of his passing. And this could get him killed. He had to force himself to pay attention. But when he would stop for the night all he could think about was, *Why am I not going back? What does my spirit know that my mind does not?* Something was waiting for him, this he knew and understood. *But what and where?*

At the trading post, after he had gotten his voucher for his furs, he said, "Mr. Stone, on this other account I want to add two names. And when they come in they won't have a voucher. Their names are Neokiowa and Little Claw of Big Eagle's tribe of the Cree Nation. These are friends of mine and I consider Big Eagle's people as my family. There won't be any trouble, will there, Mr. Stone." Not a question, but a statement and Eben looked into Stone's eyes, and repeated, "Will there, Mr. Stone. Because if I hear you or anyone giving my friends a hard time about anything, I'll make it a point to come back here, Mr. Stone, and settle the account with you. I'll skin you alive, Mr. Stone, and nail your hide to a barn door while you watch. Do I make myself understood, Mr. Stone?"

Oliver Stone didn't know what to think. He had never been talked to like this before and he didn't doubt for a second that McNinch would make his threat good. "No, I can assure you, Mr. McNinch, there won't be any trouble."

"Good, because this isn't a threat. It's a promise and I am a man of my word.

"And another point, Mr. Stone. Who better to know when someone would be leaving here heading for Fort Williams and usually with a pocketful of money and/or supplies. If I'm attacked again on the trail, I'll string the thieves up by their ankles and when I start carving they'll be all too willing to tell me who they work for. Have a good day, Stone."

Eben closed the door and Oliver Stone breathed a sigh of relief. *How in hell had he guessed that I was behind the robberies? He is one dangerous man.*

* * * *

The trail to Fort Williams was uneventful this time. Eben figured he had guessed correctly about Oliver Stone.

In Major Albert's office he reported this to the major. "When I accused Stone about this, he never denied it and there was no trouble on the trail."

"I have been suspecting something like this for a while now. Other trappers coming in are complaining about the piracy on the trail. I have decided to replace Stone with Alfons Gervais. He will be accompanying the freight wagon which is scheduled to leave tomorrow."

"I have one favor to ask of you, Major. I have set up an account with Stone under the names of two Cree natives, Neokiowa and Little Claw. There is about $500.00 in the account and here is the voucher." And he handed it to Major Albert. "I promised Stone what I would do if he did not use the two in good faith or caused any trouble for them. The tribe is like family to me. I have been living next to them and trapping on their land. They respect me because I have been completely honest with them and have protected their land from other trappers."

"What would you like from me, Eben?" Major Albert asked.

"A letter directing Alfons Gervais to give Neokiowa and Little Claw his utmost respect and fair dealings. They are good people. If the Cree were wronged, they could completely shut down trapping and North West's interests," Eben said.

"Consider it done, Eben. I'll write the letter today. Now there is another matter I need to discuss with you. Do you remember that report you wrote last year about Humphrey and Buford?"

"Yes, I remember it."

"It caught the attention of people in Ottawa and there has been a constant stream of inquiries about you ever since."

For the life of him, Eben couldn't imagine why.

"There is a Colonel Harry Benton; he arrived here last week wanting to see you."

"What's this all about, Major?" Eben asked.

"I'm not sure. But it may have something to do with the war between England and America being over."

"Who won the war, Major?"

"Believe it or not, the Americans. Between Andrew Jackson and Jean Lafitte, they really kicked ass and the British had no choice but to surrender.

"He has been told you are back and is waiting for you in the mess hall."

"I'll go see the Colonel as soon as I go see my wife. I haven't seen her for nine months."

As he stepped outside from Major Albert's office, a man in civilian attire addressed Eben. "Mr. Ebenezer McNinch, I believe. I'm Colonel Benton. I would like a moment of your time."

"It'll have to wait a few minutes, Colonel. I haven't seen my wife for nine months. She comes first," Eben said and walked off.

The Colonel went into to see the Major.

"Good morning, Colonel. Eben McNinch just left."

"Yes, I saw him. He's an arrogant cuss, isn't he."

"Not at all, Colonel. He has been away from his wife for nine months living in the wilderness."

Colonel Benton went back to the mess hall to wait.

"You're late this year, Eben. I thought maybe you had run into trouble again," Ada said with concern in her voice.

"Spring was a long time coming this year, that's all." He gave her the money from the sale of the beaver and otter.

"We now have almost $5000.00 saved, Eben. Do you think that's enough to get our place?"

"Yes, but first there is a Colonel Benton here who wants to talk to me about something."

"About what?" Ada asked.

"I have no idea and I must leave you now, Ada. He is waiting for me in the mess hall."

Eben entered the mess hall and saw the Colonel sitting with someone in the corner. Colonel Benton stood up and said, "Come over and join us, Mr. McNinch. This is Major Shelby Rigsby. Major, Ebenezer McNinch."

"I prefer just Eben, Colonel. And excuse the way I look and smell. The Colonel has seen fit to do some talking before I have had a chance to clean up."

"We're not offended, Eben," Benton said. "Let me get right to the point. Eben, I assume you are aware that the war between England and the United States is over and the Americans won the war."

"I have been told by Major Albert of this."

"I have been directed by the Provincial Lieutenant Governor to form a regiment and inspect, if you will, our border with the United States west along the 49th parallel. The treaty that ended the war was signed in Ghent and established forever the border between the two countries to be the 49th parallel.

"It is the concern of the Provincial Government, considering the Americans thirst for gold and Jefferson's westward expansion and acquisition of territory under his Manifest Destiny Proclamation. The new government is concerned that if trappers establish forts and trading posts like the Hudson Bay and North West Companies that the U.S. Military would soon move in and take control of these forts, even if on Canadian soil.

"We need you, Mr. McNinch, to guide this regiment west."

"How many men are you talking about in the regiment?" Eben asked.

"A minimum of twenty men. One will be a surveyor."

"Why so many men, Colonel?" An honest question.

Major Rigsby replied, "In case of Indian attacks. With any fewer men, it would be impossible to survive a surprise attack."

"Why would you be expecting trouble from the natives, Major?"

"We get complaints and stories all the time in Ottawa about trappers and settlers being killed and harassed by the damn Injuns."

"How much time have you spent in the wilderness, Major?"

"None, but I am a highly trained military officer," Rigsby replied.

"That may be, Major, but you don't know a damned thing about surviving in the wilderness, along with twenty men." Neither Colonel Benton nor Major Rigsby expected this kind of demeanor.

"If trappers can do it, I guess I can also."

Eben stood up and said, "Then I guess you don't need my services. Good day, gentlemen."

"Now Mr. McNinch, I can see Major Rigsby ruffled your collar some. Sit down so we can talk."

"No thanks, Colonel. Not if I have to take orders from this pipsqueak. He knows nothing of the wilderness or the natives. He won't last until January before he attacks a band of natives. If he did survive that, he would not survive the winter elements. I won't be led by someone so foolish."

The major stood up and tried to interrupt. "Sit down, Major. I haven't finished talking. I've lived in the wilderness by myself for three years. I know how to survive the elements and I know how to get along with the natives. I'm leaving now. I suggest you talk it over with Major Rigsby and I'll think on it. We'll talk again tomorrow after breakfast." Eben left and said, "Gentlemen."

Colonel Benton stood up and Major Rigsby started to speak. "Not a word, Major, not one word. He made a couple of good points. We need him, Major, more than I need you. Is that clear?"

"Have you forgotten, Colonel, who my uncle is?"

"The Lieutenant Governor. . . no, I haven't forgotten and without him you wouldn't be out here.

"Now, I'm going over to talk with Major Albert. You do whatever you want. Just stay away from me."

Colonel Benton knocked on Major Albert's door.

"Come in.

"Hello, Colonel. How was your meeting with McNinch?"

"I have never met anyone who is so self-confident and arrogant as Eben McNinch. If he was in the military, I'd have to call it insubordination."

Benton told Albert all about the meeting.

"You know, Colonel, McNinch was correct on every point. In my opinion, there is no other man who can do what or go where you want without any trouble and expect to survive the winter.

"Do you have any idea how he is known among most of the native tribes? Probably not. Big Red Beard Not Afraid. I'll tell you a story, Colonel. Sit down and have a cup of coffee."

"Thanks, but I'll have tea."

"Colonel, I asked you to have a cup of coffee with me. Do you see where I'm coming from? Out here, Colonel, when someone asks you to have a cup of coffee, it is a friendly request to socialize. Would you like to have a cup of coffee, Colonel?"

"Yes, by all means." They both laughed.

"He has been accosted many times by road pirates, thieves and other trappers. Some of those thieves were larger than he. He has often taken on more than one at a time and has always been the victor without even as much as a scratch. He was asked by Big Eagle, chief of a Cree tribe, to join them on their annual caribou hunt. He wrestled a large caribou to the ground and killed it with his knife to save the life of one of the hunters. He was attacked by a pack of wolves and he wrestled one to the ground and killed it with his knife. He still bears the scars of that attack. Native tribes all over know about Big Red Beard Not Afraid. Even our trading post on the Snake River in the United States has heard the stories about McNinch. It is said he is free to travel on any tribal land without trouble.

"You need him, Colonel, on this detail. You'll fail without him."

That evening Eben told Ada about what Colonel Benton wanted. "Are you going, Eben? This might be a rare opportunity. But I go with you. No question. Living alone nine months a year is one thing. But you'll be away for at least two years. No, I go with you."

Eben started laughing. "What are you laughing about?"

"You, Ada. You always have the last word." He laughed some more, good naturedly, of course.

Eben told Ada about the gold. "How much do you have, Eben?"

"I could almost fill a sock with it. Ada, no one can know

about this. If anyone suspected I had found gold, there'd be an onslaught to the Cree land and I made a promise to Big Eagle."

"What will we do with it, then, Eben?"

"We'll wait until we have our own place and then little by little, if we need it, we can sell some and say it came from our own land. I'm going to take it over to Major Albert and have him put it in the safe."

Early the next morning before breakfast, Eben took the pouch of gold to Major Albert's office and explained his promise to Big Eagle. "No one must ever know about this, Major. Can you do that?"

"It'll be safe here, Eben, and I'll not say a word."

* * * *

Eben and Ada sat at a lone table across the room from Benton and Rigsby. "What are you going to tell him, Eben?"

"I suppose it depends on what Colonel Benton has to say."

"You finish your coffee, Eben. I need to get to the infirmary."

Eben finished his coffee and he filled it and then walked over to Colonel Benton's table. "Good morning, Colonel, Major. The coffee is still hot if you want a cup."

After yesterday in Major Albert's office he wasn't about to refuse to have a cup of coffee with Eben McNinch. "I'd love a cup. I'll be right back."

Eben sat down and Benton came back with the cups. "Here's a cup of coffee, Major."

"I'd prefer tea, Sir."

"Have a cup of coffee." Rigsby took it. Eben was wondering what that was all about.

"Sit down, Eben. I had a long conversation yesterday with Major Albert and he has convinced me that without your knowledge and reputation this expedition will fail. I need you, Mr. McNinch, to guide the expedition. Would you reconsider if I command the detail?" Major Rigsby looked surprised and started to say something and thought better about it.

"I would, Colonel. But you must know I have a lot of concerns."

"Okay, let's talk about them one at a time. Major, take notes so nothing will be forgotten later."

"Yes, sir."

"First of all, my wife goes with us." Both Benton and Rigsby were shocked. "We will need a medical officer with us. My wife is the medical officer here at Fort Williams. And she knows more about edible herbs than I do."

"Done."

"We don't need twenty men. Besides me, my wife, and you, Colonel, five more men."

"Do you really think seven men and one woman will be sufficient?"

"There won't be any trouble with the different tribes as long as they don't think this is a military expedition. And, it'll make our winter survival much easier."

"Okay, I can understand that. Done."

"No uniforms or insignias or use of rank when talking. We use our names, not rank."

"Why is this, Eben?"

"Again, we don't want the tribes thinking in any way that this is a military expedition."

"Done."

"Also, all rifles to be carried in cases unless there is reason not to. And everyone wear holster and pistol, and everyone has the same caliber rifle and pistol.

"We take mules. Each person rides one with provisions and each will have a pack mule."

"Why mules and not horses?"

"A mule can and will eat almost anything. A horse is as finicky as a fancy city woman."

"That's certainly understandable. Done."

"During the next couple of days, I'll have a list that each man should be issued. Can you get eighteen mules?"

"That shouldn't be a problem."

"What is your timetable?"

"I would like to leave here on July 1st. No later. I think it'll take us two years to complete everything."

"You and I work together as a team. We do this together with help from the rest of the crew."

"Done."

"Does Major Rigsby go?"

"At first I had decided against it, but I think the experience will be good for him."

"Okay. What exactly will we be doing?"

"We follow the 49th parallel as closely as we can when inspecting large rivers and trails for human traffic. At each major river crossing we build stone surveyor markers. This is where you come in again. I understand you have masonry experience."

"Yes."

"If we find an American fort, even if it is a fur industry fort, we close it down and send them back across the border. The surveyor will also be a soil scientist and will measure the depth of top soils and record the type of soil. He will also record the different animal species we encounter and forest types.

"What I am going to need from you, Eben, and as soon as you can, is a list of supplies you think we will need.

"I'll give the list to the Major and it will be your responsibility, Major, to procure all supplies including the mules."

"I'll have the list for you tomorrow morning, Colonel."

"Eben, you have not asked one important question. How will you and your wife be remunerated."

"I just figured you'd get to it when you could."

"You and your wife will receive a dollar a day for each day we're gone. To be paid when we return. Also you'll be given a land grant of one-thousand hectors wherever you want."

"Will the grant be in writing and recorded?"

"Yes."

"Then we have a deal, Colonel.

"I'll get started on the list, sir."

* * * *

Eben had lunch with Ada and told her everything. "You're in, Ada. You're part of the team, and we leave July 1st." He told her how they would be paid and about the grant."

"Then we can start building our own place, Eben?"

"Yes. As soon as this mission is over."

For the rest of the afternoon Eben worked on a list of supplies they would be needing and another list of personal gear for each member to bring.

Ada went back to work the happiest she had ever been. This time she was going into the wilderness with her husband.

The next morning after breakfast, Eben gave his list to Colonel Benton.

"Now, Eben, I know we'll have to kill and forage for our own food, but what about the first part of the expedition? I mean we'll have to take some food with us."

"I'll make another list, Colonel, of food we'll have to take with us."

Much to Colonel Benton's surprise, Major Rigsby was genially happy about being supply master for the expedition and he was doing a very good job. Actually the Colonel assumed that by his taking command of the expedition he had relieved Rigsby of a lot of responsibility that he wasn't yet prepared to assume.

It was the middle of June and the mules had arrived along with all of their equipment. Colonel Benton had selected a number of soldiers for he and Eben to interview. Benton's big concern was whether a military soldier could take orders from a civilian. There was no doubt who the surveyor would be. Eugene Terrill was the only surveyor who had requested to be part of the expedition.

By mid-afternoon they had found three more good men. Fred Michaud and Pat Kelley had grown up in the wilderness north of Ottawa. They both were big rugged men. Rick Perry had formerly been a carpenter and Colonel Benton had been impressed with his military records. "I'd say, Eben, that this completes our crew and I think they are all good men.

"Major Rigsby tells me he has all of our equipment, all we need now is our food stores, and we'll be ready to leave on July 1st."

"Let's have everybody gather in the mess hall tomorrow after breakfast, even Ada. We need to talk to them as a group," Eben said.

"Good idea."

The next day when the new men realized a woman would be joining them, they were surprised. But no one objected. Major Rigsby still wasn't happy about Ada going, but he had learned to keep some things to himself.

* * * *

After breakfast on the 1st it took two hours to pack all the mules and be on their way. Instead of heading directly west to follow the Fort Gibraltar Trail until the Lake of the Woods where they expected to pick up the 49th parallel, it had been agreed upon by Colonel Benton and Eben to follow the Fort Gibraltar Trail to just west of the lake and then head south to pick up the 49th.

This was the first time Ada had spent much time in the wilderness and so far she was enjoying herself. The others, including Major Rigsby, seemed to be adapting to life in the wild and having to forage for food each day. They shot deer, partridge when they saw them and fished in the evening before dark. Along with fresh meat they were eating herbs that most of them had never heard of.

The day finally came and they turned south, west of the Lake of the Woods. With each day they became more proficient at this new lifestyle. They were able to get started earlier in the mornings and travel further than they had the first week out. They all were still excited and eager.

Two and a half days later, the surveyor Terrill announced, "We have reached the 49th parallel, Harry." It took two weeks for the men to drop the rank when talking.

"We need to build a marker here next to the lake," Eugene Terrill said.

"We'll need a lot of rocks, men, and I'll see if I can find some clay." The rocks were easy to find, but all Eben could find of clay was mud that had some clay fixed in it. "This will have to do."

He made the base four feet square and filled the inside with loose rocks and mixed the clay mud over the rocks to cement them together. He topped it at four feet tall.

While Eben was building the marker two men caught enough fish for supper. Eben would have liked to hold up for a few days and shoot a moose and take the time to cure the meat. "How many days would it take?"

"We could eat a lot of fresh meat and cure the rest, maybe four days, top," Eben replied.

"What if you and one other were to ride two days ahead of us, shoot a moose and start smoking it? That would only mean we'd have to layover for two days."

"That sounds like a good idea. I'll take Kelley with me. We'll leave at first light. To gain two days, we'll have to leave our pack mules with you."

The next morning Eben and Pat Kelley left camp and on a compass heading due west they rode hard for a day before stopping. The next day they stopped early to find a moose. It didn't take long as this was excellent moose habitat. Eben let Kelley shoot it and he helped to skin it like he had seen the Cree do it. Then he had a clean hide to lay the meat on.

"If you want to finish up here, Pat, I'll get a fire started and make a smoking rack."

That night they enjoyed roasted heart and liver with hot coffee. They both stayed up all night tending the fire and talking. "I really like this kind of life, Eben."

"Then why are you in the military?"

"Got conscripted because of the war. A lot of us did. Just in case England called on Canada for more help. I was lucky I didn't have to go."

The next day they cut green maple wood to help flavor the meat and then went in search of herbs to have with more liver and heart.

When the rest of the party caught up with them most of the meat had already been cured and they only had to layover one day. But this gave them a chance to rest and Ada made some dough for stick bread. She had cut away a lot of small pieces of meat from the rib cage and made a stew which everyone enjoyed.

Terrill took a small soil sample and dug a hole to see how deep the topsoil was. Underneath the topsoil he found hardpan clay. He made notes in his notebook about the terrain, marshes, streams, beaver, moose and tree types. He sighted in his sextant. "Hey, everybody. We're almost on top of the 49th parallel right here. That's pretty good compass work."

At night around the fire they joined in conversations. Even Ada was as excited about the trip and everyone was trying to guess what they would find along the way. Everybody was full of moose and vegetable stew and stick bread. The sky was clear and the air had the delicious aroma of roasted meat. Things couldn't have been better.

The mules started braying and Rick Perry stood up and said, "I'll check on them and see what the matter is."

Everyone else was still in conversation, when suddenly Perry broke the cheerful atmosphere. "Bear!"

There wasn't any need to say anything more. Eben jumped to his feet and ran to the mules. He drew his pistol before he had taken two steps. The others were a bit slower, but they were following Eben. Even Ada.

Perry drew his pistol and in the excitement he discharged it while it was still pointing at the ground. For some reason this seemed to irritate the bear and he stood up on his hind legs and took three steps toward Rick Perry and then he made a swipe at Rick's shoulder with his right front leg and the blow sent Rick stumbling and he fell over a rock. The bear sniffed the air and turned his attention toward the closest mule. He reared up again on his hind legs and put his front legs on the mule's back. Eben fired his pistol and he knew it wasn't a good shot. The bear was still on the mule and just as it started to bite on the mule's back, Eben went charging at the bear and screaming a blood-curdling scream that even upset his wife, Ada. He grabbed the bear by both sides and pulled it off the mule and literally threw it.

The bear regained his feet and screamed at Eben, but now he turned his attention back at Rick Perry who was still lying on the ground. The bear had his head down and his lips were curled and Perry said later he could hear him making a guttural growling noise as he came at him. The bear was too close to Perry for the others to risk a shot. Eben, to everybody's surprise, jumped on the bear's back and took him off his feet again and Eben rolled, still holding onto the bear. With his left arm Eben reached up and wrapped his arm around the bear's neck in a headlock, and began to squeeze the bear with all of his strength. At the same time he drew his knife and stuck it in the bear's throat and twisted it before he withdrew it and then he stabbed the bear in the chest and this seemed to take the fight out of him. But he wasn't dead yet. Eben kept squeezing his neck and he stabbed the bear in the chest again. The bear screamed with pain just before it died. Eben lay there exhausted with the bear lying on top of him.

No one could believe what they each had just witnessed. Perry had been close to the battle and his eyes were still bugging out of his head. He said loud enough so all hear, "Who in hell *are* you?"

Ada was crying and the first to rush up to Eben and the bear.

"Can someone pull this bear off me?" Eben asked without the slightest hint of anything out of the ordinary.

Colonel Benton tried to drag the bear off and he couldn't move it. Michaud and Rigsby helped him and the three were able to drag it enough to free Eben. Major Rigsby was probably the most surprised of any. "Maybe all the stories I have heard about Eben McNinch are true."

Ada was still crying. "You damned fool! Why did you do such a foolish thing?"

"Well...it seemed like a good idea at the time. Is Perry okay?"

"That bear broke his left arm, but he'll be okay," Pat Kelley said. "How are you, Eben? Did that bear get at you at all?"

"A few scratches, that's all." Eben got up and was looking at the bear's front right paw. "This is why he didn't do more damage to Perry. Look at his paw. There aren't any claws." Then he saw the old wound in the center of the paw. "Well, I'll be damned."

"What is it, Eben?" Colonel Benton asked.

"This bear and I met before. Three years ago when I was building my lodge. He had smelled my mules, and I shot him in the paw to drive him off. In the right front leg, just like this bear."

"Come on, Rick," Ada said. "Come back to the firelight and let me tend to your arm."

Fred Michaud was looking at the left paw and said, "About how many inches would you say it is across this pad?"

Colonel Benton looked at it, and then Major Rigsby, and they both said, "Five inches."

"Then this bear weighs five-hundred pounds."

"How can you tell by looking at the pad?" Rigsby asked.

"A hundred pounds an inch across the pad."

"This bear weighs five-hundred pounds and Eben picked it up and threw it!" Major Rigsby said. "Holy shit!" Eben had walked off with Ada and Rick back to the fire. The rest of the men just looked at each other, and all were wondering the same thing—*just who in the bloody hell is Eben McNinch.*

Ada removed Perry's shirt to see if the bone had punctured the skin. It hadn't and she said, "It isn't a complete break. There is a fracture. You can put your shirt back on and then I'll splint it." She helped him with his shirt.

"And you," she was talking to Eben. "Take all your clothes off so I can examine you. Your clothes will have to be washed before that blood dries.

"You ole fool, Eben. You get yourself hurt real bad and I'll take up with some young buck!"

"What would you ever do, Ada, with a young buck?"Eben asked.

"Have some fun!"

That shut him up, and again she got in the last word.

Rick Perry didn't know what to think about these two bantering back and forth.

When Eben had washed the blood off him, he had teeth marks on his hand, but not deep. Scratches on both legs and again, not deep. Somehow he had knocked his head on something. There was a bump on the back.

Ada was like a volcano on the inside. She was mad as hell at Eben for doing what he did and she knew it was useless to keep on badgering him about it.

After Ada fixed a splint on Perry's arm, she asked, "How does that feel, Rick? Any tightness or sharp pains?"

"No, actually it feels pretty good. How long will I have to wear this?"

"Two weeks, and then you'll have to be careful with it."

Ada washed Eben's scratches with alcohol. "OK, woman, that hurts more than the bear."

"Good."

Later as they were all sitting around the fire again, Eben said, "I think from now on we'll have to take turns standing watch over the mules. The deeper we get into the wilderness, we're bound to run into more animals—animals looking for food."

When the rest went to bed, Benton and Rigsby stayed up

talking...Rigsby taking first watch and Benton needing to talk about the evening events. He, like Rigsby, couldn't believe what they had seen Eben do. Neither one of them would ever have had the nerve to do the same.

"That bear weighed five-hundred pounds and Eben picked it up and threw it like it was nothing at all. I have never known any man who could throw five-hundred pounds, let alone a bear fighting for its own life. I have a new found respect for that man," Rigsby said.

"That's the difference, I guess, between someone who lives in the wilderness and one who doesn't. But I'll agree, Eben McNinch is a rare and unusual man," Colonel Benton said.

* * * *

They were all up early the next morning. Rick Perry's arm and side, of course, was now stiff and sore, but he tried to help out when he could. Eben and Colonel Benton rode on ahead, while the others followed all day. Terrill, Perry, Michaud and Kelley would talk amongst themselves about the night before. If they had not seen for themselves, they would not have believed it.

They camped that night on the bank of the Red River which flowed north to Forts Gibraltar and Douglas and then to Lake Winnipeg.

It was the end of August and the summer had been dry and the river was now shallow enough so they would be able to lead the mules across. Terrill got busy with his sextant and exactly determined where the 49th parallel was. The men went after firewood and got the fire going while Ada started preparing supper. Eben, Rigsby and Kelley gathered rocks and there was an abundance of clay near the river to build another stone marker. Colonel Benton and Rigsby searched the area for signs of human traffic, or temporary shelters or trapping equipment.

"This river is a major concern for the government. It begins deep into the United States and could be easily used for a travel corridor for trappers and settlers. We don't want American settlers on our side of the border," Colonel Benton said.

"Tomorrow, you and I will search the other side, Rigsby, while the others go on ahead. We'll just have to catch up, that's all."

The party crossed the Red River the next morning and there was an obvious trail following the river. "Eben, I want another marker here. Rigsby will take one other man and scout out this trail to see if it goes to any kind of American settlement or fort."

"This trail may only be a trapper's trail to the trading post at Gibraltar and Douglas. Since we are directly south of the forts and this river runs between them. This also might go to one of North West Company's outposts across the border. But I agree there should be another marker and I'll get right to it."

"Rigsby," Benton said. "Follow this trail north until noon. If you don't find an American fort or settlement, then return. You'll have to catch up with the party, but we shouldn't be that far ahead."

Rigsby and Michaud left their pack mules with the party and left. "While you're building this, Eben, I'll follow this trail into the states and see what there is. If I'm not back by the time you have finished the marker, go ahead and find a place to camp tonight and I'll catch up with you," Benton said.

Colonel Benton went off on his own, and after he left Eben was having second thoughts about him going out alone. He should have said something. He would make a point to say something that night when they were all back together.

Eben was until mid-morning before he finished the marker. Terrill was busy with his scientific work, and Ada helped carry rocks once everything had been cleaned up and the mules packed.

They had been on the move for two months now and everyone was beginning to pull together as a team. When they stopped for the night, no one had to say 'Go get some wood, or water, or unpack the mules and see that they are fed.' Everyone knew what was expected of them. Eben had another concern. He knew they would have to stop soon and build a shelter for the winter and gather food. It was early September now and he didn't want to wait until the air was cold and snow on the ground.

They only made about ten miles that day and Eben figured that was far enough. Neither of the parties had caught up to them yet. While the mules were being unpacked and tended to, Ada made a fire pit and gathered enough wood to start the fire.

At the edge of darkness, the three other party members had returned. "We came upon a party of four trappers encamped about four miles north of the 49th. They were all French trappers from Quebec. They told us that North West company trappers often used that trail to trap below the 49th," Rigsby said.

"I didn't find anything south of the 49th, but the land would be a beaver trapper's paradise. I also saw many moose, but no deer," Benton said.

Terrill was taking notes.

As the three ate supper, Eben said, "We need to be thinking about finding a place for our winter shelter. We can't wait until it is too late to gather herbs and feed for the mules."

"That sounds like a good idea. In the morning why don't you go out ahead and find a place maybe two or three days from here. You know what we need," Benton said.

"Okay, I'll take Kelley with me. And that brings up another point, Mr. Benton. I think in the future no one should go off on their own, exploring."

"You're probably right, Eben."

Terrill made note of this discussion in his journal.

* * * *

Eben and Pat Kelley traveled due west for three days and came into a huge meadow. Just before finding the meadow they crossed the Souris River which ran north to the Red River. "This will make an excellent place, Pat. There's plenty of feed for the mules, there's fish in the river, there's forest enough to protect us this winter from cold artic winds, there's cedar trees and the soil is sandy. We'll be here probably for two days at least before they catch up to us. We don't have any tools to work with, but we can catch fish and smoke-cure them."

They went back to the river. It was narrow and shallow and they could see fat brook trout in the pools.

"You start fishing, Pat, and I'll kindle a fire and build a smoke rack and get plenty of wood."

By the time Eben had finished, Pat had already caught six nice trout. Eben showed him how to fillet them and he laid them on the rack and then he joined Pat fishing.

They caught so many brook trout they had to make two more smokers. The air was permeated with the delicious smell of curing trout. "Hope this doesn't bring in another bear," Pat said.

While the fish were smoke curing, Eben and Pat went hunting for two deer. No doubt when the rest of the team arrived, they'd be hungry and then too busy building shelters to hunt. They went back to the meadow and to Eben's surprise, there were deer grazing in the meadow, but there was also a small herd of caribou. "We only need one caribou, Pat. Wait and see if that bull will come closer. He's yours, Pat. I'll back you up if he tries to run off."

They waited patiently and eventually the caribou came within fifty yards. "Okay, Pat. Now."

The shot scattered the rest of the herd and deer alike, but the one shot had killed the caribou.

"We need to make a travois now, Pat. You go get one of the mules.

Eben started to skin and flesh the caribou, but he needed Pat to hold the legs for him. It didn't take the two long to finish and they headed back to camp. The rest of the team were there and they enjoyed a meal of fresh caribou liver and heart and fish.

* * * *

Colonel Benton was impressed with the location Eben had selected. It would provide everything they would need. Eben had even found a sandy knoll in which to dig out a cave-like shelter for the sixteen mules. It had to be really large and to store grass for days to brutal to let them graze on their own.

For their own shelter another cave was dug for cold storage and supplies. The three exterior walls which butted up to the knoll were cedar log, and a stone fireplace in the front wall and door. With everybody helping it didn't take long to finish, complete with rough-hewn beds, counter top and picnic table with benches. Eben and Fred Michaud helped and he and Pat Kelley both proved themselves to be good carpenters.

Everyone, including Ada, was having the time of their life. And much to Eben and Colonel Benton's surprise, one day while working up firewood, Rigsby said, "You know I don't think that I have ever been so much alive and enjoying every day like I am now."

It was exciting and adventuresome. They were exploring the country and now at their winter camp they were building a new life, however temporary.

It took a lot of food to feed eight hungry people every day. At least two each were out foraging for herbs, nuts and berries. Then one day Rigsby and Kelley came back carrying honeycomb on a slab of bark. "I'll make something special with some of this honey, nuts and berries." She roasted the nuts and made a flour dough and spread honey, wax and all, on the dough, added nuts and berries and rolled the dough up into rolls and baked them in the fireplace.

"You keep cooking like this, Mrs. McNinch, and we'll all get fat! This dessert is delicious."

One day the men had decided to shoot a couple of caribou in the meadow. A small band of natives saw them and came in behind them. They were curious what they were doing. Colonel Benton saw them first and said, "Gentlemen, we have company about fifty feet behind us."

They all turned to look and Eben said, "Do not make any hostile movements and keep your rifles pointed at the ground." Eben leaned his rifle up against a tree and started to walk over to speak with these men.

All of a sudden there was a lot of talking amongst the six natives and the one who seemed to be the leader said in good English, "Big Red Beard Not Afraid. I can speak some of your words."

"Hello," Eben said. "How are you known?"

"I am called Tucuma. You are welcome here. This Cree land for one more day, then Assiniboine. You friend to Cree people like family, Big Eagle village."

"Would you and your men like to come back to our lodge and eat?"

"We do that. Follow you."

Their caribou hunt would have to wait for another day.

Eben noticed one of the men was limping. "What is wrong with…?" and he pointed to the man who was limping.

"He clumsy, fall down, cut leg."

Ada was working outside when the whole troop came back. She was only a little surprised. "Tucuma, this is my woman, Ada. She is medicine woman and can help the one who is clumsy."

"What's wrong?" Ada asked.

"That young brave cut his leg and I said you would look at it."

"Certainly. Have him lay down on this table out here where the light is better."

While Ada was looking at the injury, the other men were fixing something to eat for their visitors.

Ada pulled the brave's legging back and exposed an infected gash. "This isn't good. Another two days and this would have turned gangrenous. I'm going to have to open the wound and clean it out and then stitch it."

"You go get what you need, Ada, and I'll explain to Tucuma what you are going to do," Eben said.

Everybody was more interested in watching Ada than eating. Three men had to hold the patient down while Ada opened the wound and cleaned it. And then she sewed the gash shut. Tucuma and his men had never seen this done before. Then she lightly wrapped a clean bandage around his leg. "You must keep this clean. You stay here tonight, rest and eat. Tomorrow you can walk on it. But you'll limp."

Tucuma seemed to understand all this and he then stated, "He Who Is Clumsy." Tucuma pointed, "New name." Everyone there laughed.

Michaud and Rigsby had fixed a stew while Ada was tending to He Who Is Clumsy. Now they all sat inside eating, enjoying the warmth and talking. "Tucuma, how do you know English?"

"Many seasons before time of my grandfather's grandfather, before white man, a holy man taught our people many things about the Great Creator. He not white man, not native. He wore robe not shirt or leggings. He taught our people these words and some of my people today are still taught to speak these words."

"Who was this holy man, Tucuma? Where did he come from?" Colonel Benton asked.

"My grandfather said no knew where he from. He could talk Cree and other tongues, too."

"That is interesting," Benton said. Terrill noted this in his journal.

"Why you here, Big Red Beard Not Afraid?"

"We are on our way west to the tall mountains. We are exploring."

"You trapping?"

"No, only to eat."

"You looking for yellow rock?"

"Tucuma, there was a war between the Americans and England..."

Tucuma interrupted, "1812 over. Americans big warriors."

"Yes, that is so. Our people in Ottawa are afraid the Americans may try to take away land in Canada. We are here to see if this true," Colonel Benton said.

"I understand this. You stop these Americans coming to our land."

They stayed up late that night talking. Tucuma and his men were as interested in their hosts as they were with them.

Everybody ate well in the morning and Tucuma said, "We go now. How long you stay here?"

"We'll leave in the spring," Eben said.

Tucuma now looked at Ada and said, "You first medicine woman I see. You good medicine woman. You have great medicine. I will tell my chief, Nucuma, about medicine woman. You," and he looked at Eben also, "will be welcome in our village." Then he spread his arms to indicate everyone.

They left and the team went back to the meadow to hunt caribou. The weather was cold enough now so they would not have to smoke-cure the meat. It would freeze and not spoil.

They hauled the two caribou back to camp with mules. While they were being taken care of, Pat Kelley and Fred Michaud went fishing before the river froze.

They returned the next day and every day to fish until there was solid ice.

It was now late November and the daylight hours were much shorter and an artic chill blew in. The mules were faring well and had plenty to eat.

It snowed often in December, a dry fluffy snow, and the wind blew it off the meadow into the trees. Caribou were still there feeding. Around Christmas time everybody became a little somber, but nobody wanted to say anything about missing their loved ones at this special time of year.

As a treat, Ada made more of those sweet rolls with honey, nuts and berries. She surprised all. "These are sure good, Ada," Pat Kelley said.

One thing Eben had completely forgotten to put on his list were snowshoes. Right now though, the snow wasn't deep and the mules kept the path open to the meadow. There was a lot of work for eight people to survive in one shelter. They were fortunate that the caribou herd had stayed near the meadow all winter. Sometimes to change their diet of caribou meat, Eben would take one of them and go after beaver. Only it was quite a hike to the nearest flowage.

From the onset, Ada had laid down the rules when it came to living in the shelter. "There are eight of us all living together in this shelter. I want it understood, I'm not your mother or nursemaid. I'll cook for you, doctor your wounds and mend your torn clothes, but as far as keeping the inside clean, that job is you men. Mark my words if you want to eat, you'll not live like animals, not here anyways."

And every day the shelter was picked up and cleaned. With having to shoot so many caribou, they now had caribou fur rugs on the floor, except in the kitchen.

"And I won't tolerate any of you men smelling rank and you'll wash up before eating." She looked at Eben and said, "That goes for you, too, Eben.

"We're all adults here and I expect each of you, and me as well, to strip down and wash." And she did strip down and wash in front of the men. As long as Eben was there, she knew he would not let anything happen.

With January came the gawd-awful cold. Cold that only Eben had ever experienced. Terrill had a thermometer to record the readings. "Ada, and gentlemen, I'd like to announce that the temperature this morning is the coldest that I have ever seen… minus sixty-two degrees."

They kept the mules in that day and hand fed them. They were burning a lot of wood in the fireplace, but it was comfortable and they would soon have to be going after more wood.

"Eben," Major Rigsby asked, "we're all quite comfortable here even as cold as it is. There's seven of us to help with feeding the mules, gathering wood, hunting for food, but it puzzles me how you did it all by yourself? I would think, after experiencing living in the wilderness like we have, what kept you from going crazy all alone?"

Rigsby had changed the most on the mission. He had grown physically, filled out and toughened up.

"Well, I was usually busy tending a trap-line. And then drying and stretching the hides, firewood, tending the mule and fighting off wolves. I guess I didn't have a whole lot of time to be lonely or go crazy. Each day was all about surviving and trapping enough beaver to make it all worthwhile.

"Hey, Fred and Pat, have either one of you ever made snowshoes?"

"I saw it done once," Fred said. "Why?"

"Because next winter we'll camp close to the high mountain range west of here and there'll be more snow than what we have seen here. It would be good if we could make a pair for each of us."

"We would have to have something to hold hot water so we could soften the wood enough to bend," Fred said.

"I can make something from clay. We still have a lot left over from chinking the logs. How long would it have to be?"

"If you could make something four feet long, twelve inches wide and eight inches high...a trough with slots in each end so we can set the bows into the hot water."

"We could set this over the fire to heat the water," Pat said.

"We'll need ash. It'll bend easy and hold its strength. You make the trough, Eben, and Pat and I will get the trees and hew out the bows."

"We need more caribou and we can strip the hide for lacings," Rick Perry said.

All while they were discussing how they were going to make the snowshoes, Colonel Benton and Major Rigsby sat quietly listening and found it gratifying to see how the mere mention of something was coming to reality. Everyone had an idea and was contributing. This was true team work. They looked at each other and smiled. Terrill made a note in his journal.

Michaud and Kelley were excited about making snowshoes. They were both good carpenters and now they were putting their knowledge to work. They finished stripping out the first bows as Even was finishing the clay trough. The others had the whole caribou hide to strip lacings, and when it became obvious they would need more, two men quietly headed out to the meadow and shot another caribou.

It took them the rest of the winter to make eight pair of snowshoes with leather harnesses.

"Colonel, I think we should be leaving soon, but we should cure some meat first to take with us, in case food is hard to find." So for two weeks they hunted, fished and smoke-cured the meat.

When they left, Eben insisted that they rock up the entrances to both shelters, "…to keep the animals out. We might have to use this on our return trip."

There was still some snow on the ground and the nights were crisp, but everyone was glad to be on the move again. They were two days crossing the grassy meadow. "We were only in a corner of this," Eben said. "I don't think it is a meadow at all, but a grass plain. These wide ruts had to have been made by buffalo." Terrill wrote that in his journal that night and took a shot with his sextant to make sure they were still on course.

"Well?" Major Rigsby asked.

"We have moved slightly south of the 49th."

When they reached the Souris River, there was open water. But just downstream they could see that the river made up into a pond that was still frozen. Eben chopped test holes through the ice and there was plenty to support their weight.

Terrill got them back on course and they continued on.

Day after day they rode across the plains. It was mostly grass with only a few islands of trees. They saw huge buffalo herds and antelope, and a deer specie that no one was familiar with. There were no caribou or moose. Occasionally they would see black bear at a distance...and they were keeping their distance.

Once they saw what had to be a grizzly bear. It stood much taller above the grass than a black bear, and it too kept its distance and ambled off.

There were no rocks on the plain to build markers. Terrill measured the topsoil depth and was surprised to find over two feet in places. "What fantastic farm land."

They had crossed many smaller rivers and streams and no sign of any migration traffic from the states into Canada. It was late May now and they all needed a couple of days rest and to stock up with food. They made camp where two streams came together and there was a deep pool full of brook trout. They ate fresh trout for two days and smoke-cured many more. They found fiddleheads, fern roots and sorel. But to cure all the fish, they had to lay over for another day. The mules fattened up on lush green grass and they were beginning to feel frisky.

Two days later about mid-afternoon, a band of natives came riding towards them up from an old stream wash. The natives came riding straight towards them, hooting and hollering. "Sit easy, men, and don't draw your pistols. They're curious," Eben said.

Eben and Colonel Benton sat their mules in the lead and waited. When the natives saw these men were not going to flee, they stopped about one-hundred feet in front of them. The leader seemed more curious than anything. After several minutes, he said something to the others and then came forward, walking their horses.

They rode right to Eben and Benton and stopped, the leader still looking them over closely. Then he spoke. "Big Red Beard Not Afraid, I know you come to Dakota land. Wait to see you. My brothers the Cree speak well of you."

"Harry, I think we should dismount and ask them to smoke." Eben and Benton dismounted and the rest of their team did also, and the natives.

Eben pointed to the leader and then at himself and Benton and said, "Smoke pipe. Come."

He found a place to sit and brought out a long-stem pipe from his pack and filled it with tobacco. He lit it and gave it first to the leader, then Benton. Major Rigsby was watching all this with great interest. He had been so wrong about Eben and he understood this now.

"What you do on Dakota land?"

"What is your name. How are you called?" Eben asked.

"Black Elk. You?"

"Eben McNinch."

"Harry Benton."

"Black Elk, we are exploring, to see if the American settlers are coming north into this country from the United States," Benton replied.

"Where you go?"

"West to the tall mountains and winter there."

"You trap the beaver?"

"Only to eat."

"You look for yellow rock?"

"No."

"Want to see your medicine woman." When Eben looked surprised, he added, "I know about medicine woman."

"He isn't going to take me, is he, Eben?"

"No."

Black Elk stood up and looking Ada up and down, and then he turned her around and looked at her backside. "Name?"

"Ada. Ada McNinch."

"Big Red Beard Not Afraid woman. Good."

"You helped Tucuma's son."

"Black Elk, how do you know our tongue?" Eben asked.

Black Elk told him the same story about the holy man who had wandered into their village to teach them about the Great Creator, in the days of his grandfather's grandfather. When he had finished he stood up and motioned for his men to mount and ride out.

As they rode on, Michaud said to Kelley, "You know Pat, it's a damn good thing we have McNinch with us or I don't believe we'd make it through all this Indian country."

"He's a legend to the Indians, and I think he is in our world also, Fred."

For days that followed, they saw bands of natives and then they would ride off. "Just keeping an eye on us," Eben said.

"It still makes me nervous," Benton said.

"They're just making sure they can trust us. The natives are honest and trustworthy people and they have seen too many lies from the white man to trust us on face value," Eben said. "The more they see of us, the more they will trust us."

They rode on and on, day after day, never looking back. Even Rigsby was becoming a wilderness frontiersman. There was never any bickering and quarreling amongst the men, which Colonel Benton found unusual, particularly with a group of men and one woman who had been together so long. They had been on this mission now for a year and had crossed a thousand miles and seen sights that none of them would have ever dreamed about or imagined. Even Eben, who at the start was a wilderness survivor. Each day brought new wonders and filled them with eagerness and excitement about getting started the next day.

Colonel Benton was so happy that he was beginning to regret when this little expedition would come to an end. Nothing in his entire career could compare to this. He was so glad he had decided to command the expedition—with Eben's help, of course.

They were finding prairie hens and Ada would roast them like chicken. Then they started finding their nest and gathering the eggs. With the eggs, Ada could make other delicious dishes. This adventurous life was being good to them all. But that didn't mean there were no hardships. Out on the plains, there was very little shelter when it rained. There were times when it would rain so heavy they would have to hunker together under one of the canvasses. The mules had no shelter and they didn't seem to mind. Then after the rain would stop, they would have a day of soggy going when everyone's footwear would be soaked.

But in spite of these rainy times, there was never any negative talk or blaming someone. They were, they each realized, on this expedition together. If something was to happen to one member, it would have consequences for everyone, the team. So they looked out for one another. Not because they were told to do so, but because this came naturally as surviving the wilderness and the elements.

* * * *

When they reached the Big Muddy River which flowed out of Canada into the Missouri River, this was Colonel Benton's biggest concern. Settlers could come by boat or canoe all the way from the Gulf Coast up the Mississippi into the Missouri and then up the Big Muddy.

They made camp back away from the river, where they could still see it. "In the morning, Eben and I are going to explore upriver, cross over and come back on the west side. Terrill, find where the 49th crosses the river and the rest of you build the marker."

"Colonel, what happens if we find a settlement or fort, or one being built?" Eben asked.

"I have orders from the Lt. Governor to use any means that becomes necessary to make sure they leave."

"You don't think this might be considered by some to be an act of war?"

"Not at all. We're simply asking trespassers to leave."

"You said earlier that the North West Company had a fort—a trading post—on the Snake River. How is that any different?" Everyone thought that was a good question.

"Before talking with you, Eben, at Fort Williams, I talked with the administration of the North West Company and I was assured that their only interest in the Snake River area was buying fur, that the only building is the fort and all the trappers who sell to the company are Americans. The only Canadians are those who run the company. The Americans, on the other hand, have a reputation for settling in a territory, and then under Jefferson's Manifest Destiny Proclamation, annexing it."

However, they all were needing a rest. Even the mules.

"Just in case there might be something upstream, there'll be no shooting until we know for sure," Benton said.

Benton and Eben left right after eating the next morning, following the Muddy upstream on the east bank.

There was a game trail on the east side and at times it traversed along a steep side-hill. The other side was flat countryside, and this is where a trapper or explorer would have his trail.

Eben stopped. He was looking to the other shore. "Do you see that, Colonel?"

"What? I guess I don't see what you're looking at, Eben."

"That trail coming down to the river and those drag marks in the mud. Someone with a canoe has been using the path to the river a lot."

"We'll have to wade the river and look into this."

"I'm glad the water is low. I can't swim."

They each found a pole they could use to help them from slipping on rocks.

Eben and Benton both unbuckled their gun-belt and looped it over their head to keep the powder dry. At the deepest part, the water was up to Eben's underarms. Benton was taller.

"You willing to take a suggestion, Colonel?"

"What is it?"

"We wander in there posing as two trappers out scouting. And you'd better let me take the lead on this one."

"No argument from me."

Eben walked slowly along the trail. They could hear noises now, but couldn't tell what they were. A little further and they could make out voices. "Sounds like they're building something. We'll go slow and see what we're up against before wandering in."

Eben stayed off their trail now so to be less visible in the forest. "Look at that, Colonel. They're building two houses. I see four men."

They watched the four for several minutes and decided that's all there were. "Let's go, Harry."

They stepped back in the trail and walked with a normal gait into the clearing. Eben hollered, "Hello there!"

One on the roof looked up. "Hey, boys, we got company." Then, "Hello!"

Eben walked over to the first cabin, Harry Benton following. "You boys lost?" the guy on the roof asked.

"Nah, we came up from downriver a bit, scouting out beaver. We were about to head back when we heard you."

By now all four had grouped in front of Eben and Benton. "Is this your first year up here?" Eben asked.

"No, we trapped here for two years now. Decided to build something a little more permanent. This is a nice spot, really. All kinds of game and deep, rich soil in the plains. Be good farm land. How about yourselves?"

"This is our first time in this country," which wasn't a lie.

They talked sociably for quite a while over coffee. It seemed that as soon as the houses were completed, they were going to bring their families up and four more families would be up the following year.

All while they were talking, Eben kept watching the demeanor of each one. There were two he was figuring who were itching for a fight. "Why build back here, so far away from the river? There is a beautiful place on a little flateau that looks down on the river."

"We're in Canada and we didn't want any trouble."

It was Colonel Benton's turn to talk now. He had heard enough. "Well, boys, we seem to have a little problem. You see, I'm Colonel Benton and this is Eben McNinch, and we're out here looking for settlements just like this."

Everybody had now stood up. Eben was keeping a close watch on the two who seemed most antsy. The friendly conversation was now over. "So what are you two going to do about it?"

"You have no choice. You'll have to leave, by orders of the

Canadian Provincial Government."

"Yeah, what if we don't want to leave?"

"Then we'll force you to leave," Colonel Benton replied.

"We ain't going anywhere, mister," the same guy said.

Just then, the two Eben figured to cause the most trouble drew their pistols and before either one could point them at Eben and Benton, Eben rushed them straight on. He plowed into three of them bringing all three to the ground. Eben reached down and pulled one pistol out of the hand of one of the two, and smashed it on a rock. Then he did the same to the second pistol. The first one stood up. Eben back-handed him so hard, the blow broke his jaw and he went over backwards screaming in pain. The other two were on their feet by now and came rushing at Eben. He hit the first one in the side, snapping two ribs, and the other guy hit Eben on the side of his jaw. It was a hard blow, but Eben didn't lose his footing.

Colonel Benton was trading blow-for-blow with the fourth guy. Eben brought his iron hand fist-down on the collarbone of the guy who had just hit him. He crumbled to the ground. Those three had had enough. Without looking, Eben asked, "Need any help, Colonel?"

"I don't think so," and he hit the guy another blow to the head. This time he went down and stayed down.

Eben took all their pistols and rifles then and smashed them on the rock. "Now, you four get in your canoe and go back wherever you came from. But stay out of Canada. And no, you can't take anything with you. We're going to torch everything. Now, get!"

Eben watched to make sure they weren't coming back. Colonel Benton torched both buildings and threw everything on the fires.

Eben looked at Benton's face and began to laugh, and he said, "I hope the other guy looks a little worse than you do, Colonel."

Benton broke out laughing, then, "You're okay, McNinch. Glad you are with us."

They didn't get back to camp until almost dark. "We saw two canoes float by. And they looked like they had been through a meat-grinder," Rigsby said.

As they ate and drank coffee, Eben and Benton told them all about the settlers. "Those men are exactly what we expected to find," Benton said.

"You know, Colonel, I think the only way we're going to be able to control the migration north from the states is to build forts in strategic locations along the 49th," Rigsby said.

"I think you may be correct, Major."

After the marker had been built, the crew caught several trout in the Big Muddy, but not enough to smoke-cure them. Two days later, they came to a smaller river and this one was full of large orange-bellied brook trout. They caught so many fish they had to make four separate racks to smoke-cure all of them.

On the third day, they moved on and did not stop until just before dark. "Colonel, I think we still have some country to cover before we get to the mountains, and I think we'll have to pick up our pace some so we don't get caught without shelter and enough food for the winter."

Each day after that, two men would ride ahead and hunt for food. Whatever they found would have to be taken with them. They were running out of time to stop again and smoke-cure the meat.

A week later, they could see the tall mountain range to the west and they knew they were getting close to where they would have to hold up for the winter.

Kelley and Michaud came riding back before mid-morning one day while on a hunt. "We came to another river and just north of the 49th we found a fort all built!"

"Could you tell how many people were there?" Benton asked.

"We didn't get close enough."

"Can we cross the river?"

"Shouldn't be any trouble."

"What do you say, men and Ada, about riding right into the fort?"

Nobody objected.

By noon they could see the fort and they crossed the river and rode into the fort compound. There didn't seem to be too many men there.

There was a sign overhead at one office: ROCKIE MOUNTAIN COMPANY.

"This must be a fur operation like our North West Company in the Snake River. Eben, you want to accompany me."

A distinguished looking older man met them at the door. "Good day, gentlemen. Heard you were coming this way. You must be this McNinch that I've been hearing about, and you must be Mr. Benton. You, sir, are not a trapper, so why don't we talk in my office.

"My name is Floyd Kent, and I'm the superintendent here at the Rockie Mountain Company. This is our second year here. When I heard you were coming west, I knew you'd be wanting to see these," and he handed Colonel Benton a folder of papers.

Colonel Benton looked through the papers while Mr. Kent prepared a cup of coffee for all of them.

"These all seem to be in order, Mr. Kent. I must say I'm completely surprised to see you went to the extent to get permission to operate here."

"Actually, Colonel, this is our second year and we only received this permit this spring. We were ready to start and it was taking a long time to hear from Ottawa."

"How did you know, Mr. Kent, that we were coming?"

Mr. Kent looked surprised. "Are you kidding me? We have befriended the Blackfeet Indians and their runners here told me all about McNinch—Big Red Beard Not Afraid—and his woman, Ada." He looked at Eben and said, "There is no mistaking who you are, sir.

"What exactly is your group doing, Colonel?"

"We're gathering information much like your Lewis and Clark." That seemed to appease Mr. Kent as he asked, "I would like to meet Ada, your medicine woman. Hell, I'd like to meet everyone."

They went outside, "Hey, guys, Mr. Kent would like to meet the whole group."

"Ada," Eben said, "come here." When she was standing beside Eben, he said, "Mr. Kent, my wife. Ada, Mr. Kent."

"It is my pleasure to meet you, Ada McNinch, medicine woman. It is my pleasure to meet you all. Colonel, your little group has people talking. You and Eben, Big Red Beard Not Afraid, sent four men back down the Big Muddy River. You gained a lot of respect from the Dakotas, the Blackfeet—and the Cree are especially honored. You folks have cut a wide swath through the wilderness."

"Would you and your group like to stay here tonight and have supper with me?"

"Yes, sir, we would enjoy that."

"Mr. Kent, would it be possible to buy a few food stores here?" Ada asked.

"If we have it, yes. What would you like?"

"A hundred pounds of flour, coffee and apples."

"We can help you with all of that."

* * * *

Ada was glad to be eating someone else's cooking. In the morning they couldn't eat enough eggs to sate them. They were well rested and each day afterwards they were making good time, covering a lot of miles and frontier.

It was early September and Eben said, "I think we should stop here and build our winter shelter." Not far to the west they could see the towering peaks of the infamous mountains they all had heard so much about.

"Colonel, I'll take one man with me and scout out a place to build. The others should hunt and fish, so we'll not have to while we're building."

"Major, do you want to go scouting?" Rigsby had changed so much Eben now enjoyed his company. They rode north and found a nice stream. They followed it upstream to a stand of cedar trees on one side of a long heath, and on the other side was a mixture of hardwoods. There was even a sandy knoll to dig into for shelter for the mules and their own cold storage.

"This looks good, Eben. The area provides everything we'll need to build shelters and grass for the mules."

"I think you're right, Major. Let's get the others."

While Eben and Rigsby were gone the men hunted in two parties. One shot a cow moose and the other a bull elk. The meat had all been traversed back and they had not started to cure any.

Major Rigsby told the Colonel about the spot they had found and the mules were packed again and they arrived at their new site just before dark. They had a late supper of liver and heart. There was plenty to go around and none went to waste.

Two men worked on digging out a cave in the knoll and found the digging was so good—the sand had a little clay in it, so the sides or ceiling didn't crumble in on them. Two men were taking care of the meat and three men were cutting cedar logs for the camp. This time the sleeping area was inside the cave. The digging was so easy they especially made it big enough for sleeping quarters and food storage.

Cedar was lighter wood than spruce or fir, which made handling it easier and the main shelter went up first. Terrill had found a vein of blue savvy clay underneath the top soil in a hollow next to the stream. The sides of their cabin were chinked good as was the roof, and Eben was an artist when he built the fireplace. They had found a lot of quartz rocks to use.

When the mules' shelter was complete with a door, three men concentrated on cutting grass for the winter. It was hard, back-breaking work and no one liked the job, so they traded off every day.

While the men were hunting or foraging for herbs, Rigsby and Eben went off scouting. "Find me a bear so I can use the fat for lard, and find some honey," Ada more or less commanded. Eben was real happy how well she had adapted to frontier wilderness living and being on the constant move except during winter. There was very little privacy living with seven men in the same quarters, but not once had she complained. And the men had all gotten accustomed to her stripping down in front of them to wash. There just wasn't any room for modesty. Eben started smiling, thinking about her and how great a woman she was.

Eben was hoping to find beaver flowages, but there were none close by. They did see plenty of moose and elk. "Eben, look over your left shoulder. There's a bear standing up looking at us."

"Uh, it ain't black is it?"

"Must be one of those grizzly bears we've heard about," Rigsby said.

"You take the first shot, Rigsby, and I'll back you up."

Rigsby fired. He aimed for the chest and the bear still stood. Eben fired right behind him. The bear fell.

Rigsby started to run up to the bear. "Rigsby, no! Wait and reload your rifle. He may not be dead. We don't know anything about these brutes."

They both reloaded and while they waited, there was no rustling or noise where the bear had been, and they started to move up cautiously. The bear was down but not dead. "Look at the size of that head, Eben—holy Christ! Almost as big as a washtub."

"Yeah, and he ain't dead, either." Eben shot him again in the top of his head and the impact threw the bear's head sideways, but he wasn't dead. "Shoot him right behind the ear, Rigsby. That ought to finish him." It did.

"Look at those claws, Eben. Have you ever seen anything like it?" Rigsby was surely excited and all Eben could do was smile.

"He sure is a big brute. Those claws have to be three or four inches long. Don't think I'd want to wrestle him."

They had to make two traverses to haul all the meat and hide back. The hide, after it was cleaned and dried, would make a nice rug. They deboned the meat to eliminate as much weight as possible.

"Ada has her lard now." Eben sliced it off the back in two-inch thick slabs.

Once back at camp, no one there had any knowledge of grizzly bears either, and were as surprised as Rigsby and Eben had been with the huge claws. "Hope you didn't try to wrestle with him, Eben," Ada said, as she walked off with her lard.

To get enough fish for the winter they had to follow the stream a long ways downstream before the men figured they had enough for winter. They were so far downstream Kelley and Michaud had to stay out one night.

Firewood was next. There was precious little dead and dry trees standing. There were a few in the heath, but they had to finish up with green wood.

A honey bee hive wasn't found until November during an unusual warm period. One had stung Ada on her arm and she bee-lined it for four hours before she found it. Supper was late that night, but she had her honey.

Whenever someone was out in the forest working or exploring, they always were on watch for herbs and berries. One day Rick Perry came back with his coat filled with high-bush cranberries.

There was no beaver to be found and everyone was disappointed, as they all had grown to like it. It was their favorite meat, so tender and sweet.

Terrill, when he could, located where the stone marker was to be built, using his sextant. And he told Eben, "I want to build this, Eben. I have watched you build the others."

Much to their surprise November was warm, comparatively speaking, with an occasional rainy day, but no snow until December. The first storm piled up thirty inches of dry fluffy snow and then every two days it would snow again.

To keep trails open for the mules to the grassy heath, they would lead them out to the grass twice a day, keeping the pathway open.

They banked their cabin with snow to keep it warm. In the evenings Eben and Rigsby would detach the grizzly claws from the feet, clean them up , and using a nail, drill a small hole through the knuckle end to make bear claw necklaces for everyone. And they all wore them every day. It became a badge of honor for them.

The temperature eventually turned cold, but not the blistering cold Eben had experienced two years ago in his lodge when the temperature dropped to negative sixty-two degrees. But even on sunny days there was snow in the air. Terrill explained that the snow was only frost in the air.

The snowshoes they had made a year ago were a godsend now. Without them life there would have been so much more difficult. To keep busy, Michaud and Kelley made a counter top for Ada, a table and chairs for everyone, from cedar they were hewing and shaping with a draw shave.

The mules, though, were keeping them busy. They had to be let out and taken twice daily to the heath to feed.

March came in with warm weather and the snow settled and one day Eben and Fred Michaud strapped on their snowshoes to go exploring. They took some food as they were planning to spend one night out. They went further north than any of the group had been before. The forest turned into a pristine landscape of rolling hills, huge evergreen trees—Douglas fir, spruce, cedar and hemlock. There was also a spring-fed inlet stream, that was free of ice, to a small lake situated at the base of majestic mountains.

They made camp there that night after fashioning a lean-to of spruce and fir boughs. There was a warm wind blowing in from the south. "Might rain tomorrow," Michaud said, "with this warm air blowing in from the south."

"Yeah, maybe we should head back early."

It stayed warm all night and both men were awake before the sun was up. Fred got the fire going and Eben fixed a kettle of coffee and elk meat warmed up on a stick. The sun was just beginning to peak over the eastern horizon. Fred stood up to get more firewood and he stood still looking at the snow-capped mountain. "Sangreal." (royal blood) He took his hat off and placed it over his heart and crossed himself in good Catholic fashion. Then he kept staring at the mountain.

"Whatever are you doing, Fred?"

Fred Michaud pointed toward the mountain and said again, "Sangreal."

Eben turned to look, "Well, I'll be go-to-hell, look at that. The top of that mountain looks like it is covered with blood, not white snow." He stood there looking at the mountain in wonder also. He took his hat off, scratching his head.

"Sangreal…Fred, what does that mean?"

"Royal Blood." That's all he would say.

For ten minutes the top of the mountain remained colored in blood red. Then as the sun rose higher, the blood red color disappeared. "That had to be because of the sun, Fred. But a red sky in the morning always means a bad storm is coming. Come on, Fred, we need to leave now."

"I'll name this mountain, Eben. Sangreal Mountain. Royal Blood."

The warm air was still blowing up from the south and two hours before Eben and Fred returned to camp, it started to rain. Not just a drizzle, but a rain storm. Snow was sticking to the snowshoes, slowing them down. They were soaking wet but they were not cold.

Once they were inside the camp, both men stripped down

145

and hung their clothes up to dry. Fred was busy telling everyone about the mountain with the blood red top. "It was so beautiful and so strange."

As spring was approaching they all decided they still had enough food stores to start the journey back. But along the way they would have to have more. Just as they thought warm spring weather had truly arrived and they were making plans to leave, they were dumped on by two feet of heavy, wet snow. "Guess we'll have to wait now until this has melted. There was still ice in most of the streams and this would make crossing them easier.

"Colonel, we know there are some trappers crossing back and forth across the border, and the one possible settlement that you and Eben burned. But in our absence, what's to say there won't be others who will try the same thing? And did we miss any that are already established?" Major Rigsby asked.

"That's a good point, Major. I don't think we missed anything, but with the United States' westward movement, I think for certain, as you, there'll be more. I think the only way to deter and prevent this from happening, there'll have to be our own forts or blockades built along the border in strategic places. And I don't think they should be manned by the military either, but by the Royal Canadian Police. I think the natives would look more favorably on the RCMPs than the military."

* * * *

The day came when it was time to leave. They already had everything in packs just waiting to load them on the mules. "We leave tomorrow morning. Make sure everything is picked up and packed tonight," Colonel Benton said.

"What do we do with this shelter, Colonel? Burn it?" Rigsby asked.

"I don't think so. Whoever comes out here to build and man the forts might need to use this for a while."

146

CHAPTER 9

The smaller streams and rivers were still frozen, but the Big Muddy was clear of ice and full of water. "Water's too swift to expect the mules to swim," Benton said.

"We'll have to make a raft and float them across. Wish we had left sooner now," Eben said.

They made a cedar raft large enough for two mules and their packs. They anchored a rope upstream on the opposite shore and two more ropes on each end to pull the raft back and forth. This worked quite well. The upstream rope would act like a pendulum and help to swing the raft across. This took most of the day and they camped there at the Big Muddy.

Word had spread like a wildfire through the trapping communities about McNinch and Benton and no one was too eager to try to start another settlement.

Their progress across the plains was much faster this trip as they only had to stop every few days to hunt or fish for food. They saw huge herds of buffalo migrating north for the summer, bear with cubs, moose and deer with their young, but no wolves.

They were back at their winter shelter by mid-September. "If we leave now, I think we can be back at Fort Williams before cold weather and snow, or we can stay here another winter and start preparing for winter," Colonel Benton said.

Even though to a man, and Ada, this had been the experience of a lifetime, they all wanted to continue on to Fort Williams.

After two weeks of traveling hard and fast, and only eating a big breakfast and then stopping an hour before dark for supper,

Eben said, "Hope I'm not riding the rough off of you guys." No one complained.

Their last night out from Fort Williams they all were sitting around the fire talking about the expedition. "I want to say 'thank you' to you all for this expedition. Your demeanor, even when things were tough—you all should be proud of yourselves. I am proud of each of you. I have seen each one of you change and grow into what you now represent. I don't think there has been another expedition in our history where it was accomplished with so much professionalism and dedication, while having so much fun. I have enjoyed watching each of you change from working and thinking alone to becoming a team. Even you, Eben, and I mean no jest. You are probably the most self-confident man I have ever met, and instead of always going off on your own and telling everyone what to do, because you were more experienced with living in the wilderness, you became part of the team. I can't say enough to describe how I feel about each one of you.

"And Ada, I have a special sense of gratitude and thanks for you. I don't think there could possibly be another woman who could have cheerfully put up with what you have had to for two and a half years. You are an exceptional woman, Ada McNinch."

Everyone agreed and gave Ada a joyous round of cheer.

Later as Colonel Benton and Major Rigsby were sitting together and talking, Rigsby said, "Colonel, whether it is the military or the R.M.C.P.s who are sent out to build and man forts along the border, I would like to be considered for one of the posts. I really have grown to like the wilderness and living in it. After experiencing this, I can't see myself stuck behind a desk somewhere."

"When I make my official report to the Lieutenant Governor, I'm going to request to be in charge of building and manning the forts with qualified people. Major, you will be the first on my list."

"Thank you, Sir."

On November 15th, 1817, the expedition group rode into Fort Williams, mid-afternoon. No one was expecting them back this soon, this year. They rode up out front of Major Albert's office. He heard a crowd of people all talking and went outside to investigate.

"Well, I'll be, Colonel. I never expected you back this soon. Won't you come in, Sir? And have a drink with me."

"Yes, we all would like that," Benton replied, knowing Albert had meant only him. They were a team and not one, not even Colonel Benton, should be held above the others. Yes, Colonel Benton had changed along with the others.

In that moment of hesitation by Albert, Colonel Benton and Major Rigsby were smiling.

"Yes, yes, why sure, come on." He poured them all a drink and said as a toast, "To a successful expedition."

He was surprised to see them, Colonel Benton and Major Rigsby, including sporting full beards. They were all neat though.

He wanted to know all about their journey, but first he asked, "Eben, is it true you wrestled a bear and threw it?"

Rick Perry answered that, "He did it to save my life, Sir."

"And Ada, I heard you saved the life of an Indian?"

"Yes, Sir, one of Tucuma's men. We found the natives very friendly and obliging," Ada replied, making sure Albert had heard her use the term *native* and not *Indian*.

They talked for two hours and Major Albert said, "I'll let you go now. I presume you'll want to bathe and clean up."

Even after bathing and getting their hair cut, they all kept their beards. Trimmed, of course. It was a badge of their successful expedition. Ada even chose to wear pants and a shirt like the rest of the crew. She knew who she was and she didn't need the fancy frills. She was a remarkable woman.

Once people realized who these people were, they all wanted to know about their journey. One old timer asked, "Mr. McNinch,

I'm too old to go off exploring, but what's out there?"

"Most of the way to the Rocky Mountains is plains or prairies, flat grassland that took us three months to cross."

The next morning a ship arrived from Ottawa. " I have a message for you from the Lieutenant Governor," Major Albert said.

"You and your men and Ada are to board the clipper when it sails tomorrow morning. The Lieutenant Governor wasn't expecting you until spring, but the message stated that if by any chance you returned early, you were to take the first available ship."

"We'll be on board, Major Albert."

* * * *

"Eugene, while we're aboard this ship, I'd like you to write up a complete report of our expedition from your notes?" Benton asked.

"I'll have it done before we land at Ottawa, Sir," Terrill replied.

"Colonel, may I have a word with you in private?" Rigsby asked.

"When we left, I told you the Lieutenant Governor was my uncle."

"Yes, I remember that."

"He's on my mother's side of the family. Well there's something you should know. In my opinion, he is a coward. When the war started in 1812, he was absent on leave and an Isaac Brock filled the office. Then in 1816, after the war had ended, he resumed his position. I really don't know what to expect from him when we reach Ottawa. I just thought you should know, Sir."

"Thank you, Rigsby."

It was dark when the ship tied up in Kingston and they waited until morning before debarking. There was a coach waiting to take them to Ottawa. "Riding in this damn thing, Colonel, is worse than riding a mule in a thunderstorm," Eben said.

In Ottawa there were two carriages waiting at the stage coach terminal to take them directly to the Lieutenant Governor's office at Parliament Hill.

Dressed in their usual attire and wearing the bear claw necklaces, they were received with some question. "Whom do you wish to see?" the doorman asked.

"The Lieutenant Governor, please," Colonel Benton replied.

"The Lieutenant Governor does not entertain just any riff-raff off the street."

In a more authoritative voice, Colonel Benton said, "Then you take this message to the Lieutenant Governor, that Colonel Benton and Major Rigsby and the team are here at his request."

When the doorman just stood there with a blank look on his face, Major Rigsby said rather forcibly, "Now!"

The Lieutenant Governor came strutting down the hallway all smiles. He stopped and without saying a word looked each one of them over, head to toe. "I must say you people don't look very military. I was under the impression that this was going to be a military expedition, Colonel. Which one of you is Colonel Benton?"

"I am, Sir. Under the advice from Mr. McNinch, it was decided not to make it look like a military expedition. And it didn't take much to convince me. We thought a military expedition might alarm the Americans that we might have the intention of claiming their land below the 49th, and Mr. McNinch also convinced me that we would be accepted better by the native tribes if we posed as explorers."

"I don't think we have anything to fear or worry about with those ignorant savages," the Lieutenant Governor said.

"One thing we learned, Sir, is that the natives are not a bunch of ignorant people and they deserve our respect," Major Rigsby said.

"And who are you? There is no way of telling by your dress... or lack of."

"Major Shelby Rigsby, Sir."

"What's this woman doing with you?"

"This is Mrs. Ada McNinch, our medicine woman and valuable member of the team."

"You're as cocksure a bunch of people as has ever addressed me."

"Sir, there are a bunch of American trappers who will attest to that," Major Rigsby said.

"Colonel, why were civilians along on a military expedition?"

"In your absence, Sir, in 1815, the then-Lieutenant Governor Isaac Brock asked me to form a party to explore west along the 49th Parallel. It was my decision sanctioned by Mr. Brock to hire a wilderness guide." Colonel Benton then gave the Lieutenant Governor Gore his orders and request he had been given by Mr. Brock.

"If you'll notice the land grant and wages due to the McNinches also, Sir."

"And I suppose without McNinch this expedition would have failed?"

Rick Perry, who was normally very quiet and reserved, spoke up. "That's a fact, Sir. There's a five-hundred pound bear that Eben picked up and threw, and then wrestled it and killed it to protect me. The bear already attacked me and broke my arm. And Ada fixed my arm."

"I assume, Colonel, you must have a written report for me to study?"

"Yes, Sir," Eugene Terrill said and stepped forward and handed his report to Lieutenant Governor Gore.

"I asked you for the report, Colonel. Why is this man handing it to me?"

"Sir, Mr. Terrill was our scientist and he kept very accurate notes. He therefore wrote the report and it is his honor to give it to you."

"I'll send my aide for you after I have read this. You'll be staying at the barracks on the waterfront. You're dismissed."

Back in the outer office, Rigsby said, "What a complete ass." Just then Gore's aide came in and closed the door. "You were not accepted well, were you?"

"Not exactly," Benton said.

"Sit down, gentlemen and Ada, and I'll try to explain. Governor Gore won't be reading your report, Sir. He is retiring from the political life and today was his last day. I have your report and will give it to the Governor General Gordon Drummond tomorrow morning. Once he reads it, I'm sure he'll wish to talk with you all. And I can provide better accommodations for you, also, at the garrison on the hill and not at the waterfront.

"News about your expedition was reported here before your arrival, and you are all being called the Lewis and Clark of Canada. I assure you, you will be well received by the Governor General."

* * * *

Two days later the aide came to visit them at breakfast. "When you have finished, Governor Drummond would be pleased if you all would join him in his study. He very much enjoyed reading your report, Mr. Terrill. I think you'll all be surprised with what he has to say. But I'll let him tell you."

"Gentlemen and Ada, how good it is to see you. When I heard you had returned to Fort Williams, I couldn't wait to meet everyone. Colonel Benton, would you please introduce everyone? I am Gordon Drummond, Governor General of Upper Canada."

Benton made all the introductions and Governor Drummond kissed the back of Ada's hand. "When Lieutenant Governor Brock informed me of your expedition, I couldn't wait to read your report and I find it fascinating."

The Governor General was just the opposite of Mr. Gore. They talked like old friends for the entire day. "I have to ask one question, Mr. McNinch, did you really throw a five-hundred pound bear and then wrestle with it until you killed it?"

"Yes, Sir. It was about to attack Rick Perry again."

"But why wrestle it? Why didn't someone just shoot it?"

"Well, it seemed like the thing to do."

"And Ada, you lived side-by-side with six other men and as I understand from the report, they had to wash up in front of you and you in front of them. You are an amazing woman, Ada McNinch.

"Now to get down to the real contents of your findings. The plains seem to be excellent farm and cattle country. The whole country seems to be rich with fur and it all belongs to the native tribes. We can't allow this valuable resource to lay dormant and we must respect the natives' ownership. And we must protect our border with fortifications all the way west. What is your recommendation there, Colonel Benton?"

"Major Rigsby and I have talked quite extensively about this and we agreed that either forts or blockades be built all along the 49th Parallel. And we believe they should be manned by the Royal Canadian Mounted Police rather than military installations. We believe the natives would not be so upset and if it were military, then the Americans might misunderstand these fortifications as a militant move."

"I quite agree, but this will have to be approved in Parliament, you understand."

"I have a request, Sir. Whether these fortifications are manned with the military or R.C.M.P., I would like to be the administrator."

"Sir, I also agree with Colonel Benton and I would like to be in command of one of these instillations," Rigsby said.

"Geneltmen, I can assure you here and now that both of your requests will be granted. I can't think of two better men for these positions.

"Now, the matter of compensation. My aide will escort you to the Minister of Finance and you can draw your pay. And Eben McNinch, my aide will escort you and your wife to the Minister of Agriculture in the matter of your land grant.

"Colonel Benton and Major Rigsby, I would ask you to remain so we may talk more extensively about protecting our border. I'm inclined to agree with you."

Eben and Ada left the Minister of Finance with a little over $1800.00.

The land grant Eben wanted was west of Lake Manitoba, bordering the plains.

CHAPTER 10

It was too late in the year to think about traveling back to Fort Williams, so Eben and Ada remained in Ottawa. Ada went to work in a hospital and Eben worked on and off with Benton and Rigsby. R.C.M.P. manning the fortifications along the 49th passed with no difficulty in Parliament and both Benton and Rigsby had resigned from the military and Harry Benton was now the Administrator of Border Protection with Shelby Rigsby as his assistant. And believe it or not, Rigsby had chosen the outpost furthest to the west to oversee. His duties also included periodic checks at the other outposts. There would be a total of eight when finished. Rick Perry, Fred Michaud and Pat Kelley also volunteered to command an outpost each.

Eugene Terrill enjoyed his scientific work so much he had volunteered for another expedition to travel north through the middle of the plains to see how far north they reached.

Eben and Ada had opened an account with the Banque du Montreal when they explained they had about $5000.00 in the North West Company safe, the banque manager told them they could transfer their money to the North West Company and it would be deposited in the Banque of Montreal via the North West Company and they would be given a voucher of their account. They now had a little more than $6000.00 plus the gold to build a place of their own. They were happy.

Eben showed Benton and Rigsby where he and Ada were going to build their own place. "This is Cree land, but you both will be welcomed any time."

They said goodbye and Eben and Ada were aboard the first

ship sailing for Fort Williams. It was a cold voyage, but that was okay. They both felt more at home at Fort Williams than they did in Ottawa. They arrived April 7th, 1818.

Major Albert was happy to see Eben and Ada back. "How long will you be staying?"

"Not long, actually. As soon as we can travel, we'll strike out for Fort Gibraltar and then to the Cree land. We were given a land grant for our work." Eben showed Albert where they would be.

While they waited for the trail to Gibraltar to open and dry, Eben worked on plans for leaving and what they would have to take with them from Fort Williams. Most of what they would need they could get at Gibraltar. He bought four mules and Ada helped out in the infirmary. Eben made the transfer of their money and received a voucher. "What about the gold, Eben?"

"We'll take that with us and use it only in emergencies. The fewer people who know about it, the longer the Cree can live in peace."

"We have some tools at the lodge where I trapped, but we'll need more and I think we can get those at Fort Gibraltar," Eben said.

But they did purchase clothes, seeds, medical supplies and a few more items. Eben knew he wouldn't be able to get at Gibraltar. They packed the mules and said goodbye. Eben was eager to be back in the wilderness and Ada was happy they were on their first leg of the journey to building a life together of their own.

They met several trappers coming out of the woods, heading for Fort Williams. Some were hungry and didn't have enough fur to buy a mule, and some had done very well. But there was no trouble and of all the people they met on the trail, no one had said anything about road pirates or thieves.

"When I was trapping on Cree land, I would pack both mules and I had to walk all the way."

"How long would it take you?"

"Two weeks of good traveling. More if it rained. We'll go to my old lodge first and unpack the mules. Then we'll ride up to Big Eagle's village. Even though we have the land grant from Governor Drummond, I would feel better if we asked permission to settle. I don't believe there'll be a problem, but I think we should ask first.

When they arrived at Fort Gibraltar, there were many trappers who had come out of the woods with their bounty of fur. Some were drinking up most of their hard-earned money. Some were making plans for the next season.

At the trading post, "Good morning, folks. There is no doubt who you two are. I'm Alfons Gervais."

"Good morning, Mr. Gervais. Three years ago I had Major Albert send a message to you concerning Neokiowa and Little Claw. I can assume you have been cordial towards them and have used them fairly?"

"Yes, Mr. NcNinch, I received your message and Oliver Stone said what would happen if I didn't. They were here and left four days ago. They still have some on account."

"Thank you, Mr. Gervais. They are my friends. Like family."

"Yes, sir."

"Here is a list of what we'll be needing and we'll be leaving day after tomorrow, after breakfast."

When they left Gervais looked down through the list. "A ham, three laying hens and one rooster." He had some light weight crates in back he could use to put them in. "They must plan on staying awhile."

The next day as Eben was crossing the compound for the livery, three big, burly and drunk men came out of the tavern. Whiskey sometimes gives a man more senseless courage than he would normally have if not drunk. Stupidity, actually. They stopped and watched as Eben crossed the compound. The biggest of the three, Grayson, said, "Hey, boys, look at who's comin'."

"That's that McNinch everybody's talking about," Pierre said.

"He ain't as big as us," Novis said.

"Come on, boys. Let's have some fun." They went out in the compound to meet Eben.

They stopped in front of Eben. "Hey, mister," Grayson said. "You this McNinch fella we'd be hearin' so much about? You ain't half as big as folks tell stories about you."

Eben stood there sizing them up without saying a word. "What's the matter, mister, can you talk?" Pierre asked.

"Look at 'im," Novis said. "I think he's gonna turn around and run."

Eben was trying his all not to get in a fight with these three, but he also knew it was inevitable. "Hey, mister, you gonna say anything or not? Heard you was an Injun lover. That so, little big man?"

When Eben did speak it certainly wasn't what the three brutes were expecting. "You three pukes smell worse than the back end of a pig. And a pig has more intelligence than any of you."

This really made Grayson furious and he took one step closer and with a huge right fist swung at Eben's head. Eben dodged the fist and brought his iron-hard fist up into Grayson's solar plexus, breaking a rib. Grayson vomited and fell to the ground trying to catch his breath.

Pierre and Novis jumped Eben at the same time. Eben saw them coming and as they both hit him in the head, he wrapped his arms around both of them, squeezing as hard as he could. There was nothing the two could do. Eben had their arms pinned to their sides. Eben pushed them back to a horse railing and picked the two up and threw them against it, breaking the railing. Grayson was still trying to catch his breath. Pierre and Novis regained their footing and rushed at Eben again. He backhanded one, breaking his jaw, and he grabbed hold of the other's arm as he was swinging at his head and Eben broke his arm. These two were out of the fight. They had had enough.

Eben walked over toward Grayson; he was coming to his feet.

When he saw Eben coming toward him, he lowered his head and charged at him. Eben side-stepped and kicked Grayson's feet out from under him and he went sprawling on the ground. He was madder than ever now. He stood up and faced Eben and in slow motion he clenched his fist and came towards Eben. Eben hit him in the face and Grayson went over backwards and lay unconscious on the ground. Eben stood there looking around to see if anyone else was coming at him. People had heard the commotion and came outside to watch the fight. Now that it was over, they quietly went back inside.

Eben left the three men and he continued on to the livery. He looked over the mules and checked their hooves and shoes. "Can you put new shoes on all four mules for me?"

"Certainly, Mr. McNinch. That's a dollar per mule."

He checked pack harness, saddles, reins and leather straps. Everything seemed okay—just new shoes.

The three drunks had recovered and stumbled off by the time Eben came out to the compound again.

That afternoon Gervais had Eben's list completed and sitting in the corner of the store. "Add two more cans of tobacco and this jar of candy." The tobacco was for Big Eagle, the candy for the kids and now something for Big Eagle's woman. The only thing he could think of was more cookware: another fry pan and a couple of pots. If they had room after everything else was packed, he wanted a few more blankets.

Ada was asked to help out in the infirmary. Three more injured men had just come in. "What happened to you and your friends?" Ada asked Grayson.

"We picked a fight with the wrong man. We should have believed all the stories we heard about him."

"Let me guess," Ada said, "Eben McNinch."

"Yeah, that were him alright."

"I'm Ada McNinch."

Grayson jumped off the table and held up his hands in defense. "Hey, Ma'am, we ain't done nothing to rile you none."

"Sit back on the table. I won't hurt you. That is as long as you behave yourselves."

"We'll be good, Ma'am! Yes, Ma'am we will. We don't want no more of McNinch."

The three had no choice now but to walk around the compound all bandaged up, and they steered clear of Eben.

"I had to doctor those three guys today. Looks like you caught a fist on the side of your head, too," Ada said.

"Those guys were just itching for a fight. And yeah, one of them hit me beside the head. Pretty good punch, too."

"Can't take you anywhere," she laughed.

* * * *

After loading the four mules the next morning there was still some room. They bought four more blankets, more nails, two more hammers and two more rifles. "Why two rifles, Eben?" Ada asked.

"I figure we might persuade two men to help us build in payment for two rifles."

The glass window panes were wrapped separately in cloth and then packed securely.

"Mr. Gervais, Ada and I will be back here in mid-September. I would like you to have three goats freighted up here. One male, two females. I'll pay you now for them and the freight cost when I pick them up."

"I've had to do this before. $5.00 each goat and another $6.00 each for freight."

"I'll pay you the total now, then."

All during the expedition, even in storms and cold weather, Ada had remained excited about the discovery of new land. And she was now even more excited. She was again discovering new land, but even more this time, they were building a life for themselves. She was also anxious about meeting Big Eagle and his people. She had heard so much about them from Eben.

There was still some ice in shady places, but the ice had all broken up and flowed downstream in the streams. The mules were indeed loaded heavy, but not too much so, and they were making good time. "In two days we'll be at my lodge."

The laying hens, even riding in wooden crates, laid two eggs apiece each day. The old rooster crowed from sunup till sundown, every day. "I'd like to make a muzzle for that rooster," Eben said. "I'm surprised he hasn't called in wolves before now."

When they arrived at the lodge nothing had been disturbed. They removed the rocks from the entrances and left the doors open to air out. The mules were unpacked and then staked out in the heath to feed.

Ada was quite impressed how Eben had constructed the lodge. She laid down on his old bed. "You sleep on this? It's terrible. It needs more needles and boughs. But right now I'm exhausted and I'm not getting up."

After three years the lodge and mule shelter were still in good shape. No leaks or broken window. There was only the one bed and it was too narrow for both of them, so he gathered more boughs for his bed on the floor and to spruce Ada's up. There wasn't any need to make another bed. They wouldn't be staying long.

After eating and bringing the mules back they sat outside and watched the fire.

They stayed at the old camp the next day resting from the long journey and separating what they wanted to take with them to the village. "I wish we had some food to take."

"Maybe we'll see something on the way," Ada said.

"Just the same, I think I'll take a walk around and see if I can find a nice small moose. I won't be gone long."

He went downstream and circled back across the south end of the heath. He hunted up along the west side and as he was crossing the north end he saw a yearling bull. Just the right size. He waited and chose his shot. He didn't want to have to chase after it. The moose turned to the right and Eben sighted in just behind the ear and pulled the trigger. The moose dropped where it was standing. Eben cut the throat to drain the blood and then headed back to camp to get a mule and Ada. She would have to help to roll the moose while he skun it.

Ada met him in the yard. "I need your help, Ada, and one mule." He took his axe also so he could make a travois.

That night they ate fresh heart. The rest they would take with them to the village. It would only spoil if they left some here in storage.

After breakfast the next morning, the hens, rooster and mules were put in the shelter with enough feed and water to last several days. Everything else was in the lodge. The pouch of gold was buried in the sand in the storage room.

"How long will it take us to reach the village?"

"We'll be there before dark."

The morning air was cool and crisp and the sky was clear. The leaves on the hardwoods were almost in full bloom. Eben was thinking to himself as he rode along, *life couldn't be better.* They were out of the low land and bushes and about half way to the village. They stopped to rest the mules and drink some water.

Just as they were mounting up there came a terrible scream from ahead and not too far away. Instinct took over and Eben jumped down and began running towards the screaming, Ada not far behind him. Eben ran up a slight rise and saw three wolves attacking a young brave. One wolf had an arrow sticking out of it. The young brave was trying to fend off the wolves with his knife. Not stopping to look the situation over—there was no time for that   he went charging in with his knife in his right hand. He pulled one wolf away from the brave and at the same time stuck it with his knife and threw it as he would a rag doll. The other two wolves now changed their focus from the brave on the ground towards Eben. They stood facing him, growling and showing their huge teeth. But the wolves weren't expecting Eben to charge them. He grabbed one by the side of its head and held on while he wielded his knife like a sword against the second wolf. He slashed the knife down across its nose and blood spurted six feet away. But this didn't stop the wolf. He slashed again at the wolf's throat and this time the wolf backed off and laid down, but not dead. Ada came running in and drew her pistol and shot the downed wolf in the head. Two down.

Eben grabbed both sides of the wolf's head, so he could keep his jaw away from him. Eben spun around and smashed the wolf against a spruce tree. The wolf was now screaming with its back broken. Eben smashed it again against the tree and the fight was gone out of the wolf. Not dead, but he couldn't do anything now with a broken back and smashed spine.

Eben cut its throat with his knife and shot the first wolf he had thrown. It was over.

Ada rushed over to the young brave. He was still conscious, but he had several deep wounds and tears on his leg and he was losing a lot of blood.

"Eben, are you okay?" Ada asked,

"Better than he is. I have a few bite marks but nothing serious."

"Can you fashion some sort of a table so we can get him up and off the ground so I can tend to his wounds?"

Eben didn't answer; he went to work building a rough platform. He wasn't long putting together a few poles. He and Ada gently lifted the brave onto the platform. He looked at Ada and Big Red Beard Not Afraid. Then he laid back. His worst wound was on his leg where one of the wolves had torn muscle away from the bone. But a piece of tissue was hanging on one side.

Ada had to first clean the wound before she could stitch it back in place. She was two hours working on him before she had finished. With all his wounds, she had used fifty-five stitches.

"Let me see your wounds, Eben."

"There's one on my wrist and one on my leg that needs a couple of stitches. Other than that, I'm okay."

As she was stitching him up she asked, "Why didn't you just shoot that first wolf?"

"I don't know. I guess I never thought about it."

"How did you survive out here all by yourself without me to take care of you?"

He didn't have an answer and he let her have the last word.

* * * *

It was decided they should stay there for the night and let the young brave's wounds heal. He couldn't speak English and they didn't know his name.

Eben put him on the travois with the moose meat. He had a fever, but Ada said it was only normal. They traveled at an easy pace and by mid-afternoon they entered the village. Kids playing were the first to see them and they started shouting, "Big Red Beard Not Afraid! Big Red Beard Not Afraid!" Soon everyone came out to see what all the excitement was about. Then they saw the wounded man on the travois. Shouts went up then "Neokemowa! Neokemowa!" Eben and Ada assumed this must be his name.

Big Eagle came walking up to Eben. "My friend Big Red Beard Not Afraid...Neokemowa?" He pointed to the travois.

"Big Eagle, Neokemowa was attacked by wolves. Big Eagle...this is my woman, Ada."

Big Eagle looked Ada over and up and down and then he turned her around to look at her backside. "You medicine woman."

Ada answered, "Yes."

Big Eagle then examined Neokemowa's wounds and how Ada had sewn his skin together, closing the wounds. Neokemowa was lifted off the travois and taken to one of the lodges. Then Big Eagle, in his tongue, told his people to take care of the moose meat. "Tomorrow we feast."

Eben gave Big Eagle the tobacco and two blankets and Ada gave the cookware to his woman, Little Buffalo. Eben left the two rifles on the mule for now.

"You go away long time, my brother. Good you came back. Come, we smoke pipe with tobacco. You medicine woman, come too."

Everyone wanted to see Neokemowa's wounds and were surprised to see how Ada had stitched them closed. Even the village medicine man was surprised and interested how she had done this.

Neokemowa's wounds were still red and painful and he had a fever. When he tried to get up, Ada was adamant that he—for two days—lay in the sun. "The sun will help heal the wounds now." Neokiowa translated her requests. "In two days he should be able to stand and walk."

Eben stood with Big Eagle and watched as Ada took control of her patient. He didn't think anyone would interfere, not even the medicine man. Big Eagle was nodding his head and smiling. "Your woman good spirit. Must be to ride at the side of Big Red Beard Not Afraid."

Ada came back to Eben and Big Eagle and she unpacked the gifts for his woman, Little Buffalo. When Ada met her, she was indeed small, petite and very pretty and much younger than Big Eagle. Ada held out the cookware to Little Buffalo and said, "Little Buffalo, this gift is for you." Big Eagle translated for her. Little Buffalo was so happy to think someone would bring her a gift from the white man's world, she began to cry.

Eben gave the blankets and tobacco to Big Eagle, knowing he would keep the tobacco and give the blankets to those who needed them. The moose meat was already being taken care of.

"Eben, I have never seen a society of people who work so well together. Everyone pitches in and helps without being told. These are truly remarkable people. I already feel more at ease here than I did at Fort Gibraltar," Ada said.

Neokemowa said something and Big Eagle walked over to speak with him. They were having a lengthy conversation. Eben supposed he was telling Big Eagle how he became injured. Then he pointed at Eben and said, "Big Red Beard Not Afraid threw wolf." Then he pointed towards Ada and said something also.

Big Eagle said something to his people and the way they responded might have been an announcement. When he turned and saw the questioning looks on Eben and Ada's faces, he said, "Big Celebration tonight. Honor the return of our friend and his woman.

"Women, prepare food now for feast. We go my lodge, smoke new tobacco." When Ada turned away to join the other women and help prepare the food, Big Eagle said sternly, "She Who Walks Beside Big Red Beard, you not do woman's work. Come, smoke pipe with Big Eagle and your man."

Both Eben and Ada were surprised with this request. Women were never asked to smoke the pipe. "This is a great honor for you, Ada," Eben whispered in her ear.

Eben and Ada sat down on soft animal fur. Ada didn't know which animals. Big Eagle filled the pipe and to Eben's surprise he gave it first to Ada. She didn't know what to do. "Draw in the smoke, Ada, and then let it out when you exhale, then pass the pipe back to Big Eagle." She did and then Big Eagle gave the pipe to Eben. They smoked the tobacco until there were only ashes left. Big Eagle remained silent for a long pause, and then he said, "My friend Big Red Beard Not Afraid, you are great spirit. Cree people and all natives honor you. They know you always speak with words that are true. You understand our people. You I think sent here to help our people by The Great Creator. Many times you have protected my people from attacks by animals. You drove off white trappers who came on our land, you avenged my granddaughter, now you saved my grandson from being eaten by wolves. Neokemowa say you fight with hands three wolves at same time. Throw wolf, pick wolf up by head and smash against tree. I hear also you threw big bear to save friend. Then to fight bear and kill it with hands. You are great spirit, my friend. You, Big Red Beard Not Afraid Throw Caribou Throw Bear Throw Wolves, all these names I give to you to honor you."

Big Eagle turned to face Ada now. "You, Ada McNinch, you

woman of Big Red Beard Not Afraid Throw Caribou Throw Bear Throw Wolves. To walk beside your man you must have great spirit like your man. You wear gun like your man, Cree women not carry gun or weapons. Forbidden. You helped He Who is Clumsy. He walks and runs now because of you. You saved my grandson, Neokemowa, with your medicine."

"Big Eagle, why was Neokemowa out there alone?" Eben asked.

"Three of my people went hunting, two came back."

"Big Eagle, Ada, my woman and I would like to live on Cree land and build a house and have some animals."

"This will be good thing, have two great spirits on Cree land. Where you build?"

"Do you still have the map I gave you?"

"Yes," and he got up to get it. He unfolded it and said, "Show where."

"Here," and he pointed to a spot on the edge of the prairie west of Lake Manitoba.

"This good place. Plenty of game. You build home here, you live here, you are Cree people."

"Yes," Eben said and he looked at Ada and she said, "Yes."

"Good you build your home."

"Big Eagle, I would ask for you to let me have two of your men to help build our house. I will give them a rifle, a new rifle each."

"Good. Help you like you help my people. I send Neokiowa and Little Claw."

"You come here every summer for festival."

"Yes, we come every summer."

They talked the afternoon away and Little Buffalo announced the feast was ready. The tables were full of food: moose meat, beaver, smoked fish, caribou and some herbs even Ada was not familiar with. It was all very good and afterwards, after the women had cleaned up and removed the tables, everyone gathered around the fire and a lot more wood was thrown on.

Then everyone was quiet as Neokemowa was carried in and put in a special chair-like seat. He began telling everyone about the hunt he and his two friends were on. How he had got separated from the other two and having to fight off three wolves until Big Red Beard Not Afraid and his woman saved him from the wolves. Everything was translated by Neokiowa for Eben and Ada's benefit. He told them how Eben had fought with each wolf and Ada drawing her pistol to shoot one.

Then after the wolves were all dead, he told them about Ada tending his wounds. How she poured something on the flesh that burned like fire and then she sewed the skin back in place.

Neokiowa told about the first time Big Red Beard Not Afraid had come to their village, how he had saved his life. Little Claw told the story how Big Red Beard had thrown a caribou to the ground and wrestled it to death to save his life.

It was Big Eagle's turn to speak. He told them first about Ada fixing the ankle of He Who is Clumsy and how he now can run and walk. Then he had Eben tell the story about him throwing a bear and wrestling it to death to save a friend.

After all the storytelling had ended, Big Eagle stood up and stood by the fire. "My people, our friend and his woman have asked to live on Cree land to the west of here and the Lake Manitoba. Is there anyone who thinks this is not good?" He waited and when no one spoke up, he continued. "Big Red Beard and his woman, She Who Walks Beside Big Red Beard, will be Cree. Come to summer festival each year."

When Big Eagle had finished everyone came over to Eben and Ada to welcome them to the family. Ada had never felt so happy, so wanted and loved. These truly were remarkable people.

It was after midnight before people started to break up and go to their own lodges. Eben and Ada would sleep in Big Eagle and Little Buffalo's lodge and there the four talked amongst themselves for a long time before going to sleep.

* * * *

The next day Big Eagle talked with Neokiowa and Little Claw about them helping to build a home for Eben and Ada. They each already had a rifle so the new rifles were given to two other men. The natives did not know the concept of being paid to help someone, so the rifles were only gifts.

Eben and Ada stayed at the village for two more days. She was teaching or showing the village medicine man Natou about the importance of cleaning wounds and cleaning the hands before he worked on open wounds. Natou seemed to understand this. But sewing the skin together to close a wound, he was not so sure about.

The last day of their visit, Neokemowa was up and walking. Slowly, but he was walking and he had no fever. In his own words translated, he was happy to be alive and not in a wolf's stomach.

When it came time to leave, there were no tears or sad goodbyes. The village was still happy that they had become their family. Ada rode with Eben on one mule and Neokiowa and Little Claw on the other mule. They were back at Eben's lodge before dark.

With the mules all taken care of and the chickens, it was time to eat. Tomorrow morning they would pack and lead the mules and leave for their new home.

Eben showed Neokiowa the same map that Big Eagle had, showed him where they were going. "No need to go south around Manitoba." He pointed to the narrows at the north end of the lake and said, "We cross here. The water goes in and out and good place to walk across. Much shorter route."

It was mid-morning before they could leave, and all four mules were loaded. They all now had to walk which wasn't a problem. Eben rocked up the doors again like he had always done, "To keep animals out."

Neokiowa and Little Claw nodded their heads that they understood. "You use this lodge any time you want."

Before leaving, Ada had found eight eggs. The hens and

rooster were all new to Neokiowa and Little Claw. But when Ada fixed eggs and bacon the next morning, "Eggs big, much bigger than little birds. Much good."

The second night of the journey they camped at the narrows at the head of Lake Manitoba. When they awoke the next morning, the water current through the narrows was in the opposite direction of the evening before. But the crossing was indeed shallow—gravelly on foot.

From the narrows to the plains Eben saw more beaver flowages. They saw a lot of moose, a very few deer. The soil was looking good and the timber tall and straight. He wanted to be near a cold stream of water, and at noon he found just what he was looking for. A stream running north and south at the edge of the plains but in the forest. There was a flat area that was about four feet above the stream level and a sandy bank. "For this year, Ada, we'll have to build a cabin much like we had on the expedition with a dirt floor. Then during the winter I can hew some beams and boards for a real house.

They unpacked the mules and put up a temporary shelter with a piece of canvas, for now. The mules were tethered at night close to the camp and staked out to feed in the daylight.

With three men digging, it didn't take long to hollow out a cave (room) in the knoll. The three other walls were made of cedar logs. There was a nice thicket of cedar trees about three hundred yards away in a marshy area close to the stream. Eben showed Neokiowa and Little Claw how to cut the knobs and knots and high points off the logs so they would lay flat against the top and bottom logs with an axe. He showed them how to hew planks using the axe and drawshave.

With the hewn planks, he made doors and window boxes, one in each log wall and one on the door casing. The window panes would come later.

While the men were doing the heavy work, Ada would help peel the logs, keep the fire burning with the scraps and cook. Sometimes when they were low on meat, Eben would ask the two to go hunting. Food on the hoof was plentiful. And one day after they all had eaten so much red meat, they took a day to catch huge brook trout in a beaver flowage downstream of the camp.

Ada also gathered herbs, like fiddleheads, dandelion greens and blossoms, onions and early summer mushrooms. The hens were laying several eggs each day and Ada would make special sweet treats with the little sugar she had.

Like before Eben laid cedar logs on front and back into the sandy knoll. The logs were put next to each other and scarfed with the axe to remove knobs and knots. Then clay was laid in between the logs and the canvas spread over the logs and sand spread on top. Neokiowa and Little Claw both were impressed how Eben was building his cabin. Eben hoped they would take some of this building knowledge back to the village with them.

While digging out the cave for the mules, Eben found the sand was not as stable, so he had to prop up the ceiling with cedar posts. This worked well and he was also able to make a pen for the hens behind the support posts. Neokiowa and Little Claw both marveled about the type of structures they were helping to build.

By August 1st the work—or the necessary work—was done and one morning Neokiowa said, "Time we go home, my brother. Prepare for cold weather."

"Neokiowa, if you ever have any problems at the trading post at Fort Gibraltar, you tell me about it and I will take care of it, okay?"

"No trouble, but my woman wishes to go with me to see white man's world."

"Just be careful, Neokiowa, and remember what I say."

Ada had wrapped a dozen eggs for Neokiowa and Little Claw to take with them and then she kissed each one on the cheek as tears trickled down her cheek. "I will miss you."

"Next summer you come to festival."

"Yes, we come. Promise," Eben said.

Ada had insisted that Eben build them a bed large enough to sleep them both. "I'm tired of sleeping alone." While he was making the frame work, Ada spent several days gathering dry pine needles for a mattress. When she was done there were eight inches of soft needles and then on top of that she spread out a moose hide, soft hair up, and she had brought sheets with her from Fort Williams. She had also insisted on that.

They laid down together on the new bed and couldn't believe how nice it was to lay on. "Through the years, Eben, you have often told me about the Cree people and in particular about the people at Big Eagle's village, how nice they were. How honest and how well they work together. They are always so happy and so obliging. I didn't doubt you for a minute listening to you talk about them, but now that I have experienced them, they are truly good and wholesome people without any of the negative aspects you would find in a white settlement. I feel so comfortable with them and around them. I understand now why you were always so happy living out here in the wilderness. You were never quite all alone." She snuggled close to Eben feeling the warmth of his body.

"You said it better than I could ever have, Ada."

"I want you to make me a promise, Eben."

"What's that?"

"When we have the house nearly done, the one with wooden floors and such, not this cabin, I want a baby."

"Okay, so long as you give me a boy," he replied.

CHAPTER 11

During the day Eben worked on firewood and cutting grass for the mules during the winter. It would take much more grass to feed four. In the evenings he would work inside building tables, counter tops, cupboards and chairs. There wasn't any time for wasting.

Come early September, he had enough firewood ahead for winter and almost enough grass. "Ada, let's head out tomorrow morning for Gibraltar. We'll be there about mid-September like we told Gervais.

He rocked up both doors to protect the hens and keep animals out of the cabin. They took all four mules, riding when they could. They rode in a light drizzle one day so they stopped early to dry out. Ada was anxious to get to the trading post because there were a lot of things she wanted to get for the cabin.

They arrived on the 16th and Gervais was good to his word and the goats were out back. Eben gave Gervais a list of things they needed and Ada walked around the store picking up things she had forgotten to write down:

A hand scythe with extra blades
More nails
Canvass
Lanterns and coal oil
Sugar
Salt
Spices
Cookware

Blankets
Cloth
One-hundred pounds of flour
Twenty pounds of bacon
Coffee
Rope
More window panes
Boots for both of them
Medicinal supplies
A roll of chicken wire
Two more drawshaves
A broad axe
Some vegetable canned goods

"I think we'd better see if we can pack all this on the mules, Ada, before we buy the store out."

The four mules were pretty much loaded, but not heavy. They left Gibraltar that same day, just in case there were those about who might want to fight him.

With the four mules and goats in line, they looked like quite a freight-train heading north. Where they were only two weeks getting to Gibraltar, they were three weeks getting back. And all was well. By the time they had the mules unpacked and taken care of and all of the supplies stored away—"I'm exhausted," Eben said. "I hope we don't have to make another long trip in the near future."

* * * *

Ada would gather herbs every day until freeze-up and Eben caught fish and smoked them. And they had eaten enough moose so he went after a caribou. He had to go a long ways to find them and then a small herd tucked away in a corner of the prairie where the wind didn't blow so strong. He chose a large bull and pulled the trigger.

It was cool enough so the meat wouldn't spoil and he only smoked a little of it. He went exploring up and downstream looking for beaver. He found beaver but not as many flowages as at his old trapping grounds. But then again, they didn't need as many beaver hides now, either. They still had a good bankroll.

He had ten super large beaver before there was too much snow and cold for easy traveling. For the rest of that winter he worked on hewing out boards for the new house they would start to build in the spring. At first he was only hewing one board a day, then he found easier ways to hew the logs and he was making two a day and sometimes three.

He started building before it was good traveling. The logs were all peeled and the high spots cut off. It took him as long to build the stone fireplace as it did to put the floor and four walls up. It took an extra day to build a compartment on the right side where they could keep the gold and other valuables. Come the middle of July they had to set building aside and make the trip to the village for the festival.

There were two days of feasting and telling stories. Some retold many times now. They had to excuse themselves and apologize for a short stay, but they had more building to do before winter.

Come September, it was obvious they would not be moving in before winter. It was now tight to the weather and the inside would have to wait until winter preparedness was done: firewood, hay, fish, red meat and herbs. And they had to make a fast trip to Gibraltar. They took both mules so not to load one too heavy. They planned on riding back, also.

For all the supplies they bought, they was more than enough in beaver hides to pay for them. They loaded both mules and returned home. Instead of coal oil for the lanterns, there was a new fuel called kerosene. The flame was brighter and the glass globes didn't smoke up as quickly. Ada saw two women's hats and bought one for her and one for Little Buffalo.

With the Gibraltar trip over, the winter firewood done, food stores enough, Eben went back to work on the house. There were two windows on each wall and two plus a door window on the fourth wall. The roof logs he extended six feet for maybe an add-on porch later. There was an anteroom at the back for food storage and everyday things, a big kitchen with a lot of cupboards, a big table, a large living area and two bedrooms.

Eben was enjoying the inside work during the winter. On real cold days he would burn some of the waste wood in the fireplace. Ada was already moving some of their furnishings from the cabin. Their new bedroom was done as, too, was the kitchen. "Eben, the two most important rooms are done. We are moving in tonight. I'm serious, Eben. . .tonight."

"Okay, but tell me one thing. How is it you always have the last word?"

"That's just how it is."

When supper was over Ada stripped and washed up. "Okay, Eben, your turn." She stood in front of the fireplace drying off. The fire was feeling good on her bare skin.

As they were lying in bed, Ada said, "This is a beautiful house, Eben. I don't mean fancy, like a city house,—comfortable, beautiful."

"I know what you mean. I like it, too."

"Now roll over on your back, mister. It's time you got me pregnant." It was early February so that would make the birth about early November. That would be a good time of year.

* * * *

Eben did trap another dozen beaver, but that winter he was more interested in finishing the house and working around the farm as he and Ada were calling it now. The goats were giving a lot of milk and Ada was making cheese and butter from the cream. They had a few potatoes but Eben wanted to save most of them for seed in the spring.

Between gathering dead trees, standing or on the ground,

and the mules and goats, he had cleared a place in the heath for a garden. The soil was dark and rich and moist all summer.

Eben was enjoying this new life of farming and building, and Ada was happy creating a home for them. "But I never realized, Ada, how much work there is to farming. The work is never done. We had fun on the expedition, exploring new country, but now we are building this future for us and our son."

"Maybe a girl," Ada said.

The fireplace was really providing a lot of heat and nighttime light, as the firebox was larger than the cabin fireplace. There were times, even on extremely cold days, that Ada would open a door for a few minutes. "You know, Eben, a wood cook-stove would be awfully nice. I wouldn't have to bend over so much to cook our meals."

"Well, when we go out to Gibraltar we'll look at one and see if it comes apart so we can pack it in. It would be nice, though."

"We're so comfortable here, Eben, I sometimes wonder what the rest of Canada is doing." The temperatures were not as cold that winter as Eben had seen in the past. It only dropped to negative thirty degrees one night. But there was a great deal more snow. But it was dry, fluffy and the mules could still wade through it to feed. The goats could only flounder in it, so Eben fed them in their pen. A bunch of chicks had been hatched in December, and now it was obvious two of them were roosters, so Eben killed the old rooster and Ada roasted it. It was a delicious switch from red meat and fish. The hens were laying more eggs than they could eat, and often times they had to throw away eggs before they spoiled.

"Eben, I think we should make our trip to Gibraltar soon before I get any bigger. If we wait until late summer, the trip might be too much for me."

"Okay, as soon as we can travel, then."

* * * *

Eben made a point not to travel as fast as they had in the past. If it rained, they didn't travel. What used to take only two weeks now was three weeks. Ada was doing fine—just fine.

The price on beaver fur had gone up a few dollars and this year his twelve beaver brought $264.00. Still plenty to pay for all of their supplies. Ada picked out two pretty hats, one for her and one for Little Buffalo. With more hens, Eben needed more fencing. Ada wanted material to make curtains for the windows.

"Mr. Gervais, do you have any newspapers?"

"I don't have anything more recent than two weeks ago. But I have a stack of last year's."

"Could I have those?"

"I'll give them to you."

"I need a wood cookstove. Do you have anything?"

"I have one."

"Can it be taken apart?"

"Yes, it can be unbolted so there are several pieces."

"If you can do that and I can pack it on my mules, I'll take it."

An hour later, Gervais had the stove disassembled and Eben had it loaded on the mules. They bought a few more supplies and Ada said, "The rest will have to wait until September."

"Put the rest on our account, Mr. Gervais. We'll be back in September."

Along with the stove he had to have several sections of stove pipe and a top for the pipe. They were still loaded light and three weeks later they were home.

Two days out it started to rain. "It isn't raining heavy, Eben. I'm alright. We don't need to stop." He was being a little over-protective, but that was his nature.

When they arrived home, it stopped raining for two months. It took Eben two days to put the stove back together, and another day to get it set up and the stovepipe sitting on top. "This is going to be great," Ada said, "and we won't use as much wood either."

It was time to plant the potatoes, cabbage, squash and corn. He had to till a garden with only a spade. But in the soft, rich, black soil, it didn't take long. He made a bigger pen for the hens, with a small building to shut them up at night. One of the female goats had a kid and Eben was beginning to think he'd have to build a barn.

He didn't have to sleep on the idea and the barn didn't have to be built in one minute. But he did start cutting cedar trees and peeling them and stacking them to dry. He would set stanchions about twelve feet apart and then nail smaller logs to form the walls and again for a slanted roof to the back. It was big enough for his animals and a workshop. And he still had the cave he had used to shelter the animals.

When they went to the summer festival that year, it was obvious Ada was pregnant. Little Buffalo was so happy. Neokiowa's woman was also pregnant and expecting soon. When Ada gave the hat to Little Buffalo, she was so happy she hugged and hugged Ada and cried out with so much happiness flowing through her.

Big Eagle understood they could not stay long because of Ada's condition. Goodbyes were said and three days later they were home. Eben made sure the trip would not overtire Ada and cause her to lose the baby. He kindled the fires, cooked food over the fire, made their shelter and beds and tended the mules. He waited on Ada hand and foot.

* * * *

"Eben, it's time for you to go to Fort Gibraltar. We need winter supplies and I don't want you gone when my time is so near. I have made a list."

He took two mules and left the other two in the barn with enough hay and water until he returned. Ada would tend the goats and chickens.

He rode even after the sun had set when there was a moon to see by. He pushed hard and was there in ten days.

Beaver had gone up another dollar, to $23.00 for a super large beaver. He had a dozen. He filled Ada's list and bought more vegetable seeds also and more powder and shot for the rifles. He also bought six smaller traps for mink, otter, bobcat and fox. They still were not worth as much as beaver, but the prices on each were increasing a little each year.

With the mules loaded he left Gibraltar the same day and again he rode hard, pushing his endurance and the mules. The mules were better prepared for the fast pace, though. When he arrived home he was exhausted.

To keep from worrying about Ada, Eben buried himself in work. He had more than enough firewood worked up and piled. He liked using the hand scythe to cut heath grass, but it was slow work lugging it to the barn. He didn't have a wagon. All he needed, actually, were the wheels. He could have the rest of the parts on his next trip to Gibraltar. But after a while, he had all the hay he figured he'd need.

The garden did real well. They now had potatoes, cabbage and squash to see them through the winter. "If we had some canning jars, Eben, we could save all this corn. Now we'll have to grind most of it into corn meal."

"Next trip to Gibraltar, Ada."

Eben was now doing all the farm work, feeding and milking the goats, feeding the chickens and mules, and doing what he could to help out inside the house.

"Ada, I need to get us a moose or caribou. Are you so near your time that maybe I should not go?"

"My time is close, but if you're not gone overnight, I'll be okay."

"Okay, I'll be back tonight, regardless then."

He saddled one mule and brought along one more. When he got to the prairie, he tied off both and he began working his way north along the tree line. There was a slight breeze blowing across the prairie from the west. This would keep his scent in the woods and off the prairie. He had gone less than a quarter of a mile and saw a small herd grazing. They had no idea he was close. He crawled on his stomach to get close enough to make a killing shot. He crawled up behind an old rotting stump and rested the rifle on top of it. He found the caribou he wanted, but waited for it to turn so he could get a clean shot at the back of the head. Another one turned at a right angle and he took that one and fired. The caribou went down and the others ran. He reloaded before walking over to the animal. When he did walk over, it was dead and he cut the throat to drain the blood.

Then he went back to bring the mules up. Before he was halfway there, he heard both mules braying and instantly knew they were being attacked by wolves. He ran, cursing them with each stride. How he hated the wolf.

There were four wolves circling the mules. They had not yet attacked either one. They were so intent on killing one of the mules, they never saw their real nemesis. Eben had hatred written all over his face. He stopped thirty feet away and shot one that was about ready to bite into the hind quarter of one of them. He pulled his pistol then and shot another. He dropped his pistol and using the rifle for a club, hit another one behind the head, killing that one. He ran after the fourth wolf. The wolf turned its head to look at its pursuer, stumbled over a rotten log, and this gave Eben enough of an edge that he jumped on its back, flattening it to the ground and at the same time he stabbed it in its heart. He rolled off the wolf exhausted. "There, you son-of-a-bitches. I declare war against you!"

The mules were shaken, but okay. He had to make the travoises, one for the caribou and one for the four wolves. He walked beside the mules to keep them calm.

He was up until midnight taking care of his animals, quartering the caribou and putting it in cold storage and skinning the wolves.

"Do you think there were any more wolves, Eben?"

"Not in that pack, but to be on the safe side, I don't want you to go outside without your pistol. The smell of our farm animals may lure them in if they're hungry enough. Or this may have been just a roving pack. But I don't want you to take any chances."

As they lay in bed that night, Eben said, "I don't know who gets more tired each day now, you or me. I'm exhausted."

She hugged her husband. He was a good man. "Well, I didn't have to fight four wolves today, either."

He was already snoring and didn't hear her.

* * * *

At daybreak on November 7th, Ada began labor pains. "Eben—Eben, don't you plan on going outside today. The baby is coming."

Eben turned to face her. What she could see of the skin on his face was turning whiter than snow. "Oh, my God, Ada. What do I do?"

"Help me back in bed and get a kettle of warm water and some clean towels." Just then she half screamed and half moaned with another wave of pain.

"Ada. Ada…are you alright?"

"Never mind. Get the water and towels."

He came back and set the kettle on the floor and put the towels on the bed beside her. "Now what do I do, Ada?"

"We wait. When the baby is ready it'll come through the birth canal. Keep the house warm and I need a drink of water."

"I need a couple of shots of whiskey, only we ain't got none."

"Are you going to be alright, Eben? I have enough problems giving birth than worrying about you. Just keep your mind on fighting wolves, will you."

Every time Ada would moan from another contraction, Eben would start sweating and his nervousness would start anew. At noon her contractions were coming more frequently and then at 2 p.m. she said, "Eben…it's coming. This is it."

"What do I do, Ada?"

She had to walk him through it, step-by-step in between contractions, and screaming. And then the baby was there. "Ada! He's here! You gave birth to a son!"

She talked him through how to take care of the afterbirth and tie off and cut the cord. "Now wrap him in a warm towel."

Eben laid their son on Ada's breast. "What will you name him, Eben? He's your son."

There was no hesitation. "Enoch."

Ada repeated the name, "Enoch McNinch. Like it."

* * * *

Eben was still doing all the work while Ada was regaining her strength. But it was Ada who got up at night to tend to Enoch.

When Ada was able to work around the house, Eben took one day to go back where he had shot the caribou and set four traps for wolves. And then one upstream and downstream of the farm. To protect his family, he decided if he had to he would rid this country of every wolf.

He waited four days before checking his traps. Those near the farm had not been touched. Around the caribou gut pile, there was a lynx and a bobcat. Not what he wanted but both valuable pieces of fur.

He left two traps and set one a half mile behind the house and one on the opposite side of the heath, across from the farm. He waited another four days and had another lynx near the gut pile and he left these traps there. If wolves were still in the area, eventually they would come to the gut pile.

He had one wolf across the heath and a fox behind the house. He reset those traps and left them. He set traps for beaver, only to have bait for wolf sets and castors to lure the wolves to the traps.

During the winter he made snowshoe trails up and down the stream, across the heath and even a mile behind the farm. He trapped six wolves that winter and shot two more. He also had trapped four beaver, two otter, another fox and another lynx and bobcat. He wished that everything had been wolves, but he had enough he figured so maybe they wouldn't bother around the farm for a few years.

Things were changing fast everywhere, especially at Fort Gibraltar. Since 1812, the Hudson Bay Company had a similar fort across the river, Fort Douglas, and now in 1821 the two companies merged and the new fort was named Fort Garry. And there was already talk about renaming Fort Garry to Winnipeg. There were now many settlements around Red River and the Assiniboine River. There was also a school and church. Fort Garry had become the Hudson Bay Company's leading post in the region.

That spring at Fort Garry, he was paid a total of $596.00. "Not so good as your beaver, McNinch, and no castors?"

"I used them to trap the wolves.'"

"You're the only trapper who bothers with wolves," Gervais said.

Most of his money was left on account. So far the McNinches had not had to use any of their money deposited in Banque du Montreal, and he had close to $600.00 on account at Fort Garry.

Enoch had dark hair like his mother and she doted on him. When she had work to do outside she carried him on her back. She seldom left him alone, and Eben loved his son as much.

When he returned from Fort Garry, he had brought four wagon wheels and axels. The rest of the wagon parts he worked on in the barn in his spare time.

They had enough chickens now so Eben was killing one a month. Roasted chicken with potato and gravy was a real treat from a long diet of caribou or moose.

The years were passing and Eben and his family were generally happy and growing. The wolves seemed to have understood and they left the country. Life was being good to the McNinch family.

CHAPTER 12

1836

As the years passed, life was good at the McNinch farm. The wolves stopped coming close to the farm. Only on rare occasions would Eben ever see a wolf track in the snow while tending traps, and then at a great distance from the farm. It seemed the wolves had learned finally to leave the farm and Eben McNinch alone.

Through the years Eben had begun to slow a little. But whenever he and his family were at Fort Garry every troublemaker would give them a wide berth. And stories were still being told to the newcomers about the red bearded McNinch, as if the stories themselves were new.

Newspapers all the way to Ottawa, Quebec and New Brunswick had run stories about Eben McNinch, the man the natives were calling Big Red Beard Not Afraid.

Big Eagle was an old man now. He was still chief, but Neokiowa, who would be the next chief, had taken over Big Eagle's responsibilities. Little Buffalo was a bit younger than Big Eagle and she still was a beautiful woman.

Neokiowa and Echo Berry's daughter, Blue Flower, had been born two months before Enoch and with each visit to the village they became very close friends and everyone, Eben and Ada included, knew when the time was right that Enoch would take Blue Flower for his woman.

As Enoch grew older, he would journey alone to the village to see Blue flower. Everyone approved of Enoch and his closeness with Blue Flower.

Ada had been very adamant about Enoch's education. Every day she would teach him to read and write and Eben in the evenings, would teach him mathematics. They would bring home old newspapers from Gibraltar and they each would read every article. This way they stayed informed of the civilized world. Even if a year late.

More changes had been happening at Fort Garry. In 1826 the fort had been destroyed in a flood. The fur buying business was done in the back of one of the livery stables. The fort wasn't rebuilt until 1835, and the fort became the residence of the Governor of Hudson Bay Company.

Fifteen years had passed and Eben and Ada both were forty-six years old. Ada had only a few gray streaks in her hair, and Eben's hair and beard were still fire red. Enoch was six feet tall, two inches taller than his father, and with brown hair like his mother. He was tall and slender, but strong. He was a lot of help around the farm. He enjoyed hunting and trapping as much as his father.

North West Company trappers all knew Eben and Ada had settled somewhere north on Cree land, but no one knew where for sure. And even though the price for super large beaver pelts had doubled, no one was foolish enough to make the mistake and trespass on Eben's land.

Eben shared with his son the secret of his gold and told him where he had found it and if word ever got out to the white settlements, it would only bring trouble to the Cree nation. Eben made sure his son knew about the secret compartment in the stone fireplace where the gold, the land grant papers and other valuables were kept.

One day two years later, Enoch announced to his mom and dad, "When I turn seventeen in November, Blue Flower and I want to be married, and we both would like to live here and help you both on the farm. Blue Flower is already seventeen.

There were no objections. "Then we must get busy and build an addition onto this house. A separate bedroom for you and

Blue Flower and then when you have a child, he can have your room."

Ada smiled to herself. Eben was already declaring that Enoch and Blue Flower would give them a grandson and not a granddaughter.

Father and son worked tirelessly building the new addition, in between farming, winter wood and meat. But before Enoch's seventeenth birthday, the new addition was complete, with windows and an outside door.

Eben knew the visit to the village would not be a short one, so he made provisions enough for his animals. They took all four mules, one for Blue Flower to ride on the return trip. Through the years they had used the same route to the village and there now was a well-worn trail to follow and the three of them had taken the time to cut branches and remove fallen trees across the trail. A blind man could now follow the trail.

Big Eagle, although his health was failing, and Little Buffalo were the most excited about the joining. "This is good thing, my brother. Bond between us now that can never be broken."

Ada had brought with her a basket full of fresh eggs and Eben brought an old goat to butcher and roast for the celebration. The eggs were most appreciated by everyone.

There were days of celebration before the joining and some nights, even in the cold, the music and dancing continued until midnight.

The day of the joining Enoch was dressed in his best clothes and Blue Flower a deer hide dress that she had turned white and decorated. Her long black hair she wore straight on her shoulders. She was really beautiful. "Look at what I've been missing all these years," Eben said.

Ada punched him in the ribs with her elbow. "You keep talking like that, old man, and I'll trade you in for a young buck."

"Yes, dear." This time he had the last word and he began laughing to himself. And he thought, *The only time in all these years I was able to have the last word.*

The ceremony itself was short and simple. Enoch and Blue Flower stood up before Big Eagle and Little Buffalo. Big Eagle had to be carried up on a chair. Everyone else was standing behind them. "It is Enoch McNinch and Blue Flower's desire to join this day. Is there anyone who thinks they should not?"

There was a long silence as no one spoke. Big Eagle waited the appropriate time before continuing. "If not, I can see no reason why these two should not join. Enoch, you take your woman Blue Flower."

They clasped hands and walked off to a lodge especially for them. There they would remain, just the two of them learning to explore and please the other.

When they emerged the next morning, it was as if they were only another couple with no fanfare.

The McNinches remained in the village for another two days before saying goodbye and returning to their farm.

* * * *

Not surprising to either Eben or Ada, Blue Flower became pregnant early into their joining. Ada was in heaven having another female in the house to talk with. Until Blue Flower moved in, she had not realized how much she had missed womanly conversations.

1837

Blue Flower gave birth to an enormous son. "You called it right again, old man. He has your genes…also red hair and already strong arms."

Enoch and Blue Flower both agreed that since their son had so many of his grandfather's genes, they named him Ebenezer McNinch. Ada cried with happiness and there were tears in Eben's eyes.

For Ada, having a crying baby in the house was music to her

ears. Eben could have done without the music, but he loved his namesake and he said nothing.

It was decided to eliminate confusion they would call little Eben, 'Eb.'

When Eb was old enough, Ada began schooling him and Blue Flower. "Blue Flower, if you learn to read and write, a whole new world will open for you. And Eben taught the two mathematics.

Even at a young age, because of his strength Eb was good help around the farm. Eben was now fifty-two. He still could outwork most men, although he was going to bed earlier now.

1842

The whole family would make the trips to Fort Garry. This was another world entirely for Blue Flower. Eb liked the excitement and sometimes he had other kids to play with for a short while. And everyone knew not to cause trouble beause Blue Flower was Cree. Each trip Mr. Gervais, who was now an old man, would give them all of his back newspapers. Now that Blue Flower could read another new world was opening for her. She read about people and places that before were non-existent to her. She saw pictures in the papers of strange looking villages and wondered how big the big world was where all the white settlements were. She saw how some people in the pictures dressed so much different even from the McNinch family.

Big Eagle had outlived his youth and Neokiowa was now chief. The village rejoiced, knowing he had been a good leader and because of his physical restrictions the last few years of his life. He was now spirit and would be on his journey where he could not walk in his body.

Little Claw made the trip to the farm to tell of Big Eagle's passing into the spirit world. Eben would miss his friend.

They read newspaper articles about something called the Alamo, a war between Texas and Mexico, and two men, Jim

Bowie and Davy Crockett. Both had volunteered to travel to the Mexican border in Texas and fight for the republic of Texas. They had all read stories in older newspapers about the two men, their exploits as fighters. "It seems the United States is always fighting a war with someone," Eben said. "I'm glad we live here where we do."

Eb was only five years old and usually his granddad would read to him about Bowie and Crockett. There were always a lot of articles about the white settlers fighting with the Indians and Eb asked his grandmother one day, "Grandmother, my mom is a native so that makes me half native, don't it?"

"Yes, Eb, it does."

"Would I be accepted in the white settlements?"

Ada didn't want to upset the boy so she said, "Of course, Eb, why wouldn't they?" Even though with his red hair and more natural features of his white grandparents, he still was half native, and secretly she was worried if the outside world could ever offer him anything.

In the winter of 1843 the wolves made another appearance in the farmyard one night. At the first braying from the mules, Eben was out of bed and reaching for his rifle. He eased a window open and waited for a clear shot. There were four of them circling the yard. Finally a big male stopped and turned facing the house. Eben shot him and grabbed a pistol and another rifle and went running outside. Enoch was up by now and he too was outside with his rifle. The other three had already run off.

In the morning Eben and Enoch set traps where Eben had the last time the wolves had been a problem. They only tended every four days, and at each tend they would have one wolf. When they had the four wolves, they figured they had gotten them all and they pulled their traps. Then two nights later they were all awakened again by wolves howling out in the heath.

Eben and Enoch both were concerned about their family. They reset all the traps again. "You go on back to the farm, Son. I'm going to have a look around before I come in."

The snow was deep that winter and the wolves were having a difficult time chasing down enough food to keep their bellies full. Eben show-shoed out to the prairie and the moose and caribou with their long legs were having no difficulty at all wading the snow and out-distancing the wolves. The smells of the farm were drawing them in.

He followed the tree line next to the prairie south for a long ways before turning east back to the farm. He found wolf trails that were well used traveling east and west. He figured this must be the wolves' travel lane when they came to the farm. He had an idea, and he headed for home. He talked with his son about what he had discovered. "Son, I think we can make up some snares with the fencing wire that's in the barn and set them in on their run."

After breakfast and chores the next morning, the two headed out, being careful not to cross the run and leave their scent and tracks. When they found where the run would go through a close knot of saplings or trees they would hang a snare about one foot off the snow. They had enough wire to set up a dozen snares.

At supper that night Eben said, "The moon is full and bright tonight. I'm going to sit up with that window open just enough to put my rifle through. When I can't stay awake any longer, son, I'll wake you. It always seems wolves have been more active with a bright moon."

Eb stayed up with his granddad for a while until he couldn't stay awake any longer. Eben whispered, "You'd better go to bed, Eb. You're falling asleep."

Eben stayed up well beyond midnight before he woke his son. Eben laid down with Ada and he was instantly asleep. Enoch poured himself a cup of coffee and sat down at the window. There was a slight breeze blowing through the opening.

About an hour before dawn, Enoch, almost asleep, saw two shadows moving near the barn door. He waited for a clear shot. One of the wolves picked up a scent of something else and followed it towards the house. Enoch fired and the other wolf ran off. Eben came running out of the bedroom already dressed with his rifle in hand. Everyone else was also up now.

"There were two. I got one."

After breakfast, Enoch let his son skin that wolf while it was still warm. It was a beautiful fur pelt.

"Eb," his mother asked, "would you get me some bark of hemlock and break it up in small pieces?"

"Sure." He took a pail and an axe. It took longer to pound the bark into powder than to cut it off the trees. "What you going to do with this, Ma?"

"There is oil in the bark that our people use to rub on animal skins to make them soft. If you men get me enough wolves, I'll make vests for everyone." Eb liked being called a man, even though he was only six.

Eben found wolf tracks circling the barn and where one of them had clawed at the big front doors. As much as he wanted to snowshoe out and tend the snares, he didn't. Their human scent needed to dissipate first, in order for them to work.

All this was exciting to six-year-old Eb. He couldn't understand the danger of wolves being so close and so bold. Blue Flower was not as upset outwardly. Her people had lived with dangers like this for eons of time. The danger for her had become more ingrained as everyday living.

Eben kept following tracks to find their run they were using to get to the farm. There were tracks all around, but he seemed to think they had used the run that went west to the prairie.

Enoch and Eb had finished their morning chores and now for Eb and Blue Flower, it was time for school.

They didn't see any more wolves at the farm and each morning Eben would circle the farm looking for tracks. A week after setting the snares Eben and Enoch snowshoed out to the prairie checking snares and traps. Of the twelve snares they had set, they had five wolves. Two were already dead and three had to be shot. They were all tall and lengthy animals, but very thin. For now they reset the snares and spent the rest of the day tending traps. They had one more wolf and two lynx.

That made eleven wolves from one pack. Blue Flower now had enough pelts to make vests for everyone. The fur when cleaned was beautiful.

A week later they tended traps and snares again and only had another lynx and one bobcat. "I guess the wolf threat is over for this winter."

* * * *

That spring when the McNinches traveled to Fort Garry, they were all wearing their new wolf vests. They did stand out and everybody stopped what they were doing to watch them pass. Blue flower with her vest was really beautiful, the fur accentuating her natural beauty.

Whenever Eben and his grandson were together close, Eb would ask his grandfather to tell him more stories about his life and wrestling with caribou, bear and wolves. His grandfather was to him a living legend and his hero.

1849

As Eb grew older he and his grandfather would explore the countryside together, always returning home for supper. They would look for new fishing holes and keep only the biggest trout. They hunted and trapped. By the time Eb was twelve he was as skilled a hunter, trapper and hide skinner as his grandfather.

It was time for their annual spring trip to Fort Garry. No wolf pelts this year. A few beaver, lynx, bobcat and otter. After the supplies were deducted from the sale of fur, they still had some to put on their account. There was now $800.00 on account, plus their savings and the gold which no one talked about or ever thought about.

"Eben, tomorrow is Sunday and I want to stay in town tonight and all of us go to church in the morning." Enoch, Blue

Flower and Eb had never been to church and didn't know much about what went on there.

Eben and Ada had not been to church since they were married in Ottawa.

Ada was right in her glory. She had missed this living in the wilderness. It did bring back memories for Eben. Enoch wasn't sure what it was all about. It brought back memories for Blue Flower. Although what the preacher was saying was very similar to the teachings of the shaman, the preacher was using different terms. But she was sure he was talking about the same thing. Eb was confused. He believed in the Great Creator and wasn't sure about this God or the one called Jesus Christ. But he was feeling an inner glow.

* * * *

Eb had become good friends with Wenonah, Neokiowa's granddaughter. With each visit at the village, the two would spend more and more time together. Blue Flower's woman's intuition was telling her that when the time was right, these two would join. But that was still a few years off.

One night back at the farm Eben was looking through some of his personal things and stumbled across the map, like the one he had given Big Eagle. He unfolded it and laid it on the table and mentally retraced their journey along the 49th parallel. He had marked off each night where they stopped and where they had spent each of the two winters. "Enoch and Eb, come here. This map outlines the journey your mother and me were on when we guided the group west to the big mountains." He pointed to a small lake and he said, "Remember this place, and the mountain range behind the lake. Fred Michaud exclaimed the morning he and I woke up here. When the morning sun hit this mountain, the white snow cap turned blood red and he exclaimed, 'Sangreal,' *Royal Blood.* We named this lake and the mountain behind it Sangreal. We camped—it was in the winter—near a spring inlet to the lake. The water was not frozen and we could see huge schools of brook trout. We found many moose there. Big, tall beautiful timber for building a house and it all sets on the western edge of a prairie like here.

"After Ada and I are gone, if things change too much around here with the white man moving in, go west to Sangreal. Promise me you will if you can no longer live in peace here."

"Sure thing, Pa," Enoch said.

"Yes, Granddad."

1850

That November and December it seemed like it snowed every other day. Taking the mules out into the heath to feed now was Eb's responsibility. Ada was spending more time inside, while the chickens were now Blue Flower's chore, and the goats and work in the barn and outside was Enoch's. Eben still prowled the countryside, as he said, "…looking for wolf tracks," which was probably more of a reason to be out roaming than anything else. He hadn't seen a wolf track now for five years.

January thaw arrived with fifty degrees of warm sunshine; day and night for a week, much of the snow had melted. Then the ungodly cold returned with a vengeance. Too cold to let the mules out to feed. And then in the middle of February the wind blew out of the north and the northern lights that winter were really spectacular.

March came in with a warm wind from the south and longer daylight hours. Ada tended the chickens one morning and milked the goats. "It is so nice out today, Blue Flower, you and I should go for a walk along the trail."

"That I would like, Ada. Spend some time alone with you. We all have been shut up inside so much this winter."

After their walk, Ada was a little tired. "Ada, why don't you lie down for a while. You seem tired. I'll make supper and call you when it's ready."

"I could use a little nap. Thank you, Blue Flower."

When Eb saw his grandfather back in the farmyard, he ran over to greet him. "Where did you go, Granddad?"

"Looking for wolf tracks on the prairie."

"Did you see any?"

"No, and that's strange." Eb thought to himself they hadn't seen any wolf tracks for years. He let it go.

"Wish I could have gone with you, Granddad."

"Where's your father?" Eben asked.

"He's in the house with Mom."

"I have to take the mules out to feed now. Do you want to help Granddad?"

"Sure, why not."

Eb loved spending time with his grandfather. He looked so much like him. He was taller—six feet, was barrel-chested like his grandfather and of course the red hair. He was growing whiskers now but had not started to grow a beard yet. And he, like his father, was as strong as Eben. He was only fifteen, but he looked every inch a man.

Ada was up before supper and she helped Blue Flower set everything on the table. She still was a bit tired and didn't eat much. Eben was quiet also.

After supper and the kitchen cleaned, the family sat in the living room with the comfort of the fire. Ada and Eben sat on the couch. "Hold me, Eben. I'm cold."

He put his arm around her and puller her close. They talked about taking a spring trip back to the village as soon as traveling was good. This made Eb happy. He'd get to spend time again with Wenonah.

Eben was also tired after his exploring all day and he was having trouble staying awake. He and Ada went to bed early. "Hold me, Eben, I'm still cold. Eben...Eben, this has been a happy life, hasn't it."

"Yes, Ada. The best that I could ever imagine."

"I have always loved you so much, Eben."

"I have always loved you also, Ada."

Sometime during the night while Ada was asleep, she died, quietly and at peace. She was sixty-two years old.

* * * *

When Eben awoke in the morning and discovered Ada's cold and stiff body, he bellowed and roared with anger like he had when he wrestled the bear.

The whole family woke up and came running to see what the matter was. Enoch said, "Oh, Ma." Blue Flower said, "Ada." Eb said, "Grandma?"

Eben collapsed in a chair crying his heart out. "All of my life I have protected Ada, provided for her, kept her from harm. How was I supposed to protect her from this?" He looked at each of them looking for an answer. "She was too young to die, too good. I always thought I'd be the first to go.

"Please…give me a few minutes alone with Ada?"

Ada's death was difficult for everyone to accept. She was never sick a day in her life. She was always so strong and wholesome. There had been no warning anything was wrong. Eben stayed with Ada for a long time before he came out.

"Dad," Enoch said and sat down beside his father. I'll take care of Mom. The ground is frozen so we'll have to keep the body wrapped in a blanket in the cold storage room."

Enoch wrapped his mom's body in a blanket and carried her out to cold storage. He laid her body down and said to himself, "We can't give you a proper burial, Mom, until the ground thaws."

Eben couldn't eat at all that day, not even a cup of coffee. The others ate very little. "Dad, you stay here with Granddad and I'll go do chores. He needs to be with someone," Eb said.

Blue Flower was as sad as anyone. Ada always had seemed like her own mother, so kind and understanding. While Enoch went outside for an armload of firewood, Blue Flower sat beside Eben and took his hands in hers. "Eben…Dad, I know it is always sad to lose one you love. You did protect her all of her life, but when it is time for spirit to walk into the Spirit World, there is nothing we can do about it. We have to let them go and take their walk. You and Mom were like one spirit in two bodies. You two were so close, Ada's warmth and goodness was what you have always needed. And your love and protection for Ada is what she always needed from you.

"I know what I am about to say, Dad, is going to be hard to hear. But you need to hear it. You need to let Mom go and let her take her walk to the Spirit World. When she is ready she will come to you every night in your dreams."

"How do you know all this, Blue Flower?"

"I have known this all of my life. It isn't what I believe, Dad; it's what I know. Once she has reached the Spirit World she will have things there she will have to do."

"Like what?"

"She will be making a place for you, when you walk to the Spirit World."

* * * *

For days Eben moped around the house, never going out and eating very little. Two weeks after her passing, Enoch said, "Dad...the ground has thawed and I have a grave for Mom."

"Where?" he asked. "It's time."

Enoch and Blue Flower walked with Eben, each on a side, and Eb carried Ada's body up the knoll.

After the body was lowered into the grave, Eben said, "I used to know 'The Lord's Prayer.' I can't remember it now. God, my wife Ada was a good woman. I can't take care of her now, so I'm depending on you to take care of her until I can take my own walk."

They stood there in silence for a few minutes and Eben said, "Son, will you take your family back now. I will fill in the grave and I want to spend some time here with her by myself."

It was time for their spring trip to Fort Garry. "You three go ahead," Eben said. "I'm not going this year. You three go on and enjoy your trip."

"Granddad, do you want me to stay with you?" Eb asked.

"No, you go with your folks, Eb. It'll be good for you to get out. I'll take care of the farm while you're gone."

Enoch was thinking maybe this is what his father was needing. Something that was depending on him again for their survival.

Although Blue Flower probably had a better understanding about when one dies, or takes his last walk to the Spirit World than her husband or son, she was missing Ada just as much as the others. Ada had actually been the matriarch of the family and it was Ada who was responsible for the family unity, as Eben had been the protector. She was also missing the female companionship.

Blue Flower held her head up high and smiled. She was now the matriarch of the McNinch family and she would do her best not to disappoint Ada's memory.

Eben brought a chair and sat in the shade of the overhang and leaned back against the house. He was glad for this time alone now, so he could think of Ada without interruptions. He thought of Ada going out every morning, even trudging with the cold and snow to gather eggs and feed the chickens. Then to milk the goats and that reminded him he had not yet done either. He went in and got the egg basket. They had quite a flock of chickens now and he found a dozen eggs. He opened the pen to let them out to feed. They were always back in the pen on their own before dark. He milked the three goats and turned them loose in the outdoor pen.

For some strange reason he was suddenly feeling better. Maybe it was because by doing the chores that Ada had always done, that had brought him closer to her. And this made him hungry. The first time since her passing had he felt like eating. He fixed up a big pan of bacon and eggs and cut off a piece of fresh bread Blue Flower had made, and he made a pot of coffee. When he had finished eating he took his coffee cup and pot outside and sat in his chair leaning back against the house.

He eventually finished the pot of coffee and stayed there leaning back against the house reminiscing about his life. The memories started when he had first come into this country and Ada had stayed behind at Fort Williams. She had not complained at all. She was understanding, not demanding or temperamental.

The pictures in his mind changed then to the expedition west to the big mountains and he started laughing out loud as he remembered and now could see in his mind Ada telling everyone that she was not going to live with smelly pigs for two years. That each of them would take a sponge-bath once a week. He saw her disrobing in front of everyone and thinking nothing of it. And after a while how commonplace her bathing in front of everyone had become.

"You were quite the woman, Ada. I hope I told you often enough how much I loved you." Just then he thought he had heard her say, "You did." He was sure it was her voice and he looked all around him. There was no one but him. He shrugged his shoulders and thought it was probably all in his head.

These memories of Ada were not making him sad. Instead, he was happy to be reliving them again and for the first time since her passing, he knew she was beside him in spirit. Like Blue Flower had said. *How did she know so much about the Spirit World? Enoch is a lucky man to have you.*

The sun was beginning to set below the tree tops and Eben was still leaning back against the house, with his coffee cup in his hand and the cold empty pot sitting on the ground beside him. He had been lost all day in his mind, reliving the time with Ada. He stood up and walked over to the chicken pen to close them up for the night and put the goats back in the barn. He walked like a man newly in love.

Ada had worked her goodness again.

* * * *

Enoch and his family were worried about Eben but they were enjoying the trip and like Ada, Blue Flower said, "Tomorrow is Sunday. I would like to go to church." No one argued with her. They were all wearing the wolf vests Blue Flower had made when they were seated in church. Everyone knew who they were and no one stared at them.

On the way home Eb asked her many questions about The Great Creator and God and the one the preacher called Jesus Christ, and the Holy Spirit.

"The Holy Spirit, Son, is the spirit that is in each of us."

"I don't understand what Heaven is?" Eb asked.

"We call it the Spirit World."

"Okay, that makes it easier to understand."

They each were packing a few supplies on their mule and the pack mule was carrying oats for the animals.

When they arrived home at midday, Eben was nowhere to be seen. "He can't be too far away," Enoch said. "His coffee cup and pot are sitting there beside his chair under the overhang of the house."

"The chickens are out of their pen and the goats are in the outside pen," Eb said.

"Looks like he ate breakfast this morning. How about his rifle?"

"Still here," Enoch said. "If his rifle is still here, he can't be far away. Eb, you walk around the farm. Maybe he laid down for a nap under a tree somewhere."

Enoch and Blue Flower walked up the knoll to see what Eb wanted. "What is it, Son?"

"I found Granddad." He turned his head toward Eben leaning against a tall spruce tree near Ada's grave.

Blue Flower walked over and felt of the carotid artery in

his neck like Ada had taught her. "There's no pulse. He's gone, Enoch. But no more than a few minutes. He is still warm. I think he was still alive when we rode into the farmyard."

"He's actually smiling. Look."

"Look at his hand," Eb said. "He's holding it out like he was holding someone's hand."

"He is, Son. Ada came back to walk with him to the Spirit World. He reached out to grasp her hand, smiling, and he left his body behind."

They stood there, arms around each other, happy that Eben had finally found happiness again and that he was with Ada. "I'll miss you, Dad." There were tears in all of their eyes.

The saga of Ebenezer and Ada McNinch had come to a close. But the stories told and retold about them would live on for a long, long time.

CHAPTER 13

Eben was buried next to Ada on the knoll overlooking the farm. They would miss them both. There was a big void in their lives. "Ma, Dad…you named me Ebenezer after my Granddad. I want to be called Eben and not Eb, in his memory." There was no argument.

With his grandfather's absence, young Eben now had to start to take more responsibility. He had his grandfather's prowess as a hunter and trapper. He would go off on his own with a mule and bring back either a moose or caribou. He was always exploring the wilderness as his grandfather had, looking for beaver flowages, brook trout pools, and wolf signs.

The people at the Cree village were saddened by Eben and Ada's passing and that night after the feast, they all enjoyed telling stories about the two. This Enoch and Eben learned was how the native people kept alive the memories of those before them, and of their own history, nothing was ever written. The history and memories were the stories they told.

Eben stayed another two days after his mom and dad returned home. He wanted to spend more time with Wenonah. Because of their ages and developments they were not allowed to be alone. They always had to have a chaperone. Eben during the last year had filled out so, he was looking like a man, rather than a fifteen-year-old. He had developed his grandfather's barrel chest and his strength. In fact, he was stronger. But he was never one to test or probe it.

Enoch and his son were always working together on some project or other around the farm. When there wasn't any work,

Eben would take off on his own to explore. He knew where every beaver flowage was within a five-mile radius.

Enoch didn't have his father's natural abilities when it came to carpentry or masonry. But he would study beforehand whatever project he was working on and find his own solutions.

One day Enoch and his son were after firewood. They were going quite a far distance from the farm now, and they would use the wagon and chunk the trees up in the woods. This particular day the wagon was full and it was getting late. "Let's go home, son. It's getting late. We can come back tomorrow for that tree."

Eben put the bucksaw and axes on the wagon and Enoch walked beside the mule as it pulled the load. Eben reached down and picked up the butt end of the tree and put it on his shoulder and wrapped his arm around it to hold it, and started following the wagon, dragging the tree behind him like a mule. It was a dead, dry tree about eight inches on the butt. His father never looked behind him but kept up a constant conversation with his son.

When they were in the farmyard, Enoch stopped to unhook the mule from the wagon and saw Eben dragging the tree behind him. Enoch knew his son had abnormal strength. He just looked at his son without saying anything. "Couldn't just leave it there," Eben said.

Enoch shook his head and laughed.

Blue Flower was wanting some bear fat to turn into lard, so Eben packed an overnight pack and went bear hunting. He left the mule at the farm and went off on foot, figuring he could be quieter without it. He had taken along a bucket of spoiled fish and caribou meat to use as bait.

He knew just where to go—an island of trees in the prairie. His granddad had killed bear there before. He placed the bait and made a blind of boughs amongst the trees and sat down to wait.

His grandfather had told him when he was a small boy that a bear is the nose in the forest because of its ability to smell. The eagle was the eye because of its ability to see and a deer was the ear because of its sensitive hearing. The wind was carrying the smell of the spoiled meat into the forest. If a bear were to smell it, he would not be able to pass it up and it would have to come out onto the prairie where he would have a clear shot at it.

He'd only brought a small lunch and most of that was gone by the time the sun was overhead. The sun was beginning to set and his lunch was gone. Colder air was blowing in, too. He had planned to stay the night if he had to, but he wished he'd brought more to eat. The moon was bright with a clear sky, which made it colder. As much as he wanted a fire, he knew a bear would not come to the bait with the smell of smoke in the air. He pulled his knees up and wrapped his arms around them.

Just as he was getting sleepy and his head kept bobbing on his chest, he saw movement way off. He held his breath and let it out slow. Whatever it was was coming closer. He hoped it wasn't a pack of wolves. Whatever it was was certainly taking its time. It could probably smell his scent mingled in the smell of meat.

It finally came close enough, and he could see it was a bear. A not terribly large one, but that was okay also. He waited with his rifle resting on his knee and braced against a tree. When the bear reached the bait pile, it stopped and looked in the direction of Eben and pointed his nose in the air. Eben took this opportunity and pulled the trigger. The bear went down. Eben reloaded in the dark as quick as he could and then he waited to see if the bear would stand.

When he was satisfied the bear was dead he walked over. He walked back to the island and built a fire. Then he went back to the bear and cut off a piece of meat and roasted it over the fire. He'd wait for daylight to take care of it. He put more wood on the fire after eating and lay back to sleep.

When he awoke the next morning his fire was out, so he kindled another and went to work butchering the bear. He brought his back-board and tied on most of the meat and fat and then ate more roasted meat before leaving.

It was much colder than the day before, but when he walked into the farmyard, he was wet with sweat. His father wasn't surprised to see him with the entire bear on his back. He just grinned. Blue Flower went to work cooking the fat down to lard. When she had finished, she had a gallon of pure white lard.

* * * *

Two years passed and Eben had the appearance of a man, even though he was almost seventeen. He was starting to show some whiskers, but decided to wait for a beard like his granddad, until there were more whiskers.

1854

That winter Eben had trapped many beaver and lynx, but before they made the spring trip to Fort Garry, Eben went by himself to Neokiowa's village to talk with Wenonah about their upcoming joining in the fall.

He couldn't stay as many days as he would like, but he and his mom and dad had to make their spring trip to Fort Garry as soon as he returned.

* * * *

"Hey, Paul, why don't we turn around and walk out of here back to Fort Garry. I'm hungry and tired."

"Jerry, this trail has to go somewhere. Look how much it is used. We might stumble onto a rich hit." Paul and Jerry Leet, two brothers who couldn't make it as trappers, were looking to rob someone before returning to Fort Garry and then home down the Mississippi.

"We didn't do so good this winter, Jerry. We couldn't trap enough beaver for food, let alone have any fur to sell in Fort Garry. Admit it, Jerry, we're just not trappers."

"Well, Paul, if we don't find something soon, we may not make it back to Garry."

"You mean someone to rob," Paul said.

"That's exactly what I mean."

"Well, it's either that, I guess, or we starve."

"Now shut up, Paul, we may stumble onto something."

They kept on the trail heading northwest. They found where trees had been cut down. Jerry pointed to the stumps. A mile further along the trail, they saw the barn roof and stopped. "Paul," Jerry whispered, "before you turn the corner by the house, wait until you see me go in the barn."

Jerry ran to the barn door and Paul rounded the corner at the house. Jerry had his pistol in his hand and when Enoch saw the gun he picked up an axe and rushed toward him. Jerry shot him in the chest and Enoch dropped dead. Jerry saw the fur pelts all bundled together, the mules and pack harness.

Paul opened the house door and went in just as Jerry shot Enoch. Blue Flower ran over to the window and didn't see Paul until he had closed the door. He was awestruck with her beauty and forgot why he was there.

"Well, hello there, Missy. Ain't you a good lookin' Injun." She ran to the bedroom for a pistol Enoch kept there, but Paul was on her before she could grasp the pistol. He threw her on the bed and started ripping her clothes off. He didn't care about robbing. All he wanted now was this beautiful woman.

Blue Flower screamed and Paul hit her hard in the face with his fist. He had all of her clothes off and he pulled his trousers down and lay on top of her. She kept fighting him and he hit her again. He used his knee and spread her legs and as he entered her, Blue Flower took his right ear in her mouth and bit down as hard as she could. Paul screamed and pulled back and when he did she bit his ear off. He pulled his knife and slashed her throat. His ear was still in her mouth.

He pulled his pants up and ransacked the house looking for money. All he could find of value were two rifles and three pistols.

Jerry tied the fur pelts onto the mule and found a rifle and a pistol.

Eben was close enough to hear the pistol shot and he naturally figured that his father may have shot a wolf. So he got the mule to run. He came in beside the barn and dismounted. He saw Paul exit the house and Paul saw him at the same time and he drew the pistol he had taken from the house and fired at Eben. The bullet hit Eben in the head and he went down.

Jerry came out of the barn and said, "What was that, Paul?"

"There was a guy coming in from the woods beside the barn. I shot him."

"What the hell happened to your ear? I shouldn't have to ask that. You found some bitch in the house, didn't you?"

"Yeah, an Injun bitch and she bit my gawd-damned ear off." There was blood all over his face and jacket.

"Did you find anything inside?"

"Just these guns. There weren't no money at all. How 'bout you?"

"I hit a bonanza of fur pelts. I have them loaded on a mule already. Let's get the hell out of here."

As they were leaving Paul asked, "How much you figure these here furs worth, Jerry?"

"Oh, maybe $500.00 or $600.00."

"Hell, this was easier than spending all winter in the cold and come out without no fur," Paul said.

Darkness was creeping in so they didn't go very far before stopping for the night, figuring they had killed everyone back at the farm.

Paul's bullet had only grazed the right side of Eben's head, knocking him down and temporarily unconscious. He came to in time to see them leaving the farm, but he still couldn't stand. It was several minutes before he could get his feet under him. Then he staggered to the barn and found his dad, dead on the floor. He ran and stumbled for the house, falling down twice. He rushed in calling his mother's name. No answer. He found her lying naked in her bedroom with her throat slashed. She had been beaten and raped and he found an ear still in her mouth. Now he knew to look for someone who would be missing an ear.

He fell on the floor and passed out.

He woke up two hours later with a throbbing head where the bullet had grazed him. He was full of sadness and a terrible anger that he couldn't let go. He was an active volcano waiting to erupt. He had to do something. He couldn't just sit in the dark and brood about his mom and dad. He lit a lantern, grabbed a spade from the barn and dug two graves beside his grandparents. He wrapped his mom in a blanket before carrying her body up the knoll. He couldn't look at the gruesome horror again. He laid her in the grave and filled it in and then carried his dad up and filled in his grave. He remained standing there in silence for a while, then he said, "I'll get whoever it was that did this. No matter how long it takes, I'll track them down."

Back in the house, he began putting a pack together. A blanket, his granddad's wolf vest. He took the money and gold that was hidden in the fireplace. The one pistol that he was wearing. He pulled on the green knit hat his mom had made. He put his granddad's long sheath knife on his belt and he took a little smoked meat.

The two brothers had taken the mules, but Eben still had the one he had been riding. He made sure the goats and chickens had food and then he was on the trail to Neokiowa's village.

He crossed the ebb and flow narrows in the dark and by noon the next day he was at the village. Everyone was surprised to see him again so soon. Wenonah ran up to him with happiness until she saw the sullen look on his face. "What has happened, Eben? And your head? What happened, Eben?" She pleaded.

Eben didn't say anything until Neokiowa came over. "They killed my folks. Two white trash. I'm going after them, Neokiowa. I may be gone a long time. Would you have someone bring the goats and chickens here? They took the mules, all except this one."

"Where you go to find them, Eben?" Neokiowa asked.

"They stole our fur also, so they will have to go to Fort Garry to sell them as fast as they can. I will start there. It won't be hard to track them. Mom bit an ear off on the one who raped and killed her."

"I will send two of my braves with you, Eben."

"No, Neokiowa. Cree killing two white men will only bring trouble to your people. With my red hair, I'll pass as white and they will not hunt you."

"You are right," Neokiowa said.

"When I have found them, I'll return here. Now I must not lose any more time."

Eben rode all day without stopping. At sunset, he catnapped for two hours while his mule rested and ate. Then he walked and led the mule in the dark all night until dawn. Then rode all day again. He kept this routine up all the way to Fort Garry. He was there in ten days.

He went first to see the fur buyer Cedric Merrill. "Hello, Eben, do you have any fur to sell this year?"

"No, Mr. Merrill, it was stolen by two men. Maybe they stopped here and sold it. We had twenty beaver and eight lynx. And one man was missing an ear."

"They was here, all right, Eben. Yesterday. And one of them, I think his name was Paul, did have an ear gone. Said an Indian cut it off."

"What was the other one's name, do you recall?"

"I think I heard Paul call him Jerry. Paul's last name is Leet. I have it here in my books. They both talked with a southern drawl, almost like a twang."

"Are they still at Fort Garry?"

"No, they left right away. They crossed the Red River and was following that south. At the time I thought that a little peculiar.

"If you're hunting them, Eben, it must have been more than stealing your fur."

"They killed my folks and raped my ma. And now I'm going to kill them.

"I need a new rifle, Mr. Merrill. They stole all our rifles and pistols, except this one I was wearing."

"I have some new rifles and pistols right over here. They use the percussion cap now, instead of flint. More reliable."

Eben hefted the rifle and liked how it balanced. I'll take one. Now I want to look at your new pistols. You say they are percussion cap also?"

"Yes, and the cylinder holds six rounds. It's a Remington .44 caliber, same as the rifle."

"I'll take two pistols and one rifle and powder and balls for a hundred rounds. You show me how to load them."

"Sure thing, Mr. McNinch." Eben watched very closely so he wouldn't be making any mistakes. Watching Cedric, it certainly looked easier and faster to load the weapons with the new caps.

Eben took out his old pistol and tried out one of the new pistols in his holster. "It doesn't fit. Do you have holsters for the pistols?"

"Sure do," and he laid two different types on the counter. One fit his belt. "What is this one?"

"It slings over your shoulder and is carried under your arm."

"I could put a shirt or coat on over it and then it wouldn't be seen."

"That's correct, Mr. McNinch."

"I'll take both of these, then. And I'll have ten pounds of bacon, coffee and a pot, a rain slicker, and one of those green shirts. Make it extra-large to fit over this shoulder gun. And how about one of those saddlebags to put this stuff in?

"I almost forgot grain…twenty pounds for my mule."

"Certainly. Will there be anything else?"

"How much?"

Cedric did some figuring and said, "It all comes to $263.00."

"Take that off the McNinch account and change the account to only my name now. And I'll draw $200.00 in coin from the account. What's the balance now on the account, Mr. Merrill?"

"That leaves $483.00."

"Okay, I'll leave it in the account, with a voucher of course."

"Of course, Mr. McNinch."

Eben put everything, including the $200.00, in his new saddlebags. There was still room left. "Thank you, Mr. Merrill. You say the Leets left yesterday and crossed the river to the south?"

"Yes, sir, Mr. McNinch."

"If you lied to me, Cedric, I'll be back to settle up with you."

Cedric Merrill stood on the porch and watched Eben ride off toward the ferry. *I wouldn't want to be them Leets when he catches up to 'em. And I don't blame him at all.*

Eben steadied his mule as they crossed the Red River by ferry, thinking he was only a day behind them now. He found a trail on the east side of the Red, but he had to dismount and lead his mule. He patted the mule's neck. "You've earned it, fella." Once in a while he could see boot tracks in the mud, mixed in with mule tracks.

Eben had to stop at dusk that night. The underbrush was just too thick to try wedging through it in the dark. He gave the mule some grain and then kindled a fire and cooked some bacon and made some coffee. Even with the coffee he slept sound that night. He was exhausted.

* * * *

Paul and Jerry Leet were only a day ahead of Eben. But of course they wouldn't know that. They both had thought they had killed everyone at the farm. But the next morning Jerry said, "We need to find a place to cross the river."

"What on earth for?"

"I just have this creepy feeling someone is following us."

"Why would anyone be following, Jerry? We kilt everyone at the farm."

"I don't know. Maybe someone there at Garry saw us bring these furs in and suspects we're carrying a lot of money."

"I think you're worrying about nothing, Jerry, but if you want to cross the river…we cross."

At daylight the next day, Eben was on the move again. There was only one occasion when he could ride, so he chose to walk along, following the Leets' tracks. But the next day he lost their trail. Not knowing whether they were still on this side of the river or maybe had crossed over, he kept heading south toward the U.S. border. He figured there had to be someone on the Canadian side who might know something about the brothers.

At Emmerson, he found a R.C.M.P. office and went inside. "Hello, can I help you?" an older gentleman asked. Then he looked up to see who had come in.

"Eben, is that you? It can't be. You're too young. Eben McNinch would be my age."

"I am Eben McNinch. So was my grandfather. How do you know him?"

"My name is Rick Perry."

"Yes, I know who you are now. The expedition west along the 49th."

"Yes. How is Eben and Ada now?"

"They both died two years ago."

"Oh, I'm sorry to hear that. They were both remarkable people. What brings you to Emmerson?"

"Three weeks ago, two brothers, Paul and Jerry Leets, killed my folks and raped my mother and shot me." He turned his head to show Mr. Perry the scar. "They stole our fur pelts, guns and mules. I lost their trail halfway between here and Fort Garry. Have you or any of your men seen them? My mother bit Paul's ear off. They sold the fur in Garry and may be spending a lot of money wherever they stop. I have good reason to believe they are from some southern state in the U.S. They talk with a twangy drawl."

"There were two men who passed through here two days ago. I didn't talk with them or see enough of them to tell if one was missing an ear or not. If you'll wait here, I'll go out to the barracks and inquire of the men. Sit down and have some coffee. I won't be long."

Rick Perry was back in fifteen minutes. "It looks like those two are the ones you're following, Eben."

"What would likely be their next stop, Mr. Perry?"

"I'd have to say Grand Forks."

"And from there, where would they be likely to go?"

"My guess would be Fargo, then overland southeast to the Mississippi River to Fort Snelling at the junction of the Mississippi and the Minnesota Rivers. It's a big settlement.

"What will you do, Eben, when you catch up to them?"

No hesitation. "Kill 'em."

"The law won't be on your side across the border, Eben. But I understand how you feel."

"Thank you, Mr. Perry. I've always been two days behind them. Is there any way I could get ahead of them?"

"Only if there was an overland route from the Grand Forks to Fort Snelling. If I were you, I wouldn't waste my time stopping to inquire at Grand Forks. I'd push on to Fargo. Across the river is Moorhead. They both have drinking establishments. Once there, they might feel safe to stop and drink for a time. I'll send a letter with the next courier going south to be on the watch for these brothers."

"Thank you, Mr. Perry."

"I know you want to be going, but on your way back, I'd like you to stop so we can talk."

"I'll do that, Mr. Perry. Thank you."

Eben picked up more bacon, then he was on his way south. South of the border traveling was only a bit better now, but he wouldn't stop until well towards dark, when he had no choice but to stop for the night. During the day, he stopped looking for their trail and concentrated on getting to Fargo before them.

One day it rained all day. He slipped on his slicker and rode through it. The moon was full that night and the rain stopped about sunset. He stopped long enough to rest his mule and give it some grain. He was running low on grain. He had bacon and coffee and at midnight, he was on the trail again.

There was a small farm on the river just south of Grand Forks. He stopped and bought some grain and fresh bread. He wanted to ask if they had seen two other men traveling ahead of him, but decided against it, just in case they happened to be ahead of them now. He didn't want anything to alarm them.

He figured the brothers had probably traveled this route on their way to Fort Garry. And they surely would have taken the easiest route and then followed it back south. *But how far south were they going?*

He rode into Moorhead after dark. He checked first at the livery stable and no mules were stabled there, and the old man tending the horses had not seen anyone come into town on mules. "Would you feed my mule some grain?" Eben gave him $2.00 for the feed and information. "If someone does come by, I'd appreciate it if you not mention me."

"Certainly, sir."

Eben walked the streets looking for mules tied up to a hitching post. When he didn't find any, he went into the local restaurant for something to eat. He chose a table in the corner so he could watch the door. There were a dozen men there. Most were drinking, a few playing cards.

He ordered a beefsteak, potato and squash, "...and a pot of coffee, please." When he said please, everyone turned to look at him. He gave them no mind.

"Hey, Mister, we don't serve coffee in here. It's beer or whiskey."

"Beer, and I still want a pot of coffee."

"Yes, sir."

He could tell the others were sizing him up. What for, he didn't know. He did notice that the big brute standing at the bar spoke with a twangy drawl like he had heard the Leets. There was a possibility he knew the Leets.

Eben had let his whiskers grow since leaving the farm, and

already he was supporting a beard almost as full as his grandfather, and it was just as red. He was wearing his wolf vest and it seemed some of the conversation at the bar was about his vest.

When his meal came, the big fellow at the bar was still talking. Eben ordered another beer. When the barkeep came back with the beer, he said, "Hey, mister, be careful of that fellow. He's saying some stupid things."

"Thanks. I'll be okay." That surprised the barkeep. He went back behind the bar.

The steak was cooked just right, almost blood red in the center. *Oh, that was so much better than either caribou or moose.* He wasn't long finishing his meal and the second beer. He knew something was going to happen. He heard his granddad whispering to him and he smiled. This didn't set well with the big brute.

"Hey, you," the brute said.

Eben ignored him and paid for his meal and beer.

"Hey you!" He said a little louder. "I'm talking to you."

"Oh yeah, pig breath. Then take the shit out of your mouth so I can understand you." Eben stood there looking at him.

Everyone there was shocked to hear someone talk like that to the brute. The barkeep noticed the gun on Eben's side and how the holster strap was still attached. He made no move to remove it and everyone was also noticing, wondering about this red beard.

The old timer in the other corner stood up and said while laughing, "Big Red Beard Not Afraid," and he continued laughing as he walked down the street.

The barkeep looked at Eben and wondered what that was all about. But somewhere he thought he had read or heard of someone called Big Red Beard Not Afraid.

"Well, pig breath, what in hell do *you* want?" Big John stood two inches taller, and probably outweighed Eben by twenty pounds. Big John was getting mad and this is what Eben's granddad had told him: "An angry man can't fight without getting hisself hurt."

"Well, pig breath, what is it?"

"My cousins said to watch for someone with red hair and wearing that vest."

"You must mean those piles of pig shit named Jerry and Paul Leet. You're almost as stupid as those two idiots. So, just what are you going to do, stupid?"

Big John drew a knife and before he knew what was happening, Eben charged him and grabbed the arm with the knife, side-stepped and twisted the arm behind Big John with so much force, he dislocated Big John's arm. He screamed in pain just as Eben picked him up and pushed him back eight feet to the back wall. He hit the wall so hard the wind was knocked out of him. He couldn't even scream any more.

Big John was able to hit Eben in the side of his head which did little to stop him. He grabbed Big John's left arm and broke it. Everyone there heard the bone snap.

"Where is Jerry and Paul?"

"Go to hell."

Eben punched him so hard in his left side that he broke two ribs. "I'll ask you again, where are your cousins?"

"Go to hell."

Eben broke ribs on his right side. "I'll ask you again. If you don't tell me we can do this until I've broken every rib in your chest. Then I'll start on your legs. Now, where are they?"

"Overland to Fort Snelling."

"Now that wasn't so hard, was it?" Eben let go of Big John and he fell to the floor. Just then two more guys Big John had been talking with jumped Eben at the same time. He backhanded one so hard he was knocked unconscious over the bar. The other guy he hit in the stomach and then picked him up and threw him through the window. Then three more jumped him. He threw the first against the wall and hit the other two in the stomach and they both collapsed. He turned around to face the other patrons. "Anyone else?"

He walked over to the bar and laid $50.00 on it. "For the damage."

"You're him, ain't you?" the barkeep said. "Big Red Beard Not Afraid."

"That was my granddad." Now he knew where to look. Outside, Big John was still lying in the dirt. He couldn't get up without using his arms.

"You be careful, Eben. Big John and the last three guys are Leets, also. A bunch of no-goods. Just what did the other two do to you?"

"They killed my folks and raped my mother and stole everything we had. Paul shot me, also." He showed the barkeep the scar.

The old-timer walked by still laughing. "I warned you, Big John."

Eben went to the livery and asked the old guy, "How do I find the overland trail to Fort Snelling?"

"You go straight out of town on this road."

He had wanted to sleep the night in the stable, but he figured it would be a good idea to get out of town.

He had a road to travel on now and not through the forest. He could keep going with little light. If the Leets had suspected that he was following and had made it to Moorhead, they would assume that their cousins would have taken care of him and they might not be so careful about looking for him. He doubted if they would be traveling at night or pushing as hard as he was.

He met a freight wagon two days later heading for Moorhead. "Hello, there," Eben said. "I'm trying to catch up with two friends of mine. Have you seen them? They're riding mules like this one."

"Yeah, they're about a half-mile ahead of you."

"Thank you so much."

* * * *

"Paul, let's rest a spell on top of this slight rise. We can see in both directions for a ways. I still have this odd feeling someone is following us," Jerry said.

"You've had that feeling ever since we kilt that farmer and his wife. There ain't been nobody following us, Jerry. It's a good spot to rest, though. Maybe a rich dude will come along and we can relieve him of his burden."

They dismounted and tied off their mules. "Who was that third person you shot, Paul? The one with that there fancy vest?"

"I don't know. Kin, maybe. I wish I'd taken that vest."

"You watch the road in that direction, Paul. I'll watch this here'n way."

"How come we ain't spent none of that money we got from those pelts, Jerry? Every time we come to a fort or settlement you don't want to stay long enough for a decent meal, or have a few drinks," Paul whined.

"'Cause I think someone is following us, Paul, and I don't want him to catch up with us."

"Well, who'd you suppose it be?"

"I don't know, but I won't feel comfortable at all until we get home."

"You mean we're going all the way to Memphis?"

"No, stupid. We done got run out of there, remember?"

"Oh, yeah. Our whole clan had to move to Rockford, Illinois. Yeah, but Jerry, Pa… he won't be none too happy with us'n goin' to Canada trapping," Paul said.

"He'll change his tune when we show him this $800.00."

"Yeah, but Jerry, we done stole that money."

"He won't know the difference."

"Hey, Paul, hush up. We got one comin' my way. Get behind that rock there. I'll stay behind this tree. We wait and see who it is before we do anything."

They waited in silence, then Jerry whispered, "He's riding a mule like ours." Then a few seconds later, Jerry said, "Oh, my God Almighty! It's him, Paul. The one you shot with that fancy vest. He's the one been following us all this time."

"Can't be, Jerry. I shot him in the head, remember?"

"Yeah, but that's him alright. You keep down. I'll pick 'im

out of the saddle. I'm a better shot than you'n."

Jerry sighted in on Eben's chest and pulled the trigger. But he flinched and hit the mule right by Eben's left leg. The mule went down and Eben crawled behind him for safety and then off the road for cover in the trees.

"Damn you, Jerry, can't you shoot straight? You kilt his mule, not him!"

"Oh, shut up and stay down."

Eben crawled to a large pine and just kneeled behind it for a few minutes listening. His mule was dead and he realized it could have been him. This was a valuable lesson. He needed to keep more alert if he was going to come out of this alive. The first thing he did was to remove the throng from the hammers of both pistols. Now they were free to be drawn from his holster. He slid each one out and then in. Checking.

He stood up slowly, making sure he wasn't exposing himself around the huge tree. He could hear them talking and knew about where they were. Then he saw movement. Only a little on the ground behind a tree. He waited and waited and finally he saw the same movement. Only now he could see a foot. He braced his new rifle against the side of the tree and took careful aim at the foot and pulled the trigger.

Jerry screamed in extreme pain, "Yah! That gawd-damned son-of-a-bitch shot me in the ankle!" He screamed again, "Yah! Paul! My gawd-damned foot been shot off. You git, Paul. Ain't no way I'll be leaving here. You git and I'll hold him off as long as I can."

Paul was already running for his mule. He knew he'd shot him in the head and kilt him and he didn't want anything to do with this apparition. Jerry had the $800.00 and he didn't care. He wasn't wasting any time. He mounted the mule and took off at a run down the road.

"You son-of-a-bitch, you come out where I can see!"

Eben reloaded, taking his time to make sure he was doing it correctly with the new rifle, then he bounced a bullet off a rock and he hit Jerry in the ass. It hurt true enough, but didn't do much damage.

"You crazy son-of-a-bitch!" Jerry tied his handkerchief around his leg to stop the blood loss. He couldn't even stand up. He was done for and he knew it, but he was going to go down fighting and give Paul as much time as he could.

Eben wasn't sure if he would have one of the pistols with him that they had stolen or just the old rifle. "Which one are you? Jerry or Paul?"

"Paul kilt your mother, not me!"

"Then you're Jerry and you killed my father. Now who's the son-of-a-bitch?"

He decided he needed to get Jerry to shoot again, then while he was reloading he'd rush him with his two pistols.

The best way to get him to shoot would be if he ran to another tree. In Jerry's condition, he doubted if he could hit a moving target. Then he'd go rushing in with his pistols. "Hey, you piece of shit, I can smell you from here. You stink. Does Paul smell as bad as you, you pig breath? You know, pig breath, you and your stupid brother are poor excuses of men. Have you got the guts to fight me with your fists? Oh, yeah, I forgot. You can't stand, can you. I shot your foot off."

That's all it took. He didn't have to run to another tree. He had gotten Jerry so mad, he wasted his shot and fired into the tree he was standing behind. Eben rested his rifle against the tree and drew both pistols and ran up towards Jerry.

Jerry couldn't reload lying on the ground, and he was trying to pull the pistol out of his belt when he heard Eben running. Eben shot him in the chest.

Killing Jerry didn't make him happy, nor was he glad he had done it. It was just something that had to be done. He went to find his mule. When he smelled Eben, a familiar scent, he started braying. "Hello, boy. It's me, Eben." He scratched the mule behind his ears and led him back to the top of the knoll and tied him off. He then went down to the dead mule and removed his gear and dragged the mule off the road. He gave some grain to the mule and decided to make camp there. It was almost dark already.

He went through Jerry's pockets and bedroll and pack and found the $800.00 for the sale of the beaver. He pocketed that. The rifle and pistol both belonged to the family, as did the saddle.

He wrapped the body up in a blanket and set it aside. He built a fire and made a pot of coffee and cooked some bacon with a little bread.

Before the bacon had finished cooking he heard, "Hello there, by the fire. I'm alone and mean you no harm. Would like to share your fire and warm up these old bones."

"Come on in. But your hands better be empty."

"You're learning," the stranger said.

He dismounted and tied off his horse. "My, that coffee and bacon sure does smell good."

"Tell me who you are and maybe you can have some."

"Fair enough. I was the old timer sitting in the corner of that saloon back in Moorhead that you tore up."

"I guess you're alright. Sit down. Here's some coffee. The bacon will be done shortly."

"You know, young fella... how old are you? Seventeen? Eighteen?"

"Seventeen."

"You handle yourself real good for someone so young. A long time ago, before you were even born, at Fort Gibraltar... do you know where that is?"

"I do."

"Thought so. Well, anyhow, a long time ago at Gibraltar I ran into you. My friend and I were drunk. Except it weren't you, was it? But you are the spitt'n image of him. I know, because I never forgot it. This other you gave me and my brother the beating of our life, not that we didn't deserve it... 'cause we did. My friend has passed on now—some years.

"When we sobered up we learned we had started a fight

with the man the Indians everywhere called Big Red Beard Not Afraid. I can't get over how much you look and handle yourself just like he did."

"That was my granddad. I was named after him, Eben McNinch."

"How is your granddad now, son?"

"He and my grandmother both passed away two years."

"I'm truly sorry to hear that. In spite of the beating he gave us, I always liked him. I would like to have ridden with him.

"So, you're way down here hundreds of miles from Fort Garry, now... who are you after?"

"The two men who killed my mom and dad. One of them raped my mother before he killed her. She bit his ear off."

"Do you have a name for these two?"

"Leet brothers, Jerry and Paul. Paul killed my mother and shot me in the head," and he showed him the scar. "Jerry is lying behind those bushes.

"Who in hell are you, anyhow?"

"Excuse my manners, sir. I'm Joe Attle.

"That big brute you roughed up a little back there—Big John? He's a Leet and three others there were Leets, also."

"He told me."

"You going after Paul in the morning?"

"Yes. This bacon is done. Here, help yourself. And here's some bread."

"This is quite a feast, son."

They ate in silence.

"You know Paul won't stop at Fort Snelling. Not now that he knows you're on his tail."

"Where will he go?"

"The whole Leet family came out of Tennessee. Around Memphis, I think. Paul, the one you are after, raped a woman there and the whole clan moved to Rockford. They've been a real nuisance ever since. When they left Moorhead two years ago, no one knew where they had gone.

"This bacon and bread is good."

"Want more?"

"If you have it.

"If Paul reaches Rockford before you, you'll have the whole clan after you."

"How can I get there before him?"

"Well, he'll probably go right through Fort Snelling without stopping. Then he'll probably take a boat down the Mississippi and get off at Dubuque. From there to Rockford is only a day trip by horse—or mule.

"If you get him before he reaches Rockford, you're still not home free. When word gets to the family, they'll come after you. And it won't be one-on-one. There'll be more likely two or three after you. I know you can take care of yourself in a fistfight, but these people will likely wait in ambush. And you're easy enough to identify.

"I watched you back there in Moorhead. I have a few suggestions if you're interested."

"Go ahead."

"Number one, whenever you see someone approaching you in the wild, whenever you ride into a settlement or fort, take the leather throngs off your pistols. You'll never know when you have to use them.

"Number two, wear your gun-belt on your left side with the butt pointing towards your middle and have that big knife on your right side. You're right handed and you'll find it more convenient.

"Number three, also keep your back to the wall and don't make camp close to the road like this.

"Number four, the name Eben McNinch is legendary and some young punk will try to take you. They'll hunt you down to try and prove they might be better than you. Eben McNinch is known from the East Coast all the way to Californy. There have been newspaper articles written about your granddad.

"But most of all, always keep your wits about you. If you start day-dreaming, or thinking about your dead folks...well, that's when they'll attack. There is one more suggestion. When you ride, you should have a pistol readily available either in your lap or hanging from your saddle horn. And have it cocked and ready whenever you encounter anyone on the trail.

"What you did back there in Moorhead will eventually reach the newspaper. Do what you have to as soon as you can, and go back across the border."

It was late and they both were tired. Eben had stopped thinking about the dead body lying behind the bushes.

* * * *

In the morning as they were eating, Eben asked, "How many days are we from Fort Snelling?"

"Three, with easy riding. A day-and-a-half if we push it into the night."

"We'd better push it, then."

They rode hard all day and only stopped at high noon to rest their mounts. Eben still had a bit of grain. "I've been thinking this morning, Joe. Paul has no food and no money. He either goes hungry, shoots something, which we would hear the shot, or robbery."

"Maybe he is scared enough of you so he'll go without food. That is, at least to Fort Snelling. But all the way to Rockford? I don't think so. My guess is he'll try to steal."

With their mounts rested, they continued on and stopped at dark to feed their mounts and give them a rest. Eben made a pot of coffee while Joe fried up some bacon and warmed the bread. After they had eaten, they rested for another two hours and then moved on.

As they rode, Eben asked, "Joe, you seem to know quite a bit about surviving in a clandestine world. What is it you do?"

"After your grandfather beat some sense into me, I decided it was time to grow up and be more responsible. I eventually became sheriff in Rockford."

"That's why you know so much about the Leets."

"Yes. After a few years, I was appointed to U.S. Marshall of the Minnesota Territory. I'm too old, now, to be marshalling, so I am a courier between Fort Snelling and Grand Forks."

They pushed on all night until about an hour before daylight when they took another break and fed their mounts and themselves, and rested for two hours. "We made good time last night. We should be in Fort Snelling by noon.

"Let me take the body in, Eben, so you can ride on. I know the commandant and I'll tell it just as you have told me.

"Before you leave Snelling, though, I'd check with the steamboat company at the river and see if Paul booked passage anywhere. If he doesn't have any money, he may not have gone by boat. If there's a boat leaving today, even if you have to wait for the afternoon, it still will be a quicker trip to Dubuque. When you get there, ask around for Paul Leet. People there should know who you mean. If not, a man missing one ear. But once you leave Dubuque, you'll be in Leet country, so be careful."

Eben had only seen pictures of what Joe was calling a steamboat. "Are you sure, Joe, about boarding this steamboat to go downriver?"

Joe tried to explain about the steamboats and how important they had become traveling the mid-central west, up and down the Mississippi River.

"I'll go see the commandant, Eben, and you head for the terminal on the river. Good luck, and remember what I have told you."

"Thanks, Joe."

Eben rode by the fort to the terminal. It was easy to find as there was a steamboat tied up to the wharf. He dismounted and walked inside. People stopped whatever they were doing to watch him pass. He walked as a man with composure.

"Can I take this steamboat to Dubuque?"

"Yes, sir. She leaves at 2 p.m., sharp."

"And my mule?"

"You can take your mule, but it'll cost you."

"How much for me and my mule to Dubuque?"

"$5.00 each; $10.00 total."

Eben paid him and asked, "I'm looking for a friend who may have left yesterday. His name is Paul Leet."

"I was here all day yesterday, and I don't remember anyone by that name. Can you give me a description?"

"He had a mule like mine, and he was missing an ear."

"No sir, no mules were boarded yesterday, nor anyone missing an ear. I'll need your name, sir, for my records."

"Eben McNinch."

Next door was a trading post and Eben wanted to purchase a few more supplies. Not wanting to miss the steamboat's departure, he decided to wait onboard. People everywhere were looking at him, more from curiosity than anything else. He stood tall and straight; he was clean and wore clean clothes and all were impressed with the wolf-fur vest. This truly was someone from deep within the wilderness. But what was he doing here?

Once they were on their way downstream, it was at a fast pace, faster than Eben had assumed. He was quite impressed. There was a buffet-style lunch served in the big dining room. Eben had never seen anything quite like it. At the Cree village their feast was served in a similar way, but not with such a variety of food. For $2.00 you could go back for more as often as you wanted, until the buffet lunch closed. He went back twice before he had had enough.

He noticed that most of the passengers clung together in small groups, whereas he stood back in a corner observing.

After he had finished eating, he went back out on deck with his mule to watch the scenery. At this speed, there was no doubt he would arrive in Dubuque well ahead of Paul Leet.

The boat was making a few stops to take on more passengers and some were getting off, and there was more cargo. But even with these stops, Eben knew he would be at Duduque ahead of Leet.

There was another $2.00 buffet for supper and although he hadn't done anything to be hungry, he was. There was the same variety as earlier and this time he chose a different selection. It was all good. It was obvious that some of the men had been drinking. Eben drank several cups of coffee.

He didn't want to socialize with anybody, so when he'd finished, he went to check on his mule. As he sat there at the bow, on the deck, the voices from the dining room were getting louder. Some was because of the drinking, but there was something causing an argument. Something to do with north and south. This was all confusing.

It was a warm evening and some of the passengers had come out on deck for the cooler air. They brought their arguing and bickering with them. A group of well-dressed men kept working their way forward, bringing their arguing closer. Eben turned his back to them and suddenly one of them came up to him and asked, "What is your view on secession, sir?"

Eben stood a little taller and he looked at the well-dressed intruder and said, "I don't have an opinion," and he turned away from him."

The others were getting more courage from their drinking also, and they walked over to join the first fellow. "What do you mean, you have no opinion," another asked.

Eben turned back around and said, "I have no idea what the five of you were discussing. Whatever it was does not concern me."

"Are you in favor of the North's stance on no slavery, or the South's position?"

"I said before, none of this has anything to do with me. Now, if I were you, I would mind my own business."

They were inching closer, "My, you're an uppity one, aren't you?"

"Look, you guys obviously have had too much drink. Why don't you move on. I have no interest with what you are talking about."

"You trying to insult our intelligence, mister?"

"If you had any intelligence to begin with, I wouldn't waste my time insulting you." This wasn't playing out how the six planned it. They had intended to cower this guy and rob him, but he wasn't cowering.

"Before you and your friends get hurt, why don't you just leave."

Just then, Eben saw a shiny knife blade come out and he took the guy's arm so fast, he let go of the knife. But Eben didn't let go. He broke the man's arm and backhanded him. He lay on the deck screaming in pain. Eben grabbed the heads of two more and hit them together and now they lay unconscious with their friend. The remaining three all charged Eben at the same time. They swung and hit Eben, but they were no match for him. They all were on the deck unconscious or screaming in pain. One-by-one he lifted them and dropped them into the back of an empty wagon.

Eben climbed up to the wheelhouse and asked, "Are you boss on this boat?"

"I'm the captain. What can I do for you?"

"I was just attacked by six men and I believe their intent was to rob me. One of them pulled a knife on me. I put all six in the back of an empty wagon."

"Yeah, I saw a little scuffle up forward. I'll have to have your name for my report and why I threw them off the boat before Dubuque."

"Eben McNinch."

"Captain Elijah Samuels. Captain Sam. I don't put up with thievery or fights on board. Can you watch those boys until I can put ashore somewhere?"

"Sure can."

"Been watching you, Mr. McNinch. You don't drink, play cards, socialize with the other passengers. You always stand or sit in a corner, so you can watch the others. You have looked over every passenger like you're looking for someone. My take on you, young fella, you're on a mission. You're looking for someone in particular."

"You have a keen eye, Captain Sam. I am looking for someone."

"What did he do?"

"He raped and then killed my mother and he shot me," Eben showed Captain Sam the scar.

"His brother, Jerry, killed my father. They also stole over $800.00 in fur, our guns and mules. I caught up with Jerry. The two tried to ambush me between Snelling and Grand Forks."

"What's the name of the one you're after now?"

"Paul Leet."

Captain Sam began laughing then. "Sir, you just missed him when you first came aboard. He said he didn't have any money but would work for passage to Dubuque. I know the Leets and I told him to get off my boat. You came on board two hours later."

"He's heading for home, alright," Eben said. "I've followed him and his brother from Lake Manitoba. He's running now, knowing for sure I'm after him and have already killed his brother. He has no money, and no food. He'll be desperate."

"He's known around here and I don't believe there would be anyone who would help him until he gets to Dubuque. He has family there."

"Where is he most likely to go?"

"Probably to Rockford. That's where his folks have a small, hardscrabble farm. They grow some corn, cotton and tobacco. They own a few slaves and they are hard on them."

"Can you tell me how to find the farm, Captain Sam?"

"Sure, you take the main road from Dubuque to Rockford. It'll be marked. Five miles before you get to Rockford, you'll cross a river. There's a covered bridge. You cross the bridge and take the first road to the north. This road is only a short distance from the bridge. The farm is at the end of this road, eight miles from the main road. Some of the houses on this last road will also be Leets, so be careful."

"Are there any Leets living on the road between Dubuque and Fort Snelling?"

"I know there are some that live close to town on that road, but that's all I can tell you.

"You have already kicked a hornet's nest son, when you killed Jerry. When the other Leets learn of this, they'll come after you. You kill Paul, you are sure to have them come. You'd be doing the family a favor actually, by killing Paul, but they won't see it that way."

"Thank you for the information, Captain Sam. I'd better go forward. They might be coming to by now."

"You be careful, Mr. McNinch."

A few of the would-be robbers were coming to. "You guys stay in the wagon. Captain Sam is going to put ashore as soon as he can, so you can walk off this boat and not have to swim ashore. Now sit back and relax."

Eben sat on the deck next to his mule.

* * * *

At LaCrosse, Captain Sam tied up at the wharf only long enough for Eben to escort the six off the boat. Then they were on their way again. Eben decided it was time to get some sleep. He spread out his bedroll on the deck next to the mule.

He was sleeping soundly at daylight and Captain Sam's night relief blew the steam whistle at another steamer going upstream.

Captain Sam was back in the wheelhouse at 8 a.m. "Any more folks you want to put ashore?" Sam asked, and they laughed.

"You could do me a favor, though. Is there some place you can put in before Dubuque?"

"Just below the Wisconsin River there are a series of islands. There's one with a sandy beach that I can stop long enough for you and your mule to get off. That's a good idea you have. You're learning."

Eben had a big breakfast and a pot of good strong coffee.

232

He wasn't sure when he'd be able to eat again. Then he gave his mule some grain and water.

There were several islands in the river, but no major river yet. Captain Sam had to slow to half speed as he maneuvered through the islands. He could see the river coming up on the left and then more islands. Toward the last of the islands, Captain Sam pulled in and stopped briefly on a sandy beach. Then he reversed it, blew the whistle to say goodbye to Eben.

He had to work his way through a tangle of bushes and vines near the river. Then it was small hardwood trees all the way to the road from Snelling. He had decided he would prefer to encounter Paul away from his family and on the trail, rather than following him to the farm.

He didn't figure there was any way possible for Paul to have already gone through Dubuque, so he rode north away from town, looking for a good place to wait for him to come through.

* * * *

Paul was mad as all hell because Captain Sam wouldn't let him work for passage to Dubuque. But as mad as he was, he also knew Captain Sam wasn't someone he would want to tangle with. Not even at Captain Sam's advanced years. Actually, Paul Leet was a coward and what made it worse was he knew he didn't have a backbone. Everything he had ever done in his life had always been underhanded.

For days now he had been surviving on squirrels, fish he could catch with his hands in shallow pools or anything he could steal. He was hungry and worst of all, he was afraid of the man with the wolf vest and red hair that was following him. His brother was dead. Although he took off running before the final shot, he was still certain of it. He was certain he would be coming after him now. But he didn't know Eben was onboard the steamboat and would now be in front of him, waiting on the road to Dubuque.

Before leaving Fort Snelling, Paul had just enough money to send a telegraph message to his father Ezra in Rockford, telling him a man had been following him from Canada and killed Jerry and was now after him. He asked his father to send help and he would meet them in Dubuque.

Paul stopped at his Uncle Boufford's place in Tomah. He had always liked him and his brother, Jerry.

Paul explained his version of why the man was after him, and it didn't include raping and killing the man's mother.

"Pa and some help are going to meet me in Dubuque. Will you ride with me, Uncle Boufford, as far as Dubuque?"

"I can't leave now, nephew; I have too much work to do."

"How about me, Pa?" Brodie asked. "I'll ride with Paul to Dubuque."

* * * *

When Ezra received the telegram, at first he was furious with Paul, then he thought about losing his son, Jerry, and then became even angrier that someone was hunting his youngest son. Regardless of what Paul had done, nobody had the right to hunt down any son of his. So he and another son, Alfred, packed some supplies and headed for Dubuque.

When they arrived at Dubuque, Paul had not arrived yet, so they headed for Ezra's brother's house in Tomah, not knowing who they were up against.

* * * *

Eben found a perfect spot to wait for Paul. He was on a slight knoll off the road, and he could see in both directions. He settled in for a long wait.

The second morning about mid-morning two riders from Dubuque came along. They looked like father and son and as they rode closer, there was the unmistakable resemblance to

Paul with the older man. The older man was even talking about getting the guy that had killed his son, Jerry.

Eben figured they must be on their way to meet up with Paul, and ride with him back to Rockford and his father's farm. Eben would have no idea that Paul had sent his father a telegram. Eben had no idea what a telegram would be. But one thing he had learned from his granddad was to be patient. He knew the man he was after would be back along this same road. Perhaps with others, but he would be back.

Eben decided that if he were to fell a tree across the road in front of them, then they would have to stop. He found the right size hardwood with many branches and he cut partway through it with his axe. When he could see them coming from the Tomah end, he'd finish cutting the tree and drop it across the road, blocking it. He doubted if they would be back through that day. Probably they'd wait until the following day. But Eben had everything ready to go.

He only took short catnaps all night, watching the road for a night passage. At daylight Eben made a pot of coffee and cooked up the last of his bacon. He nursed a hot cup all morning. Then about noon he could see four riders coming from Tomah. He had no doubt this would be the Leets. He dropped the tree across the road and then went about where he figured the four would stop. He already had an evergreen blind made to conceal him close to the road.

He waited patiently with no excitement nor remorse with what he was about to do. He laid his rifle on the ground and un-holstered his handgun. He could hear them talking and laughing now. But not what was being said.

When they rode over the rise and saw the tree across the road Ezra said, "What's goin' on here'n?

Eben was a little behind them and to their left. He had both handguns drawn. He said in a simple flat tone, "Don't move and don't go for your guns. All I want is Paul."

"Why do you want my son?"

"He didn't tell you? No, he wouldn't. He wouldn't have backbone enough to tell you he raped my mother and then slashed her throat and he shot me and left me for dead."

"Then why did you kill Jerry?"

"He killed my father. Did Paul explain how he lost his ear?"

"He said he was in a fight with an Injun."

"My mother bit it off while he was raping her."

"And you saw this?" Ezra asked.

"No."

"Then you don't know for sure if he raped her or not?"

"I know." He put one gun under his belt and tossed something to Ezra. He caught it and Eben withdrew his gun again.

"That's Paul's ear. I took it out of her mouth before I buried her.

"Get down, Paul," Eben said.

"Pa! You can't just let this crazy man kill me," Paul begged. He was almost crying.

"Whether he raped and killed your mother or not, you can't expect me to just hand over my son."

"All except Paul are free to leave. If I have to, I'll shoot him out of the saddle."

Just then Eben saw the one called Alfred draw a gun, cock it and point it at Eben. Eben swung his arm and fired and struck Alfred in the chest, blowing him from the saddle. Then Ezra drew his gun and Eben shot him and Wilford, Ezra's nephew. Then Paul drew his flintlock pistol and Eben blew him out of the saddle. Then he swung on Boufford. He had not pulled his gun out, but he was raging with anger. "You're nothing but a gawd-damned killer. I haven't drawn my gun! You going to murder me? Damn you."

"You sit there and blame me. If not for that first one drawing his gun and cocking it, none of this would have happened."

"You shot my son Wilford."

"But it was okay for Jerry and Paul to kill my folks and steal everything we had of value? They were scum. I've done what I came to do and now I'll go back to Canada."

"This ain't over by a damned sight. Just who in hell are you?"

"My name is Eben McNinch. And now I'm leaving and if I find you following me, I'll kill you."

"You shoot my brother, my son and two of my nephews and you expect me not to do anything?"

"I expect you'll take the scum and bury them."

Eben walked back to his mule and mounted and left, keeping an eye on Boufford until he was at a safe distance.

Fort Garry

CHAPTER 14

As soon as Eben was out of sight, he could almost hear his granddad talking and he suddenly turned uphill off the road and circled back and watched to see which way Boufford would go after he had all the bodies tied down to their horses.

Boufford wasn't a strong man and it was a long time before he had all the bodies secured. And he headed back towards Tomah. Eben went to Dubuque.

Word would not have arrived at the town this soon, so he had a good meal and he left the mule at a livery for feed and new shoes. He purchased more food supplies and grain for the mule. Then he went down to the steamboat terminal and made passage back to Fort Snelling.

"Yes, sir, where are you going?"

"Fort Snelling."

The agent started laughing. "Young fella, if you were to ask me that tomorrow I'd say there was no such place as Fort Snelling. Tomorrow the old fort will be sold and the settlement will be called Minneapolis."

"When is the boat leaving?"

"In four hours, sir."

Eben went to sit down. "Excuse me, sir. The captain, Captain Sam, is requesting that you join him in the wheelhouse. I'll see that your mule gets aboard, sir."

"Thank you."

Eben boarded the boat and climbed up to the wheelhouse. "Good day, Captain Sam."

"Sit down, son. Coffee? Sure you do. I think you survive on

238

coffee." Captain Sam handed Eben a cup and then continued. "I hear you found your man." Not a question. A statement of fact.

"Yes, I did."

"And a whole lot more as I hear tell. You've stirred up quite a hornet's nest, now. I have no doubt the other three got just what they deserved. But this country is full of them Leets. They breed like flies on a rotten carcass.

"Old man Boufford Leet stopped at the first telegraph office on his way home and sent out a message to the family about their kin being shot by you. He gave your name and description. Them Leets will be looking for you from here all the way to the border. They won't come at you one at a time. It'll be more likely two, three or more."

"What's this telegraph, Captain Sam?"

Captain Sam began laughing uncontrollably. Eben stood there dumbfounded. Finally, "Have you noticed wires strung along the roads on poles?"

"Yes."

"There is a device—there's one in the ticket terminal—let's say at each end. A code, a series of taps, sends messages through the wires to the other end, and the person there changes those taps into letters and spells out messages. Information about you, son, has gone out through all the lines, gathering the Leets together to chase you down.

"The agent here in Dubuque for the steamboat line is a Leet and I know he has already sent out messages that you are aboard and where you are going. Do you see those two men standing near the gangway?"

"Yes."

"I recognize one and he is a Leet. Do you see what I mean now, son?"

"I'm beginning to."

"You best stay right up here with me. I can have your meal sent up when I take mine. I can let you out at Red Wing, a short ways before Snelling. Only it ain't called Fort Snelling now. It's

Minneapolis. You take a wide berth around Minneapolis and I'd suggest to the west.

"Remember this, Eben, you can without a doubt take care of yourself in the wilderness and outwit all of them. But you're not as used to the towns and villages and I think if you stay too long in one, the Leets will outwit you."

While the boat was being loaded with passengers and cargo for upriver, Captain Sam and Eben talked over a pot of coffee in the wheelhouse.

"I have read stories about your grandfather. I always figured that's just what they were. But since knowing you, I can tell you are a lot like your grandfather and his stories are true."

They talked to while away the time, waiting for the boat to be loaded. Eben wanted to know all about the things he had read about that he had no understanding of. And now he kept after Captain Sam to tell him all about this new world of the white man.

"Captain Sam, what makes this boat go?"

"Steam." When Eben didn't show any signs that he understood Captain Sam, "You must have seen the steam from a coffee pot when the water boils?"

"Yes."

"Well..., would you like to go below to the engine room and I'll show you. Don't worry about the Leets. We won't have to go out on deck." Eben followed Captain Sam down into the belly of the boat.

"This is the boiler, Eben. The fire boils the water and makes steam. The steam is allowed to build up pressure and then the steam under pressure flows through these pipes to this throttle valve, allowing the high pressure steam to flow into the cylinders. When the cylinders move back and forth, they cause the crankshaft to turn. The side-mounted paddlewheels are connected to this shaft."

The engineer was beginning to warm the engine up and build up steam pressure and the cylinders and shaft were moving slowly.

"Okay, I think I can see this now. I've seen pictures in the newspapers of something called a steam locomotive. What is that?"

"Right now there aren't any around here. But they operate under the same principle, except the locomotives, trains, turn iron wheels on iron rails that are laid on the ground. The train engine pulls many rail cars on top of those rails all over the country."

"My world back home is not so complicated."

They returned to the wheelhouse where Captain Sam blew the steam whistle signaling that the boat would be leaving in fifteen minutes.

Eben told Captain Sam all about his world back near Lake Manitoba. He didn't tell him that his mother was Cree, making him half Cree. He didn't want to bring trouble to the Cree people with him killing white men, even though they were Leets, and with what they had done to his family. To look at Eben with his red hair and beard, no one would ever imagine that he was half native.

Captain Sam wanted to hear the stories about his grandfather wrestling with the caribou, wolf and bear. About his grandfather's life living with the Cree.

"Well, he didn't live with the Cree. He lived on their land and would visit them. He and my grandmother would help them. My granddad said once that he had never known a more honest and friendly people in his whole life."

Captain Sam blew the whistle again, meaning the steamboat would depart in five minutes.

"Eben, do you see those two on the forward deck?"

"Yes."

"I know one of them is a Leet. The one with the face of a weasel."

"He looks like the others."

"His friend must be a cousin," Captain Sam said.

Sam blew into the engine room tube and said, "Okay, Henry, reverse...slow."

Eben could feel the vibrations of the engine through the deck. The steamboat started to back out into the river clear of the long wharf. Captain Sam blew in the tube again and said, "Okay, Henry, slow ahead."

With the reversed direction, now the boat was really vibrating. Captain Sam saw the worried look on Eben's face and said, "Don't worry, young fella, she won't fall apart. She's just like any woman, temperamental at first but she'll smooth out here soon.

"It'll be interesting to see if those two have any more friends on board. I know what I'll do," Captain Sam said as he rang the stewars's bell. In a few minutes, a steward knocked on the wheelhouse door.

"Yes, Captain Sam?"

"Come in, William. Do you see those two men standing alone on the forward deck?"

"Yes, sir."

"Have someone keep an eye on them at a distance. I don't want them to know they are being watched. I need to know if they have any friends on board."

"Yes, sir, Captain Sam."

The captain had signaled for full ahead and the boat picked up considerable speed. Eben had decided he liked traveling like this. One could cover great distances with little effort.

"Captain Sam, I don't want those two knowing where I get off, nor departing at the same place. I'm going down and talk with them."

"There's no stopping you, is there?"

"No, sir."

Eben walked down to the main deck and started forward, keeping out of sight as much as possible. They were looking forward as Eben boldly walked up behind them. He stood there momentarily before either of them knew anyone was there. When they did turn around, they were shocked to find the man they were after and wanted to kill had walked up behind them and they were unaware. They were unsettled to say the least, to be now confronted by the man who had killed five members of their family.

"You two stupid idiots looking for me?"

When they didn't answer, Eben said, "What's your name?" and he poked one in the chest with his finger.

When he still didn't answer, Eben said, "I asked you a question."

This wasn't how it was supposed to go. They figured they would just back-shoot him and ride off. They weren't expecting to be accosted by the prey.

"You're Leets. What are your first names?"

"I'm Seth," the one on the left said. "That's Noah."

"How are you pukes related to Jerry and Paul?"

"We're cousins. Noah and I are cousins."

"So, you're here to kill me." Not a question. Just a statement.

"You killed our cousins," Noah said. "For what, a dirty Injun squaw?"

Eben backhanded Noah so hard the blow sent him over the railing and overboard. "Well, you going to stand there and let Noah drown, or are you going to jump over and save him?"

"You son-of-a-bitch!" Seth jumped over to save Noah who was still unconscious.

Eben went back to the wheelhouse. Captain Sam grinned and said, "I thought that went well. Why did the second fellow jump over?"

"I suggested he save his cousin."

"Just what did he say to you?"

"He called my mother a dirty Injun squaw. She was Cree, very beautiful and educated.

"That makes me half Cree, Captain Sam. I don't want this to become whites against the natives, so I'd appreciate it if you'd keep this bit of news to yourself. I'm not ashamed of being part Cree, in fact I'm proud. I just don't want to cause any trouble for the Cree or any native."

"They won't hear from me, son. Hell, I've enjoyed my time with you. It's about time someone stood up to the Leets."

Captain Sam ordered supper for two. Catfish chowder with biscuits.

"That's a nice looking vest. Wolf, isn't it?"

"Yes. Where we lived the wolves had been after granddad for years. One year he had had enough of them and he and my father set out traps and snares and shot a few. My mother, Blue Flower, made vests from the fur pelts for each of us. I wear it now to honor her."

"When you return to your farm, Eben, do you think you'll miss what you have seen here?"

"Life on the farm, Captain Sam, was so uncomplicated and simple. There was very little need for money. It is a quieter life-style. You take nothing for granted."

"I suggest you get some sleep, Eben. My first mate will be taking over for me until 6 a.m. tomorrow. There's an extra cot in my cabin."

* * * *

Eben laid awake for a long time that night, wondering about the Leets and where would they strike again. Would he have to fight them all the way to the border? Would they cross the border and follow him to the Cree village? This he couldn't allow. *Would they ever get tired of the chase and give it up?*

He was awake before 6 a.m. and he went out onto the flying deck for some fresh air and to stretch. One of the stewards woke the captain and at 7 a.m. they had breakfast while Captain Sam also was at the helm.

"It'll take some time to maneuver through the islands between LaCrosse and Red Wing. The current is strong and I'll have to maneuver at full ahead to keep it in control. You'll have to jump off near Red Wing. I don't think they'll be looking for you there. But you'd better watch yourself around Minneapolis. I'd make a wide detour of the town."

Two more men had wandered up to the forward deck and were watching the passing islands. Eben wondered if they might be part of the Leets gang. But these two men were well dressed and they carried themselves like gentlemen. I'm getting paranoid, he thought.

"Eben, you'd better get yourself and mule ready. I can only stop long enough for you to get off. But remember there are dozens of people on board who will know you debarked in Red Wing and it won't be long before the Leets learn of it also."

"Thank you, Captain Sam," Eben said as they shook hands.

"You be careful, young fella. I don't want to read in the newspapers that the Leets got you. Here, you'd better take this, it might help you." Sam gave Eben a map.

"Thanks again, Captain Sam." Eben left and readied his mule to leave.

Captain Sam pulled the steamboat into the wharf at Red Wing only long enough for Eben to jump off. Now Eben needed to get out of town as fast as he could. There was no way of knowing if any of the Leets would be in Red Wing or on this side of the Mississippi. All he knew now was he had to go west to detour around Minneapolis.

No one seemed to pay him much attention at all as he walked through the village streets. He found one road heading west and followed it. When he came to the Minnesota River, it was too wide to try and cross. He'd have to find a ferry somewhere. Downstream toward Minneapolis was out of the question. He turned southwest and began following the river upstream toward Mankato. It was almost dark before he found a ferry on the outskirts of the town. The ferry was still manned with only a few people around. This would be better now than waiting for daylight to cross when there would be more people out and about.

He paid his two bits, not knowing exactly how much that was, so he held out a handful of coins. There were only two others crossing. He was feeling relatively safe.

He circled back toward Minneapolis and there were no houses on the west side of the river. Still he found a secluded spot for the night. There was no moon and he had had difficulty to make it as far as he had.

In the morning before leaving, he looked at the map Captain Sam had given him. If he traveled due north and stayed in the forest, he figured in two days he'd come to the road between Minneapolis and Moorhead. He checked his compass and left, letting the mule forage occasionally.

He had no idea how many family members were hunting for him or how widespread they would be. There were smaller streams he had to cross, but they were shallow. About halfway across land to the Mississippi North Branch, he found a heath. He staked the mule and did a once around the heath and the immediate area to make sure there were not any traveled trails or huts. He didn't like stopping so early in the evening, but he was tired and he and the mule needed rest and a full belly. As much as a cup of hot coffee would taste good, he did not build a fire until about midnight when everyone would be at home and asleep. He ate until he was full and then he put the fire out and lay back to sleep.

* * * *

The cold water of the Mississippi brought Noah Leet back to consciousness as soon as he hit the water. His cousin Seth had jumped overboard to save Noah. When he grabbed the back of Noah's shirt to pull him back away from the boat and the sidewinder paddles, Noah from his dazed stupor thought it was Eben and he struck out, glancing a blow off the side of Seth's head. "Noah! Noah! It's me, Seth."

Seth was a good swimmer, but Noah wasn't. He could swim some, but not enough to get ashore and Seth knew this. He swam beside Noah trying to help him, but Noah kept grasping at Seth and pulling him under. Finally Seth had to stay away from him and he tried to coax him to swim. That was not working either, and finally Noah went under and never surfaced.

Seth walked to Red Wing and sent a telegram to his uncle Boufford who was supposed to be in Minneapolis at another family member's house. When Boufford got the message, he was furious. First at Seth and Noah for not stopping Eben and then as he saw it, it was Eben's fault Noah had drowned. He sent out all the younger boys to all of the Leets in the area to meet at St. Cloud.

He also sent a telegram to Moorhead to have the family there watch the trails and roads from Minneapolis.

Big John was still recovering from his encounter with Eben and he couldn't help, but there were enough other Leets that wanted to help to watch every road and trail.

"Damn him!" Boufford exclaimed. "He has killed six Leets now. Put Big John in the hospital and severely beaten three others. It's damned time we find him."

Leet men from all around dropped whatever they were doing to help hunt down the man who was supposedly terrorizing the clan. Not any of them had any special fondness for either Jerry or Paul, but when someone attacked one Leet, they all got involved.

From Grand Forks to Dubuque and west of Minneapolis, there were now forty Leet men out looking for Eben. Everybody traveled in threes. Nobody by himself. He had proven too capable for even two men.

"I want one group of three to work their way upstream to Grand Forks on the west side of the river and another group of three to do the same on the east side. If you get to Grand Forks without seeing anything, turn around and work your way back to Minneapolis. And if nothing, work back to Moorhead. Look for us at Aunt Emma's in Grand Forks.

* * * *

Eben had no idea of the extent of the Leets' search for him. The countryside was dotted with small lakes, marshes and ponds, much like the country back home. He rode the mule when he could, but often found it easier to lead it. When he came to a high prominence, he could look down and see the river and there was a road following on the other side. He sat down to rest and study his map.

Looking off toward the northwest, the country looked like it opened more like grassland. For two days he had been struggling through thick stands of small softwoods and then low-growing bushes. He decided to head in that direction and see if it was open grassland.

It was getting late, so he decided to spend the night. He was out of food. He was able to gather a few edible herbs and berries. This would have to do until he could take the time to hunt. There was no need of a fire that night and he would save what little coffee he had for the morning.

Before going to sleep, he stood to stretch and across the river he could see a fire. It could have been the Leets or anybody traveling between towns. He suspected the Leets, but they were on the other side.

The next morning he left the prominence and headed northwest toward what he hoped was grassland. If the Leets were indeed on the other side of the river, then they probably would have Moorhead tied up and he'd never be able to make it through.

At the end of that day he came to country that wasn't so choked with forests or undergrowth. He made camp at the edge of the open country and he saw a deer and wanted to shoot it. But on second thought, he didn't know exactly where the Leets were. Maybe they were using dogs to follow his trail.

He caught fish in a small stream and gathered edible herbs. The mule had all he wanted to eat.

The next day before mid-morning he found an active beaver flowage. He didn't want to chance a shot, so he sharpened the point of a stick for a spear. He broke away some of the dam and broke off a small fir tree and stood it up, sticking the end in the mud, to hide behind so the beaver would not see him waiting.

He didn't have long to wait. A beaver swam up and looked things over, but didn't come close enough. It swam off and in a few minutes, it was back carrying moss and mud in its front paws. It went to work packing the mud and Eben took this opportunity and drove the wooden spear into the beaver's back.

He skinned it and built a small fire of snapping dry softwood limbs, so the fire would not smoke. He sat back roasting beaver meat over an open fire, remembering similar times with his family while in the wilderness and making trips to Fort Garry. That was a happy time, and all of that was now gone. He was missing his mom and dad and tears filled his eyes.

He had to stop thinking like that and concentrate on getting home without encountering any more Leets. He dried his eyes and began to think of other things. When he bit into the first piece of meat, it was the most delicious food he had eaten since starting on this endeavor. He thought, *How long have I been gone?*

Soft maples in the marsh were beginning to turn color... but they always turned color first and early. He had been finding mushrooms that were normally found only in the fall. He had seen brook trout spawning in clear spring-water streams. *It must be early autumn.* Then the nights would soon be getting colder, the daylight hours were already shorter. He hoped he could make it back before snow.

He spent the night roasting the rest of the meat to take with him. He did get two hours of sound sleep and was ready to go at dawn.

The next morning, he decided to have some more beaver meat. It would be a long day and he'd need the energy. While he was eating, he looked at his map again and decided to go further west and hit the Minnesota River and follow that to the height of land and cross over to the south end at Red River. He felt safer traveling west and then turning north, and he wouldn't have to be so cautious about shooting game for food or stopping at a trading post for supplies. Traveling in this direction was easier and he made good time to the Minnesota River, and he found a small but adequate trading post.

He wanted to buy some grain, but decided he didn't want the extra weight. He picked up bacon, coffee and two loaves of fresh bread. Even with the bacon, he still caught beaver to eat.

After he left the trading post, a trapper stocking up for the season said, "Do you know who he is, John? That big fellow who just left?"

"No."

"That's Eben McNinch. He was up in Moorhead earlier this summer and Big John Leet and his cronies started a fight with him. He broke some of Big John's ribs and an arm and threw him through a window. There were six in all and I guess he broke up a couple of others pretty good, too, as I heard it."

The storekeeper said, "I'm surprised. Big John has never lost a brawl in his life. He seems like a nice enough fellow. Where's he from?"

"I don't know. Maybe he's looking to do some trapping around here," the trapper said. "If he knows what's good for him, he'll stay out of Sioux country. I had friends went west to trap last season and no one has heard a word from 'em."

Eben wanted to come into Fargo from the west. He figured the Leets probably wouldn't be watching that trail. He had to cross several other rivers, before turning north again.

As he rode, he always was watching for the Leets. Before making camp at night he would circle an area on foot, looking to see if he had been followed or someone might be waiting to ambush him, which the Leets seemed to prefer. He knew he must be getting close to Fargo, which was situated just west of Moorhead. He killed two more beaver and spent half the next day roasting the meat to take with him. If he encountered the Leets, he would have little time to hunt for food and his bacon wouldn't last long.

He continued north until he came to the road between Bismark and Fargo. He stayed off the road, but followed it east towards Fargo on the north side.

* * * *

Boufford sent men out to tell those out in South Minneapolis, around Red Wing and the group of men on the road between Minneapolis and Moorhead, "I think he may be north of us now and I want to concentrate between Fargo, Moorhead and Grand Forks. There is still a group on the road south of here and men already spread out at Grand Forks. He may have crossed the rivers and may now be traveling cross-country to Grand Forks. I want six each to work their way north along the Red River. Six to a side, those on the west side of the river, spread out more. If he's between Grand Forks and Fargo, we'll box him in and we'll surely get him."

If Eben was to get by them and north of Grand Forks, then their only chance would be to wait for him to cross the border.

Eben didn't go right into Fargo. Instead he turned north about a mile from town. There was a road on the east side of the Red River and a horse trail on the west side. He led his mule back away from the trail on the west, just close enough so he could see if anyone was on it.

It had been days since he had encountered a Leet—those on the steamboat. He wanted to think that maybe they had more productive things to do than hunt him down, and had gone home. But in all honesty, he doubted it. He was too close for a fire if they were still looking for him, so he ate the beaver meat cold.

When he was feeding his mule the next morning, he could smell smoke. *So they are still after me.* He checked the wind direction. It was coming from the north. The smoke smell was strong and he knew they weren't far away. He decided to leave the mule tied up there. There was water and he brought in some grass for it. He was going to hunt them and he didn't need the mule along making noise. He hated to leave his belongings there, too. The money and gold and his bedroll, but he didn't have a choice. He had his two pistols and he left the rifle.

Actually, he was glad. Now he knew for sure who they were and it was to his advantage to be behind them. He could move along through the trees effortlessly without the mule, without a sound. It wasn't long before he found their camp. They were still there, six of them sitting around the fire talking. Then one of them got up and doused the fire and they split up into two three-man groups. One group stayed pretty much with the road and the other group went west. He did hear one of them say they would all meet up with Boufford in Fargo. So there were more of them to the north.

He followed the group west, always staying back far enough not to be seen. They went about a mile and then they spread out about a hundred feet apart. *They're trying to drive me toward the others.* When evening came, instead of meeting up with the other group, they made camp for the night.

Eben lay on his stomach only about a hundred feet away listening to them talk. They talked about the family members that had already died chasing him and wondered why he had set out after Jerry and Paul to begin with. Apparently they didn't know the two had killed his folks. They talked some about girls.

He waited, his stomach growling with hunger pains. More wood was put on the fire and then all three lay down on their bedrolls. He waited until he was sure they were asleep and then he crawled toward them one inch at a time. When he reached the nearest one, he drew out his pistol and hit him over the head. Then he crawled to the next one and hit him, and then the third guy.

Then he put more wood on the fire until he had quite a bonfire. He smashed the actions of their rifles and pistols and threw their knives in the fire. He cut strips from their blankets and tied their ankles and hands. He put more wood on the fire and waited for the three to regain consciousness.

He didn't think he had hit them so hard. They were still out. He got some water with their cooking pot and poured it on their faces. Then he sat back and waited.

"What the hell is the meaning of this?" one of them raged.

"Do you know who I am?" Eben asked.

The same guy shook his head to clear it and said, "Ain't you the one we've been after? The one who kilt our cousins and uncle?"

"How many are there of you Leets?"

No answer. Eben dragged him by the feet a little closer to the fire. "How many?"

No answer. Eben dragged him closer to the fire. He was sweating now. "How many?"

Still no answer. Eben dragged him even closer and put his feet up on one of the rocks. The heat was getting hot on his feet. Eben stood there waiting.

"Damn it! Okay! Get my feet off the rocks."

"How many, first."

"Maybe forty, all tolled."

"How many north of here or around Grand Forks?"

"Don't know for sure. Twenty, twenty-five maybe."

"Do you three know why I killed Jerry and Paul?"

"Not for sure."

"They killed my dad, raped and killed my mom, Paul shot me and they stole everything we had.

"You three are out here trying to kill me. I think it only right since I caught you that I kill you."

All three were scared now, and they each were wishing they had never joined up with their Uncle Boufford.

Eben put more wood on the fire and cut the boots off the other two and threw them in the fire, along with their pants and everything they had. Food and all. "I'm not going to kill you. But before you walk all the way to Grand Forks in your stocking feet, you'll wish I had killed you. Remember this: you'll never know where I'll be. I'll be watching for you three and if I ever

253

see you again, I'll kill you on the spot. Is that understood?"

"Yes, mister."

"Now you take a message to Boufford. If he doesn't call off this hunt, I'll kill every Leet. Do you understand that?"

"Yes, mister."

"Boufford knows why I killed Jerry and Paul. I let him live, once. He should have let it go. He's pushed me as far as he's going to."

"He won't stop, mister. But I'll give him your message. He has a meanness about him like his brother, Ezra, Jerry and Paul's father. He won't give up."

"You tell him if he doesn't, I will kill him."

Before leaving, Eben looked around to make sure he had thrown everything on the fire.

"What are you going to do with us? You can't leave us here tied up."

"You'll work free eventually, and that'll give me enough time to put some distance between us. Know this: I'm letting you three live so you can take the message back to Boufford. Don't come after me again."

Eben then disappeared into the darkness without making a sound. He hoped he had put the fear of God into them.

* * * *

Quite a few minutes passed after Eben left before any of the three men could speak. "I don't know about you two, but when I get out of here, I'm going to take his advice. I'm going home and forget Eben McNinch."

"Yeah, me, too. He's scary. This wilderness is too much like home for him. We wouldn't have a chance going after him again."

"I'm afraid what Boufford will do. He won't be happy we three getting caught like this and him still walking free."

"Yeah, but I'm not going after him, are you?"

"No."

Those three wouldn't be hunting him anymore and he knew the other group of three were to the north and near the river. So when he got back to the mule, he built a fire, warmed up some beaver meat and had some hot coffee and then slept soundly until dawn.

He kindled the fire again and made another pot of coffee and studied the map Captain Sam had given him. He liked the old captain. He surely had given him a lot of help. *Hope the Leets don't come after him for helping me.*

He now knew there were at least twenty-five men in and around Grand Forks looking for him and probably also all the way to the border. If he tried now to go north, he surely would run into the Leets again. And even if he didn't, before he got back to the farm, the ground would be covered with snow.

It would be safer to wait until spring before crossing the border. But he had had enough of the white man's world. He decided to go west and find a band of Dakota Sioux and see if he could spend the winter with them.

CHAPTER 15

It took the three Leets three days to walk out of there. They had no pants, no boots, no guns, no food. They had nothing. They came limping into Grand Forks wearing a shirt and torn and tattered long underwear. Their feet were bleeding and they were dirty and starving. Eben had been right. It would have been more humane if he had shot them that night.

Uncle Boufford was furious. "What do you mean you had him and let that bastard go!"

"We didn't have him, Uncle Boufford. He had us!"

"How can that be? There were three of you."

"He came sneaking into our camp at night after we had gone to sleep. He cracked each of us over the head with his pistol. He tied us up and burned our pants, boots and everything we had. He smashed all the guns we had. There was nothing we could do."

Boufford was so mad he looked as if he might explode.

"He gave me a message to give you, Uncle Boufford."

"Well, what is it?"

"He said if you don't call off this hunt for him, he will hunt you down and kill you. And, Uncle Boufford, we three are finished with this. We're going home. We've had enough of Eben McNinch. Leave him be, Uncle Boufford, or he will kill you, too."

"Go home, damn it! You three arc useless. Go on, get out of here. Go back home."

* * * *

Eben was feeling good about his decision to ride west and hopefully winter out with a band of Sioux. He really was longing for home and to see Wenonah again, but he knew Boufford Leet wouldn't give up the chase so easily, and probably many more felt as Boufford did. No, trying to go north now would only invite trouble. He'd have to wait for spring.

There was no hurry now. He took his time and enjoyed the countryside. He speared brook trout in the streams, he shot a small crotch-horn deer. He gathered edible herbs in the forest and he was living quite well. Only colder weather was coming and he needed some sort of a shelter. So he packed the deer meat and fish on his mule and continued west. He had no idea how far west he'd have to go to find the Sioux. He naturally supposed they would find him.

Each day he stopped early for the night and built a fire and put on green wood and some pine boughs on the fire to make smoke, hoping a brave out hunting would see the smoke and investigate.

He shot another deer and took the time to smoke the meat. Maybe this would cause a curious brave to come to his fire. While the meat was curing he had time to reflect on his life since the death of his mom and dad. He had seen much of the white man's world and although there were some things he liked about it, there was just too much he didn't. He really liked the old timer at the bar in Moorhead and he liked Captain Sam. They were both good and honest men, not like those who were chasing him. It didn't seem as though the white man needed much of an excuse to fight, drunk or sober.

When he awoke the next morning there was a dusting of snow on the ground and the stream had glazed over with ice. He packed the meat on his mule and he decided to walk and lead him.

* * * *

Running Dawg and Short Feather were back at the village talking with Chief Tall Feather, Short Feather's grandfather.

"We find this white man with fiery hair on his face; the one other whites look to kill. He is coming west. Builds smoke like he wants our people know he is here in Dakota land. No travel some days. Stay, make meat over fire. Spears fish like a Sioux, knows what plants to eat. He more like one of us than white man who hunts him."

"I think I know who this man is. Go find him and bring him to me."

Running Dawg and Short Feather left the village the next morning and traveled all day on foot before they found the fiery haired man. He was still traveling toward the setting sun. Eben had stopped early for the night again, and had made a smoky fire. When he saw Running Dawg and Short Feather coming toward him, he laid his rifle on the ground in front of them, a sign that he meant them no harm.

Eben greeted his guests using the Cree language. This surprised Running Dawg and Short Feather. Even though his words were different, they could understand enough of what he was saying.

"You travel as we do. Like Indian," Short Feather said.

"I am a native Indian. Cree." This really surprised the two. They had never known anyone of their color to grow hair on the face.

"Sit," and Eben made a motion with his hands. "Are you hungry?" He gave them some deer meat and they ate hungrily.

In between mouthfuls, Running Dawg said, "Good meat."

When they had finished eating, Short Feather said, "You come with us to village. Leave now."

Eben replied, "We go in morning. We sleep now."

This also surprised Running Dawg and Short Feather. They had not expected to be rebuked like this.

In the morning, Eben made a pot of coffee to have along with the deer meat. They seemed to enjoy the bitter taste of coffee. He was glad he had shot the last deer. Now he would have a gift to present to the chief.

Short Feather stood and said, "Go now," and he and Running Dawg started walking, Eben following and leading his mule. Running Dawg and Short Feather seemed to be in a hurry to get back to the village. The only time they stopped was to drink water and then they were traveling again. Eben didn't mind, really; he was used to walking.

It was almost dark when they arrived at the village. Eben was escorted to Tall Feather's lodge and Running Dawg and Short Feather disappeared. Eben didn't have long to wait. Tall Feather came out and stood before him. Tall Feather towered above him. He paused standing in front of Eben and then he began laughing, and everyone was watching him and wondering why.

In between bouts of laughter, Tall Feather was finally able to say, "Big Red Beard Not Afraid, you not change. You still young."

Eben waited until Tall Feather had stopped laughing. "Tall Feather, I am his grandson. I have his name, Eben McNinch."

"You and my two braves eat. Then we talk. Much to talk."

Eben took the smoked venison from the mule and gave it to Tall Feather. "I need to care for my mule, Tall Feather."

Tall Feather said something to two young boys and they led the mule off. "Boys care for mule; bring your things here. Now eat."

While Eben, Running Dawg and Short Feather ate, the rest of the village were busy in conversations. When they had finished, Tall Feather said, "Come, we talk." He led the way into his lodge and the two sat on animal fur and leaned back against a rolled up hide, much like a pillow.

Tall Feather lit a pipe and handed it to Eben first. He took a long draw and then exhaled and gave it to Tall Feather. Tall Feather didn't say anything until the tobacco was nothing but ash. "I remember your grandfather and grandmother. She good medicine woman. Was with a hunt long time ago. One of the men hurt his ankle; your grandmother fixed him. Talked much with grandfather. You look like grandfather. Big Red Beard

Not Afraid. Tell me about Grandmother, medicine woman, and Grandfather, Big Red Beard Not Afraid."

"Three summers ago they walked to the Spirit World."

Tall Feather was surprised with Eben's words of walk to the Spirit World. He decided there was more about Eben McNinch that he wanted to learn.

"White men that want to kill you. Why?"

Eben started at the beginning, how his mom and dad had been killed and how he had hunted and killed the men that did this, and now these men's families were hunting him.

"You avenged your mother and father. How is this wrong?"

"In the white man's world, they have what they call laws, and we are supposed to let the law make good the killing of my folks."

"You are white like grandfather. Law no good for you?"

"I'm only half white. My mother was Cree, Blue Flower."

"You have blood like me?" Tall Feather found this exceptional, since Eben had so much red hair and on his face. "You have home here. You stay as long as you want. I send out braves to hunt these men who wish to kill you."

"No, Tall Feather. You can't. The white men that are wanting to kill me think I am white also. If you send your men to kill them, Native Indian against the white men, it would start a war against all the native people and bring trouble to your people."

"You are wise for someone with not many years. I will watch. If these men come to Sioux land, I will stop them." Eben nodded his head.

Tall Feather wanted to know all about the white settlements and how they lived.

"People there seldom help each other unless they are given money for their help."

"I not understand this money."

"Do you know gold? The yellow rock white man looks for?"

"Yes, have seen this yellow rock in waters. Why this rock drive white man crazy?"

"The yellow rock, or gold, is very valuable to them. They can use it to trade for food, clothes, blankets, everything. The more gold you have in their world, the better you can live. When this gold is found on Dakota land, white men will come into this country like water in a river. There'll be no stopping them."

"Dakota Sioux strong, have many good braves."

"That may be, Tall Feather, but there are more white men than all natives. The more you fight against them, the more they will kill your people." Tall Feather wasn't liking this talk. He could see the end of his people and his world.

"How do we stop them? I old man. Not long now and I walk to Spirit World. My son Red Cloud will then be chief."

"Tall Feather, maybe Red Cloud should be here to hear my words."

Tall Feather went outside and made hand motions to Red Cloud and he joined them.

Tall Feather told Red Cloud in his own words what he and Eben were talking about, and said he should hear what Eben had to say, also.

"The greatest defense you could have against the whites pouring into Sioux land like water in a river is to learn their ways. Your people, Tall Feather and Red Cloud, must know how to talk with the whites with their tongue. Your people need to be able to speak the tongue, read printed words and know how to write. This is the only way you'll be strong against the white man.

"You need to educate your people, to teach your people these things so they can understand and talk with the white man. Ultimately, what you'll need is a lawyer. This is a man trained in the ways of law, settling disputes with law and not fighting."

"Is this what you do, Eben? Did you kill those men because of the law?" Red Cloud asked.

"No, there is no law where I live. And now I have many men looking to kill me. You don't want or need this happening to you or your people. In years to come, you need to send one of the young men out to the white towns and learn how to use those laws."

"How do we do this, Eben?"

"If I were you, I would find a white man's mission where they help the native people. A missionary can teach your people how to read and write and talk the white man tongue. How did you and Red Cloud learn to speak my words?"

"A missionary, many years ago. He was French, but he taught us your words."

"See, this is a start."

It was late and they agreed to talk again. Now they would sleep. As Tall Feather had said, the two young boys had brought Eben's saddle, pack and bedroll, and left them outside Tall Feather's lodge.

Three days passed before the three talked again in Tall Feather's lodge. In the meantime, Eben wandered around the village, getting acquainted.

In a society like the native peoples', everyone had a duty or job to do that benefitted the entire tribe. Some men were scouts, some runners, some hunters and some warriors. Women were the tender caregivers and they were the food gatherers and cleaners of the hides for their use. But no matter what each individual did, it benefitted the whole tribe, and everyone was expected to do their share. Eben was asked to teach some of the people, first to speak his tongue and then to tell them about the white man's world and how he lived. He taught the old as well as the young. Since he could speak fluent Cree, the people could understand him. Then he just had to translate everything to English. They were willing pupils, and they all were fast learners. Everyone wanted to know more about the mysterious white man.

Shortly after he started teaching, Tall Feather asked, "Eben, come to my lodge. We talk."

Eben followed him inside and there were two pretty young women there. He thought maybe fifteen or sixteen. He sat down and Tall Feather began speaking. "Eben, these two women are gifts to you for as long as you stay in village. You will have your own lodge and these women will keep you company, cook for you, make clothes, anything you desire."

"Thank you, Tall Feather. I have a woman in my Cree village back home."

"You need woman to keep you warm while you here. My people need your blood in our people to make my people better, stronger. You leave your seed in these two women and they have your babies. We have your blood in our blood, now make tribe stronger."

So this wasn't so much a gift, but a request to leave his genes in the babies these two women would give birth to.

"I know you leave in spring, so no joining with women, only you leave seed in each to grow."

Red Cloud's daughters, Ula and Serena. Both very pretty girls and that's what they were, but probably not in this culture.

Eben agreed as long as everyone understood he had to leave in the spring to return home and to his woman. At first, Eben felt a little awkward having two girls as his own, doing everything for him that a wife would do, and all that was asked of him was to make each girl pregnant. And he certainly found it awkward having sex with the other girl there watching. Sometimes if he wasn't too tired, he'd have sex with them both. In the evenings when they were alone, he taught both Ula and Serena to speak English. They learned very quickly. During the day, each day, he taught his other pupils, as he liked to call them. They were eager to learn and they especially enjoyed listening to Eben tell them about the white man's world. He wished he had the things necessary to teach them to write. Perhaps this would have to wait until a missionary was found.

* * * *

Boufford Leet and his son Brodie and Wilfred, an older brother of Jerry and Paul's, were obsessed with finding Eben. The rest had returned home for the winter, but most had agreed to continue the hunt in the spring, as soon as weather permitted travel. They would all meet in Saint Vincent, next to the border.

Once a week all winter, they would ride along the 49th Parallel to see if anyone had crossed. All they ever found were moose tracks.

During the January thaw, they took a trip to Fort Garry and talked with Alfons Gervais. "Mr. Gervais, me and the boys are looking for a friend of ours and we were wondering if by chance he had gone through here recently. Eben McNinch."

"And who are you?" Gervais asked.

"I'm Boufford Leet. Have you seen McNinch go through here?"

"It's been a couple of years since I've seen Mr. McNinch. If he stops by, want me to tell him you were looking for him?" Gervais asked.

"Ah, that won't be necessary."

Ever since Eben had gone south of the border the previous year, there were stories about Eben and his confrontations with Jerry and Paul Leet and their family, and how the Leet clan had vowed to avenge the killing of so many family members. There had even been stories printed in the newspapers about Eben.

Gervais had suspected something was afoul as soon as the three had entered the store. He wasn't about to help them.

Boufford and the boys hung around Fort Garry for a week and then headed back for Grand Forks. They checked all the establishments in Grand Forks and since much of the town was Leet, Boufford felt pretty certain when told Eben McNinch had not been seen. "He couldn't have just dropped off the face of the earth. He has to be holed up somewhere, but where. Wherever he is, once spring and warmer weather get here, he'll be moving north."

* * * *

Eben was having the time of his young life there at the Sioux village. Two pretty girls to care for him—cook, mend, carry firewood and keep him warm at night. He was enjoying sleeping with and having sex with Ula and Serena. That winter he often thought about staying permanently. Then he would think of Wenonah, the Cree people and his home. No, if he stayed, it wouldn't be right.

The weather was warming each day, melting the snow and ice and the daylight hours were getting longer. He knew he'd have to leave soon. Ula and Serena also knew he would be leaving soon, as each day he kept looking to the east with a forlorn look on his face. By now the girls were pregnant with Eben's babies, his bloodline. They each were very much in love with him, but they understood their role and would not ask him to stay. He had also grown a fondness for them, but his true love and desire was Wenonah, his childhood friend, and returning to the land he loved and understood.

One afternoon, Tall Feather asked Eben to his lodge to council with him and Red Cloud. "I know you leave soon, Eben. Red Cloud and I would ask you to stay and be one of our people, but we know this cannot be. You look to the east and north like someone looking for a friend to arrive. Your heart is with the Cree. You may not be done with those who hunt you. We have heard stories now from runners that some of those same white men wait for you to cross the border. There is a spirit who walks with you, my friend, and as long as you are not careless, this spirit will let no harm come to you.

"You have crossed the darkened valley of death many times without harm. This spirit that walks beside you is great and protects you and when you return to your people, you will be happy for a time. But this spirit will cause you to move on. You have much to give to native people that you cannot begin to ever imagine. It is because of this that you are protected by this Great Spirit.

"Ula and Serena both tell me they carry your child now. This way you have given our people a great gift. Your blood will now be mixed with the Sioux people and maybe with each generation we can now learn more of the white man's ways."

"My heart wants to lead me back to the land of the Cree and my woman, Wenonah. If not for this, I would stay with my Sioux brothers. You are a good people. Someday when I can, I will return for a while. Until then I will always remember my days here. I have found much friendship here and I will miss everyone.

"Tomorrow morning I leave, but I take with me a goodness in my heart for the Sioux people."

That night in his lodge with Ula and Serena, there were no sad tears. It was a time for joy and one last sexual fulfillment. Both girls knew this would be their last sexual joining. Over and over they would moan with silent screams of ecstasy. Eben was young and virile, but after so much he had to rest and the girls each lay in the crook of his arms and just as he was about to fall asleep, they would start all over. Tonight there was no sexual satisfaction with either Ula or Serena as they kept Eben awake all night with their sexual play and love-making.

* * * *

The whole village knew Eben would be leaving after daylight and everyone was awake and up at dawn. Eben ate a good breakfast. He knew he would soon have to shoot something for food and his next meal may not be for a while.

He cleaned up, pulled his wolf vest on that Ula had cleaned and repaired, over a buckskin shirt Serena had made. He hugged each one and kissed them passionately and said, "Goodbye, my loves."

He looked at Tall Feather and then Red Cloud and slightly nodded his head at each and they returned his nod and its meaning.

One small boy led his mule over, saddle and gear already secured. "Goodbye, my friends." They all watched as he rode out of sight.

CHAPTER 16

1855

Eben thought it was spring. The air was cool. He rode steadily toward the east, not fast, but at a steady pace. A bear stood up on its hind legs not fifty feet away. The mule shied and stepped sideways. Eben's confidence and quieting tone calmed the mule. The bear was still standing. Probably it had just come out of hibernation and was hungry. "Look fella, I want no trouble with you. You let me pass undisturbed and I won't hurt you." The bear, back on all fours, walked off.

The ground was still frozen and the prairie was wet, as the water had no place to go. He rode all day up until dark before he found a dry knoll to make camp and sleep. He had no food or coffee, so he slept.

The next day he stopped at midday. The sky was gray and threatening to storm. He found another dry knoll and built a shelter of fir boughs. He spread his slicker on top in case of rain. He tied off the mule to graze and he went hunting. If the Leets were still looking for him, he didn't want to shoot his rifle anywhere near where they might be. He still was feeling safe for now.

He saw doe deer heavy with lambs and passed them up. He had just about figured he'd have to go hungry again when he saw a deer with antlers in velvet. It was lying on the top of a dry knoll facing into the wind coming from the east. He carried the deer over his neck and shoulders back to his camp before he dressed it. This way he wouldn't get blood all over him. He set the heart and liver to roasting, then he gathered more wood for his fire and built a rack to smoke the meat. The weather was looking like he was going to have to stay for a couple of days, anyway.

The liver and heart sure smelled good while they were roasting. He skinned the deer and sliced off strips of meat to lay over the rack to smoke. He would keep some fresh to eat.

He buried the remains away from camp. The smell would surely attract a bear. He sat up most of that night tending the fire and meat, only taking short catnaps. During the night the air cooled and it snowed by midmorning. The snow changed to a drizzling rain. He broke up the rib cage and roasted ribs over the fire and snacked on those. He broke open the leg bones and ate the marrow—some raw, some he cooked. He liked the cooked marrow better. It was full of nutrients.

While waiting for the meat to finish curing, he studied his map, trying to decide how and where to proceed. He wanted to find a trading post before he crossed the border.

He remained at his camp on the knoll for three days. The meat now was all cured and the ribcage had been roasted and picked clean. He made tea from bunchberry leaves. He still didn't have a plan, only he wanted to find a trading post. He had been doing a lot of reminiscing about his winter with the Sioux tribe and in particular about Ula and Serena. He hoped he was doing the right thing about going back. Then he heard Tall Feather telling him the spirit that was walking with him would lead him away from the Cree village. He would finish what he had started.

The snow was wet and heavy and Eben's progress was slow. He didn't want the mule to slip and break a leg. After two days of this, the sun came back out warmer than before and the snow was soon melted. The ground thawed and ice left the streams.

Water in the rivers was high, of course, and he had to hunt at each river for a shallow place to cross. Sometimes he had to go a couple of miles out of his way.

Not wanting to come to the Red River south of Grand Forks,

he turned north and a day later he came onto a trail running east and west—only a horse trail and no wagons. It was used often and the last tracks were traveling to the east, toward Grand Forks. He checked the tracks carefully. There were two horses and traveling light.

It was the right time of year for trappers to be returning from a winter of trapping. *Or?* Or it could be Leets out looking for him. He decided to follow, to be sure. Whoever it was, was not traveling fast. They made several rest stops, and had a fire at each one.

He didn't mount up. Instead he walked, leading the mule, so he could study the tracks and signs as he progressed toward Grand Forks. It was obvious whoever it was, was still not in any particular hurry. If it had been trappers, they would have been more eager to get to a trading post to sell their fur. He had no idea what was to the west along the trail. But because of the slow progression of the two, he was convinced the Leets were ahead of him. He decided it was time to turn the table and hunt them

* * * *

"Brodie, you and Sam ride the Missouri Trail west three days from Grand Forks. Don't go so fast that you can't read the sign along the trail. Go out three days and then back. If you meet anyone on the trail, ask questions. That son-of-a-bitch has to be out there somewhere," Boufford ordered.

"What makes you think he'll be coming to Grand Forks, Pa?" Brodie asked.

"He stayed the winter somewhere west of the Red River. As soon as he can travel, I suspect he'll either head for the border or a trading post.

"Elmo and I will be riding both sides of the Red River to Saint Vincent. I don't want any screw-ups this time, boys."

Elmo was an older brother to Ezra and Boufford, and he didn't take part in the hunt the year before. Now he was riding with Boufford and couldn't understand why it was so difficult to hunt down one man. And this man had killed and maimed so many of the family.

Brodie and Sam rode three days west on the Missouri Trail and stopped at Rubgy Trading Post. "No, sir, I ain't seen no one looking like that this spring nor last year. Not at all."

A day and a half east of Rugby, they stopped in the trail on top of a rise. Brodie looked behind them. "Sam, somebody is coming up behind us. Let's go on ahead and look for a narrow place in the trail where we can ambush whoever that is." They disappeared off the rise and around a couple of sharp bends.

"Here, Wilfred, you on that side and I'll stay here. Put your horse far enough back so it can't be seen."

They each hid their horse and then found a place to hide close to the trail, and they waited for the stranger to come riding up.

Eben had been reliving his last night with the girls again and didn't see the movement on top of the rise.

Eben had spent so much quiet and relaxing time at the Sioux village he was off-guard. As he crested the knoll and started around the sharp bends, his mind was way off and not paying attention. All of a sudden two men with rifles, one on either side of the narrow trail, pointed them at him, and Brodie said, "Hold it right there, mister!" His rifle was in the scabbard and one pistol was hung over the saddle horn. He sat there just looking at the two without saying a word, and this was making Brodie worried. He had the red hair and beard and he was wearing a wolf vest. This had to be the man they were hunting, McNinch.

"You're McNinch, ain't you, mister?"

Eben just stared at him with anger. Anger, because he had been caught day-dreaming.

Sam could see the rifle in the scabbard. "You carry a handgun. Where is it?"

"Hanging from my saddle horn."

"Throw it down." Eben dropped it beside the mule.

Brodie had taken a step or two closer to the trail and said,

"Get off the mule, you son-of-a-bitch."

Brodie took another step closer as if he intended to physically pull Eben from the saddle.

Brodie was careless and over-confident and Eben saw a slight chance. He started to dismount and he swung his right leg up and over the mule, while still standing in the left stirrup. Brodie started to reach up and grab Eben by the back of the collar and as he did, Eben struck out with his right leg and his foot caught Brodie in the shoulder and he went over backward. As he was falling, he pointed his rifle at Eben and pulled the trigger. The shot went wide. The mule ran off. Eben jumped at Brodie and pulled him behind some trees so Sam would not have a clear shot. He pulled on Brodie's right arm so hard to get out of the line of fire, he actually heard Brodie's arm break and Brodie let the screams out of him.

Brodie pulled a knife while still screaming, and Eben brought his iron-hard fist down on his wrist and he dropped the knife and his wrist was now broken. Eben drew his pistol from under his arm and cracked Brodie over the head to shut him up. He lay unconscious. Sam fired and hit a tree in front of Eben's face. He turned and ran at Sam before he could reload or draw a pistol. Sam saw him coming and dropped the rifle and started to draw his pistol when Eben hit him in the stomach, knocking the air out of his lungs and breaking two ribs. He couldn't scream yet, because he couldn't draw any air into his lungs yet. When he could, Eben decided to break his gun arm and he snapped it over his knee. Now it would be a long time before either one of them could shoot a rifle or handgun or continue the hunt for him.

Like before, Eben built a fire and cut off their boots and pants and burned them. Then he smashed their guns. He retrieved his mule and tied it to a tree and brought both of their horses over. He burned their saddlebags, bedrolls and saddles and shot his pistol behind the horses' rumps, scaring them off.

He dragged Brodie up to the fire and then Sam. By now they both had stopped screaming. "Where's Boufford waiting for me?"

No answer.

"Either you tell me where Boufford is or I'll take a stick and hit your broken arm and maybe break some more ribs. Where is he?"

"He's on the trail north of Grand Forks."

"How many men besides you two pissants?"

"Just Boufford and his older brother, Elmo. That's all."

"You can't expect us to walk out of here with no boots and all busted up like this, mister," Sam said. "We need a doctor."

"You were going to kill me. Do you want me to kill you instead? You're not bad off. Not as bad as you'd have me believe. You're still breathing and you both can still walk. Although by the time you get to Grand Forks, I'll have put miles between us. And probably your feet will hurt like hell, but think of the only alternative you have."

"No matter where you go, mister, Boufford will come after you," Brodie said.

"He won't have to. I'm going after Boufford. I would tell you to tell him this, but by the time you two pissants get out of here, I will already have found him."

Eben stirred the fire, making sure everything would be nothing more than ashes. "It'll be a long painful walk out of here, but you'll make it, if you don't starve to death first. But as I said before, it'll give me time to put some miles between us."

Eben mounted his mule and rode off. He found both horses not far off. He caught up to them and removed the reins and bits. Even if they were able to catch their horses, there was no possible way either one of them could mount the horses and ride 'em.

He rode until just before dark and then made camp off the trail on a slight rise where the mule could feed.

As he sat watching the fire that night, he decided he had better keep his mind on surviving and stop thinking about Ula and Serena. Maybe this is what Tall Feather had been trying to warn him about. He had learned two valuable pieces of information from Brodie. There were only Boufford and Elmo now still looking for him, and he now knew where they would be.

In spite of the minor setback that day, Eben managed to sleep well and was up at dawn and ate a good breakfast, and then saw to his mule. Two days later he found a Northwest Company trading post about a mile west of Grand Forks. This trading post made him feel like he was back in familiar country.

The store was empty except for the storekeeper. Eben didn't want to spend too much time here in Grand Forks. "Mister, I'll have ten pounds of bacon and two pounds of coffee."

"What's your name, mister?" the storekeeper asked.

Eben glared at him and asked, "What difference does it make? My money is good."

"If you're this McNinch, then it makes a big difference. Boufford told me I shouldn't sell you anything."

Eben reached across the counter and grabbed the storekeeper by his shirt and pulled him off the floor and across the counter. "You must be a Leet, then."

"Cyril Leet."

Eben pulled him up right to his face and said, "Ten pounds of bacon and two of coffee. Now! Or I'll throw you through that window. Is that understood?"

"Yes, sir." Cyril was scared for his life and he was literally shaking.

"And you keep your hands away from any weapons or I'll stomp you. Wrap them up, please."

"Boufford, he ain't gonna like this none."

"Well, if you ever see Boufford, you tell him Eben McNinch is looking for him." Eben put his money on the counter and left.

He knew the main trail to the border was on the east side of the Red River, but there was supposed to be a less used trail on the west side. He decided on the west side trail.

* * * *

Boufford and Elmo split up and Elmo crossed the river and headed north on the west side. Boufford was on the east side. "We meet in Saint Vincent, Elmo." There were a lot of travelers

273

on the east side, trappers mostly, returning from their trapping grounds. Boufford stopped and questioned them all, if they had seen a lone man wearing a wolf vest and riding a mule, "He has red hair and a red beard." No one had seen him.

Elmo's progress on the west trail was slower as it was not in as good condition. He met no one. He was five-and-a-half days reaching Saint Vincent.

"What took you so long, Elmo? I was here in three days."

"The trail isn't as good. I'll try to pick up the pace on the way back. I need a few things at the trading post first, though."

Although Elmo had a son that had been severely beaten by Eben, he was not as obsessed with killing him. But he did wish to settle the score. He had never met or seen Eben and was a little curious how one man hunted by forty men could do so much damage.

Elmo's trip south this time only took four days, but it rained every day and night, and cleared up as he was approaching Grand Forks. They met at the trading post. "Have you seen anything of McNinch, Cyril?" Boufford asked.

"No, and I've asked everyone who has come in. No one has seen him," Cyril said.

"Do you suppose he went through late last year or during the winter?" Elmo asked.

"Maybe," Boufford said, "but I doubt it. I think he found someplace to hole up for the winter and he'll be through here or around Grand Forks.

"Okay, Boufford, but this time I'm going to slow the pace and take time to look at things. So far I haven't seen evidence that anyone has used the west trail this spring."

"Alright, meet me in Saint Vincent when you can."

Elmo stopped and checked every mud-hole to see if there were any tracks. He looked for out-of-the-way places to make camp and still found no evidence.

* * * *

As Eben leisurely rode up the west side of the Red River, he began thinking that he didn't want to spend the rest of his life worrying if Boufford Leet was still hunting him. He wanted to end this once and for all. He figured he had traveled about half the way to Saint Vincent, and he found just what he was looking for, a dry knoll with only a slight rise. From there he could see a short ways behind him and about two-hundred yards to the north. What he didn't know was that two minutes earlier a lone rider had disappeared around a bend in the trail.

He made camp just off the trail on his left side. He tended to the mule and then he built a fire and cooked some meat and coffee. Then he waited for Leet to smell his fire and meat cooking and come in, and he would get this over with now. He sat up awake all night waiting for one of the Leets to show.

Come morning he built up the fire and stayed right there. He would let them come to him. He was done with running. He staked the mule with new feed and water, and gathered wood for the fire. He ate little, but drank coffee, cup after cup. After dark, he cooked up some bacon and more coffee.

Still, no one showed up. He wasn't discouraged, because sooner or later he knew one of the Leets would show, and he hoped it would be Boufford.

The next day was a repeat of the previous day, only the air was cooler. At dusk he put a piece of smoked venison on a stick and then wrapped some bacon around it and set it over the fire to cook. There was a slight breeze from the south. He made some coffee and sat back watching the fire and his supper cook. He began thinking about Ula and Serena again, but stopped. He would stay focused this time.

He wrapped a blanket around his shoulders as the air was still getting cooler. The stars were out bright but the night was as dark as a closed closet. He pulled the blanked up around his neck. He turned the meat over. It was almost cooked and he poured another cup of coffee.

"Hello, there, by the fire," a strange voice called in the shadows of darkness.

"What do you want?"

"To share your fire and warm my hands." The voice didn't sound twangy and no southern drawl. He didn't sound like a Leet.

"My damn horse has a sore foreleg and I've been walking for hours."

"Come in, but your hands better be empty." Eben drew his revolver and held it concealed under the blanket.

As the stranger came into the firelight, he sure didn't look like a Leet. His face was heavier. He was heavier and taller. And his horse was limping.

"I could smell your bacon and coffee a long way back. Smells good."

Eben didn't say anything and he didn't know if this guy was a Leet or not.

The stranger picked up the horse's bad leg and rubbed it. Eben doubted if any of the Leets he had encountered would be concerned about their mount. The stranger then took the saddle off and laid it on the ground, unbuckled his gun belt with sheath knife and laid that with the saddle.

Eben didn't know what to think now.

"You can un-cock that revolver you're holding under the blanket." Then he added, "I would have done the same thing. I'm hungry, tired and cold. I mean you no harm."

"Sit," Eben said, and picked up the stick holding the meat and handed it to the stranger.

"Thank you."

Eben started cooking some more. "What happened to your food? No one comes out into the wilderness without food."

"While I slept last night, a damned fisher-cat carried off my pack and ate all my food. This is good, wrapped with bacon."

"Coffee?"

"That would be good. How come you ride a mule and not a horse?"

"A mule will eat much coarser feed than a horse and they're easier to care for, and they may not be as fast, but they have more rigor."

"What kind of fur is that vest? I'm color-blind and really can't make out the detail."

"It's wolf." Eben waited to see how the stranger would react to that.

The stranger put more wood on the fire. "I'm cold to the bone."

Eben's supper was cooked and he started eating, always keeping an eye on the stranger. When he had finished eating, he laid the stick down and said, "What are you doing out here? You're obviously not a trapper, and the trail on the other side is better traveling."

"No, I'm no trapper. Farmer, actually. I'm looking for someone."

Eben didn't want to believe it, but he knew now this guy was a Leet. But he was so much different. He was a gentleman, well dressed and groomed and he didn't talk with that twangy drawl. He had Eben puzzled.

"Who are you looking for?"

"Eben McNinch."

"Why are you looking for this McNinch?"

"He's killed six of the Leet family and beaten the hell out of others."

"What are you going to do once you find him?"

"My brother Boufford want s him dead."

"And you?"

"I'm no killer. Like I said, I'm a farmer."

Eben poured him another cup of coffee and filled the stranger's cup also. He took a sip and said, "You must be Elmo. I would recognize Boufford."

"You must be Eben McNinch." Elmo sipped his coffee. "Like I said, I'm color-blind and couldn't tell if your beard is red or black or what color the fur vest is. But you are too candid for a usual traveler. Too cautious."

"And you came into my campsite, regardless?"

"I'm no match for you, McNinch. I figured if I was unarmed you'd understand I mean you no harm."

277

"Then why are you out here looking for me, when you should be planting your crops?"

"Family is family, McNinch."

"What now? What do you want?"

"Let's talk. We have all night. Why were you hunting Jerry and Paul?"

"Jerry shot my father in the back. Paul raped my mother and then slashed her throat, but not before she bit off his ear. Paul shot me and left me for dead. They stole our mules, our guns, our fur, which they sold in Fort Garry for $800.00, and they took food."

"I wasn't told the whole story. Actually, I never knew why you were after them."

"I confronted Jerry and Paul on the trail. They had tried to ambush me. I got Jerry while Paul ran off. I later caught up with Paul. He was with his father, Ezra, Boufford and Boufford's son, Alfred. He drew down on me first. When I shot him, Ezra and Paul drew down on me. I shot both of them. Boufford didn't even draw his gun, so I let him ride off and told him to let it alone."

"I was never told any of that. All Boufford said was that you were a cold-hearted killer."

"So, unless you have a change of heart, Boufford is out here alone after me."

"There's Brodie and Sam on the trail west."

"They won't be any problem. In fact they may be back in Grand Forks now. I made them walk barefoot to give me time to increase the distance between us. They ambushed me and they both shot at me. I left them able to walk in but they'll need a doctor to set some bones."

"You say they shot at you? How come you didn't kill them?"

"I needed some answers and there's been too much killing."

"My brother Boufford should have done some thinking on this before organizing the family to hunt you down. But he always was too impulsive. He always let his anger control him. Now because of him several lay in graves and even more with broken limbs."

"What are you going to do now, Elmo?" Eben asked and

poured each more coffee.

"Sit here and drink your coffee. I'm no match for you, Eben. I came in to your camp like I did so you would know I mean you no harm. You killed members of my family, but I guess if I had been in your place, I'd have done the same. I'm older than Ezra or Boufford and Ma always called me the mediator. I'll return to my farm and try to bring the family back together and explain things as you did here tonight.

"What about you, Eben? What will you do now?"

"Go home and try to put the pieces of my life back together."

"I want you to know, Eben, I am truly sorry about your folks. After talking with you tonight, I know they were good people."

"Thank you, Elmo. That means a lot to me. What about Boufford, though? Will he give up the hunt?"

There was a long pause before Elmo answered. "I wish I could say he will, but he won't. He's obsessed with killing you and I don't know why. He's acting like a crazy man.

"We are supposed to meet tomorrow in Grand Forks. So you know where he'll be and you'll be safe from here to the border. When we leave in the morning, I'll take my leisurely time to the Forks, to give you more time. My brother will be furious when he learns you and I spent the night together drinking coffee and talking. He may try to kill me. But I think before reacting and I'm bigger than Boufford. I'll try to talk some sense into him, but in the end he'll continue the hunt."

They continued to talk and drink coffee and eat warmed up smoked venison all night. When morning came, they mounted up and Elmo said, "Boufford will know you are now riding for the border. I'll delay him as long as I can so don't waste any time getting to Saint Vincent. And Eben, I hold no grudges for those of my family you had to kill. I understand. But as long as Boufford lives, he'll always be a threat to you." With that said, Elmo turned his mount and rode off, and Eben quickened his pace for Saint Vincent.

* * * *

When Elmo rode into Grand Forks, he knew where to find Boufford. He walked into the saloon and sure enough, Boufford was standing at the bar with a whiskey in his hand. "Well, what took you so long, brother?"

"I spent the night talking with Eben McNinch."

With the mention of his name, Boufford threw his drink against the back wall. "You what?!" he bellowed. "You bastard!"

"Brodie and Sam spent the last three days walking here barefoot and broken ribs, arms and wrist. It'll be a long time before either one of them will be any use. You bastard!"

"After Brodie and Sam ambushed him and shot at him first. He told me a different story about why he was hunting Jerry and Paul. And frankly, I would have done the same.

"Haven't we lost enough men in the family, Boufford? You're no match for him. You saw firsthand what he can do when outnumbered in a fight. And you, Boufford, sat on your horse as he shot your own son, Alfred, Paul and your brother, Ezra, and you didn't lift a finger to help them. And I think this is what this hunt for Eben is all about. The fact you didn't do anything when you should have. You're no match for him, Boufford. He's a better fighter and he's smarter than you. Give it up, Boufford."

Boufford was so angry now he started to swing at Elmo, but Elmo punched him so hard in the face it knocked him out and onto the floor.

"Barkeep, you got a room in the back where I can put him?
"Sure."

Elmo put Boufford in the back room and went outside and mounted up and started back for home.

CHAPTER 17

Eben rode through Saint Vincent without stopping and crossed the border. He was running out of meat. His bacon was gone and he only had a couple of pounds of smoked venison left. His coffee was also gone. He pushed on through the night and stopped for a catnap and to feed the mule. He ate some venison and then continued on. He wouldn't feel completely safe until he reached Winnipeg.

A half day out of Fort Garry, he finally had to stop and sleep. He was too exhausted to go on. He didn't bother looking for anything to eat. He could do that tomorrow when he was in Fort Garry. He fed the mule and then he lay down to sleep. He slept until dawn the next morning.

He was in Fort Garry by mid-morning. His first stop was the new restaurant. He sat in the corner and ordered a whopping breakfast and a pot of coffee. He sat back sipping his coffee when the door opened and a distinguished looking gentleman entered. He looked directly at Eben. Eben had never seen him before, but he started walking over to him.

"I can't believe it. Eben McNinch." Everybody stopped what they were doing. Not a word was spoken. Everyone there knew the name Eben McNinch, but maybe not the person.

"I can't believe it, Eben. You haven't aged a day in what… thirty-eight, thirty-nine years?" He extended his hand to shake Eben's.

Eben shook his hand and said, "I think you have me confused with my granddad, Eben McNinch."

"It's remarkable. You're the spitting image of your grandfather. How are he and Ada?"

"They both passed away three years ago."

"Oh, I'm so sorry to hear that. They were good people. Remarkable, actually. Oh, my name is Shelby Rigsby."

"Yes, Major Rigsby. My granddad told me about you and that expedition."

"I didn't care much for your grandfather when we first met. I was young and thought I knew it all. I thought the natives were dirty, ignorant savages. He straightened me out in short order and working and living beside him for two-and-a-half years I learned the difference. I wouldn't be where I am now if it hadn't been for him.

"After the end of the expedition, I resigned my military career and joined the Royal Canadian Mounted Police and chose the Milk River Post near the 49th Parallel on the western edge of the plains where we wintered out in 1816. Your grandfather and Ada transformed me. I married a beautiful Blackfoot woman and have two sons and a daughter.

"We have all heard of the stories of Eben McNinch chasing down the two Leets and then being hunted by their kin. All this time I thought it was your grandfather people were talking about. I just can't get over how much you look like him. He too would have chosen a seat in the corner so his back would be against the wall and he could watch everything going on.

"Is this matter with the Leets finished?"

"For the most part. There is still one who vows to hunt me down and kill me. Boufford Leet. But he is all alone now, and I don't know if he'll come across the border or not. His brother and I had a good long talk and he was going to do what he could to stop Boufford."

"What are your plans now?"

"Go home and try to pick up the pieces and sit by the graves of my mom, dad and grandparents and talk with them. Then there's a girl, a Cree girl in Neokiowa's village and we'll be married as soon as I return. My mom was Cree and she was a beautiful woman. Probably like your wife."

"I have an idea, Eben, and I want you to hear me out."

"Okay."

"I live here at Fort Garry now and I have recently been promoted to Governor of all of Canada's western territories. I could use a good man like you to oversee the Canadian Native Affairs. You would have people working for the Canadian Provincial Government through you. You would be the spokesman in Parliament for the native tribes. You would be their liason to Parliament and to the white man's world. You could do a lot of good for your Cree tribe and natives all over Canada."

"It truly sounds inviting, especially if I could help the native people. I have a few ideas how to help. Who would I have to see to get this position?"

Shelby Rigsby began laughing uncontrollably. Then he said, "Son, I am Governor of the biggest part of Canada. What I say goes. All you have to do is say yes."

"This would be a nice way to honor my mother. I'll do it, Governor Rigsby, but there is one provision, though. My granddad talked of the Sangreal Mountains and how beautiful the mountains are and the country there. I'll need time for Wenonah and I to go out there to see this Sangreal Mountain. Then when we return, I will take the position."

"Done. You have one year."

"Make it two."

"This is the last of March, 1855. You be back here at Fort Garry mid-September, 1856. That's a year-and-a-half."

"Okay."

"My wife's people live not far from Sangreal Mountain and it is a beautiful place. My wife and I would go there quite often.

"The trip west won't take you as long as the expedition. There is now a road that goes all the way to the west end of the plains. You can make the trip now in two months. That's why I shortened your time frame.

Eben finished his breakfast while all the time listening to

Governor Rigsby talk. "I must excuse myself now, Eben. I'm so glad to have met you like this and I am so sorry about your folks and Eben and Ada. And if you have any more trouble with Mr. Leet, you tell me. In fact I'll send a notice to our post at the border not to let him ever enter Canada. Goodbye for now, Eben. Be sure to look me up before you leave for Sangreal."

Eben finished his breakfast in disbelief. His future had certainly taken a change for the better. And now he would be in a position not only to help his people but all Canadian natives.

At the trading post he bought new clothes and food enough for the trip home. He bought a flowery dress for Wenonah and a flowery hat for Neokiowa's woman, tobacco for Neokiowa and candy for the kids. "I assume my account is still good here?"

"Yes, Mr. McNinch. Do you wish that I deduct these purchases?"

"Yes."

Eben left Fort Garry feeling better about life than he had for a year now. There was a real purpose to his life and future now, and he couldn't wait to see Wenonah, Ula and Serena now forgotten.

* * * *

It was strange to see the farm so empty. The first thing he did was go visit his mom, dad and grandparents. He sat down and leaned back against a tree. He sat there a long time, telling them everything he had been doing during the year. About meeting Shelby Rigsby and in a year-and-a-half he would be in charge of Indian Affairs. He was happy to be talking with them and then sad knowing he would never see or talk with them again.

The house was clean and that night he cooked supper in the kitchen and not out on the trail somewhere. He slept in his own bed and had forgotten how comfortable a real bed was.

He was up early the next morning and walked around the farm. It had weathered pretty good in his absence. He was surprised. He caught trout in the stream and had those with fresh fiddleheads.

He still had the pouch of gold and decided to leave it in a safe in Fort Garry when he and Wenonah left for Sangreal. That evening before he ate he washed up in the stream and packed a few things for the trip to the village first thing in the morning. He wanted to see Wenonah and he needed to talk with Neokiowa.

On his way to the village he could almost feel the happiness of going as he had before his parents deaths. Even now there was a terrible sadness with the memories of his family that he had loved so much. First with the passing of his grandmother, then his grandfather soon after, and the brutal murders of his mom and dad. Everywhere he went he saw memories of them. But still he was happy to be on his way to see Wenonah.

When he rode into the village, there was such clamor and yelling, it was almost deafening. Neokiowa soon appeared exiting his lodge with a big smile.

"It is good to see my friend. Is it over?"

"Yes. Those who killed my mom and dad are dead."

"Good, we will speak no more. No good to keep bad memories awake."

Eben gave the tobacco to Neokiowa, the hat to his woman and the candy for the kids., and when he turned around, Wenonah was standing there and smiling. He held up the dress to her body and she was ecstatic with joy and excitement.

"Neokiowa, you, Echo Berry, Wenonah and I need to talk." They went into Neokiowa's lodge…Wenonah last.

Eben said, "It is time for Wenonah and me to join."

"Yes, it is time. We will have days of feasting and celebrating."

"Two days only, Neokiowa. Then Wenonah and I must leave."

"Speak."

"There is a white man, Shelby Rigsby, who was with my granddad and grandmother when they took the expedition west. He is now Governor of the Territories of Canada and he and his Blackfoot woman now live at Fort Garry. He has offered me a job where I will be able to help my brothers the Cree and all

Canadian natives. But first I want to take Wenonah and go west to the Sangreal Mountains. Then we will return and I will work with the Governor."

"How will you help my people that you don't already?"

"While I was hunting those who killed my parents, I saw many things in the white man's world and discovered how to help the Cree. Education. Writing, reading and speaking the same tongue as the white man, so everybody will better understand them and not so easy to cheat the Cree. This can only be done through education. Teaching your people these things."

"And you can do these things working for the Governor?"

"Yes, but I'll actually be working for the Cree and all native peoples."

"This all sounds good, if you can do this."

"I can, Neokiowa, and Governor Rigsby will help me. You see, he also likes the ways of the native peoples and how they live and he wants to help all of the tribes."

"What you do with your farm?"

"Keep it, so we can come back some."

"I would not like someone taking my granddaughter away to live in the white man's world. You can. I know your heart is in the right place and you will take care of Wenonah. We have joining tomorrow. Woman, you have work to do." Echo Berry and Wenonah left the lodge to start preparations for the joining and the feast.

Eben and Neokiowa talked for a long time. Neokiowa was curious about the white man's world and wanted Eben to tell him about what he had seen.

Neokiowa was especially interested in the steamboat where many people and wagons rode and no one paddled. This was difficult for him to understand. And it was equally difficult to understand the telegraph. How messages could be sent over the wire to someone many miles away. "And Fort Garry will soon be a city, Neokiowa. They already have a name for it. Winnipeg. The country and people, Neokiowa, outside of Cree land, are changing fast. And this is why your people need education. When I start my job, I'll see to it that teachers come here to teach your people all these things."

"I worry you might lose your way in the white man's world and forget you are Cree. You are a great man like Big Red Beard Not Afraid. You look like grandfather. You are Cree. Don't forget."

"How could I forget, Neokiowa? Yes, I could. I look white like my granddad. But was not his heart truly Cree? Don't you forget, Neokiowa, that my mother was your daughter. I am Cree. And this is why I will take the commissioner job, because that way I can do more good for my people then Wenonah and I living on the farm, near this village.

The next morning after eating, Neokiowa said, "Eben, come with me. We prepare for your joining."

Neokiowa led him to a sweat lodge and both men stripped and entered the lodge. It was so hot and humid Eben found it difficult to breathe. But after several minutes, he adjusted to it. It was difficult to carry on a conversation, so both men sat in silence.

Eben sweat so much that after an hour he stopped sweating and Neokiowa said, "It is time." He got up and walked out to a nearby stream and waded out and sat down. Eben did the same. Although the water was very cold, they were hot and did not notice the cold.

Afterwards, Eben felt really clean and refreshed. There was a lodge specially for Eben and Wenonah and he went there to change into new clothes that Wenonah had been making all winter. Tanned deer-hide pants and shirts. They fit perfectly. He was now feeling more like a native than he had all of his life.

Wenonah had planned to wear a white deerskin dress until Eben had given her the flowery dress. It was too long, so she shortened it, which accentuated her natural beauty.

As they stood before Neokiowa and Echo Berry they were a handsome couple. And of course no one objected to their joining and they spent the rest of the day in their new lodge, while the rest of the village celebrated.

Before leaving the next morning Eben took one of his revolvers and gunbelt and buckled it around Wenonah. "You won't have the protection of the village now. We'll be traveling through the wilderness. You wear this gun everywhere you go. In the wilderness we look out after each other."

The others were surprised to see Wenonah wearing a gun. It just wasn't heard of in the village. Neokiowa nodded his head that he understood.

They had little to take with them, so they both could ride on the mule. They rode all day and stopped at the farm for the night. This was the first house Wenonah had ever seen and she was quite impressed. He took her up on the hill where his grandparents and parents were buried.

Wenonah marveled over the wood cookstove and all the cooking utensils. And the bed. It was so simple and so comfortable. "My grandparents built this house."

"Will we have house like this?" Wenonah asked.

"When we return from the Sangreal Mountains, yes."

"Nice. I like," she said.

They stayed at the farm only one night and then they were on the way to Fort Garry. Before leaving, Eben took the gold pouch and money and his family's papers.

Eben walked beside the mule as Wenonah rode.

When they arrived at Fort Garry, Wenonah was nervous. There were so many white people and they all were looking at her. "Why all these people look at me, my husband?"

"Because you are so beautiful. They mean you no harm."

They tied the mule up in front of the trading post store and down the street…, "Eben McNinch!" came a thunderous voice. Everybody heard it and stopped to see what the outburst was about. "You bastard! You killed my son, my brother and four nephews and maimed many more in my family! I'm going to kill you, you son-of-a-bitch!"

Eben knew immediately who was shouting. Boufford Leet. He turned to face him. "Wenonah, you stay behind the mule."

Boufford was fifty feet away and all this so far had occurred in a very few seconds. But Eben was aware of everything. The people all around him. His wife, Wenonah, Boufford and his anger. Time didn't slow down or stop for Eben as he made all these observations, but his conscious awareness had risen to the point that he was cognizant of everything and he decided in that moment to take the attack to him and surprise Boufford Leet. He charged at Boufford. To the horror of Wenonah and surprise of everyone there watching.

Boufford saw the charge coming and there was no one more shocked and surprised than he. And he hesitated a fraction of a moment too long and Eben was on him. Eben, like his grandfather, grabbed Boufford by his sides, snapping ribs in doing so. Then all in the same moment, he lifted him up and threw him twenty feet. Boufford still had his hand on his handgun when he hit the dirt and now he drew it and pointed it at Eben. Then the explosion of the gun firing, except it wasn't Boufford's. Eben looked across the compound and saw Governor Shelby Rigsby standing there with his handgun in his hand and smiling at Eben.

Everybody there knew Rigsby was the new governor and any questions they might have had about his abilities were answered.

Governor Rigsby started walking across the compound to Eben and he began laughing. Not at having to have just shot and killed someone, but…, "That's just what your grandfather would have done, Eben. You remind me so much of him. I really miss Eben and Ada." His eyes were watering, remembering his friends.

"That must be Boufford Leet. I don't know how or where he crossed into Canada. It shouldn't have happened."

"That's Boufford and according to his brother, Elmo, he is the last of the Leets that were hunting me.

"Governor Rigsby, I'd like you to meet my wife, Wenonah. Wenonah, this is Governor Shelby Rigsby."

"It's certainly a pleasure to meet you, Mrs. McNinch."

"Are you going to be in town tonight?"

"Yes, we'll leave tomorrow morning."

"Then you must come and have dinner with my wife and I, and spend the night. We're in that house there," and he pointed. "Now, I must leave you. If you have any problems getting supplies, let me know."

Eben had to purchase two more mules, one to pack their supplies. He knew there would be trading posts along the route and he wouldn't have to pack too heavy. There was still enough money in his account to more than pay for the supplies. The Banque de Montreal had opened a bank there in Fort Garry and he checked the account and deposited the gold in the safe, in a safety deposit box.

Wenonah marveled at the grandeur of the Governor's house. Supper was superb and their bed that night was the softest and most elegant that either of them had ever seen. "Do all white people live like this?"

"No."

The next morning they said their goodbyes and Rigsby reminded Eben, "Remember, Eben, you only have a year from this September."

"We'll be back, Sir."

* * * *

Eben and Wenonah crossed the plains and stood at the small inlet his grandfather had described, by the end of July. There were towering spruce trees on both sides of the cool spring fed inlet. The water looked like ice it was so clear. Brook trout were jumping for flies on the surface. A beaver slapped its tail at the intruders. Behind them were the grassy plains and standing majestically in the background were the Sangreal Mountains.

They made a quick shelter and caught brook trout for supper. The next morning they were up before daylight to watch as the morning sun hit the snow capped peaks. And just like his grandfather had said, the sun filtering through the morning haze turned the snow caps the color of blood red.

"Sangreal, Granddad."

The End

Author, Randall Probert

Randall Probert lived and was raised in Strong,Maine; a small town in the western mountains of Maine. Six months after graduating from high school, he left the small town behind for Baltimore, Maryland and a Marine Engineering School, situated downtown near what was then called "The Block". Because of bad weather, the flight from Portland to New York was canceled and this made him late for the connecting flight to Baltimore. A young kid and alone from the backwoods of Maine finally found his way to Washington DC and boarded a bus from there to Baltimore. After leaving the Merchant Marines, he went to an aviation school in Lexington, Massachusetts.

During his interview for Maine Game Warden he was asked, "You have gone from the high seas to the air. . .are you sure you want to be a Game Warden?" Mr. Probert retired from Warden Service in 1997 and started writing historical novels about the history in the areas where he patrolled as a game warden, with his own experiences as a game warden as those of the wardens in his books. Mr. Probert has since expanded his purview and has written 2 science fiction books, *PARADIGM* and *PARADIGM2,* and has written a mystical adventure, *AN ESOTERIC JOURNEY.* Mr. Probert is also currently working on another historical novel, which should be available in the spring, 2015.

Acknowledgments

I would like to thank Laura Ashton for her help with this book and Eleanor Goodman for letting me use her painting for the cover.

Other Books by Randall Probert

A Forgotten Legacy

An Eloquent Caper

Courier de Bois

Katrina's Valley

Mysteries at Matagamon Lake

A Warden's Worry

A Quandry at Knowles Corner

Paradigm

Trial at Norway Dam

A Grafton Tale

Paradigm II

Train to Barnjum

A Trapper's Legacy

An Esoteric Journey

The Three Day Club